# TERROR POLITICO

Edited by
Cin Ferguson and Broos Campbell

# Terror Politico
## —a Screaming World in Chaos

Edited by Cin Ferguson and Broos Campbell

Copyright © 2019 Scary Dairy Press LLC
All rights reserved.
ISBN: 1732094608
ISBN-13: 978-1732094604

All rights reserved. No part of this publication may be reproduced or transmitted in any form or by any means without the prior written permission of the publisher. All characters in this publication are fictitious, and all places in this novel are used fictitiously. Any resemblance to real persons, living or dead, is purely coincidental.

# DEDICATION

This book is dedicated to all of the people who suffer from inequality, political ineptitude, effects of climate change (ignored by political and big business powers) and the lack of social and political freedoms. May all humankind act peacefully to change things for the better. May equality, religious and political freedom and compassion rule the world.

This book is also dedicated to the people of Puerto Rico, and in memory of those who suffered and died from Hurricane Maria. Ten percent of this book's first year of profits will go to the UNIDOS Disaster Relief and Recovery Program, an organization dedicated to providing immediate and long-term needs of families and communities in Puerto Rico.

# INTRODUCTION

Dear Reader,

There are thirty-five authors represented in this anthology. In numerology, thirty-five represents business and material accumulation as well as creativity and the freedom of self-expression. It is a number geared toward the achievement of goals, political effectiveness and creating systems with long-term social benefits. Thirty-five is the number that embodies the qualities of optimists and those who are tolerant, adventurous and curious. The number thirty-five is reflective of this piece of work you are about to read.

When Scary Dairy Press put this anthology together, we specifically chose not to obtain blurbs and accolades regarding its content. A lot of politics goes into achieving a name and recognition in an anthology. We made the decision to avoid that. This piece of work stands on its own and the authors have worked hard to bring meaningful pieces of work to you for you to read. We hope you enjoy their stories as much as we have.

Sincerely,

Cin Ferguson
November 6, 2018

# CONTENTS

## ALIENS AMONG US

Rad Bodies by Querus Abuttu   3
Is It Really Genocide? by Stephen M. Coghlan   7
Wrong Side of the River by Morgan Duchesney   19
End Credits by Stuart Hardy   31
I've Been Waiting for You by Larry Hodges   41
They Bleed Green by Laszlo Tamasfi   47

## MONSTER MASH

Red Hats by Eddie Generous   67
What Crawls Beneath by Sin Fergus   83
Everybody Listens to Buck* by Nicholas Manzolillo   91
Only a Dream by Tahni. J. Nikitins   101
Making a Monster by E. F. Schraeder   121
Heal by Rider Sullivan   131

## PRESIDENTIAL PAUCITY

Greatest Art of the Deal by Gregg Chamberlain   145
In My Mind by Leadie Jo Flowers   159
Run! by Thomas Logan   181
Application to Teach the Future Patriots by Donna J. W. Munro   195

Seeds* by John Palisano   221

## SOCIAL DISTORTION

Stone in Stream by Broos Campbell   231
Thaumaturgy by Michael R. Colangelo   241
Defend Atlantis by David L. Day   251
No Such Thing as a Free Lunch by Kev Harrison   263
Mexico City by Russell Hemmell   271
Voodoo That You Do Do by Andrew J. Lucas   281
Wish Granters by Adrian Ludens   287
Buried Alive in a Sallow Grave by Alice van Harlingen   301

## CLIMACTIC CHANGE

Highway 99 by I.A. Green   319
Trinidad by Jessica Palmer   333
Destitution Terminated by Catrin Rutland   363

## UNFAIR AND UNBALANCED

Each New Twist of Fate by Bob Freville   381
How I'll Lose My Career by Edmund Colell   395
Crossroads by Michelle R. Lane   415
Insider Trading by Ken McGrath   435
Freedum by James Musgrave   445
Affection by Proxy by Jay Seate   453
Secret Ballot by Frank Oreto   465

Author Bios   477

# ACKNOWLEDGMENTS

This project is a success because of the people who worked to put it together. We thank the authors who were diligent, getting edits and information in to us as quickly as possible, and to the editors, Cin Ferguson and Broos Campbell, who read and reread these stories to make sure all of the edits were done as completely and correctly as possible. Our thanks also to you, dear reader, because without you our stories would go unread and unheard and would remain inert. By reading these stories, you've helped our words live.

# ALIENS AMONG US

# RAD BODIES

by
Querus Abuttu

K.J. chuckled, showing all of his teeth in a wide, predatory smile. His plump cheeks rose so high that his eyes squeezed into fleshy stilettos.

"What you think, Worm?"

Truth? I wasn't sure how to respond. With my man Kim, things could get slick like dice on ice. One minute it was sevens—the next, snake-eyes.

"Maybe we can show 'em how to get active 'round the rim." I air dribbled, jumped and imagined a swish.

K.J. nodded. My Korean sucked, but hell—I tried. He'd sent me personal tutors in the language and gifts for my ying and yang. All he wanted from me was to teach him American culture. Still, the last thing I ever expected was *this*.

Sure, the man had tossed some pocket-rocket payload over the Japs. His peeps needed to know he's strong—not a "bend over, I'm gonna be yo bitch" state leader. I mean, dude's barely out of his dead pop's ball-sack and already he's statist. Don't wear no bling, but the man stabs some meat.

The assembly line was something I never seen before. Metal workers melting scrap and adding something to it that made it porous like bone yet harder than steel. Next were the frame makers. Tweaking 206 puzzle pieces into a full skellyman. Different sizes. Tall. Short. They seemed extra careful when attaching the skull.

"My missile launches have, of course, been decoys." K.J. gestured to where two rail-thin chicks used their slender fingers to fit skelly-heads on the frames. Strange. The skulls were packed on the inside with something. Two men slid by us holding electronic instruments. Similar gadgets were on the walls near the workers.

*Are those Geiger counters? Damn.* I pushed down the urge to cover my balls.

"It's a helluva operation, K. J." Luckily, it was cool in here or I'd be sweating bullets. Kim pointed to a golf cart. He got behind the wheel. I grabbed shotgun. Dude was stylin his own ride through a nuke-skelly factory. Nerve.

"Lot more to see this way," he said with a glint in his eye. We followed alongside a conveyor belt that smoothly transported the completed skeletons into another part of the warehouse. Up ahead, I saw a gate. Each set of bones passed through it and a green light lit up after every one. Kim saw the question in my eyes and grinned.

"Metal detector. From the same company used by your Homeland Security."

"How . . . ?"

"A process we have for years. Change the structure of metal so it no longer electromagnetic. The principal behind the scanners now completely useless."

Machines whirred. Odd. I realized no one in this place spoke a word.

My lips felt dry. I licked them before asking what I knew was a stupid question. Decided to dish out some props first. "Amazing, K.J. Freaking mind blastin. These guys could jet through any airport, right?"

Kim nodded. His eyes burned me as I watched workers use hand-held devices to squeeze lumps of a gelatinous wack over the bodies. First it spread out and quickly took the shape of muscles, veins and arteries. More globs were squeezed into the ribcage and belly. The stuff congealed and then separated to form internal organs. Heart, lungs, liver and stomach. Unreal! The stink in the air was like a combo of outdated raw chicken and melting plastic.

"Your country has so many limitations on its scientists. We've cloned humans for years now, of course. We've used stem cells, and discovered how to grow all kinds of cellular tissues. We can create fully functional brain tissues the size of . . . " He paused, at a loss for the word—then grinned, pleased with himself. "A walnut! I order them programmed to follow my orders. No questions ever."

This game was goin too far down the court for me. I hadn't signed on for this. "Very cool, dude. Very cool. Yeah, our scientists don't have any freedom when it comes to that shit. Damn! You must have hundreds of these."

Kim's mini-whip eased to a stop, and he rolled out of the cart. I followed suit. A guard pushed his palm against a panel, opening up a large metal door. I walked through, and a gigantic part of the warehouse lit up in front of me.

"Not hundreds, Worm. Thousands." The mirth in his voice was unrestrained.

There were at least six different levels of bodies all packed closely into each space. The peeps were actually breathing. A collective heartbeat pulsed through the air. Stanky sweat, pungent, reached my nose. Very human. And each fake human sported a different skin color. It was as if Kim had kidnapped up the entire city of Los Angles and squeezed them in here. Mexican. Asian. White. Black.

We rode a lift to the bottom floor, where a few of Kim's creations were clothed and actually mobile. They were speaking, some in different languages. I noticed them receiving passports, briefcases or backpacks. Some sat in chairs.

"The time has come for us to part, my American friend. I have enjoyed seeing you again, and our exchanges were mutually beneficial. It is time for you to go home."

Home? My flight wasn't scheduled until tomorrow. I let Kim know.

"There have been other arrangements," he said. Two guards gripped my arms. "No worry, Worm. You fly first class, all the way." His face glowed. He was actually jovial. The closest to happy I'd ever seen the man.

An entire wall of the warehouse slid open, and a 747 jumbo sat on the tarmac. Kim's rad humans were boarding it. Manufactured families, talking, laughing. Heads full of nukes flying to America.

The leader of North Korea waved a hand at me before his boyz ushered me onto the plane. His next words would ring in my ears until they rang no more.

"Say hello to your president from me."

# IS IT REALLY GENOCIDE

by
Stephen M. Coghlan

Senator Ti'kakali'ti'mana'hwanaban of Wick'ta'ta'la'ma'sa-bo, or Tiki of Wicki, for short, listened to his aide with only one and a half ears, as the remaining half an ear was actually a cybernetic replacement and was currently soaking in a bath of polishing oil.

He wished that he could find a way to turn off his organic hearing. The news he was forced to listen to was both expected and unwelcome.

Captain NikNikNikNikNikKnock, or Nik, as she was known, collapsed the first holosheet she just completed reading, sighed with only two of her six lungs, and opened another.

"Bratch managed to fix the fuel leak, finally, but we lost enough from stocks that we're going to have to shut down another 'minor' function to conserve energy."

"Let me guess," Tiki of Wicki growled as he rubbed one of his tentacles over his head, which was presently the color of rotten Hlarg grass. "Primary illumination?"

"How did you know?" Captain Nik asked sarcastically. "Was it the flickering lights?"

The look that Senator Tiki shot the captain was filled with scorn, but then he remembered the last time he had cast that look upon her, she thought he had been implying that they should mate. It led to a fight that took dozens of letters back and forth before everything was smoothed out.

"Have any of our distress beacons been noticed?" probed the politician. Captain Nik paused, swallowed air, and then opened an entirely new holosheet by tapping the implant in her palm, clapping her hands together, and then spreading her limbs apart until the hovering illusion was large enough to read in the dimmed light.

"We got word that at least two different ships have heard the message and are inbound. One of them has a capacity capable of holding at least two percent of our passengers."

When Nik hesitated, Tiki spun the end of one limb to encourage her to continue.

"The other is a butcher ship that's offering to buy up as much meat as we can sell."

Swallowing against his dry throat, Tiki mentally engaged his respiratory gear, and its humidifier filled his lungs with moistness before he responded.

"What are they offering in return?"

Wiggling her arms, Captain Nik made her species' equivalent of a gesture of concern. "Depends. They suggested the price would be competitive. I took the initiative of asking them, and they said if we provided enough 'material' that they would even consider giving us some of their spare faster-than-light equipment."

At that, Tiki sucked on his lips. "Butchers always drive a hard bargain," he said to himself. There was no doubt that the meat merchants made a good deal.

With the choices running through his mind, Tiki stood his great bulk into the air and slid himself across the floor. His office was almost at the center of the great vessel, for which he was the elected leader. At that location, gravity was very light, which made mobility so much simpler for him. Captain Nik was in fine condition for her species, and often resented the low friction.

Peering out his observation window, Senator Tiki looked across the vast interior of the ship that was their responsibility. All around the perimeter, peoples of all species labored and built, farmed or slept. Most were supposed to be asleep in cold cryo, but power to the chambers had been the first things cut, in order to save energy after the "incident."

If only he had listened to Captain Nik, he wouldn't be faced with such a decision. She had advocated to avoid the third planet from the system's sun. The comet that was heading towards it had thrown off dangerous radiation, and chunks had continually broken away, but Tiki of Wiki had ignored her pleas, and had ordered their entire vessel forward. She had refused still, until he had challenged her pride by asking if a better captain could have done it.

She had risen to the challenge and had guided their vessel, which was almost the same size as the planet's moon, to the doomed world. There, they had rescued the dolphins, who had paid well in international currency for their salvation. At the same time, under urging from both the dolphins and another species, known as the Greys, Nik's crew rescued a small portion of the other supposedly intelligent species to occupy the planet, humans.

They had not escaped unscathed. The severity of the comet's impact had flung planetary debris far and wide, some of which even the advanced space vessel had been unable to avoid. Radiation and other amorphous particles which the comet had dragged with it also had various ill effects and had played hell with the ship's system.

At first, the ship had been able to maintain some faster-than-light travel, but within only a few relative hours, it had failed.

By then, they had managed to escape the solar system and were out of immediate danger, but that was the best news they had.

It only took a few more "days" for the primary generator to fail, and with it, hopes to wait for rescue in cryo-sleep. Normally, a fail in the cryo-chambers would only mean a slightly longer travel for the passengers, because thanks to time dilation, a journey that took "years" only took "weeks" to those who traveled.

Without FTL, without cryo, the entire complement was looking at a minimum of twenty "years" before they made their first safe haven, and at least five before their own company would send relief.

That was why it was vital to repair their systems as soon as possible. They only had enough food and supplies to feed everyone for six months, or a year, ship time, on a starvation diet.

"Show me how much they want for a new FTL, and the parts we need for a generator," Senator Tiki said.

The improvised shovel bit into the soft moist earth of the parkland, and with it, the last of the saved Leiberg's panic grass was torn away, making room for the dandelion seeds that had been salvaged from a camping family's clothes.

With a sigh of regret, Perkha Ahmadzi looked at the results of her toil. Flat earth stared back at her, and the turned soil was slowly and methodically being poked, prodded, then tamped back down by the others, who did their best to revert what little space they, as a species, had been given, into something that would sustain them for however long they had left as a whole.

"Do you think it is enough?" she sighed. Beside her, Imani, her second in command and recent friend, ran one hand through his short curls before he replied in slow and carefully measured words.

"I think it's enough for the day." He smiled softly, showing his perfectly aligned teeth, which stood out against his dark skin. "There is no point to keep going. No weeds have shown, and we don't have enough cold compost to spread. Let the children sow the seeds, and let the others water. You need to rest."

"I'm fine," Perkha said, crossly, even though she knew that Imani was right. She had not been raised a farmer like Imani had. No, Perkha had barely survived her early years. She had grown up in a refugee camp until she and her mother had found themselves sponsored, taken in by the country of the maple leaf. School was tough, but she adjusted, excelled, and worked her way through university on a political sciences scholarship.

With her background, she was prime United Nations material. She had led teams into the field to investigate, collate, gather, but she had never thought that all of her training would become vital to the survival of the entire remaining human race.

It was not the kind of success that she had ever dreamed of, nor ever wanted.

"I'm sorry, Imani," she said a moment later.

"That is okay," her friend replied, although he was already looking elsewhere. Switching to French, the farmer yelled at a youth who was supposed to be passing a bucket of water along the brigade, but had instead stopped and was staring into the "sky." The response was fast and furious.

"It appears as if we will have visitors," the old farmer explained.

Looking towards the center of the ship, Perkha saw the lowering arm that signified they were about to be blessed by the presence of their "saviors." Dusting her hands off on her pants, she trudged across the turned earth. Imani followed closely behind her while chanting out further orders. His makeshift shovel never left his side.

As the pod finished its descent, both humans felt the tickle in their necks that meant the translator implants were coming online.

The doors opened and three different aliens, and a very familiar porpoise, beckoned the welcome party inside. Captain Nik looked regal in her uniform, as she towered well over everyone else. Her long arms practically dragged on the floor. If Perkha had not been entitled to a copy of their saviors' version of an encyclopedia, she would have never known that Captain Nik was a female of the species.

Senator Tiki of Wiki was bulbous and round. His tentacle limbs crossed themselves in greeting. Emulating the motion as best as she could, Perkha hoped to keep her relationship in good standing with him. Back when the survivors had been brought aboard, the senator had introduced himself with an air that only experienced politicians seemed to be able to summon. It had both been as charming and as frightening as Perkha was used to.

Wearing a suit to hold moisture to her skin, Pa'pa rested in her cart. The bottlenose dolphin wore the helmet that allowed her to speak using telepathy. She had also accompanied Senator Tiki on their first greeting to the humans, and had helped to cement Perkha to the rank of leader.

"Thanks for all the fish," Pa'pa projected into Perkha and Imani's head.

Lastly, a thin amphibious creature stood on its four legs. It was rather like a centaur of myth, but instead of a body of a human mounted on a horse, the entire being was covered in a thick white pelt, not unlike that of a harp seal.

"Representative Perkha, a pleasure to meet you," the quadruped whistled melodiously. Bending its forelegs, it attempted a bow, which the two humans mimicked in kind. "I am biologist Rivkha. I am sorry for your homeworld's destruction."

"We thank you for your sympathies." Perkha spoke in a monotone, hiding her emotions so her grief did not overwhelm her.

"Would you please join us?" Pa'pa bleated, and without looking at each other, the two humans entered, the doors sealing behind them to isolate the few occupants from prying eyes.

"To what do we owe the pleasure of your visit?" Perkha asked.

"There is good news and bad news," Senator Tiki began, harrumphing as he hoisted his heavy shape about until he was comfortable. Reaching out, Perkha grabbed for Imani's hand as the pod began to move.

"Please, senator," Imani said calmly. "Do not take your time to fancy your speech for us. There is much farming left to do if we wish to have any chance of survival."

"That is precisely what we are going to talk to you about," Pa'pa said, rather sorrowfully.

"We have a possible solution to the problems that our ship received during your 'rescue'." Captain Nik was curt. "But it comes with a cost."

"What do we have left to give?" Perkha asked.

"Lives." Senator Tiki's answer made the two humans' blood run cold.

Rivkha interrupted before anyone else could comment. "Thirty thousand, to be exact."

"That's three fifths of our current population!" Perkha yelled as she felt the anger rise in her chest.

"Why do you want those?" Imani remained calm, but his voice was icy with threat.

"There is a butcher's ship nearby. It can be on us within two of your weeks. They claim to have the material required to repair all of our issues, but they won't give us anything for less than the estimated weight of so many of your kind," the captain replied just as coldly.

"What about the other species on this vessel?" Perkha demanded.

"They are paying clients, you are refugees," Nik fired back.

Interposing his great bulk between the two, Senator Tiki ordered the captain to silence and begged Perkha to remain calm. Once order was restored, the senator continued. "It is true that we did not have to rescue you, we only did so out of favor to the species that admire you for certain qualities."

"You are proposing a genocide!" Imani whispered.

"Is it really a genocide if your species was already doomed?" Tiki responded, just as quietly.

Standing on her hind legs, Rivkha caught everyone's attention. When she fell back onto her front limbs, she landed quietly on thickly padded feet.

"We aren't proposing genocide, entirely," she began. "Yes, we would be drastically shortening your species' chance for survival, but we will not be ending it. I've run some calculations, and I believe that the minimum viable population for your species is around the five-thousand mark. We will be leaving you with four times that amount. If we are repaired, we can drop the survivors off on a planet that is rich enough to support your species. You will have a chance to rebuild."

"The other option," the senator continued, but his tone was flat and level, as if he was a professor explaining to a class of sleepy students, "is that we don't give them their demands. We all work and labor, we convert our lands, live on survival rations and what we can grow. If we're lucky, and by a miracle the backup generator holds, we can expect relief in five earth years from now."

"The problem," Captain Nik said, "is that we only have enough fuel for two years, if we cut primary lighting."

"The chances of us surviving it, you humans most of all, are very, very slim," Rivkha whispered. "I'm sorry," she added, as if it was an afterthought.

"This is too much," Perkha said, numb with shock.

"We can always use your people as rations for ourselves." Nik's comment was murmured, but heard.

The pod began to descend.

"Please, consider it as an option," the senator burbled. "We will await your decision."

"This is heinous!" someone from the back of the room yelled. He was a troll of an individual, a former person of wealth who always interjected himself into places of power.

"What they are asking for is impossible," another man, who wore the tattered remains of a three-piece suit, yelled. He claimed to have been a youth counselor, although he was known for his short temper and hatred of physical labor. He had been dragged into the farming operation only when promises of ejecting useless survivors were made.

"I say go for it," a Caucasian in a white polo shirt added. "Let us cleanse our people of all inferiors once and for all."

The punch that landed across that speaker's face was sudden and brutal, and the meeting descended into a brawl worthy of any House of Commons—or shack, in their case. The building they argued within was built out of scavenged metal and wood. Its sides were open, and some who had joined the meeting watched in amusement as people battled each other.

"Should we stop them?" Imani asked, sounding slightly entertained.

"What's the point?" Perkha asked a question of her own. "They will only start to fight again. We have already stopped them twice before."

"Then let them finish on their own. Duck." Imani laughed as a rock sailed over their heads. "Let's take a walk."

Only too happy to agree, Perkha stepped into the artificial sunlight. When they were far enough away from the shack for safety, she sighed and rested her hands on Imani's shoulders.

"We don't have a choice, do we?"

"For not the first time, I am glad that you are making the decisions." Imani's voice was tired.

"But why? Why me?"

"We chose you." Her friend took her hands in his and looked into her eyes. "When we first arrived, we were lost, worthless. You gathered us together, you organized us, and you took a census and decided for us to stand together. Now you must choose if we are to survive."

Her mouth was dry when she finally replied. "I don't know what to do."

"Then I will pray for you." Imani smiled, sadly.

Behind him, the shack collapsed as the counselor was shoved through a supporting pillar.

"I should go." Imani chuckled, and he found one of the shovels, with which he advanced on the unruly mob, all the while yelling in the myriad of languages, commanding onlookers into order.

Seeing as she was not going to be of any help, Perkha turned away from the chaos of politics and instead strode through to the barriers of their borrowed lands. It did not take long before she was staring at the clear casing that separated their individual world from that of the dolphins, who swam in a vast artificial ocean.

It was a utopia she wished to join. Unlike on earth, their water was clean of debris, having been strained carefully during the evacuation. Only good food sources had been left, and it amazed Perkha just how pristine the waters looked. Free of trash and debris.

A pod raced by, flipping out of the water, diving beneath the waves. They looked so at peace, so carefree that she wished she could join them in their frolicking play and freedom of mind, but her thoughts were broken as another woman impacted against the glass beside her.

Wondering what had transpired, she saw the same polo-shirted man from earlier. His victim was a woman of possible Latin origins. Her eye was already swelling and her two children tried to form a protective barrier between the monster and their mother.

"You got mud on my shoes!" the man roared, ignoring the fact that his footwear was already caked in earth, and combined with a growing shiner of his own, and the bloodied hole in his gums where four teeth had once been, he seemed irate. He had received quite a beating back at the shack, and it appeared that he wished to take his vengeance out on someone else.

Someone whom he perceived as weaker.

He advanced, fists raised.

Frustrations came to a head, and Perkha stepped in front of him. Raising her arms, spreading her feet, she sank into a combat stance.

"You've done enough," she whispered harshly.

Pausing, the polo-shirted one seemed unsure of what to do. Then he spat in Perkha's face and walked away.

Only once he was out of sight did Perkha lower her guard and help the woman to her feet.

"Are you okay?" the leader of humanity asked.

"*Sí*," The woman answered. "*Gracias*."

Perkha smiled.

Resting upon a rock that was too large to move, Perkha found herself watching in silent awe as the woman removed a needle and thread from the folds of her clothes and repaired a rip that had begun in her shirt. There was majesty and confidence of skill in the performance, and when she was done, the lady walked away with her family, but Perkha didn't notice.

Standing numbly, she found a carpenter at work, building shelters using crude tools. She found a father teaching his children how to build a campfire. She saw a young woman weaving grass into a rope with the help of a man who, although clumsy, smiled lovingly at his coworker, while he talked about working metal with fire.

Returning to her own shack, which was one of the only ones with power, Perkha sat at her desk, opened the computer provided by their saviors, and began to write.

The pod descended into the inky blackness of night. Perkha never looked away as it touched down. Her mind was made up. For a moment she wished Imani was beside her, but she did not want her friend to stop her or turn her from her decision. Straightening her clothes one last time, she entered to face the same four representatives as before.

"Close the door," she ordered, automatically placing herself in charge.

The pod began to ascend.

"I have your list," she continued, and offered the pad to the captain. Holosheets appeared for all to read.

Pa'pa spoke. "This is too small a list for the butchers."

"It's not for them." Perkha was ready with her answer. "What I gave you is the name of those who *won't* be fed to the butchers."

"But there are only three groups of five thousand each," the dolphin protested. "You could choose anoth—"

"There aren't others," the human interrupted. "Each group is to be dropped off at a different planet. You are going to use the remaining 'payment' for food and supplies." She purposefully called the remaining survivors currency, dehumanizing them and distancing herself from the atrocity she bargained with.

The senator looked as if he was about to speak, but she cut him off.

"And you will check in on them once per human year, and provide medicine and services for the first two decades. Can that be done?"

A whistle escaped from Pa'pa, which the others seemed to take as assent.

"But what about you?" the senator said, confused. "I don't see your name here."

The smile of victory that she wore was bittersweet. "I have done the unthinkable. I have damned many thousands to their doom for the salvation of a few." Holding out her hands, Perkha continued. "As such, let me be the first, or the last, to sacrifice herself for her kind. Do you accept?"

The pod continued to climb until it reached the very center of the ship.

# WRONG SIDE OF THE RIVER

by
Morgan Duchesney

*I gotta get outta this place,* Simon Fraser thought as he neared the squat, gray rectangle of Gatineau's U.S. consulate. *I guess Soviet architecture isn't dead yet*, he reflected caustically while surveying the ugly source of his frustration. Reaching quickly into his pocket, he touched his wallet and passport. *If they refuse again, I'll just escape. I'm done with this place and all the nonsense. However, I should go through the motions once more, like a nice, polite Canadian. No need to attract attention.*

Thirty minutes' passage found him fuming in the sunny park beside the consulate, cursing softly as he dragged hard on another cigarette. *Those bastards! No one leaves the province until further notice, including public servants.* Driven to rage, he shouted to the sky, "To hell with that!" drawing nervous glances from a couple of strangers.

After calming down and reviewing the situation objectively, Fraser decided to ask Marie Godard and Donald Burton to join his escape plan when he met them later at Donald's place. Marie was Fraser's Quebecois girlfriend, and his cousin Donald as another expatriate, a Cape Bretoner with a taste for risky adventures. Eager as he was to talk, he ignored the nearby payphone and started walking the seven blocks to Donald's apartment. Extra care was now vital and he had to assume that everything electronic was being monitored by the U.S. military.

Fraser quickened his pace just as a Marine foot patrol rounded the corner. The platoon commander nodded coolly to him as the column of hard men strode past. When Fraser's anger flared he reminded himself that the U.S. military presence was as unstoppable as it was inevitable. Besides, it wasn't wise to mouth off to twenty big guys with machine guns. Fraser stood and watched them disappear around the corner.

As he continued along Gatineau's narrow, sloping streets, Fraser reflected on what his plan might mean for Marie, a lifelong Quebecer whose huge family were scattered across the vast province. No matter what she said, he had no intention of remaining trapped in occupied Quebec any longer than necessary. He was sure he could convince her to leave. Who knew how long the Americans would stay and what onerous conditions they would impose next? While the situation hadn't yet deteriorated to extreme repression, Fraser had little faith in the goodwill of the U.S. military.

After entering Donald's apartment building, Fraser bounded up the stairs towards the open door, where Donald and Marie stood gazing down at him. After the trio entered the apartment, Donald locked the door and they all seated themselves at the small kitchen table.

Momentarily, Fraser leaned forward and said, "Now that we're alone together I've something important to tell the two of you. I'm leaving Quebec secretly and I want you both to come me; Donald with me immediately and you a few days later, Marie. It will be easy for you stay in Ottawa after work. What do you say?" He gazed at Marie while reminding himself that her situation was delicate. Marie's secret exit from Quebec meant painful separation from family and friends, who might face harsh reprisals from the American authorities.

While Marie's features betrayed hesitation, Donald instantly replied, "I'm in! Definitely! When do we leave? I can't get out of here soon enough and I admit I've been considering something desperate. It worries me that they are being so tough with non-Quebecers like us; especially ex-military members with combat training. Things may be nastier than we thought. There's no other way out; I think we'll have to swim the river. It's still early October so the water won't be too frigid."

Marie broke her silence and demanded, "Why such a drastic course of action, Fraser? Is there no other way? You know how hard that swim will be, not to mention the danger."

Fraser looked out the window for a moment before replying. "First thing, Marie, you are at risk just from knowing us now. We can't involve you on this side of the river. Beyond that, all the interprovincial roads, bridges, rail lines and airports are guarded and none of us has official permission to leave. We don't have the connections or the time to get forged papers. Please just think about it while I lay out the situation."

After Donald nodded affirmatively, Fraser carried on, "OK, good. We'll have a moonless sky in a couple of nights and my scuba gear is ready. I had the tanks filled last week. As far as I can tell, the only safe place to cross is under the Portage Bridge just below the rapids. The current will be brutal but the turbulence will hide most of our bubbles. What kind of shape are you in, Donald? The other man quickly answered, "About the same as you, I guess. I've been doing a lot of underwater laps at the YMCA pool."

Fraser, while a smoker, was also a serious swimmer and a military-trained diver. "I can handle it. It'll be cold, though. It's mid-October so we'll need to use our dry suits. I'd like to go tonight but it's too risky with that sliver of moon. We know exactly what the Marines will do if they see us. Technically, this territory is under martial law and they likely have orders to shoot suspicious swimmers. That's a scary thought." Donald lit a smoke before commenting, "They wouldn't hesitate for a second."

Fraser considered Donald's answer and turned to Marie. "You both know what this means, right?" he asked but immediately felt like a bastard when Marie answered tearfully, "I will miss my family constantly but they all oppose the occupation and will certainly support my decision to leave. They have their reasons to stay but I've no worries about informants. In fact, they really like you guys, even if you are *Anglais*."

Donald chuckled and said, "Not quite *Anglais*. We're Celts, Marie. There's a world of difference." Marie's considered this and declared, "*Anglais* or Celt, how do I know this? My current work as a French-English translator for the Americans involves frequent visits to Ottawa so all I need do is cross over and drop out of sight to await your arrival. My cousin Louise in Embrun will gladly shelter me as long as necessary." Louise Godard had lost her only son in Afghanistan and, while publicly conservative, had little love for government.

Marie continued, "Later, I will take my chances with the Canadian authorities. Who knows, I may be required to sign a loyalty oath of some sort. That's fine. It is unlikely that the American authorities will pursue a lowly translator and I've never held official membership in any of Quebec's separatist organizations. Everything really depends on the goodwill of the Canadian government. In any case, I can advocate for my family in Canada."

"That sounds solid, Marie. Lay low until I contact you," Fraser stated. He then rose and lit a smoke before looking out the third-floor window to survey the armored vehicles rumbling down Boulevard du Portage. He coughed heavily and excused himself momentarily to consider the gravity of the situation. Automatic-weapons fire popped and crackled in the distance, punctuated by the ugly thud of mortar impacts. *The Marines were especially busy today and a number of militant cells had been eliminated recently by a Force Recon platoon.*

"They're on Maloney Boulevard, too, Simon," said Donald, who had joined him at the window. "Looks like more Marines. I think I can hear tanks in the distance, too."

Fraser replied that it was unusual for the Americans to deploy armor so close to the Canadian border. Something big must be up. Over the last few weeks the QLA had been operating close to Ontario to irritate the Canadian government and provoke an overt military response. That response had never materialized, and instead the Americans had seized the initiative to neutralize the separatist irritant. So far, Canada had limited its military support for the U.S. intervention to logistics and intelligence. Officially, the Canadian government was protesting the occupation of Quebec at the United Nations but the U.S. was indifferent to that.

"I hear the Americans will guarantee Canada a twenty-kilometer strip of Quebec territory along the south shore of the St. Lawrence to protect access to the Maritimes from Ontario to New Brunswick, at least for the interim," Fraser remarked to his friend, who replied, "Do you think they will keep Quebec or give it back to Canada once the separatist movement is destroyed?"

Fraser continued watching the Marines as he pondered the question. "Quebec is too large to completely control militarily but most of the separatist operatives are located in urban centres like Gatineau, Montreal and Quebec City. I think the Americans will offer Canada a shared occupation deal with tough conditions. Once the Marines completely suppress the militants, they will likely demand that Canada deploy troops in the province, especially up north. God knows what the James Bay Cree are going to do."

Donald replied, "I agree with you. Quebec has things the U.S. needs: hydroelectric power, freshwater and all that oil in the Gulf of St. Lawrence. Not to mention the value of an Arctic port on the North Atlantic."

The men entered Donald's bedroom and laid their dive gear out on the neatly made bed. A careful inventory satisfied them that they were well-equipped for a nocturnal passage under cold and rough conditions. In addition to air tanks, they possessed cold-weather dry suits, masks, fins, depth gauges, compasses, flashlights, dive knives and a sturdy mesh bag with flotation bladder. As well, the two had always been fond of heavy dive watches, their only real concession to jewelry.

It had been a while since either man had negotiated cold, turbulent water but their mutual experience dramatically reduced the risk. They once again agreed to minimize their time under the surface by swimming directly under the bridge. This was the really dangerous part because the strength of the current required extra effort to keep a straight course, since the water below the bridge would be clearly visible to Marine guards equipped with night-vision goggles. Once Donald and Fraser were on the Ottawa side, the shore current would pull them downstream to a beach where they planned to surface in the calm shallows behind the shelter of the huge boulders placed there to protect the beach.

Donald looked up from the dive gear and said, "All that dive gear is fine for the swim but we'll have to hide it on the other side? Scuba suits will look a bit odd on the staid streets of Ottawa."

Fraser chuckled softly, gestured towards the carry-all in the corner and remarked, "Oh sorry, I forgot to tell you. That bag contains a few special things for us to drag across in the dive bags. Your stuff is in there too, but you better check it."

Donald's walked over and examined the contents: two leather jackets, jeans, shirts and sweaters, shoes, passports and a pint of brandy. Turning to Fraser with a quizzical look, he asked, "What's with the booze?"

Fraser replied, "I figure we could both use a drink after the swim. He paused to light another cigarette and spoke again. "Go home now; get your IDs, passport and anything else you deem necessary. We may need proof of citizenship back in Canada. Bring it all over here and be careful on the way."

Donald nodded and turned to leave with a promise to return quickly. "I'll pick up some smokes and beer on the way back. At least the Americans haven't closed down the *depanneuse*," he said over his shoulder as he exited the apartment.

After reaching his place, Donald quickly collected the necessary items, filled his car and returned to the darkened streets. The heavy dive tanks clanked loudly as Donald's jeep bumped through a deep pothole. He knew the tanks should have been better secured but time was short. After a few blocks he checked his rearview mirror and noted the presence of a large dark truck behind him. "Goddammit! I don't need this shit!" Donald swore as a large engine's growl shattered the nocturnal air. With shocking speed, the other vehicle was suddenly beside him and Donald turned quickly to face the ugly muzzle of an automatic shotgun held steadily by a large man who gestured for him to pull over. Donald slowed the car, steered to the edge of the deserted street and willed himself to present a calm demeanor. This scenario had disastrous potential but at least he didn't have Fraser's pistol in the car. Still, the scuba tanks were suspicious enough considering their explosive potential.

Donald kept his hands in view as the big man angled up to his window. He remained silent, waiting for the other to speak. Besides the shotgun, the man was laden with grenades, ammunition and a long combat knife. "What ya dooin' out here, boy?" the soldier demanded in a slow drawl that indicated his Southern U.S. origins. "You gotta know you breakin' the nine o'clock curfew drivin' this here car around. What ya got in there, son, and where the hell you goin' to or comin' from? Speak up right quick, now!"

Donald glanced down nervously at his watch and noted the time. It really was after nine. What the hell was had he been thinking, forgetting the curfew? In spite of the dire situation it suddenly occurred to Donald that he might be able to save himself. Subtly, he pressed a button on the edge of his Seiko. "It really is nine o'clock, isn't it," he replied blandly. "I don't know what I was thinking, losing track of time like that. I haven't changed my watch back from Alberta time. It's set for a quarter after seven." He slowly raised his arm so the soldier could see his watch.

The huge American seized Donald's forearm with gorilla fingers and studied the timepiece for a moment before exclaiming, "Goddamn that's a nice one! I got me one of the older models. Lookee here." Donald found himself staring at the nearly identical Seiko dive watch adorning the other's meaty wrist and he offered his compliments on the soldier's good taste in chronographs. "Yeah, boy; it done served me well in Eye-rak and Afgannystan. Damn dusty hell holes they was, too. You move on now!"

Donald smiled nervously, rolled up his window and drove off slowly with his heart throbbing in his chest. Thank God the older watches didn't have the time zone button.

Back at the apartment, the three conspirators reviewed their plans and sat down to what would probably their last shared meal in Quebec. Later, Fraser and Marie left together, returning to his apartment as was their habit. Hopefully, any observers would notice nothing amiss. When the next day dawned, the couple separated, with the understanding that they could attempt no contact until Fraser and Donald were safe in Ottawa.

Forty-eight hours later, Marie took a morning drive across the Portage Bridge, performed a series of translation jobs at the U.S. embassy, emailed her manager and proceeded straight south rather than back to Gatineau. Within an hour she was sitting in Louise Godard's bright kitchen, drinking wine and nervously as she recounted recent events.

"What the hell was I thinking, Louise! What's gonna happen to my family in Quebec if the Americans notice my absence and start poking around?"

Louise noted her distress and said reassuringly, "I admire your courage, Marie. You had to make a move or be in Quebec for God knows how long. If anyone official comes around, I've the dogs outside and Dad's old bomb shelter up on the ridge. We all thought he was crazy to build it; but now I'm glad it's there. I've stocked it with water, food and the necessities. He actually dug a basement tunnel to the barn so people can leave the house unseen. Hopefully it won't come to that, but thank God for Cold War paranoia."

Marie replied, "He was quite a character; I miss him, Louise," and the cousins settled into a companionable silence as Marie's thoughts turned to Fraser and his friend Donald.

Following the passage of another jumpy day, a moonless midnight arrived. Fraser and Donald slid out the back window of Donald's apartment, navigated the fire escape and crouched with their gear in the shadowy alley. The men already wore their matte black dive suits to speed the passage from exit grate to water. After methodically scanning the streets the pair jogged a hundred yards to the nearest sewer grate, shoved in a taped crowbar and gently slid it aside before descending the ladder into the dank, slimy tunnel that sloped to the cold river eight hundred meters distant.

"Get back up and replace that fuckin' grate, man!" Fraser hissed. Donald, behind him on the ladder, scurried back up and gingerly pulled the heavy steel slab back into place. All they needed was a Marine patrol to notice the dislodged grate and throw a few tear gas canisters down the tunnel, followed perhaps by grenades.

After thirty minutes of soggy trudging, Fraser and Donald peered through the thick bars of the exit grate and scanned the blackness for evidence of human presence. They had seen Marine bridge guards directing search lights over the nighttime river, and such illumination was their greatest fear. Fraser waited a full twenty minutes before unscrewing the grate and carefully lowering it to the gritty concrete ledge above the river bank.

After a final survey, the pair donned masks and fins before descending the muddy bank to enter the icy channel beneath the massive bridge. Immediately, the crushing current generated by the upstream cataracts threatened to drag them into the open channel, where calm water would reveal their bubble trails. Linked by a rope and burdened by lead dive weighs, they struggled against the water's force, desperate for contact with the slim safety of the river bottom below the bridge. Though the cold bit into their extremities and exposed faces, both were fiercely determined to complete the crossing.

The men braced themselves against the bridge foundations to rest briefly before setting out. Moments later, Fraser's lead momentum was suddenly halted by the pressure of rope around his waist. The trailing dive bag was caught on something. The distracting delay broke his concentration and he thought suddenly of Marie being apprehended and subjected to RCMP interrogation. Fraser willed his mind clear as the touch of Donald's hand refocused him on the present danger. He directed Donald's gaze to the rope that disappeared into the gloom behind them. Donald nodded and staggered back to investigate. Within moments, the snag was cleared and the divers returned to their plodding course.

Fraser nearly spat out his mouthpiece when the first bullet split the dark water before him. The Marines were firing their rifles down through openings in the bridge rails. The first round was followed by a swarm of projectiles that pierced the icy river, surrounding the struggling men with scores of lethal bubble trails.

Fraser caught Donald's attention, signaled acceleration. The two swimmers drove forward as the glare of powerful searchlights joined the hail of high-velocity lead. After forty feet of progress, the two men felt safer and began pulling themselves along the slimy stones in the near total darkness. Donald tapped Fraser on the arm while pointing to the luminescent wrist compass glowing in the murk. The two adjusted course, hugging the bridge foundation and hastened for the safety of the far shore. With subterfuge irrelevant, speed and depth were imperative.

Within a minute, Fraser felt Donald's cold hand clawing desperately at his arm and he turned his hooded dive light to see his friend's agonized expression through the shattered lens of his dive mask. A random bullet had slammed into the frame of Donald's mask, bending it and shattering the tempered glass. Miraculously, the round had failed to drive any shrapnel into his face and Donald's eyes looked undamaged. However, the mouthpiece of his air hose had been shredded by a second bullet that also smashed the delicate valve of his air tank.

Fraser took a deep breath and passed his bubbling mouthpiece to Donald, who seized it for a few desperate breaths. What he wouldn't have given for a bubble-free air tank, Fraser thought grimly. He understood that only the iron discipline of their military dive training could save them now, as surfacing was out of the question. As occasional bullets continued to slice the water around them, the friends continued with agonizing slowness as they shared their lone means of survival.

After a seemingly endless river bottom crawl, Fraser bumped into a wall of stone and they let the current pull them a kilometer downstream, safely out of rifle range. After a few minutes, Fraser slowly rose to the surface, dragging his injured friend behind him. He seized an outcropping of jagged rock and gingerly raised his head for a survey. This far from the bridge, there were no Marines visible, only rock, river waters and the lights of Ottawa.

Donald's glistening head suddenly appeared, and they grinned at each other in the darkness of the cliff base.

"We made it, buddy!" Fraser whispered breathlessly. "Just a few hundred yards to the beach and we're there." The two friends drifted down the river towards their exit point at Victoria Island as Marine searchlights swept across the river's surface.

Minutes later, the pair paddled through the shallows and secreted themselves behind the boulders at the east end of the small beach. Shivering uncontrollably, they quickly removed their sodden dive suits and pulled on the warm clothing and boots from their waterproof dive bags. Fraser examined Donald's face and was amazed to see only minor cuts and bruises. After hiding their gear under a screen of leaves and brush, they turned simultaneously for a final look at the opposite shore. Things might get interesting now but hopefully Canadian authorities would welcome them after the inevitable debrief. Fraser's pushed aside tender thoughts of Marie and concern about her fate. If all went well, he would see her soon enough and Donald also had friends to consider.

Turning to his companion, Fraser declared, "I never thought there was a wrong side to this river. I was wrong. Let's move out." The two men turned abruptly, shouldered their rucksacks and started up the dark path to a world of fresh uncertainty.

# END CREDITS

by
Stuart Hardy

Jen and Mark would never forget the day they were woken up at five in the morning by a strange booming orchestral score just blurting out of the sky all of a sudden. They jumped in shock out of their respective dream states, looked at one another in hazy-eyed terror, and then decided to scramble into their dressing gowns and go outside and have a look at what was happening.

They weren't the only ones. All over the world in all of the different time zones there were people being woken up in the middle of the night, interrupted during lunchtime conversations, jerked back to life in boring classes as the sound rattled through the windows around them. People in clubs late at night looking to hook up were deafened by the loud long note that dwarfed everything and everyone around them. Deaf people all over the world could feel the vibration ringing through their heads so violently that they just had to go and find out what it was.

Jen and Mark left the small rural house they'd moved to a few years back to get away from the noise of the city, and just like everyone else, they stood watching the sky, bewildered, dazed and wondering if they were dreaming.

Streets and fields everywhere started filling as everyone stared up at the source of the still droning chord.

Painted across the sky in an ethereal glowing font were the words:

## THE EARTH

No explanation. Nothing. Just two words somehow visible from all corners of the Earth in everyone's respective languages.

The words stayed there for approximately sixty minutes.

Jen and Mark both phoned their places of work (hers a local graphic design company, his an estate agency) and they both just sat on the side of the road outside their house, staring up at the words, trying to figure out what this was.

Everyone else did pretty much the same thing. If you tuned into any TV or radio station that day, you'd find pretty much everyone in the media talking endless garbage about it. No one had managed to come up with any theories that made total sense of the situation yet.

Most of what was being said was connected to religion. Maybe whichever God turned out to be the right one was about to reveal him or herself to the world. One theory going around was that one of the world's governments had decided to label the planet so that any passing UFOs could find it more easily. That one may have been a bit of a stupid theory but it was the best that anyone could come up with beyond something equally ludicrous like a mass hallucination or something.

Jen and Mark sat and watched it in a state of pure bewilderment. Both were beginning to get a bit of a headache from the chord emanating from the heavens that was still ringing its way towards the end.

The world collectively held its breath as the chord rung its way out. As the final vibrations echoed across the world, the text began to inch itself upwards ever so slowly. The music then progressed into a recognisable tune; a classical piece that most people had definitely heard at least once in their lives, but no one could quite remember where from. The heavenly strings were a lot more pleasant than the chord, and you could listen to them without getting a headache. The words floated upwards and fizzled out into the atmosphere and disappeared forever. They were then followed by two slightly smaller columns of floating words written in that same ethereal font. These words were a bit harder to make out. Some people went to find binoculars, but discovered that if you looked directly at the words, when magnified, they burnt out your retinas.

It didn't really matter that much though, because everyone who successfully managed to take a closer look after taking the necessary precautions weren't able to read them anyway since the words were written in a multiplicity of what can barely be described as languages that weren't spoken by anyone living.

Upon further inspection and analysis and being filtered correctly for public broadcast, the floating words were found to be spelled-out grunts and onomatopoeia that usually read something along the lines of "Urguburga" or "Raruraurawa" or something equally apparently meaningless.

Everyone stood around that day muttering to one another, not managing to say anything that was of any more consequence than the indecipherable gibberish scrolling across the sky. What did this mean? Why was it there? What happens now? Where do we go? What do we do?

By the end of the day, well after everyone had gotten bored with standing around debating the meaning of the floating words, people started wondering whether this was even anything to worry about at all. Peoples' frail elderly relatives went back inside to have a bit of a lie down; children started playing games with each another; and friends, family, and colleagues started moving the main topic of conversation on and wondering what was going to happen now.

Jen and Mark, still sitting with their neighbours on the side of the road in their dressing gowns, then had phone calls from their respective managers. Both of them said that no one was going to get anything done if they just sat around thinking about the words in the sky all day (if they could legitimately be called words), and they were both expected to be at work tomorrow at 9AM sharp.

Jen and Mark didn't know what else they could do; they didn't have any excuse not to go back to work. Should they just sit here and watch the words go by until something happened? What would that achieve if they did?

So the adults went back to work, children went back to school, half the planet went back to sleep, and life carried on as normal for the time being.

The radio and TV wouldn't shut up about the still-scrolling words, of course. TV channels were opened across all continents broadcasting in all countries, entirely dedicated to the live streaming of and rolling news concerning the words in the sky. Jen and Mark would sometimes watch the UK's iteration of the same idea, "SkyWords News," when they got home from work, but it was getting a bit dull after a while because there was never anything new. The experts were still scratching their heads, the journalists were still saying nothing of consequence, the vox pops were useless, and any politician they had on so they could waffle some meaningless drivel was just as clueless as the rest of them.

By about three months down the line, life had gone almost totally back to normal. The continuing orchestral music just sort of faded into the background for most people. It became like the low humming of aeroplanes, birdsong, or the neighbours' dog barking. It was always changing as the song went on, so you never annoyingly got a repetitive catchy bit of it stuck in your head.

Sure, it was annoying that people could only just about look up at the clouds in the sky now without getting a searing pain in their eyes from the scrolling text, but who has the time to just sit and watch the clouds all day anyway? Layabouts!

The governments couldn't be bothered to do anything about it. Sure, people complained about light pollution, but nowhere near enough people saw precisely what harm the words were doing to anybody. Doing anything about it would be a waste of public money. I mean, yes, all right: the words lit up the night sky like a never-ending firework display, but if you can't sleep then just buy a blindfold or get thicker curtains, you cheapskates! Honestly, this isn't that much of an inconvenience!

So the gibberish kept scrolling across the sky for years, and the years ended up becoming decades. Jen and Mark got married and had two children in that time. They named them Luke and Samantha, and Luke and Samantha grew up in a world where the scrolling words in the sky were normal; they'd always been there, always would be, there was nothing they could do about it and nothing was going to change. Luke and Samantha grew up and went to school, Jen kept designing websites and logos for companies, Mark sold houses. Life was generally good for everyone.

There were the occasional issues that arose that got everyone thinking about the words in the sky again, but not for very long. Scientists had noticed something strange about the still-scrolling words in the years since they had begun. They'd been keeping an ongoing transcript of the words, and they found that as time had gone by, the spelled grunts and onomatopoeia had started to resemble actual words. Most of the words were from long-dead languages, but there was something that looked like a noun here and there, and then there was a long section which sort of looked like Ancient Egyptian hieroglyphics, but that was probably just a coincidence. The human mind tends to see patterns in things that aren't there; they see shapes in clouds and such; it was probably just a lot of worry over nothing.

No one thought much of it until one day about four decades later when everything changed. Samantha had gotten married and had children of her own. She and her husband had gone to visit Grandma and Grandpa, and there'd been a sudden newsflash interrupting some film that the family were watching together in the evening while the burning gold in the sky outside was still lazily scrolling by.

It was a bit of a shock, as breaking news always is. Was a major political figure dead? Had a war started? The newsreader's grave expression as the incidental music rang out said that it might even be worse than that.

Jen gripped Mark's hand tightly as he began.

"The writing in the sky, first identified as ancient Sumerian approximately five years ago, is now comprised mainly of Hebrew, Tamil, Basque and the occasional bit of Macedonian," said the newsreader. "A new theory among scientists is that the words that we have been seeing all these years were the names of cavemen from the first two-point-eight million years of human existence, and now we're beginning to see the credits of dead civilizations," the newsreader trailed off. His face had gone a pale grey; he was visibly shaking and appeared barely able to make it through the broadcast.

"They are beginning to believe that what we are seeing are the end credits of mankind."

Households around the world sat in stunned silence for a while, not really sure how to react to that. Jen, Mark, Samantha, her husband, and the grandchildren all got up and headed for the door. They stepped out into the wordlit evening and gazed up, careful to shield their eyes from the bright light of the still-moving text.

All of them were now thinking the same thing.

"Is this really happening? When am I going to see my own name, or the name of someone I recognise?"

They only thought that for a little while though. More questions followed, and those questions were batted back and forth through everyone's minds and all the news channels in the years that followed.

Typical broadcasting was suspended once again so everyone could jabber about the writing and ask all the necessary questions and fail to come up with meaningful answers. What does this mean? Why is it happening? Are famous people going to have more prominence than non-famous people? Should I buy one of those adapted pair of binoculars and spot the famous ones like Genghis Khan, Alexander the Great, Jesus or, when its gets further down the line, John F Kennedy, Elvis and Martin Luther King Jr.?

However, the questions then moved away from the writing and on to why the birth rate had dropped.

It had been going on for several years now and most people had ignored it. A higher number of couples had just sort of decided on their own not to have children for some reason; they wanted to live their lives first, it would be too much hassle, maybe they'd get round to it later if they could be bothered. Births were still going on, but impotence was on the rise and the doctors were struggling to explain it. Couples in a perfect bill of health would find that, no matter how many times they had sex, the test would always come back negative. IVF became a lot more difficult, so many failures, the occasional success, but the birth rate just kept dropping off and this last year it had been the lowest figure recorded in centuries. Scientists, doctors, journalists, politicians, and everyday folk had been arguing about the cause of it for years. Was it societal? Biological?

Until now, it had only ever been a mildly eyebrow-raising set of statistics, the type of story that the papers and news channels jabber about incessantly but ordinary people don't really pay that much heed to. It was only now that people were starting to connect it to the writing in the sky. The evidence wasn't firm in any way, the connection was only an arbitrary one, but a theory was going around that maybe the world was being prepared for the last line of the end credits of mankind.

Everyone did still get on with their daily lives, but it wasn't like it was before. This time everyone was tense and on edge, certain that the words in the sky meant something now. How much time did they have left? How long would a dead language last? Ancient Sumerian had vanished from the text a long time ago.

Grandma and Grandpa had a bit of a falling out with Samantha one day when she came to visit with the kids. Samantha had been angry at them for a while. She kept asking them about the words in the sky. What had been going through their heads when it had first appeared? Just what the hell did they bloody think two columns of scrolling text in the sky were? Wasn't it obvious that something really ominous was happening and that they should do something about it? Just why the hell hadn't anything been done? Why didn't the government fund research into it? Just who the hell decided that everyone should just carry on with their lives in spite of the fact that the end credits for the human race had been scrolling across the sky this entire time and no one had realised?

Jen and Mark didn't really have much of an answer. They got a bit defensive for a while, offered up some petty excuses and started to blame everyone but themselves.

"Well, why didn't anyone else sort it out? You can't blame us here! We always thought someone else would deal with it, how were we supposed to know? Samantha, please, we just didn't understand . . . "

It was that day that the news announced they'd spotted Jesus of Nazareth.

It wouldn't be too long now. All of history being considered, the post-Jesus period of mankind was basically nothing. Of course, governments were talking about it again—there were summits, collaborations between superpowers—but no one could agree on any one strategy. Sending shuttles up to examine the words hadn't done any good; they'd just floated through the words as if they weren't there. No one could identify what they were made of; it was as if they didn't exist at all. All that the space stations orbiting the Earth could do was just watch the backwards credits scrolling across the Earth and vanishing into nothingness. The Americans tried launching nuclear missiles at them just because why not? But the missiles had just passed through the ghostly apparition and floated off into space.

They were all out of ideas. The writing was on the sky.

Mark died a few months after Jesus appeared in the credits. Heart attack. He was a chain smoker most of his life, ate a lot of fatty products, and rarely exercised. He was seventy-two. He and Samantha hadn't made their peace in the end, but strangely that didn't seem all too tragic to either Jen or Samantha. Everyone was too preoccupied with what was going to happen when the credits reached the end to think about anything going on in their own lives.

No babies at all had been born in the last year. Every man and woman on the planet had been made infertile somehow. Maybe the words were radioactive? Who knows? Who cares? All that mattered was that the list of potential names was finite now. It was all going to come to a head eventually, and what would happen then? Would everyone left alive just suddenly drop dead? Would the world fade out of existence like the end of a movie? Were the credits going to end by listing the production company? At least absolute proof of whether there was a God or not would be some small comfort in the Earth's final moments.

After she got back from the hospital, where she'd said her final goodbye, Jen sat on her porch just across from where she and Mark had sat all those years ago staring up at the writing in the sky wondering what it all meant. She had really bad cataracts by that stage and everything was all just a fuzzy blur to her, so she didn't care about the pain caused by the intense light of the words or if she would end up going completely blind just by looking at them.

His name would be scrolling up to the heavens soon, and then hers would follow. She wasn't too worried like everyone else was because at least they'd be together; Jen and Mark would have peace where they were going.

Everyone will have their peace when the world ends.

# I'VE BEEN WAITING FOR YOU

by
Larry Hodges

President Smith rubbed his hands in excitement as he sat behind the Oval Office desk for the first time. He'd moved in that morning, January 20, but had avoided the desk until now, after the official inauguration. It had been a grueling election year, but half the American people are chumps—useful idiots—and he'd lied, insulted, and conned his way into office—like all his predecessors, though none were quite the master of the game as he. But now the election was over. He'd given President Jones a thumping, sending the one-term president back to the footnotes of history. Now he could go about the job of being the greatest president ever.

Something caught his attention in the corner of his eye—did the top desk drawer just move? He stared down at it. He leaned forward and then stopped—what was that stench? He wrinkled his nose. Had Jones left a rotten tuna sandwich in the top drawer? That would show real class.

It was customary for each president to leave a note there for his successor. What type of note would that loser president leave for him? An apology? A plea not to unravel his pitiful legacy? Perhaps a temper tantrum as he once again ripped into Smith for all the outrageous stuff he'd pulled in the election, one last outburst from the worst president in the history of ever, who just didn't get this "winner take all" election thing? He'd met with Jones that morning, but the man seemed dazed, as if he couldn't believe he was no longer president. He swore nothing like that would ever happen to him, and that eight years later he'd be having a much happier meeting with his hand-picked successor.

Many said James Buchanan was the worst president ever, while Lincoln, his successor, was the best. Jones had taken over the worst spot, and history would repeat itself. There'd be a fifth head on Rushmore, even if he had to force the budget item through himself. Maybe he'd grow a beard to match Lincoln's. He himself was almost as tall as his supposed idol, with piercing blue eyes that he often used to skewer opponents. Perhaps he'd have to colorize Rushmore.

It was time to see what note Jones had written for him, and find out what was causing the stench. He reached down and opened the drawer. The rotten tuna fish stink increased a hundredfold, the stench of a dead presidency.

"I've been waiting for you," said the slimy green alien in the president's desk drawer. The words appeared directly in Smith's brain. He gasped as he pulled his hand back. It was like a big green cabbage, flattened slightly so it could fit in the drawer, with bits of mucus dripping off its leaves. A pair of tentacles sprouted from the top. "We're going to have a great four years together."

"Who and what are you?" asked the president. "How are you talking to me?"

"It's called telepathy, stupid," said the alien.

"Nobody calls me stupid!"

"That's factually inaccurate; I just did." The alien waved its tentacles about. "But you never worried about facts, did you? As to who and what I am, I am the president." The alien slowly oozed its way out of the drawer and onto the desktop. "Well, not really. Just the acting president. Who do you think ran everything these past four years?"

"President Jones?"

"Nope," said the alien. "He was almost as bad as you, though of course every election brings a new low from you humans. No, the very day he took office, I took over, just as I've done for so many past presidents."

"I'm calling security," said the president.

"Feel free. Except you'll find time has come to a stop for others while we have this little chat. They won't be able to react until we're done. Why don't you pick up a pen and drop it?"

Smith hesitantly picked up an official presidential pen from the desk and let it go. It hung in the air, gently rotating. Smith waved a hand over it to check for strings, but there were none.

Smith had started the election campaign an unproven novice at campaigning, but had quickly figured out how to react to any situation. In all cases the answer was to counterpunch, using lies and distortions to change the subject back to the villainy of his adversary, and never forgetting that the big lie is more believable and effective than the small lie. He thought he'd seen everything, knew everything, and was ready to respond to anything. But conversing with a slimy green alien telepath while watching a pen float in the air was not something he'd prepared for. But when in doubt. . . .

"So what type of losing demon-spawn are you?" he asked. "If you're the devil looking for a soul to steal, you've come to the wrong guy. Our military will destroy you so fast you'll—"

"Ah, the joy of stupidity," said the alien. "Let me know when you're done so we can continue our discussion. And then we can get back to normal time in no time." The alien laughed hysterically at its joke, which was disconcerting to Smith since it came from inside his head.

"Funny thing about time," continued the alien. "One minute, you're sitting in the Oval Office, talking to an alien . . . ," the alien waved one of its tentacles for a moment, " . . . and the next thing you know, four years have passed and your presidency is over."

A wave of nausea passed through Smith. The pen dropped to the desk.

Smith pushed the button under his desk that called security. Somehow he felt a bit drowsy, even dazed, like a bad early morning before his coffee.

"The security you find outside may surprise you. But that button doesn't work anymore—I disconnected it." The alien pointed a tentacle at the Oval Office door. "You have a visitor." The alien quickly oozed back into the top desk drawer, but with the drawer still open so Smith could see it.

Senator Reed waddled in. If the guy ever became president he'd break Taft's weight record, move Carter to No. 2 on the presidential scold rankings, and make them all forget about Bush 2's smug factor. But for now, Smith needed to be polite so he could con and swindle his agenda past the opposing party's majority leader.

"Did we have an appointment?" Smith asked.

"Funny one," said Reed. He sniffed the air. "You need a shower or something?" Then he froze in place, a stupid grin on his face.

"Okay, I get it, you've stopped time again," said Smith to the alien. "What's going on?"

"Just thought I'd give you the heads up that four years really have passed. You governed—well, I did—according to the stupid stuff you campaigned on, and you were a crummy president. You just lost re-election in a landslide to Senator Reed, who will be sworn in at noon today, two hours from now. Sorry, you won't be going down as any type of Lincoln."

"I don't believe you!" Smith exclaimed. Why, he'd just been sworn in an hour ago!

"Why not look out the window?"

The curtain behind the desk was pulled closed. Hadn't it been open before? Smith rose and walked over. His hand began to tremble as he drew open the curtain, squinting his eyes against the expected sunshine.

There was no sunshine. Outside the White House grounds, the local buildings had been burned to the ground. Smoke rose from nearby buildings and covered the sky. Tens of thousands of people encircled the White House.

"Civil war," said the alien. "You liked to compare yourself to Lincoln. He said, 'A house divided against itself cannot stand.' You divided that house with everything you said and did to reach this office. Unlike Lincoln, you had to deal with a civil war you brought on yourself."

"But I didn't do it!"

"Oh, really?" asked the alien. It waved a tentacle side to side at him with a tut-tut gesture. "The masses gathered outside are not here for you. They are here for President Reed. He brought the country back together from the mess your policies and rhetoric brought on. Though of course shortly I'll be taking over again. You humans aren't capable of governing yourselves."

"So what do I do now?"

"That's up to you and your lawyers. You're a private citizen now, so there's no need to impeach you through a corrupt congress. The police are waiting outside with arrest orders. Good luck."

# THEY BLEED GREEN

by
Laszlo Tamasfi

Aaron was on the verge of crashing after a three-day coffee binge. In the last thirty-some hours he'd only gotten off of his computer to put on another pot or to nuke some pizza rolls in the microwave. He always got like this around election time.

And this year, the frenzy continued well beyond the inauguration.

THEY BLEED GREEN, he typed. He was in caps-lock mode, which was frowned upon on the Forum, but he was losing his patience.

I DON'T CLAIM TO KNOW WHAT THEY ARE, BUT I KNOW THEY'RE NOT HUMAN. THEY BLEED GREEN.

He shoved his cigarette butt down into the two-liter soda bottle that had turned into his improvised ashtray two days ago and now was almost full.

LOOK AT THE KENNEDY ASSASSINATION! THE SECRET SERVICE GUY IS HAULING ASS AFTER THE CAR TO CLIMB ON AND COVER UP AS MUCH OF THE BLOOD AS POSSIBLE.

JACKIE IS FREAKING OUT WHEN SHE SEES IT. MAYBE SHE DIDN'T KNOW.

He wasn't sure if he made sense, but he hit 'post' anyway.

It was five A.M. in Washington, D.C., and the only cats on the Forum were the guys in France, and that one kid in Japan who was using that awful Google translator. Nobody liked him.

He stared at the monitor for a long second. Nothing. No response from anyone.

The lines on the screen blurred as he dozed off for a moment. He shook his head; he couldn't afford to stop. Not now. The power was changing hands in the White House, and this was their only chance. The only frail moment in this age-long conspiracy. Different puppet masters were coming in to move different pawns on the same old global chess board. They were playing us.

THEY ARE PLAYING US, he typed. His eyes were burning, partly from the cigarette smoke but mostly from exhaustion. THEY'RE NOT HUMAN. JUST LOOK AT TRUMP'S HAIR. HIS ORANGE TAN.

He closed his eyes to stop the burning. He squinted and looked at the screen.

IT'S LIKE HE DOESN'T EVEN TRY TO BLEND IN ANYMORE.

He squinted again…

… only to wake up to the sound of the doorbell.

He was confused. A message on his monitor said TGRTRRRRR-RRRRRRRRRRRRRRRRRRRR, which was the record of his head hitting the keyboard. His mouth was dry. He picked up the soda bottle but saw that it was filed with cigarettes and ash. He gagged as he put it back down.

The doorbell rang again.

And again.

"I'm coming!" he yelled, but not as loudly as he meant to.

He stumbled to the door.

"Who is it?"

"What do you mean? It's me. I've been texting you for the last hour."

It took Aaron a moment to place the voice. It was Charlie. Aaron's only mate from the Forum who actually lived in town.

"What do you want?"

"Are you kidding me?! You really didn't get my messages?"

"No. But I'm busy. I'm working on something."

"I know. That's why I'm here! I got you proof, brother. Proof!"

Aaron paused.

"I have it with me," said Charlie. "I couldn't bring it home. Sarah would freak out if she found it. Let me in!"

Aaron started unlocking the door. This always took a while: He'd had two sets of steel security bars installed by a friend. It was, of course, against every fire code imaginable, but on the upside it would stop the police from ever bursting into his apartment.

"Hurry up, before somebody sees me. I just bought Obama's skin from a homeless guy."

Aaron stared down at the box.

It was a very unassuming box, a case for canned green beans. It had obviously been put to good use since then. It was weathered, with water stains, and it had several layers of duct tape holding it together.

"I got tipped off by one of the guys I work with at the shelter. He thought it was a joke and he knew I'm into this stuff." Charlie opened the box. "But it's not a joke."

And there it was. President Barack Hussein Obama's skin, neatly folded, like those uniforms in the military.

"Holy shit."

Aaron was putting on the powder-free latex gloves he kept around just in case something like this would happen.

"I think it's a 'Phase Three's skin . . ." Charlie pointed at the scalp. "Look at how his hair *just* started turning gray!"

"You're right. 2011, maybe. 2012?"

"That's what I thought. Definitely reelection era."

Aaron reached for it but paused at the last second. "Do you mind?"

Charlie shrugged. "Not at all. Let's make sure it's the real thing before we get too excited."

Aaron pulled the skin out of the box. It wasn't quite like anything else he'd ever touched. It was stiff and elastic at the same time but softened up wherever he touched it. Maybe it reacted to his body heat? Who knows?

"I heard that there's a changing room right below the East Wing. It's set up to look like an emergency bunker, but its real purpose is to coat the president in a new skin, in case something unexpected happens," explained Aaron, as he lifted it closer to his eyes.

It was amazingly detailed: the hair, the fingerprints, everything was there.

"Ha. I wonder what it's made out of."

"I don't know, but it's incredible. It looks freakishly real," said Charlie.

"There's a guy in Philly who created a program that analyzes the president's photos. It looks for inconsistencies. He concluded that a skin has a shelf life of about three months. At most."

"This one seems to be in pretty good shape."

"I think they're getting better at it. Even Bush W. had to change his a lot more than Obama."

Aaron could feel something hard inside the skin suit. Small and paper-thin, like a potato chip, stuck inside the right arm. Or more like a guitar pick.

"Wait a second," Aaron said.

He tried to reach in for it, but his hands would only go in up to the elbow.

"Sorry. There's something . . ."

Aaron started carefully turning the skin inside out.

". . . in there."

The skin's inner lining had a deep red, raw flesh color, and it was veiny. Aaron wondered if it was really organic, or if it was designed this way just to sell the illusion even more.

"I got it." It was wedged in right by the wrist. It gave only a little bit of resistance as he pulled it out.

For a long moment, they stared at the tiny object in Aaron's hand.

"I think it's okay to get excited now. I'm pretty sure it *is* the real thing."

"No shit." Charlie nodded. "Wow."

It was, of course, a scale.
A giant lizard scale.

*"He thinks he can do anything he wants. That he's above the law. He lies, and lies, and tweets, and the same people who were freakin' out over Hillary's emails don't give a shit about somebody hacking his Twitter account and starting World War Three with a hundred and forty characters. That's all it takes. Somebody to type in HEY CHINA, ENJOY THE NUKES!, and that's it! You know, I guarantee you, there is not a government on Earth that wouldn't believe that the president of the United States sent that message. Maybe end it with an obnoxious SAD! Or misspell something, to make it look right."*

The words seeped into Aaron's consciousness like a lullaby. The voice was soothing, and familiar, but the words didn't even matter. It just had a nice rhythm. He only woke up fully when the car made a sudden stop.

"Hey man, you okay?" asked Charlie, as he turned the radio off.

"Yeah. Sure. I'm fine."

But of course he wasn't fine. He was sleep-deprived and didn't know where he was.

"I'll be right back."

And with that, Charlie got out, leaving the car running.

They were in a parking lot. It was, according to the clock in the dashboard, ten in the morning. The sun was out, but it couldn't muster up enough heat to take on the winter chill. It was a gray, smoggy day, and everything felt like a headache coming on.

Aaron looked around. They were parked between a coffee shop and a pet store, and he really hoped that Charlie had gone into the coffee shop.

He rolled down the window and lit a cigarette. After a moment of silence, he turned the radio back on.

"... *I mean, don't get me wrong, we had some seriously shady people in the White House before. Bush destabilized the Middle East and started spying on the American people. Clinton was a sex addict. And you can go back, really, to how Reagan lied about his Alzheimer, and Nixon used the FBI like they were his personal henchmen.*"

It was *The Eric Rant Hour*. A shortwave radio broadcast from the bowels of D.C., hosted by a communist liberal who was proud to be a social justice warrior. Aaron really liked him.

"*But this? How did this pussy-grabbing monster get in there?! He's insane, he's dumb as a brick, and the worst of it, he's greedy and selfish and an egomaniac!*"

Aaron pulled his phone out and logged on to the Forum.

"*He's a giant man-baby.*"

There was a single reply to his rant from last night. He clicked on it.

YOU'RE AN IDIOT.

Three words. That's it. Of course from that douchebag in Japan. Aaron imagined that he meant to type in something much nastier but couldn't get it through Google translate. That made him smile.

He put the phone away without replying. He wasn't an idiot; he had proof.

He looked at all the people in the parking lot and wondered if this was the moment that everything would change. Is this where the veil falls off of everyone's eyes and they finally see that we've been slaves all this time? We have overlords. Lizard overlords. As crazy as it sounds.

"*A racist, who entered politics by spreading birther conspiracies. Trying to delegitimize the first black president by saying that he wasn't born in the U.S.*"

"He's right," said Charlie as he got into the car.

"What?"

"Trump. He's right about Obama. You know, not being a natural-born American."

Aaron nodded. "Hadn't thought of it that way before."

"They're all the same. It's all just a circus to keep us entertained."

Charlie had a large paper bag in his hands. Sadly, it wasn't coffee. It had the pet store's logo on it.

"What are we doing here?" said Aaron.

"You wanted me to take you to the guy I got the skin from," said Charlie, "and this is what he wants."

He pulled a plastic container out of the bag. It was clear, and Aaron could see that something was moving inside of it. Took him a second to recognize what it was.

It was full of live crickets.

"I'm pretty sure he's one of your lizard guys."

Aaron knew the neighborhood. He'd grown up on this side of the river, only a mile or so north.

"I still don't know why he would pretend to be homeless," he said, staring at the container in his hand. He thought he could feel the crickets moving inside, their tiny bodies pushing against it as they were crawling and hopping and doing whatever crickets do. It was gross. Gross, but fascinating.

"What do you mean *pretend*?!"

"The lizard man or whatever it is. Why would it disguise itself as a homeless man?"

"He's not faking it," Charlie said. "He lives on the corner of St. George and Varella, in a tent made out of moldy plywood and an old recycling bin. Maybe he really doesn't have anywhere else to go."

He was driving really slowly, to the point that it was a traffic hazard, but Aaron knew not to give him a hard time. It was an occupational habit with Charlie. As a social worker, he was always looking at the people on the sidewalk, trying to spot the ones who were in trouble.

"He's hungry all the time," said Charlie, "and he gets cold just like anybody else."

"How long exactly have you've known him?"

A black BMW behind them started honking, so Charlie turned his hazard lights on.

"About six weeks. Hard to tell." Cars were passing them. "I think he used to stop by the food bank wearing a different skin. He used to be this Jamaican woman, and only became a tattooed traveler-type dude about a week ago." They were passing a dodgy-looking gas station and Charlie waved at someone filling up his tank.

"What the hell makes you think it was the same person?!"

"Oh, wait till you see him. He's like six-foot eleven, for starters. Also . . . you just know." They turned onto a side street. "You have to understand, this guy is scary!"

He looked at Aaron as if to make sure he was listening. "Your subconscious senses that something is wrong. That primitive part of your brain . . . the part whose job was to ensure that you'd survive in the wild. It knows that this man is an impostor."

A chill crawled up Aaron's arm, all the way to his back where it made the hair stand up.

"And it wants you to run away as fast as you can."

Aaron could tell why Varella Avenue would be a popular spot for someone stuck outside in this weather. There was steam coming out of the manholes. Islands of warmth, where the snow always melted and you could stop shivering.

He lit a cigarette. His throat was dry and his lungs were burning, but he didn't care. It was helping him stay awake.

"Do you know what you're going to say to him?" asked Charlie as he stopped to light one too, holding the reptile feed under his arm. "We can't just go there and stare at the guy."

"I'll think of something. Let's see if he's there first."

They walked by chain-link fences and old warehouses.

"I want to know if it's real," said Charlie. "If he really is one of our lizard overlords, living on the streets of D.C. for some godforsaken reason."

A woman passed them, pushing a baby carriage full of clothes.

"Maybe he's been banished," said Aaron "Maybe he chose to leave his kind. Either way, he was willing to sell the Obama skin for pocket change, so he must be down on his luck."

They climbed under a gate, and while it didn't have any signs on it, Aaron had the feeling that they were not supposed to be there.

"I always wondered if I was crazy," he said. "I believed, with all my heart, that we were slaves and that there was a secret society of lizards running our lives. But I knew it was crazy talk. It's nuts, if you think about it."

The street was about to end, behind a shopping strip with delivery trucks and giant trash compactors.

"But it's true. That's the crazy part."

"I know the feeling," said Charlie. "It's like a bizarre addiction that I even have to keep hidden from my own wife. She would think I have brain damage if she knew half the shit I think . . . the shit I *know* about the world. I once made the mistake of telling her *why* we can't drink the tap water when we visit her parents in Colorado . . . "

He stopped and looked at Aaron.

"We're almost there. We have to put our cigarettes out."

"He doesn't like the smoke?"

Charlie laughed. "It's not that at all . . . he'll try to bum the whole pack off of you if he sees that you have some."

The tent where the lizard overlord was living was a real shithole.

It reeked. Not like the stench of body odor people on the street have. It was something alien. Something you might smell in the zoo if they let you in with the crocodiles.

And Charlie wasn't exaggerating about the moldy plywood either. It was nasty black mold, the kind that makes you sell your house and move to a new city.

"Where is he?" asked Aaron as he peeked into the tent.

"Who knows?" said Charlie.

It was cold, and they'd been standing there for what felt like an hour but was probably closer to ten minutes.

"I'm going in," said Aaron.

He entered the tent before Charlie could object. It was very tall, but not very wide: He could easily stand up, but not without his shoulders touching the walls. The canvas was torn up on one side—that's where the plywood was propped up—and one area was soggy with . . . something. Aaron realized that whoever or whatever was living there liked his environment different than a human would. That maybe for this creature, living in this gray, damp city was paradise. At least this time of the year.

"Hurry up!" said Charlie.

Aaron was standing on rags; not clothes, just rags, in a giant pile. Like a nest.

"It's okay. There's nothing in h—" The ground started shaking before he could finish his sentence.

He fell against the plywood. Steam was coming up, and the nest of rags started to move. He realized that the tent was set up on top of a manhole.

The lid lifted up. Long hands emerged to grab the edge of the concrete. Then the rest of the body came out, naked, wet, and covered in tattoos. His skin was hanging, wrinkled; his head was bald; and he had a long, gray beard.

Aaron panicked. He was, after all, in somebody's house. Uninvited.

The creature seemed stunned to find Aaron there. It stood silently for a minute, towering over him. It was huge. Yet . . .

To Aaron, he looked just like an old, frail man. Like someone he could take down.

He could hear Charlie yell at him, but he didn't care. He launched himself at the creature.

And there it was. That primitive part of his brain that Charlie had told him about. It went into overdrive the moment he put his hands around the creature's neck.

The old-man skin glided on top of the scales underneath, inhuman, wrong, different. His brain screamed at him to run. That this person was not who he pretended to be. That he was an impostor.

He let go and stepped back, which was enough for the creature to knock him down.

"You fuckin' assssshole. You almosssst ripped my only sssssuit."

Aaron could feel something land on his face. Something tiny, with six pointy legs and a couple of antennas. It wandered around on his cheek for a second, then came the fingers. Slimy, long fingers that picked the cricket off of him.

And then he could hear crunching.

And with that, he fell back into the darkness once more.

His back was hurting, and that's how he knew that he'd been lying there for a while. That, and he was cold. The cold seeped deep inside his bones, to the point where he wasn't even shivering anymore.

He was afraid to open his eyes, until he heard Charlie's voice.

"Of course I can spare one more."

A moment later he heard the lighter clicking, and he knew then that the creature was taking one of Charlie's cigarettes. He was okay.

He sat up.

It was dark out, but there was a small fire burning in a tire. Charlie was sitting on a crate, pulling his jacket as tight as he could. The old man . . . no, the creature . . . the creature was sitting there, smoking a cigarette and playing with something in his lap.

The creature looked at him, and then back to Charlie.

"Ssso, this is your friend?"

"Yes. That's Aaron. A nice guy, when he's not panicking."

Aaron looked around. The tent was all shredded to pieces. The plywood was bent—it was too damp to break, but it was nonetheless unusable. Clothes were everywhere.

"Sorry I fucked your place up," he said with a shaky voice.

The creature laughed. Or hissed. It was hard to tell.

"It'sss okay. No harm done." His eyes were two burning dots in the darkness and they reflected the fire. "But I would've crushed your skull open if you messssed up my suit. This is my last one."

The creature pulled on his skin to move it back into place. It was sliding down his body in an unnatural fashion.

"I've been trying to sssalvage this one that I got when Andrew Holness was in town. You know, the Jamaican prime minister."

And that's when Aaron realized what the creature was doing. He was sewing.

In his lap was skin. Dark skin, with big breasts and long dreadlocks. He was trying to close a big tear down the side.

"I loved diplomatic visitsss. They were like Halloween, you could play dresss up and no one could judge you!"

He smiled, and it was terrifying.

"Ww . . . what happened?" asked Aaron, as he carefully scooted closer to the fire. "To you, I mean?"

The creature looked confused.

"I thought you knew," he said. He took a drag of his cigarette. A deep, satisfying drag, and he held it down for a long moment.

"I thought that'sss why you're here. That you knew."
The smoke gushed out of his lungs as he spoke.
"We losssst."

"God knows, we tried. We had Jeb Bush ready to go, with the family dynasssty and the whole nine yards. Same with Hillary. But nooo . . . you guys didn't want to have anything to do with that." He spat into the fire "It'sss okay. The times were changing. You wanted excitement and you had enough of the establishment."

The skin was slowly drooping down his face as he spoke, and Aaron could see something green underneath.

"And that's where we fucked up. We meant for Ted Cruz to be the outsssider candidate, and it didn't work. He was stuck in the 'uncanny valley.' He never learned to behave like a human being, and the voters noticed. Fuck me, they noticed big time. I know that the guy who was first wearing the Cruz skin got forty lashes for that disastrous performance. He should have gotten eighty. It was really amateur hour."

The creature took the lid off the container and grabbed another cricket.

"The lassst one for the night. Want to leave some for the morning." He popped it into his mouth. He didn't bite down on it at first, but let it run around for a moment. Then finally came the satisfying crunch, and a smile.

"Cruz never passed for a human, and by the time we realized that nobody would trusssst him it was too late."

Aaron lit a cigarette. "What about Trump?" he asked.

"Trump?" said the creature. He stood up from his crate. The skin of the Jamaican woman fell on the ground next to him. "What about Trump, you asssk?!"

He screamed—or laughed, it was hard to tell—but the blood froze in Aaron's veins as he sat there. Dogs started howling somewhere, as if they were answering him.

"He's all yours, my friend. Trump isss all on you!"

It took Aaron and Charlie a couple more visits to piece the picture together. The creature would hold information back until they brought more snacks. They got him a space heater and a generator, although he must have sold them because they were both gone by their next visit.

It was difficult to talk about Trump around him. It made him furious. The lizard overlords were just as caught off guard by his popularity as anyone else. But Trump was only one symptom of a bigger change.

"There's only a few of usss left. Trudeau in Canada, the last one guarding North America. And for Europe?" he revealed one time. "What. A. Fuckin'. Shit. Show. Merkel is hanging on by a thread, and she's already planning her new life after politics. She doesn't have illusions about where it's all going. We lost the U.K. with Brexit. We lost Hungary and Italy. France is about to sssink."

Aaron thought that to an outsider they must look like just some guys sitting around a fire, drinking beer and talking politics. It was almost a joke.

"What about Russia?" he asked, and he took a sip.

"We never really fit in with the Russians. They threw usss out in the revolution back in 1917. Never recovered from that." The creature was chewing on a snail he'd found crawling on the side of a dumpster. It was stomach-turning. "I, for one, don't really mind. Not a big fan of that hard freeze."

He smiled at Aaron.

"Ssso you can't blame us for Putin either."

Apparently, they had all scattered after the 2016 election. All the lizard people of the Shadow Government. They got fed up.

Politics was so toxic that they just couldn't deal with it anymore. Some of them went on to learn a trade. They learned how to fix cars or do drywall. Most of them took menial jobs; Aaron knew that it was more than possible that a lizard overlord was stocking the shelves at night at his local grocery store.

And some chose to just live on the street. It was still better than putting up with Congress and fighting Trump.

THAT'S THE DUMBEST THING I'VE EVER HEARD.

Aaron wasn't all that surprised at the reaction. It was a weird conclusion to their pursuit of the truth. They were onto something, that was for sure. The Illuminati were real, the Freemasons, the secret symbols on the dollar bill, the secret messages hidden in the blueprints of the White House.

All true, yet none of that mattered anymore.

Not quite a letdown . . . it was terrifying more than anything. They'd been bashing him on the Forum pretty hard lately.

HOW COULD YOUR MOTHER PUSH OUT SUCH A TURD?

Even the Japanese guy had decided to look up some decent insults.

He cracked his fingers and started typing.

THEY LIVE AMONG US. THEY LOOK LIKE YOU AND ME, BUT THEY'RE NOT HUMAN.

THEY GO TO WORK AND TAKE THEIR KIDS TO SCHOOL AND GO ON VACATIONS, BUT THEY'RE JUST PRETENDING TO BE NORMAL.

They'd hidden President Obama's skin in a safe place. They knew that they were about to stir up some trouble, and they didn't want to be caught with the skin of a black man. There'd be no easy way to explain that to the police ...

THEY BLEED GREEN, AND IF YOU EVER GET TO TOUCH ONE YOU CAN FEEL THE SCALES UNDERNEATH THE FAKE SKIN.

The creature was gone. He'd left the tent behind, but eventually the spot was taken over by a different homeless man. Someone who reeked of body odor and was terrified of bugs.

THEY HISS LIKE A SNAKE WHEN THEY LET THEIR GUARD DOWN.

Aaron suspected that the old-man skin finally gave in, and that he'd never managed to repair the Jamaican-woman suit. He'd most likely slid into the sewers one final time, and now lived underground.

SOMETIMES THEY LIVE UNDERGROUND. He was on a roll. IN THE SEWERS.

He looked at his message and hit 'post.' That was as good as it gets.

The coffee maker had been beeping for a while, and he could smell the bottom of the pot burning.

He got off of his chair and stumbled into the kitchen. It was two A.M., and it perhaps had been a mistake to brew another pot.

He stared at the table for a moment. There it was, the last container of lizard feed, the one he never got a chance to give to the creature. He picked it up and shook it. The crickets weren't moving anymore.

He was scared.

He was scared that mankind was in charge of its own destiny. It reminded him of being a young child and realizing that there were no adults in the house. All of a sudden everything felt dangerous. He would look at his cousins playing in the kitchen, and his little sister opening the cabinets in the living room, and realize that he'd still prefer to have a babysitter. That they were not ready to take care of themselves.

He poured himself a coffee and went back to the computer.

One reply.

He didn't expect much, but he clicked on it.

WE'RE FUCKED, AREN'T WE?!?!

Aaron exhaled. Seemed like someone believed him. Or maybe not yet, but it was a good enough start. They would believe him, eventually, when things *really* started to turn to shit.

He lit a cigarette and typed in his answer.

# MONSTER MASH

# RED HATS

by
Eddie Generous

Unacknowledged, a golden brown, sunbaked world passed by the windows of Dr. Christopher Osumi's Volvo S90. Fury blocked all but the physical autopilot: left two county roads and up the fourth dirt path. Blind rage nearly drew him into a driveway pothole big enough that would've swallowed the luxury automobile whole.

The dry-packed dirt driveway was raised several feet above sandy ditches. Crowding the peripheral landscape was a grey forest of primarily dead swamp growth. Osumi stared at the massive hole and considered his options.

He could back out the driveway, cool down, call the school, call his lawyer, call the police, or he could get out of his car and stomp the rest of the way up the excessive and winding path to whatever kind of abode housed the family.

Scott's bloody nose, Scott's black eye, Scott's swollen lips, and the backpack strap welts along Scott's back paraded in a gruesome showcase before the eye of his mind. Images mingled with the heavy words he'd known as a boy. They came despite the promise that words could never hurt him. His mother was a liar—words slash. Words linger and revolve.

Worse, words embolden action, and the man at the top had picked his side.

Osumi kicked open his door and slammed it behind him. Anger took him forward. Osumi stomped with fists clenched, ready to throw the first *real* punch of his life.

Osumi and his wife, Jennifer, had taken all the necessary steps to raise a pleasant, honest, humble, and caring son. They'd promised him good things for being a good boy. One trashy schoolyard bully had made their words worthless. Dr. Osumi had called the school. Jennifer Osumi had called the school. The school was at a loss about what to do with Arnold Walton, *especially nowadays*. The Waltons had no phone, they never answered their mail, and rarely had anyone seen them in town.

Arnold Walton rode a bus.

The same bus Scott rode despite a monstrous social and economic divide separating one county concession from another.

The trouble had gone to simmer in recent years. The country had seemed to be moving forward. The election had it jumping ten steps back almost weekly. The old trouble rolled anew, coming in waves, crashing against every visible minority.

Arnold Walton spent a week at home when Scott told the bus driver the boy was a bully and that he gave Scott an Indian burn and a wedgie. There were insults, things a good boy like Scott didn't dare repeat.

That was strike one and this was strike two, so heavy there couldn't be a strike three.

Scott was in shock. He was a civilized boy in a civilized world. 2017 and Scott heard the things Christopher heard back in 1993, things Scott's grandfather heard when he'd first migrated to the country.

"Unacceptable," Osumi grunted as he rounded the final turn.

About sixty feet ahead was a home on stilts. It looked like a boys' clubhouse, clapped together with whatever the occupants could fetch. A fresh and bright Confederate flag dangled over the stoop.

"Are any of you people home?" he shouted.

A screen door opened and a frumpy, heavy-breasted woman stepped forward in shorts and stained T-shirt, no bra. She had long greasy hair.

"Doug, you 'spectin' someone?" she called back over her shoulder.

"What?" a voice shouted from inside the house.

"I asked if you 'vited over some Chink prick in dancin' shoes."

That ignorant confidence slowed Osumi's pace, but the fury was a residue not so easily rinsed away.

"Is your son the criminal named Arnold Walton?"

The woman frowned at this and a skinny pale man pushed her forward so he could see the figure declaring his son a criminal. The man wore his head shaved to fuzz. The man had tight lips and yellow teeth. Eyes icy blue. He wore cut-off jeans and a yellowed undershirt. Inordinately large hands rode ropey-veined arms. A red ball cap transferred from hand to head. Those four sweat-stained words that put a megaphone to the country's lowest creatures seemed to shout out.

"What you say, Chink?"

The voice was high and grating.

Arnold Walton followed his father out. The boy was big, at least one and a half times the weight of Scott. As if part of the uniform, a red hat lifted and sat loose atop his head. It was bulky and ill fitting. An ugly article with uglier sentiments attached under the guise of betterment.

"I asked if you're the parents of the criminal named Arnold Walton. Your kid has been bullying my—"

The word choice was cause for laughter.

"Bullyin', listen to this. Rich Chink come out to talk 'bout bullyin'? What you think you was doin' comin' out here?"

Being intelligent and learned did not guarantee forethought. This was a question Osumi should've posed before visiting the swamp slum.

*Can't back down now. You came out here because Scott is a good boy and good boys don't deserve torment from social boot sludge.*

"I came out for an apology from your son. I came out for an apology from you as well. I can see your kid has loser parents, so his actions are partly your fault."

A tremble began in Osumi's chest as he spoke. As if lightning struck, the awareness that his car was a half-mile away and that he was another ten miles from much of anything rattled the seeds at his core like a maraca.

The smile never faltered. "Loser? Sounds 'bout right, don't it? What's an apology gonna do? Well, I'm so sorry, Mr. Ping-Pong. Sometimes my boy acts like a boy."

*That's it? That all you need?*

"Anythin' else?" the woman asked.

Although he didn't buy it, his adrenaline dumped sand on his fury. The wise thing to do was to jog back to his car and let the police deal with these people.

*And why should the police care?*

"I suppose not," Osumi said.

He turned and started away, getting only two steps when he heard some of the nastiest words a man of his profession could hear.

"Sic 'em, Meat! Sic, 'em, Stink!" the man said.

Osumi stopped dead and spun slowly as a snarling dog came closer. It was a mangy mutt, genetic traits of Rottweiler and St. Bernard overshadowing any others. The dog had bare patches up both sides from scratching, but otherwise it appeared as healthy as it was nasty.

Bending his knees and spreading out his stance, the twelve-year veterinarian and lifetime animal lover had a pretty good idea of what he ought to do.

*Sure, maybe with one. Didn't he call two dogs?*

Too late for worry. Osumi saw and braced while the dog leapt toward him. Teeth sunk into his forearm and he cried out, turning slightly to use the dog's momentum against it. The fat, furry head lost its grasp. The veterinarian wedged that head beneath his arm. With his free hand, Osumi grabbed onto the dog's hind legs, shifting as he moved, and then slammed the dog down into the dust.

He used his knee to pin the dog at the throat. "Call him off or I'll—!" A second set of teeth sunk into the flesh of his shoulder.

Man and dog rolled, and then, out of nowhere, the offending jaw relented. The dog whined. There was blood and a lot of it. A lucky turn for Osumi; the teeth of a rusty and mostly buried rake tore three long holes in the poor dog's stomach.

*That'll need surgery.*

The pointless thought drained as quickly as it came when the first dog resumed its attack. Teeth entered the back of Osumi's neck and he stiffened, screaming from pain and fear. The vet reached over his shoulder, grabbed fur and jumped as if trust falling. They thumped and the dog reacted like a winded squeak toy. Osumi fixed his grasp. A body follows the head. Control the head, control the body, *survive this mess.*

"Stink?" Arnold Walton's voice joined the wet snap of the dog jerking within Osumi's bear hug.

Osumi wrestled for hold.

"Stink?" The boy's voice was closer.

Osumi leaned against the fighting dog and finally took control. He lifted a knee and stuffed his shoe in the dog's jaw, pressing down while jerking the jagged mandible skyward.

Panting, bleeding and overdosing on adrenaline, Osumi screeched, "Call off the dog or it's dead!"

"You hurt Stink!" Arnold shouted from right behind Osumi. Stink whined. "Dad, Stink's dyin'!"

"Call off this dog or I'll have to do it!"

"Dad! Meat's gonna die too!"

"Call this damned dog off or—!" Osumi wrenched and drove the weight of his knee into Meat's throat.

The bang echoed through him, but he hadn't heard anything. Fresh hot pain in his shoulder worked like earplugs. Dust scattered over Osumi's face and somewhere deep, where survival instinct dwells, he recognized that a second shot had come at him. Up to his feet, he broke for the barren forest.

"Dad, don't let'm get away!"

"Jammin' bugger," the man grumbled, trying to jerk a bad round from the chamber.

"Shoot'm again!" the mother added.

Osumi's senses returned and he listened. If it was left up to them, he was a dead man. He raised a good boy, he was a good dad and a good husband, and the backwoods criminals were in the mood to kill him. This was not how it was supposed to be.

Osumi ran until he no longer heard the Waltons.

*Get to the car and get the hell out of here. Hurry now before Meat gets up and does what those monsters trained him to do.*

Keeping to the trees, Osumi sloshed through the muck and soft moss. Comparatively dry much of the year, the property now was under a foot or more of water, minimum. Huffing and tense, Osumi meandered toward where he'd left his car. It was so far, much farther than he recalled.

It was as if heaven shone down on him when he finally spotted it.

Hell's laughter filled him up on the first step he took from the edge of the dead forest. There was the wife. From the ditch, she'd retrieved two thick, foot-wide boards. The crater wasn't just a worn-out pothole. It was a dry moat…

Osumi patted his pants for keys, already knowing they dangled in the ignition. He hoped that the woman was so far out of touch that she wouldn't understand the push start. There were grumblings accompanying the ding of the open door, and then the gentle purr of the engine sank a dagger into Osumi's chest.

*OK, follow the car. Get to your phone, call for help.*

As the car drove back up the laneway, Osumi heard a boy talking to his dog. It was close and the doctor dropped down onto his face, to peer at the greys and browns from an inch above the mud.

Arnold Walton approached him and at his side was a limping dog. Osumi slid on his belly until he came to deeper muck. He rolled onto his back and let the swamp cover him in murky water.

*Let's see, there's garters, the ribbon, the queen, milk snakes, oh and don't forget rattlesnakes! It's probably dry enough that they'd wander the marsh for food… Stop that, hold your breath and stop all that.*

Stopping was impossible and his imagination slithered fanged and venomous creatures over his vulnerable body, many that weren't even local. He gasped and sprang forward. The boy and the dog were right there. Arnold fell backwards and the frantic doctor grabbed onto the startled dog. He pushed the dog's snapping head under the water while Arnold ran.

"Dad! He's got Meat!"

Bubbles rose.

Legs splashed.

Osumi gazed into space and time, sick about what he did.

Meat was dead. Meat never had a chance to be a good dog.

*And given the chance, he'd have torn your throat out.*

Meat was just one of the family, head the wrong shape for a hideous red hat.

Arnold had not run back to the house. From the laneway, the boy called to his father. The image of an aiming redneck pegged a splinter home and the doctor started off deeper into the woods, back toward the house, in the direction where his car had gone.

*Get the car. Get the phone. Call the police. Get home. Get safe. Hug your family.*

Osumi paused against a tree. The wounds announced themselves more fully than previously. The cool mud stung and countless organisms mingled with the open flesh. So much goes on beyond the eye. So much more goes on beneath the skin.

The image of Scott's damage rose again. The bullies from his own childhood climbed aboard.

Osumi fought off a scream.

The house came back into view. The car was a lagoon in the middle of the desert. The Walton woman sat on the porch, donning a red hat now. She husked corncobs. A rifle leaned against the doorframe. It was older and smaller than the weapon the man wielded. It was plenty big enough to put a hole in Osumi.

"You Chinese prick, you killed my dogs!" a voice filled a distant air and surfaced enough for Osumi to understand. "You come on my property and kill my dogs?"

The woman on the porch nodded with the message.

"You're all insane," Osumi whispered and pushed onward. It was imperative that he understood the landscape and any options he had for sneaking up on the woman. He needed the vehicle and…

Behind the little home was an old Mercury truck. It was pale blue and rusty rainbow.

"Chink!"

The voice was a good distance away and the woman was at the front of the home. Osumi risked it. He crossed the high grass of the backyard to reach the old truck. It was rougher than rough. The keys sat on the dash as if awaiting him. He opened the door and heard the thick buzz. It was not the door-ajar buzz. Bees climbed out of the dash-length hive and targeted the intruder.

Osumi slammed the door and sprinted. He tripped and fell in the high grass. Feet swished through the dry straws as the woman approached in a meaty sprint. Osumi held his breath amid the sun-bleached strands that reached for the sky.

"It's all right, rice eater. You can come on out, I won't hurt ya," she whispered.

Osumi cast a sideways glance, saw only the top of her head across the yard and knew she held the weapon in the ready position. A hollow feeling drummed within and the adrenaline that had washed in and out filled him with highly animated gas. Shivers splashed like vacated bathtub surf.

The woman tracked nearer the truck, moving in a mostly straight line toward Osumi. An imagined muzzle flash bloomed and he cringed. Fantasy would meet reality any second. Like steam burst from kettle.

He tackled the woman. They rolled. She screeched.

"No!" Osumi shouted, driving his fist three times before she took a shot. The report announced how ill equipped he was for battle. After kneeing the downed woman's immense chest, he sprang to his feet and broke for the woods.

Another shot echoed, but no more pain invaded.

Moving beyond his body for a time, right until a crash pervaded his abilities. Crawling, breathing in short, hot sips, everything hurt.

"Rice eater!" the woman screeched.

The husband joined her soon after. "Chink! You don't touch my woman! You don't kill my dogs! You hear me? You'll pay!"

The earth was solid in the woods behind the house. There were more fallen trees and Osumi got an idea. It was no good sneaking in the daylight. Light was a problem. There were two hours until sundown. If he kept close, but hidden, he had a chance to get to his car safely.

*Could always chance the woods.*

Stupid thought. The woods spanned almost the entire county, butting up against the power station ponds and the river.

A few gnarly trees had limbs that cradled in palm-like baskets where they crossed. One of these palms faced away from the house and was about twenty-feet up. He looked at the drooping limbs, calculating the steps necessary to reach the cradling surface.

"Ricer! Chink!" the mother shouted. An ATV kicked into gear. "You ain't gettin' away!"

Time was nearly up. The first limb reminded Osumi of the bites and the shot that seared the flesh of his shoulder. A grunt escaped his lips as he swung up to his stomach. There were three more steps. The ATV approached, though not directly.

Osumi crawled out to where the distance between limbs sank to a manageable four feet. Fingers dug into the bark as he pulled himself upright. The bark slipped from the tree and his body slipped with it, knocking the wind from his chest. He wheezed and moaned, barely holding to the branch only just above eye-level.

"We ain't no losers, we won!" the woman screeched over the crawling ATV. "Beat that crooked bitch and we gon' send you home!"

*Up. Up!*

Osumi tried again and swung his body skyward. He kicked his toes parallel to his hands. A muscle on his hip seized. His foot dropped. Again, he swung, his toes skidded and his hip roared. Down.

"Goddamn chink!"

*No.*

His foot swung higher than his hands. Twisting and clinging. Osumi got to his knees. He looked through the flora. The woman zoomed crossways past his tree and he hurried to the next limb. Only a couple feet, *no problem*.

The final stretch was tricky as the limbs that cradled like a palm did so as if built on top of another tree. The ATV was directly below and the vet latched with his arms and then his legs, crawling upside down. Everything screamed for an end. His muscles. His heart. His mind most of all.

"You tresspassin', get out my country!" the woman called out and killed the engine.

Osumi's chest banged and his airless lungs raged. Sweat dripped from his scalp and fell on the peak of the woman's red hat. A small whine left Osumi's mouth as he wrenched his tired, aching body upright, into the palm.

The bed was hard, but it felt wonderfully safe. Behind him, in the distance, a truck engine started and the ATV kicked back into life. Rolling away.

Osumi basked in a situational peace.

In purgatory's waystation, the man drifted between full awareness and near unconsciousness. There were sounds and then silence. Hours passed. The falling of the sun promised as much. Still he waited, shivering from the new chilliness attaching itself to his soaked clothing and from the fear of sacrificing relative safety in the sky.

Thoughts of his worried family finally moved his tired and pained body. Climbing down was easier than climbing up. Moving on the ground, his arms and shoulders had come to an agreement and only throbbed.

Crickets and frogs sang incessantly. The natural soundtrack had a lulling effect as Osumi made for the quiet, shadowy home. The darkness within was a new mystery.

*How long was I in that tree?*

Osumi stepped to the edge of the opening and crept into the comparative light out of the shade. There was a half-moon casting a white glow on the yellowed world. With slow and careful steps, Osumi moved past the Mercury toward the unfamiliar side of the house. There were two open windows, but no hint of life. A second truck, a Dodge, sat amid the weeds. It was much newer than the Mercury. The rust reigned king as with the other, but where the Mercury's aura suggested death, this vehicle appeared functional, ready to come to life.

Every step closer to the home put a weight on Osumi's breath and a painful, shard of glass into his bloodstream. Feeling naked, he crossed the shadows. Through an open windows came a heavy snore.

The grass swished underfoot until he reached a mowed and traffic-trampled area. It was spikey and crunched beneath his steps. When he was thirty feet from his Volvo, the snoring hitched and Osumi stopped. He closed his eyes and waited for the new pain. None came. The snoring resumed after a few lip smacks.

Twenty-five, twenty, eighteen—the snoring hitched again and this time Osumi lowered into a crouch. He listened and waited. The snoring resumed and he moved on. Fifteen, ten, seven, so close that he saw his reflection in the window on the moon's shine. Broken and beaten, in a sense, but in another, Osumi was putting up a fight and winning. It was hard, but the right side would win.

Four, two, the final foot. His hand cupped around his face. The key dangled in the ignition. Osumi put his hand on the handle and stopped. The snores had silenced.

*How long since…?*

"Chinker," a voice whispered, something hard poked into Osumi's shoulder. "I got you. Dad's gonna hurt you for what you did."

The screen door swung open and Osumi ignored the hardness of the voice and the hardness of what he assumed was a rifle barrel. He turned to face the door.

"Chink," the father seethed.

Papa Walton lowered his red hat in place, standing in muddy boots and off-white underwear. He aimed.

Osumi dropped and the shot rang out. There was a fleshy thump. Behind him, the boy stumbled, fell, gurgling.

*Bad dad. Very bad dad.*

"Arnold?" the father's voice had heightened into a squeak. "Chink, you made me—"

The rifle shots began tearing into the steel body of the car and Osumi rolled backwards. The body of Arnold Walton huffed below him.

Another shot.

Another.

Dust flared and metal creaked.

Backed away, the doctor made it fully behind the Volvo.

"Chink!"

"Whud you do?" the mother shouted.

"He made me!" the father shouted back, approaching Osumi.

Arnold gasped at the air and Osumi dragged his body to assess opportunity. A .22 rifle clenched in the boy's hands. There was a black hole through the bridge of his nose.

"Fucking Chinaman! I'm-a send ya to Chinese hell!"

Osumi hadn't shot anything since he was a kid and joined a friend in the back fifty to fire at old beer cans. Twenty-five years in the past… the lightweight rifle seemed almost like a toy. There was a bolt and a trigger, a magazine tube running beneath the barrel.

"You made me shoot my boy! That's three, now I gots to take a third!"

Osumi aimed generally, his shoulder blades against the bumper. Images of his wife and son, the three of them cascaded in a kaleidoscope of painful hope. The shadowy man stepped into view and pointed at Osumi.

"You chink, let'm go!"

The boy was on the ground staring to the world beyond the sky, his arm strewn onto Osumi's thigh. The rifle in the man's hands clicked four times. He hissed and fumbled in his pocket. Osumi fired.

The man straightened and touched the skin of his left elbow. A graze wound. He laughed. Osumi yanked back on the bolt and leaned forward while Walton filled his weapon. The tiny rifle had a minimal report and no recoil.

The father fell backwards onto his ass and blinked away his final two seconds as the hole in his chest leaked three bubbles of blood. One inch from center.

"No, you… you!" the woman screamed nonsensically.

Osumi felt her before he saw her. The big knife slashed at his hand and he swung his arm, butting away a second strike with the wooden stock of the .22.

"You killed'm!" She slashed a third time and Osumi rolled sideways and jerked the bolt. A spent case seemed to float on air and the woman's voice slowed. "Rice eatin' sonofabitch!"

The bolt slammed back before the casing fell and Osumi fired. The Walton mother and wife had leaned in. The shot bent her. She teetered back before falling, pawing at a blood-spewing hole beneath her chin.

The night grew silent but for Osumi's short breaths. He sipped air, verging toward hyperventilation.

"Why are you like this?" he shouted and fell back into the gravel.

Next to him was the dead man, the red hat fallen. Osumi glanced within at the tag: *MADE IN CHINA*. Eyes inching over the yellowed interior. The stitched lettering of the forehead panels read in reverse: *NIAGA TAERG ACIREMA EKAM*, the true intention of the words revealed.

The woman coughed and rolled onto her spine. She sat up and looked around dazed. There was a chip from her chin. Blood poured.

"This is America," she mumbled, her jaw fractured. She reached for the knife.

"No!" Osumi screeched and jerked up, belted her face with the stock of the .22.

She dropped and Osumi popped the casing and readied for a resurgence of Walton, any one of them. Minutes passed and his pulse slowed. Up, the doctor dragged the body of Arnold Walton away from the back of the Volvo. A quick glance affirmed that the father was dead too. The mother was alive, but in bad shape. The shot had gone right through her chin and thick neck. She was wet with blood that ran black in the moonlight.

A three-point turn, just as he'd learned in driver's ed way back in the days of Nelly and a preteen Harry Potter. He started out the lane, for the first time noticing the heavy scent of gasoline and the loudness of the interior of the car. The bullet had gone through the woman and the rear end of the Volvo, puncturing the gas tank.

At the crater, Osumi got out and worked the boards into place. Across and up the vast winding lane. The red light on the dash demanded that he feed the gas tank. The road came into view and the engine died.

The center console was empty. His phone was gone.

*What's a few more hours?*

The dampness chilled him so he donned his suit jacket as he started toward the highway. It was surreal, more so than many dreams he'd had. A bad family drank bad political Kool-Aid and raised a bad kid.

"Chink, you ain't getting away," he said, reliving the fear. "Oh yeah? What do you call this? And guess what, I'm American! My grandparents were Japanese, not Chinese, you inbred hicks!"

On and on. It was six miles to the highway, three hours in his sluggish drag. His blood had clotted, though continued dripping.

"I'd do it again, too," he said knowing that was a lie.

The sun had begun inching. The darkness had become grayness. Osumi stood at the road. Home or the hospital?

"Home, of course."

He stumbled along, miles yet to his large house on the double-length lot.

"Chink! Rice eater! That's three, now I gots to take a third! Ricer!" Osumi imitated all the things they'd screamed at him, reveling in the faults and failures.

A thought struck him to a standstill on the dusty shoulder. What had that scumbag meant when he said he had to take a third? The Osumi household was a threesome and *Walton already took two...*

"Oh God."

Osumi took a step, replaying the words, *I gots to take a third*. Was that where the man was while Osumi hid in the tree cradle? Was he off taking eyes for eyes? Loved ones for dogs.

"Oh no, no," Osumi moaned and broke into an ambling jog.

His home had never seemed so far and he silently begged the skies to preserve his family. Those damned voices of the dead faces, *CHINK!*

"Let them be alive!" he wailed.

"Chris?"

Osumi turned to the voice and the car he hadn't heard approaching. It was a county blue and white, and the man behind the wheel was Officer Brian Tallen. This particular officer had two cats, Churchill and Oscar, and a dark brown skin tone.

"Brian! I need a ride home!"

"Sure, what did you get into?"

Osumi cramped in next to the computer, a shotgun, and a lunch pail. He gave the brief version of what occurred, finishing just as the police cruiser pulled into Osumi's laneway.

"Chris, we've got to go make a statement. You're sure they're all dead? What were you doing, going out there? You should know better."

"I don't know. I don't know, the man said he had to take a third! I mean... oh hell, Brian!"

"You got to be careful these days. You know how it's getting," the officer said as he helped the tired and filthy man rise.

Together they entered the home through the side door.

*That's three, now I gots to take a third.*

"Please, please no..."

It was nonsense shouted by an insane man. Nonsense until Osumi saw the streaked blood that ran much of the length of the kitchen.

"No!"

"Chris, calm down," said the officer as they peered into the empty kitchen.

Blood dripped from the walls and ceiling. Blood ran in rivers, stealing his family in a scarlet wash. Osumi wailed a nonword.

"Chris!" Jennifer Osumi rushed to her husband. She wore a sweater and jeans, creasing rode her form on every angle. She'd obviously slept in her clothing. "Where have you been?"

Osumi looked up from his palms and the blood ran in reverse. It had looked bad, but the good overcame, as it does.

"Dad?" Scott's small, sleepy voice carried up the hallway.

Father draped his filthy, infected arms around his wife and son. A scream rose from next door. Brian Tallen burst out and the reunited Osumi family followed him with their eyes.

"Somebody killed my cats!" Jamie Kimble screeched. There were two cats on her porch, ooze stained and dried around them like fiery auras.

Osumi stared out the window at the dead things as he held his family tightly.

# WHAT CRAWLS BENEATH

by
Sin Fergus

03 November 2020 03:00

Jake, the security watchman, saw something fleshy and pale undulate on the screen.

*Rats, maybe?* No. Too big. They were the wrong color too. And there were hundreds of them.

He watched, mesmerized, as he ate the Tofurkey sandwich his husband had fixed him. It was slathered with Veganaise, thick and delicious.

The things on the screen got closer. Was that a flash of metal? Coat hangers? Sticking out of some of their heads?

*No. Dear God, could it really be?* Jake knew he must have fallen asleep. He pinched himself and it *hurt*.

*Not a nightmare.* This was his first real emergency since being put on nights, since being assigned to watch the security cameras in the sewers that ran underneath the White House. His own office was right next to the Executive Mansion. Underground. In the path of these things.

*I need to call someone,* he thought. *Holy hell, they'll never believe me.* He took out his cell and snapped a picture of what was on his monitor. He texted it to Gina, his boss. She'd know what to do.

Jake stared at his cell, realizing the text hadn't gone through.

*Landline. I need the landline.*

Jake continued to stare at his cell as a wave of fleshy monstrosities rippled along the sewer. Something in the vents rattled. He looked up. The vent popped open. A moist, flaccid creature fell into his lap. The size of one of those Men-in-Black dogs, only a bit smaller.

*A fetus?* A fetus was in his fucking lap! And its head was encircled by wire coat hangers.

Jake nearly toppled over in his chair, trying to get away from the putrid thing. It looked up at him with glowing yellow eyes.

"Hey, dude," it said, "I'm Borticia. Send a message to the president and his right-wing gang of Justice mobsters, will ya? Tell him, tell *them,* we can't lose the election!"

Jake's fingers couldn't find the phone as he stretched his arm out. Another fetus plopped to the floor and started crawling toward him. Then another, this one without a head. And another—only a head—moving across his desk, using tentacles that had grown from its neck.

"What?!" Jake was frantic. Was he going to die, a case of death by fetal ingestion or something?

One of the creatures grabbed his Tofurkey sandwich and stuck it in its mouth, making yummy num num sounds.

"What do you want from me?" Jake screamed.

Borticia grinned with a mouth that should never belong to any fetus. Needle-sharp teeth poked out from her gums. "Tell those cronies we're mad as hell and we're not going to fake it anymore! Hell. Maybe I should just tell the big man himself."

She crawled up Jake's chest and he pushed backwards, trying to get her off of him as she lunged and then attached her lips to his nose. And then he was falling, falling, falling into black clouds, dreaming about hundreds of undead fetuses attacking his face.

Borticia had achieved the first wave of their mission. Terrorize the enemy. That's certainly what *their* enemy was doing to the women above. And that was good. Very good. It helped the Bort agenda.

Ever since Justice Crabinraw was confirmed to the Supreme Court and managed to overturn *Roe v. Wade*, the D.C. Underground was teaming with undead. Aborted babies left and right. Strained from the refuse and sludge of the city's sewers, their population kept gaining numbers. Soon, it would be time to move to other cities. Infect other undergrounds.

Borticia raised her head and yowled. Her following of Borts answered with howls and yips. She was off to see the president while her mate, Borty, scrambled to find the Supreme Court chambers. Together, they'd make sure that the Underground stayed populated with their twisted kind. The votes had to be for their side. They had to win!

Getting into the White House was easy. While security was always on high alert for intruders, they wouldn't be ready for hundreds of squalling, undead fetuses storming the president's chambers. Borticia wiggled along a duct, her crown of coat hangers jingling. Ahead of her, a laser security system threatened to ruin their secret approach. Borticia motioned for her Borts to get as low as possible and crawl under the red line. They weren't successful. Megga-Bort, one of the largest of them all, triggered the alarm with the coat hanger poking out from his buttocks. In seconds, security was outside the vents, shouting orders.

"Keep going!" Borticia waved them on. "We've gotta make it to POTUS before it's too late!"

The mass of wriggling, undead fetuses squirmed quickly along their chosen path.

"I hear something," a voice yelled from below.

"Get up there and take a look," a voice called back.

Borticia glanced behind her. She'd have a hundred Borts with her before the Secret Service and the military security teams opened the vent, and she knew just where the president's room was. After all, she'd been there before.

She used her nimble tentacle-fingers to open the vent. It was surprising how easy it was to plop right onto the president's head. Ha! She hadn't remembered it being so easy, but perhaps she was getting better at her job.

POTUS woke, issued a strange squeal, started hyperventilating and pushing her away with his hands. Until he realized it was her.

"Yeah, PO Man, it's me again. We got trouble."

POTUS shook his head, looked at the bedroom door. "Borticia, what do you want now?"

"I need to know that today's election is in the bag. I need to know I'll keep getting subjects to rule because you'll still be in office and the abortion clinics will remain closed. As long as the clinics are closed and women can't get their contraception, I remain Queen of the Underground, you hear?"

POTUS nodded, and then pursed his lips. "You got a good team there."

"Yeah, yeah." Borticia jutted her chin at him. "You got a thing with Russia again or you only going to use the Chinese this time?"

POTUS raised his thick white eyebrows.

"Yes, I know about the Chinese, PO Man. It's the one thing CNN and all of the investigators haven't found out about yet, but they will—soon—unless you win this election."

"Don't worry. I got it covered, all right? The election's a done deal. And the next one too!"

"The next?" Borticia stared at POTUS. "Third term, eh? You thinking of carrying this post Kim Jong Il style? Supreme Leader instead of just president? I gotta admit, last year's military parade—"

"You gotta go, Borticia. Secret Service is coming."

Borticia was already disappearing through the vent.

"Until next time, PO Man. Good luck with the election!" She laughed on her way out, but hoped he was right. Some of her undead had cyber skills too, but not enough to control the entire nation.

In their residence under the O-Street Sewer Pumping Station, Borticia and Borty watched the election returns on a small television they'd hooked up. Meanwhile, their fetal undead hacked online computers and found ways to wreak havoc with computed votes. One of the greatest threats to their success seemed to be an online presence called Classy Emails. It threatened, at one point, to take down their network.

"Block it!" Borticia called out. "Stop it, no matter what! Can we find out where that bitch is at?"

One of her lead men, Borticeye, replied, "No, ma'am. New York, maybe. We can't pin it."

"We can't let the Warning woman win! A female president would be bad, very bad for us, my fellow Borts! Now get online, block the assaults and change those votes!"

Borticia grew disheartened as the hours passed. Her plan to win for POTUS was failing. All because of Classy Emails and that Warning woman.

She thought and she thought until her thoughterer was thought out, and then she got a beautiful thought—a betterer and even more thoughtier thought.

"What if we could get POTUS declared a king? A rightful monarch to the United States? Ordained by God to carry on a line of kings?" Borticia said the words to no one in particular, but her generals heard her.

"Great idea!" one said. "For that, though, we'll need to hack into one of those DNA registry sites. Hit all the plot points that would make POTUS close to divine."

"And then?" Borticia was still thinking out loud, and letting her generals suggest more ideas.

"And then," said another, "we hack into Wikireadia. Erase all information about past presidents and declare POTUS the king of the USA!"

Cheers exploded around the room. It was a ludicrous idea, but the country was so divided these days, no one would know or probably even care. The lefties would laugh it off as a hoax and the righties would swear it was truth because it was in Wikireadia. It was the source of proof, after all, from scientific research—or so said the righties. Once monies were diverted from the national treasury to POTUS's account on a regular basis, everyone would accept he needed those funds to support his monarchy. And when he died, well, he had sons! His youngest by the last marriage was the son he wanted to succeed him.

*Ah, back to the good old patriarchal days.* Of course, those days were only good for humans, and not undead fetuses.

"Maybe we can even make him king of the country of Puerto Rico," Borticia mused, "and from there, the Samoan Islands, Mexico, Panama and even Venezuela."

They were getting new undead deposited into the sewers every single day. Soon they'd number in the millions. Borticia's fetal body hummed with excitement as she thought of it. Maybe one day she'd be queen over all of them. And why not? If POTUS could do it, then why couldn't she?

*Yes. Why not me?*

And, of course, there'd need to be balance in the global population. Which is where her Borts came in. Each one of them had been born with the hunger for human flesh. Each of them devoured helpless living beings wherever they found them. Aging veterans—those were the best. And it made sense to eat them first because of the horrible drain they placed on the social system. It might seem unpatriotic, but it was a service to the country, really.

Bortimer burst into her chambers.

"Bortimer! You better—"

"Ma'am. I m-mean, your m-majesty. The b-blue wave has risen! The b-blue wave has risen!"

*No,* Borticia thought. *This can't be happening.* POTUS had promised, and all of her Borts had worked so hard together to manipulate the outcome. How could it be? And yet, CNN showed a number of the states turning blue.

"Check Fox again!" Fox would tell the truth. Fox knew better than to exagger—

Borticia's dead heart sank to the floor. Even Fox was declaring a projected winner, and it was not POTUS. *That Warning woman. She could not be president. Never!*

Borty spoke up. "What about that West guy? Maybe we could get him to do an election promo on the networks? Get the news involved? He got coverage in the Oval Office, for Suction's sake!"

It was a good idea.

"Definitely! Get West out there," she told Bortimer, "and have him wear the MAGA hat!"

"Y-yes, ma'am, er, y-your majesty!" Bortimer scuttled out of the room.

Borty patted her tiny hand, and leaned his misshapen head toward her to give her a kiss, jangling her coat hangers. "We will win, my love. We will win!"

"Not if the younger population gets out and votes, we won't. Where are we on the latest video game release? Is it ready?" Borticia had scheduled a top game release starring all of her people. A game called "What Crawls Beneath." It was about the scary world that existed in the D.C. Underground. The one no one knew really existed. It was risky, but most people wouldn't think it was true. They'd think it was some twisted, weird fiction.

Borticeye's one eye sparkled. "It went out at midnight, your majesty! Sales are through the roof!"

*Ah, then many of America's brightest won't venture to the polls. They'll sit in front of their monitors using my cyber-Bort creations to kill off annoying cockroaches and rats. They'll challenge themselves at the puzzles beneath the Pentagon, and search for thermonuclear bombs, AK-47s and other weapons of destruction. They'll throw biological weapons at each other in a mage biowarfare creation so that each of them can win the Bort throne.*

Borticia hoped the game didn't give any of her minions ideas of glory, but it was a good game. Well done. She'd have to thank the game designers personally.

"Good," Borticia said. "Now, we wait. All of our pieces are in place."

And wait they did, until midnight. The race for the presidency was close.

Bortimer burst in again. "Y-your majesty. There's been a p-problem."

"Do you ever knock?" Borticia wanted to bite back her words. She forgot Bortimer had no arms. "Go ahead, what's the problem?" She knew her voice sounded terse, but this entire scene was killing her.

"The people from Puerto Rico," he said. "They voted. All of them, it seems. And all of the Latinos. Each and every one who is a U.S. citizen. Their votes are through the roof!"

"Wait! Puerto Rico? Didn't POTUS say that was a country? And the young people? The gamers?" That group can't have voted. Not with her latest game in play.

"Their p-parents literally drove them to the polls, your m-majesty."

Borticia stared at the predominantly blue-colored map on the television. "No. No. No-no-no!"

Then she paused. Joy filled her and she was nearly giddy with glee. She remembered. Why hadn't she realized the obvious? And she reveled in her next announcement.

"That's just the popular vote, my Borts! And we know, no matter what, that doesn't count! Borticeye, are all of our Borts in place to speak to the Electoral College?"

POTUS would win again, she was sure of it. And she and her Borts had the next four years to plan for his dictatorship, or even a monarchy. In the meantime, it was time to plan for the presidential parade!

# EVERYBODY LISTENS TO BUCK

by
Nicholas Manzolillo

I drive a little faster when I see the *Vote for Monagan* sign stuck into the white colonial's front lawn. Surrounded by two oak trees and a sparkling flower bed, it's a beautiful house tarnished by that one red brick of political prompting. The neighborhood stretching ahead of me is a battlefield. On either side of my car, red and blue squares adorn each front lawn. This town can't have more than a five hundred residents, tops, yet it feels like every single one of them is the loudest political panderer. What's funny, though, is that Thanksgiving's a week away. Isn't this crap supposed to be over with by now?

In my experience, travelling as much as I do, small towns can go one of two ways. Either the residents think they're a part of something big or they believe themselves to be nothing but dirt, literally seizing every opportunity to quote that Journey song: "I'm just a small town . . . " blah, blah, blah. Forget I said that, it doesn't sound right. It's not funny enough, not distinct enough. I'm supposed to be funny, being a professional joke teller and all, but there's not much to laugh about in the middle of the day.

I pass by a man dressed as a . . . milkman? Or something like that, standing in his front yard staring straight up at the sky. There's a blue *Vote for Harrison* sign to his left. Maybe it's the showman in me, but I debate laying into the horn just to pull his head out of the clouds.

When I pass by a woman standing on her front porch in old-fashioned lingerie I honk my horn as loud as my little Ford can, which is about as loud as a newborn puppy's squeak. Even in what amounts to granny panties by modern standards, the middle-aged blonde is just my type. You don't get to date much when you're on the road, so excuse me if I follow the instincts of a hound dog. My attention's for nothing though, because the woman—who has a red sign on her lawn—just stares at me with wide, bloodshot eyes. Christ, they're red enough for me to notice and I'm in the middle of the road. Poor lady must be on so many uppers she's in her undies. Then again, it's almost nightfall. Maybe she had a long, shitty day and she's unwinding.

The GPS on my phone's a piece of crap but it does its job, bringing me down a cutesy main street, past a firehouse next to a barbershop and a library practically attached to a church, until I arrive at the community center, Jefferson Memorial. At least I'm not planning on spending the night—two-hour drive back to Knoxville or not, there's at least life in the city. Bars and Chinese food and, plus, I've built up a bunch of reward points at Marriot hotels.

The community center looks like it did on Google, an unimpressive white square that could be something a colony of birdmen would build out of their own excrement. Can hardly hold more than eighty people, but I've performed in clubs for less than three drunken old ladies, so that's not an issue—if it's even a sold-out gig. I wouldn't be here if they weren't paying me a whopping three grand for just an hour set. I didn't believe the voicemail at first, so I had a hell of a time asking for verification, especially because nothing I found online indicated there's ever been a comedy event at old Jefferson "Bird Shit" Memorial. Just listings for dated art festivals and the like.

A white and blue banner is slung over the double door entrance with «Welcome to Lacey Meadows, Jamie Rudolph!» in all bubbly letters—it looks like it could›ve been crafted by the local high school›s art division. If this hick place even has a high school art division. They sure got their politics, though; while no red or blue signs claim the strips of grass beside the community center, there are numerous colorful fliers just below my banner that say, «Vote here, November 8!» Jeez, I›ve been invited right into the dragon›s den.

There's one other car in the parking lot and, figures, from the looks of my fake Rolex, I'm an hour and a half early for my seven-thirty show. I've already made peace with the idea that I'll have to deal with a few awkward, small-town community event planners or some shit. Maybe it's worth forgoing my professional integrity and finding a bar to hole up in until thirty minutes before showtime. They're paying me good money, and for the sake of all the hot wings that'll buy—I owe the show-runners some loyalty. Plus, do I really want to go to a bar as a stranger here? First thing I'll be asked is what brings me to town and then there'll be the always typical "how about you tell us a joke" bullshit and, if I've got drinking to do, it's always better to save that for after my set.

I stroll into the community center expecting to find Marcy, the chubby-sounding woman with a real thick Southern accent that booked me. Instead there's a bald fucker in a tuxedo staring at a big clock on the wall. Guy's head is newly shaved but, as if a toddler were his barber, there are mismatched patches along his skull where the razor kissed his head, creating a pink rash. I remember buzzing my head when I was younger.

«Hey,» I mutter, but Mr. Tux, complete with a pink bowtie, doesn›t move from his staring contest with the hands of time.

I guess that "vote here" banner's the extent of the mood setting. The community center is like a church without crosses; it has mismatched folding chairs where my poor audience is going to be placed.

"Hey, buddy, hey." I walk over and tap the deaf older guy with a bad (no) hair day on the shoulder. He turns, slowly.

"Hey, I'm the show, what's going on? Marcy here?"

The man stares at me like he's senile, and maybe he is, though I'd guess he's only pushing fifty. "Buck said seven-thirty. It's not seven-thirty yet." He turns to stare at the clock but I grab his arm.

"Professional courtesy to arrive early." I try getting something out of him, at least a smile, but nothing.

"Everybody listens to Buck," the man says. He sounds weary, like he's been staring at that clock all day.

"Who's Buck?" I ask before the double doors behind me swing open.

"Mr. Rudolph," a nasally woman says behind me in a Southern accent gone out of tune.

"Ah, Marcy?" I flash her a smile that has yet to land me anything other than bit parts in serious detective dramas on NBC that are cancelled before my episode can even air.

"You're on at seven-thirty," she says, in almost the exact way my fuckin' GPS told me how to get here. "Buck wants to see you as soon as you get here. Follow me to see Buck."

"Who's Buck?" I figure he's probably the rich guy that bails the town out. Maybe he's the Jefferson this place is named after. Seems like there's always a Jefferson.

"Buck is our mayor," Marcy says, like she's giving me directions. "Everybody listens to Buck!" She says that last slogan-like bit with a touch of cheerfulness. "Follow me." She's back to being nasally. When she turns her back and Mr. Tux is once more staring at the clock, I raise a middle finger to his head.

Stepping outside, Marcy points toward a squat little building with white columns. Mayor fucking Buck? Maybe this place is smaller than I thought. Maybe there's something in the water around here worse than lead.

What is a mayor anyway? What are they even worth? Place like this, Marcy here could be leading me to the local high school principal and it wouldn't matter much. Place like this, mayor's just a title and a paycheck and maybe the authority on who plays at their community house.

I don't like how Marcy walks, and while she's nothing to stare at, I stare anyway, at how stiff her back is, at how her legs march in sync with her arms like she's a windup soldier. She keeps staring straight ahead like there's a magnet pulling at her sparkling earrings.

"So how many people you think are going to show up?" I ask, but Marcy doesn't so much as look at me as I follow her into the town hall.

The building is crowded with freaks. Three women in their underwear are standing as still as mannequins on either side of a long hallway leading to half a dozen little offices.

There are framed old-fashioned pictures on the walls, showing how much of a boring turd the town has been its whole lifetime and, jeez, there are more half-naked women filling each doorframe. By this point I'm begging Marcy to tell me what's going on. She's silent as ever as I snap my fingers in the flesh-and-blood mannequin's faces, and get no response. Being a pervert's in my job description but there's something off about the glazed-over look in each woman's eye. Two of them probably aren't natural blondes, either; they're wearing wigs.

"You dumb bitch!" I hear a man with a high-pitched voice shout. Marcy's disappeared around the bend of the hallway.

"Where is he? Bring Mr. Rudolph to me!" the pipsqueak of a man who may or may not be Buck shrieks, and then the admittedly attractive women on either side of me spring to life.

Well-manicured fingers grab me on either side of my dwindling head of hair. My leather jacket's practically ripped off my shoulders and I've always been on the noodley side, so three boney damsels still manage to push me forward through the narrow hallway. Maybe it's the rising panic jabbing my thoughts but I envision a snorting pig, some kinda boar coming my way. Around the corner turns an actual man wearing a pink pig mask with no shirt and massive man boobs flopping around. He's running toward me, snorting and coughing. Behind the pig man there's a woman in a green spandex onesie and a sun hat, and then there's Marcy.

"Hey, hey, hey!" I'm full of many wonderful words ranging from "what the fuck?" to "fucking quit it, what are you doing?" But I can only keep repeating the same exclamation as if my dying breath is trapped in an echo.

At one point my feet leave the ground in the throng of six crazy people, and at first I thrash out and kick before my better instinct about harming a woman chimes in. I go limp as I'm carried none-too-gently by my hair, ears, arms, and the scruff of my shirt toward the man himself, Buck, snug in his office.

"Oh y'all," he says, "everybody that's not called Mr. Rudolph, leave, leave the building! Actually, not you two, no."

I feel a chill ripple through my brain and down my spine as I'm dropped to the coarsely carpeted floor of an office lined with bookshelves and centered by a desk carved from a fancy tree I don't know the name of. A man in stocking feet steps in front of my face, his hands on his hips as he shakes his head and watches the office door close before reaching down to help me up.

With a face covered in stubble and wearing a loose purple tie over a grease-stained white button-down is the man who must be mayor of this crazy fucking place.

"Oh, I apologize, this, they..." He grimaces, forgets to complete his sentence. He claps me on the shoulders and this guy's my age, half a millennial. There's something weird about his eyes, it's like they're dry. The lights overhead don't reflect in them. His pupils aren't mirrors.

"I'm Buck and they, they're a literal bunch, ya know? Fuck." He runs a hand through his hair, flattening it out.

I notice his fly's unzipped but for some reason I'm not in the mood to point it out.

"Well, welcome to Lacey Meadows. You want a drink?" He leans over the desk, pulls open a drawer and slams a bottle on the counter. "Most expensive shit I've ever seen," he says proudly.

I realize the shirtless man in the pig mask and the woman in the green onesie are standing behind me, hardly breathing, not moving an inch.

"Is this a reality show?" I ask, only because I've submitted a few audition tapes to a couple shows that seemed on the iffy side. This entire situation could be a prank or maybe my old manager sent something out before I fired his ass for—well, let's call it mismanagement. Guy sent me to a high school one time.

"Well, it's just, uh—" Buck shrugs. "Look, excuse me if I don't tell you what to do. I'm a big fan, man, I saw one of your shows in Knoxville like a year ago. I loved you on that show *Living It Up*, thought you shoulda been the star instead of that fat bastard. I know this is crazy, but I'll give you an extra grand, no problem. I'm going to gather everybody up, since you're here early. We can just start the show and—"

"Buddy, what the fuck?" I stop him. He's talking a mile a minute and my head's hurting and I'm still frazzled after being woman-handled in the hallway. I point to the two dressed-up bozos behind me. "Where's the hidden camera, bro?" I laugh because, fuck, if I am being filmed I want them to get my good side.

Buck laughs too, shakes his head and raises his hands, trying to think of something, some explanation.

"Well, those are…were the two mayoral candidates and, uh, well, shit, Rudolph, I've gotten so used to how crazy things are around here that I forgot someone like you would be thrown off. This is like an, uh, initiation, yeah, and everybody in town does this for the new mayor. It's, like, a strange weeklong thing . . . that ends the day before Thanksgiving. So, like, everybody around here that's of age and wants to be included in the raffle does whatever I tell them. It's funny like that."

"Dude, what the fuck?" I turn to look at the man in the pig mask.

"All right, well, I tried to lie to you. Look at me."

I turn around and look at Buck. I shiver and there's pain in my head, not in the frontal lobe like most headaches.

"You are going to stop asking questions," Buck tells me.

"Okay," I say, and the Scotch on Buck's desk looks tasty.

"Don't worry about what's going on. I've told these guys so many things that they've short-circuited a bit. Maybe 'cause of all the pranks. I won't do that to you, okay? I want you to trust me," Buck says, and he's a hell of a guy. I like his purple tie. He's got a winner's smile and, shit, he's the mayor.

"All right." I wish I had a seat. I reach for the bottle of Scotch and Buck nods as I flick off the cap, take a long sip. The cold spot in my head doesn't go away as my throat fills with fire.

"Now let's go start your show. Follow me. I'm excited, man, really. I even downloaded the Serendipity app just to watch that college special of yours. Lead the way, you two." Buck points over my head and together we follow the silly-looking mayoral candidates in costumes.

Buck orders the woman in the onesie to get him a microphone and then we head out a back door. There's a real nice green Cadillac with little American flags propped up on either side of the front bumper. We slide into the leather backseat and Buck makes the pig man drive. We drive around town, and Buck casually bellows into the microphone, "Come to the community center! The show starts now! The once-in-a-lifetime stand-up set by Rudolph! Rudolph the great!" It sounds corny, and I'm a little embarrassed, but I trust Buck. I watch as people leave their homes and shuffle down the streets.

At the community center, Buck makes sure I have whatever I need set up in a little closet of a backroom that doubles as a dressing room. Beer, soda, chips. He asks if I'm hungry and I tell him I am, even though I never eat before a set. I can't lie to the guy. It's like he's got the lasso of truth around my belly.

He makes Marcy run to get me a burger. While waiting, I peek out at the crowd. The main hall is filled with silent, staring townies. Some of the women are in various stages of undress, but I trust Buck, that he's not *that* evil, he's just a voyeur that gets off on humiliation. He has a politician's way with words, that's all. He's so good, he didn't even need people putting signs up in their front yards for him to win.

I don't need to ask, because I was told not to ask, but I'm pretty sure Buck was just some guy before this past election. He was some guy with something to say, fed up with the way his town was being run, and he found a way to make people listen to him. What a guy, that Buck.

With a burger clogging up my digestive tract, I begin my show and it's strange, being distant from my own material. I say my opening lines, I laugh, I smile, but I don't feel what I'm saying. I don't feel the fun irony when I tell a joke about the short girlfriend I don't have. It's almost like I'm outside myself, watching my own act and finding it boring. Even saying my favorite word, *motherfucker*, doesn't bring the usual hop to my step.

Buck is the only one that laughs, at first. He sits in the front row, in a comfortable leather office chair that he had someone drag over from his office. He's the only one giggling out of the hundred or so blank, still faces, until he leans over his shoulder and yells, "Laugh at everything he says!" Then all of my jokes become winners.

I end my show to a recording of "Good Times, Bad Times" by Led Zeppelin, but when I bow, there's something missing, as the audience lets out a chorus of full belly laughs instead of breaking into applause.

"Bravo! Bravo!" Buck shouts before yelling "Clap, clap, you monkeys!" The crowd begins to clap, as do I. Standing there on the short, unimpressive stage, with the mic in my hands, I clap and clap, boom-booming over the PA system. I can't stop slapping my hands together as Buck shakes his head before erupting into laughter. He stands and then twirls around to get a good view of his sea of clappers before he steps up to join me.

"Stop clapping," he says, leaning down into my mic. The room goes silent, even though the people in back surely didn't hear him. It's as if his words can leak from one person to another. He hands me a check for four thousand dollars, which likely belongs to the town. "Thank you for coming." He smiles, reaches to shake my hand, and then he notices my watch.

"Hey, could you give me that?" Buck asks.

I slip off the fake Rolex I bought after my television debut and hand it to him.

"Drive safe," he says with a smile.

The crowd is silent, watching. I can't help but chuckle. I know what he is, and his saying that is kind of hilarious. I am now a safe driver.

"And be sure to mention our little town in your act, to any funny friends you meet. Tell them to contact my office. It gets dull out here, sometimes." Buck grins and admires his new watch. I don't tell him it's a fake piece of crap that's meant to complement my persona full of jokes and sweet lies, because he doesn't ask.

I leave down the center isle of the community center. Nobody turns their head to look at me. My brain freeze is overwhelming and I ache to be free of this place, to put as many miles as possible between me and the all-powerful Buck. I'm getting out of here, and unfortunately, I'm going to have to recommend touring this place to as many people as possible.

*This story was previously published in the Dread State anthology by Thunderdome Press on December 7, 2016

# ONLY A DREAM

by
Tahni J. Nikitins

Amy went to bed at the usual time, though her mother stayed up late, anxiously gnawing her fingernails as election results rolled in. Her mother's wavy black hair was pulled into a bun and she wore sweat pants and an oversized T-shirt. Amy couldn't think of a time she'd seen her mother look more worried, except maybe when her father left and they had to move to this tiny apartment.

The apartment was so small and the walls so thin, Amy could hear her mother crying in the next room. She crept out of bed and into the hall, peering through her mother's ajar bedroom door. Her mom curled up in bed beneath the strange print that hung overhead, which Amy had asked about, though her questions never received answers. It was an image of a woman whose hair was streaming out of its knot. She lay amid scrawled Japanese characters and jagged formations that must have been waves, because there were also octopuses. There was one small octopus on the woman's face with its tentacle sliding into her mouth and another large one between the woman's legs, its mouth pressed up against her vulva, its tentacles coiled around her.

Amy's mother lay beneath that strange framed print crying with the phone to her ear. The scene made Amy so uncomfortable that her stomach squirmed and ached. She withdrew and went back to her room.

At thirteen years old, Amy looked like a smaller version of her mother, though her hair was straight. It cut straight across her shoulders with bangs cut across her eyebrows, which looked pleasant on her oval face. She'd started to feel less comfortable in her body than she had just a year ago. She now had to wear a bra, and the gazes of men began to linger. These men did not lick their white teeth like Big Bad Wolves made flesh or make kissing noises her way, but the way their eyes lingered for a few stretched-out seconds made her skin feel like wriggling maggots.

She wasn't sure why those gazes lingered. She did nothing to draw them. She used none of the tools she remembered seeing on her mother's dresser alongside her three mirrors, back in the old house where they perched serenely beneath that strange print—nothing to color her lips or make them appear plumper. Nothing to add blush to her pale cheeks or cover the occasional pimples that had become common on her pubescent skin, or the faint scars they left behind. Mostly she wore jeans and T-shirts, and when the jeans wore out she cut off the legs and wore the shorts with tennis shoes whose soles were slowly flaking off.

Nonetheless, her existence had been rattled not only by the uneasy glances cast her way, but also by a classmate who had taken to following her through the halls between classes. Sometimes he whistled and sometimes he commented on the frayed hems of her jean shorts or, worse, just stared at her so the maggots in her skin got jittery.

His name was Lance. Lance had never spoken to her before her tiny breasts betrayed her.

When her alarm rang in the morning, she remembered her existence would further be shaken by an election that had reduced her mother to tears. How an election could go so terribly wrong she really didn't know. Those politics were so far away—what did it matter which way it went?

Waking from strange sea dreams, she lay in bed with the entirety of the ocean in her skull, weighing it against the pillow while she stared at the ceiling and tried not to think about what awaited her at school. It had been almost a year since Lance had started noticing her, and though the thought of having to be in a room with him repulsed her to the point of nausea, she managed to drag herself out of bed and to the bus every morning. This morning was no exception, though the cramps made it more tempting to skip class.

Amy shuffled to the bathroom to relieve herself and take Ibuprofen. The cramps, if not a symptom of anxiety, were just premenstrual. Nothing to be done about it. Sure enough, when she stood up from the toilet there were droplets of blood unfurling in the water with the urine, spreading out like thin water paints.

She put a pad in her underwear, never having dared to try a tampon, and went to the kitchen. Her mother, eyes swollen and pink, served Amy some food and coffee, which seemed to ease the cramps while the Ibuprofen took its time.

Amy considered asking her mother for a ride to school, but she could tell by her mother's pencil skirt and button-up blouse that she had an interview. These days, her mother always had an interview. She still commuted to her current job most days, but the commute was long and it had been taking its toll, leaving her looking more worn every day. Amy stowed her question.

After her mom rushed out, she put her dishes away and got dressed. She locked the door before winding down the stairs and making her way down the street to the bus stop.

She had been sitting for a few minutes, thinking perhaps it would be a peaceful day after all, when a car screamed around the corner a few blocks down—the tires screeching against the pavement and a shifted belt wailing in the engine. Amy flinched at the sound. The car was an old brown beater she recognized from the high school parking lot. As it drew closer she could see it was packed with teenage boys.

Before they zipped past one of them stuck his head and shoulders out the window, pointing at her. "I'll grab *you* by the pussy!" As the car was tearing away, he put two fingers to his mouth, flicking his tongue between them. The cackling of the other boys faded as the car screeched down the road and around the corner.

*Oh.* She remembered hearing words like that, during an election-related media kerfuffle she hadn't really understood. Now, even with the car out of sight, she felt her skin wriggling like maggots again and thought maybe she understood why her mother had been so upset.

It began to itch between her legs. She shifted uncomfortably on the seat. Boys at school often scratched their dicks through their pants, and if a teacher saw and chastised them they quietly moaned about it when the teacher was gone. How, the boys seemed to wonder, was it not socially acceptable to scratch an itch just because the itch was on your genitals?

Amy had often wondered the same thing, albeit more quietly than the boys, but this itch was a doozy. It felt like a fire tucked between her labia. She twitched her hips back and forth, hoping the pressure and the motion would do the job of scratching her itch without being too obvious. It didn't.

The itch didn't subside until the bus rolled to a stop in front of her and she found a seat immediately behind the driver. She didn't like it farther back on the bus, where boys spit at each other or talked loudly about how you can tell a good girl from a bad girl because good girls cross their legs, among other things. Amy hadn't yet realized, but she'd started crossing her legs four years ago when she first overheard that exchange on a different bus in a different city and felt a strange, misplaced sadness in her belly.

By the time the bus rolled up at the school she'd forgotten about the itch between her legs and the cramps had softened. They were still more than her period usually brought so she waited until everyone else was off the bus before getting up and leaning on the hand railing for support as she lowered herself down the steps. The cramps felt like what she imagined a small volcano must feel like when erupting, overflowing and far too hot.

The school was buzzing with its typical morning activities, but there was a different sensation in the air. Junior and senior girls were huddled in quiet clusters, their eyes flashing like paranoid deer as they spoke in hushed tones. One girl named Eva, a popular soon-to-be cheerleader with dyed blond hair who usually batted her lashes at every passing boy with football potential, turned on one of those boys as he grabbed her ass and squeezed. Amy locked her eyes on the scene as Eva tuned on the boy, a furious flush coloring her cheeks while he laughed. Eva slammed her hands into his chest and, through his laughter, he told Eva to calm down.

"It's so pretty," he said while Eva huffed, her fists clenched and shaking at her sides. "I had to grab a feel."

Amy wrenched her eyes away when Eva threw a punch. Everyone gasped, all these kids she didn't mind so much, though she hadn't yet figured out what to say to them, and ran to watch while Amy walked away. It wasn't her business, she told herself, and tried not to think about it.

Since being here she hadn't done much except homework, studying, and watching *Gilmore Girls* with her mom, when her mom was around. Maybe that's why she'd never bothered inviting Lucy over. Amy wanted her mom to herself, when she was around.

Lucy was cool though. They sat next to each other in English class and talked before the bell rang. Lucy also liked *Gilmore Girls*, and had recommended *Supernatural* and *Buffy the Vampire Slayer*, which Amy promised she would pursue once she was done with *Gilmore Girls*.

Her gait grew stiffer while her guts dully twisted and ached, and she started toward the east hall. She pushed through the door and started toward her locker but there was Lance up ahead, blond-haired and blue-eyed with a hooked nose, wearing a blue plaid button-up shirt and khaki shorts. He didn't see her, not yet. She ducked into the girl's bathroom before he did. She'd seen what other boys felt comfortable enough to do today. She didn't want to find out what Lance might feel comfortable enough to do.

The itch started up again, so angry it stung. The cramps spiked too, roiling in her stomach as though she'd swallowed a live squid and it was looking for a way out. Fighting the urge to scratch, she slipped unnoticed past a girl fixing her tear-streaked makeup and her friend talking to her in urgent but kind whispers.

Ducking into the first open stall, Amy closed the door and began furiously scratching through her jeans while lewd, permanent-inked drawings and messages telling the toilet-user to call various girls for a good time, phone numbers included, looked on. The scratching didn't do much so she dropped her bag, undid her zipper, and attempted to scratch through her underwear. The pad was in the way.

The cramps pushed at the lower edges of her belly, creeping like electric fingers into the flesh around her pubic bone. She pushed her pants and underwear down to find the pad already soaked with viscous blood. The tangy iron smell of it assaulted her nose.

"Fuck." She sat down on the toilet and opened her bag, rifling through it for a fresh pad.

Outside the stall the girls were still tersely talking. Amy tried not to listen but couldn't help overhearing something about a stepfather. She rifled a little louder and her cramps got a little sharper. She bit her lip to quiet the whimper perched in the back of her throat, then curled her lip back from her teeth as she realized she had forgotten to bring any extra pads.

Slumping forward, she put her elbows on her knees and her face in her hands. She supposed she could wear the pad a little while longer, but the idea of sitting in the blood as it continued to pool added a subtle layer of nausea to the cramps.

Gritting her teeth, she leaned forward to peer under the wall of the stall at the Converse-clad feet of the other two girls. "Um...hello?"

The girls fell silent.

"I'm sorry, but...do you guys have an extra pad?"

They were quiet a few moments before one, in a tear-stained voice, said, "I don't have any pads but I have a couple extra tampons."

Amy's stomach sank. The idea of sticking a wad of cotton inside herself had always been wildly unappealing. Besides, the risk of toxic shock was far greater than with pads, and the videos about toxic shock in sex-ed had been terrifying. There didn't seem to be any option, though. The sanitary napkin dispensers in the girl's bathrooms had been notoriously empty for years and no one had done anything to refill them. "Would you mind if I had a couple?"

The girl sniffled and said, "Of course." She unzipped her bag and Amy heard things being shuffled around. The girl came to the door and passed her three tampons under it. "Gotta have each other's backs, right?"

"Thank you," Amy said as she took the tampons. "What's your name?"

"Diedra."

"Thank you, Diedra."

The bell rang and Diedra's feet moved away from the door. "Have a good day," she said as she left, her friend joining her.

Amy tucked two of the tampons in her bag and began to unwrap the third. It was inside a plastic torpedo-shaped cover that she assumed was there to make it easier. Shoving a wad of dry cotton up there couldn't be easy.

Putting a hand between her legs, she felt around to determine where exactly she needed to put the thing in. She poked and prodded with her fingers and, frowning, felt several large bumps on her labia.

"What the . . . " She put her fingers between her labia minora and labia majora. There were normal little bumps and ridges but, among these, were oblong, lumpy protrusions. They itched when she touched them, and scratching was compulsive. Her fingernails scraping across the tender meat ached like a burn, but it also felt good.

The second bell would be ringing soon, then class would start. As it was she would have to run to get there. She'd never gotten marked with a tardy, but at least she would avoid seeing Lance.

It felt gross to have his name cross her mind while she was feeling for her vaginal opening. She did her best to push him out of her mind and found what she believed to be her vagina and put the tip of the tampon's plastic sheath against it and pushed.

There was some resistance before what felt like a small *pop* and the tip of the tampon sheath pushed in. It didn't hurt, but when she moved to push it deeper it pinched and she winced. "Ouch ouch ouch," she hissed under her breath as her shoulders hunched and her back bent and she pushed it farther in. She considered giving up—getting the tampon farther in felt like a long, slow kick to the crotch as her vagina clearly rejected the thing, but her options were limited and sitting on a filthy pad all day was not an appealing alternative to bearing her teeth through the pain.

Though her body clenched against it, she got the tampon in and pressed the plunger. She could feel the wad of cotton pressing against her, scratching as it went, while the plastic sheath pushed itself back.

When she pulled the plastic thing out she looked at it and was surprised to only see a couple thin streaks of blood. She thought there would be more. When she looked at her other hand though, at the fingers she'd scratched with, she found them slicked violent red.

Amy stood up and bent over—her throbbing guts twisting as she did—trying to peer between her legs to see what was happening. The dull lights over the sink didn't, however, do much to illuminate the stalls so all she could see were shadows.

Grabbing a wad of toilet paper, she scrubbed her labia and wiped off her fingers, discarding the bloody tissue in the toilet before sticking her hand between her legs. There were those bumps, but they seemed larger now. Swollen from the aggressive itching, probably, but the oblong shapes were troubling. She could pinch them between her thumb and forefinger and hold onto them without having to pull or stretch the skin.

Something was wrong, but the second bell was ringing and she had to get to class. Cursing under her breath she threw out the soiled pad and rushed to wash the fresh blood off her hands. Like Lady Macbeth, she scrubbed her skin with her fingernails and soap until there was no more blood to see, but her hands remembered it and her fingers remembered the strange, alien lumps.

Itching and crampy and with nothing else to do about it, Amy ran to class, the dry tampon scraping her insides the whole way.

Amy sat at an odd angle in her seat, with her hips tipped up. It put less pressure on the tampon though it strained her back and compressed the cramps in her belly, seeming to push them lower until they sat heavily in the cradle of her hips.

Through the first two classes she rocked a little in her seat, the itch flaring up, especially in her second period class, where she could feel Lance's eyes boring into the back of her skull. She scooted her chair as close to her desk as she could to put as much distance between the back of her head and Lance's face as possible.

When the bell rang she gathered her things and ran gratefully to third period, the AP English class where she could chat to Lucy before the bell. It was hard not to think about the horrible, strange bumps and she hoped talking to Lucy would help distract from whatever was happening in her underwear.

She dropped herself into her seat and Lucy scooted as close as she could without leaning out of her desk. "Oh my god," was all she said.

Amy pulled herself tight against the desk, gripping its edge and grinding her teeth against the flaring itch. "The election?" It seemed like all anyone could talk about. Her first period teacher even set aside class time to address it. She may have only been nine when the last election rolled around, but she couldn't remember anyone acting like this. Had she just been too young to notice?

"What'd your mom say?"

"Nothing," Amy said. "She cried last night but didn't say anything about it. Did your mom?"

"She said our country is embarrassing," Lucy whispered, her voice as conspiratorial as though she were talking about the latest dirty rumor. "My dad said she was overreacting and she'd get over it."

"Is this the way elections always are?" Amy asked. "Because it seems stupid."

Lucy shrugged. She didn't know what else to say about it, but it seemed like something they should be talking about. Everyone else was preoccupied by it.

The itch subsided as they talked, but the cramps were persistent. They struck with a new vigor, as though the writhing tendrils of pain were cutting their way out.

Amy winced and lowered a hand to her belly. "Man...I have the worst cramps today. I don't think I've ever had cramps like this."

"Cramps are the worst." Lucy slouched even further in her seat. "The first time I got my period I thought I was dying. My friend Ruby had appendicitis and said it felt like getting shivved. I thought maybe I had appendicitis."

"How'd she know what it feels like to get shivved?"

Lucy shrugged and the bell rang. The class fell silent while Mrs. Lewis stepped in front of them, a broad-shouldered woman with bespectacled brown eyes. Her wildly frizzy, curly black hair was tied in a ponytail that expanded like a cloud high on the back of her head.

She wore a white blouse with the sleeves rolled to her elbows and a black skirt. Her sharp heels clicked on the sickly green linoleum floor as she walked. While running attendance she fanned her shimmering face with a fan made of pear-inlaid wood and bamboo paper, painted in a Japanese ukiyo-e style with cuttlefish. She must have been having her hot flashes again.

The cramps began to subside after attendance was taken, drifting to the back of her mind while Mrs. Lewis fanned herself and paced, jotting notes on the chalkboard and calling out questions about the first three chapters of *The Scarlet Letter*. Amy was even able to raise her hand a few times, forgetting about the strange bumps and the irritation of the tampon while she gave her answers and they discussed the book.

By the end of class, she almost felt like herself. The bell rang, signaling a fifteen-minute break in which she would take herself to the bathroom to struggle with replacing her tampon. She collected her things but as she stood, Lucy grabbed her by the arm and pulled her back into her seat.

"What the hell?"

"You bled through your jeans," Lucy whispered.

Amy could feel a humiliated flush rushing like boiling water to her cheeks. She sat in her seat and stared at the desk. How was she supposed to move from this spot without revealing she'd bled through her jeans?

"Take this." Lucy pulled off her plaid shirt, revealing the white tank underneath and leaving her pale, freckled shoulders bare.

"You'll get dress coded," Amy said weakly.

"It's fine," Lucy said. "I'm going to go grab some Kleenex for the seat."

Numb, Amy nodded. She tied the shirt's arms around her hips and stood up, worried about smoothing the shirt over her rear-end and getting blood on it. While Lucy was fussing with the Kleenex, Amy glanced at the seat. The blood was smeared liberally on the chair. She felt sick to her stomach and light-headed all at once.

Lucy reappeared beside her and shoved a wad of Kleenex into her hands. Amy scrubbed the seat with one half of the wad of Kleenexes, then with the other. It seemed clean so she wadded them all together and, pulling her bag over her shoulder, rushed to stuff the tissue to the very bottom of the trashcan.

"I think I have a spare skirt in my gym locker," Lucy said, taking Amy by the elbow. Amy clutched at Lucy's hand and Lucy squeezed her fingers.

"Thank you, Lucy."

In silence, Lucy led Amy to the locker room. They passed Lance's locker and he stared at them as they walked by. The itching returned with such force Amy had to bite her lip to keep from crying out. Tears perched at the rims of her eyelids.

The skirt was there, left over from an extra change of clothes Lucy had brought the week before. Amy accepted the skirt and withdrew to the bathroom stalls.

"That must be the period from hell," Lucy said on the other side of the brown stall door while Amy tossed her plaid shirt over it.

"You have no idea." Amy pulled her jeans off and inspected the stain. The crotch was red and the red streaked back onto the buttocks. Her face continued to burn while she folded the jeans, careful to conceal the blood, and put them in her bag. "I think I might have an infection or something, too."

"You mean, like…an STI?"

"No! Nothing like that." Amy's nose curled and she made a gagging face as she rifled through her bag for a tampon. "How could I have an STI? I'm a virgin."

"Well, you never know."

"It's just, I've had this itch." It was embarrassing to say out loud. She couldn't imagine having to say it to her mother, but if it didn't go away she would have to so her mom could take her to the doctor. "And I felt these bumps—these really big bumps." She pulled her bloody underwear down and reached to find the tampon string. "It can't be normal."

"My big sister once told me she got something on her junk that she thought was a tumor at first but it also was super itchy," Lucy said. "Then it popped one day. Turned out to be more like a pimple or something, I don't know."

Amy couldn't speak. Her hand had reached for the tampon string but now it cradled alien wads of meat—smooth, soft flesh that hung down and tapered. One of the things wrapped itself around her finger and she yanked her hand back. The burning blush in her face had drained, leaving her white and cold as shock.

"Are you okay?"

Shaking her head, Amy put a hand on the stall wall and choked out, "Yeah. Fine." She looked at the blood on her palm and tasted bile. She reached down again, doing her best not to gag as she felt for the tampon string while the protrusions explored her hand, and yanked it out. The tampon came away bloodless. "Just, um, a lot of blood." She dropped the tampon in the trash. "I've never had a period like this."

"You should go to the nurse," Lucy said. "Ask to be sent home, or call the doctor?"

Everything in Amy bristled at the idea. She pulled a wad of toilet paper from the dispenser and began to wipe at the things between her legs, her throat constricting and her stomach recoiling as she felt the toilet paper on them, as though their nerves were her nerves. This, she assured herself while the world began to spin and grow dizzy, was just a nightmare. Like those nightmares where your teeth fall out, or someone made of shadow is chasing you down alleys but your feet stick like glue to the pavement.

"Are you sure you're okay?"

"I'm fine. Thank you, Lucy," she said while she wiped herself. "Thank you for helping me. You've really got my back—it's really, really awesome of you."

"That's what friends are for," Lucy said, her voice drifting with concern.

"I'm going to clean myself up. You should head to class."

"Are you sure?"

"Of course. Don't worry about me. I'll wash your skirt and get it back to you tomorrow, okay?" The toilet paper came away just as bloody as it had this morning. She dropped it in the toilet.

"Okay. If I don't see you later I'll call you tonight? To make sure you're okay."

"Thank you, Lucy. You're a great friend." She swallowed thickly as she unraveled more toilet paper. "You should...you should come over to watch *Gilmore Girls* sometime. Or, maybe I could come over to your house."

"Absolutely," Lucy said, a smile clear in her bright voice. "That sounds wonderful. Good luck, Amy. I'll call you."

"Okay. Bye." She waited for the sound of the squealing door hinges to die down before she put her hands firmly on the stall door. Her shoulders hunched and she reared her head back, slamming it forward. She gritted her teeth as her skull cracked against the door and everything went white for a moment, the sound of the impact ringing through the empty locker room and through her skull. The pain bolted all the way to her spine like a shock of lightning, and rippled out dull and aching.

She felt dizzy and nauseated. The green tile under her feet felt as unsteady as ocean waves. Shaking, she took two stumbling steps backward and dropped herself onto the toilet. Sitting, she raised a shaking hand to touch her throbbing forehead. She winced as she rubbed the quickly raising knot there, her brow furrowing and her lips grimacing.

She was, unfortunately, still awake. Worse, she now had a headache and a quickly forming lump and bruise to accompany her cramps and itching.

What was happening? Lowering her hand from her forehead she reached between her legs again, to feel the things dangling there. They had nerve endings—nerves which could feel her fingers touching them and, somehow, they recoiled.

Her hand snapped back as well, her heart hammering. She sat there, rigid, listening to the thrum of her heart in her ears and the rush of breath in her lungs while the things growing out of her touched the toilet water and the inside of the toilet bowl. They were moving, of their own volition, but they had nerves through which she could feel. And it felt like they'd already grown even larger.

How was this possible? Her stomach didn't know whether to sink or rebel. When she reached down again, hoping against hope that this was all some horrible hallucination—a stroke, perhaps, or maybe someone somehow slipped her drugs—her fingers brushed the alien flesh and her stomach decided to rebel. She launched off the toilet while her mouth filled with saliva and she spun around, falling to her knees and gripping the toilet seat while her stomach lurched and she emptied its contents into the toilet.

While she vomited the bell rang. She tried to spit out the stinging taste of bile but couldn't get it all. She climbed back up onto the toilet, afraid of being seen by students making their way in, and pulled out more toilet paper to wipe her mouth with.

With shaking hands, she stuffed her bloody underwear with toilet paper and pulled them up. She didn't bother with the tampon this time—menstruation clearly wasn't the problem. She pulled on Lucy's skirt and checked its hem. It came down just past her knees. She pulled on her backpack, flushed the toilet, and let herself out of the stall. She went to wash her hands and checked herself in the mirror.

Aside from the shockingly pale face and the forming bruise on her forehead, both of which would help her convince the school nurse to let her go home, there was no sign of anything wrong. But now that she knew about the growing flesh, she could feel it. She could feel it crammed between her legs, wriggling like little fingers, and would never be able to un-feel it.

"It's a nightmare," she told her reflection while she washed her hands. She cupped water into her mouth, swished it around and spat. She washed her face before confronting her reflection again. "It's just a nightmare. You'll wake up soon." But in the meantime, she'd go the nurse and ask to be sent home.

While other girls began to change for P.E., Amy limped out of the locker room and started toward the office. It was near enough the second bell that most other students had retreated to their classrooms, leaving Amy alone in the breezeway with a few careless stragglers finishing stolen cigarettes.

She shouldered open the door to the west hall, prepared to shuffle along to its end where the office was located, but halted to see Lance just exiting the boy's restroom only a few yards ahead. He heard the door and swiveled his head, his eyes lurching toward her. She recoiled.

"Hey sweet cheeks." He smiled with his too-white teeth while his eyes crawled like spiders up and down her. "What's wrong? You look sick."

Every muscle in her body went rigid as stone while the cramps in her stomach reached a new fever pitch and the itching set her genitals on fire. Even the strange, itching flesh between her legs coiled up tight. Her eyes moved from Lance to the office door at the end of the hall.

"I'm trying to be nice." Lance approached her in full swagger, reaching for her.

Ignoring the pain shredding her lower stomach, Amy sidestepped his hand and, as though it no longer belonged to her, her own hand rose like a claw and slapped his arm away. Her shoulders seemed to drop and her chest to puff up as the pain in her guts subsided.

His lips pulled back from his teeth, baring them like fangs as his eye narrowed on her, a few huffing breaths escaping his parted lips. "Bitch," he managed to say as he moved toward her again, hand outstretched.

She didn't know where the bold move had come from any more than he did. It seemed they had their shock in common, not that she appreciated the common ground. "Leave me alone, Lance." She stepped backward, bumping into the lockers, but her spine remained as rigid as though a metal rod had been inserted into it. "I just need to go to the nurse's office and I don't need your help."

"You don't gotta be a bitch about it." His hand was on her arm, his fingers gripping tightly while he stepped forward, so she could smell the mint gum on his breath as he said, sounding genuinely confused, "Just accept the offer."

A door across the hall opened. The algebra teacher stepped out, his eyes catching for a moment on the students in the hall. Amy and Lance both looked back at him, silently, while he stared. Amy, with her teeth grinding, willed him to come over and do something—anything.

But he didn't.

"Get to class you two," he said, dipping back into his own classroom and closing the door.

"No—" Amy tried to call out to him but Lance shoved her off the lockers and against the door of the girl's bathroom. He stepped so close that she had no choice but to step back, even as a sensation of bold aggression was swelling inside her once more. She stumbled as the door gave way under her weight and he followed her in.

Amy tried to run. She ran to the end of the bathroom, where the light from over the sink was dim. Some part of her knew hiding in the stall wouldn't do anything at this point, but she didn't know what else to do. She ducked in amid the graffiti and shadows, too overwhelmed by fear to worry about the possibility of her name ending up on these walls within the week: "For a good time call Amy Washington," next to her phone number, which would bring her a cascade of gross requests for her body broken and contorted. Her mother would probably hear the rumors but she was too afraid to worry what her mother would think.

She tried to slam the stall door but he had been on her heels the whole time. He threw up his hands and caught the door, thrusting it back at her and knocking her against the toilet. "I'm sick of you ignoring me, you—you dumb bitch." He stepped toward her, his fists balling at his sides, looking like he was struggling with how to insult and intimidate her next. "Didn't you hear? There's a new president in town." He said it like it was a triumph. "It's time for bitches to learn their place."

Lucy's skirt was wet. Amy could feel the toilet water soaking onto her leg and her stomach felt like it was tearing itself apart. She could feel the flesh between her legs crawling out around her bloody underwear and as it did, the fear in her transformed. A sneer crossed her face, her lower jaw jutting out.

Lance grabbed her by the shirt and hauled her up, slamming her against the wall so she stood with the toilet and its low-sitting metal hardware between her splayed legs. He kept his hand on her shirt as he leaned forward, his other hand reaching for her crotch—*I'll grab you by the pussy*, the boys had yelled, pulling from the words of their new president—and she spat in his face.

He lurched back and the meat between her legs grew wild. He snarled, lifting his free hand with his knuckles angled toward her face, ready to bring it crashing down.

Amy felt her voice rising from the very pit of her and heard the guttural, wordless roar emitting from her throat. She felt her face contorting like a demon as her hands set on Lance's wrist, her fingernails digging into his skin as her underwear ripped. The tentacles fell out of her and the cramps released her, the itch relinquished its grasp on her. Her body flushed with a welcome peace.

Before Lance could cry out the tentacles were around him—wrapped around his throat and face. He made a bid to recoil but Amy gripped his wrist tighter and wrenched him back, thrusting her face toward him, her chin jutting out and her lips peeling back from her teeth. Her eyes pulled wide as she hissed her every ounce of fury, her every iota of disgust and hatred through her clenched teeth.

A tentacle thrust itself into his open mouth and cut off the sound of a scream. It shoved down his throat while Amy watched the bloody tentacles wrap around his face and arms.

They pulled him apart. They grasped him tightly with their muscles and suckers and they ripped his arms out of their sockets, ripped his throat out of his neck, ripped his legs off his hips. They tore him apart until his blood painted the green tiles red and the tentacles were satisfied.

Then it was silent, save for the sound of Amy's breath on the air and her heart beating like drums in her ears. She looked at the arm in her hand and dropped it with a squeak. The mangled corpse lay at her feet and the blood pooled around the toilet while the tentacles coiled playfully around her legs, all slicked in blood—hers and, now, his as well.

She closed her eyes and sunk her teeth into her lips. She could smell the blood and feel the tentacles testing her skin with their suckers.

Lance was dead. Lance could not have been deader and there she was, standing over what was left of him, with tentacles dangling out of her borrowed, wet skirt.

How in the ever-loving fuck was she supposed to get out of this?

First she reminded herself that this was a nightmare, something formed out of the memory of that print above her weeping mother, the haunting gazes that she could not escape, and the election that had shaken the girls and women all around her to their very core.

It was nothing more than a dream, she said while she used paper towels to remove her bloody shoes and torn underwear to leave them in the garbage can. It was nothing more than a dream, she told herself while also telling her tentacles to get back under her skirt as much as they could. They obeyed, coiling up around her thighs while she stuck her head out the bathroom door and looked both ways.

Clear. She left the hallway, then she left the school. She cut through the park behind the school and found the bike path that wound its way through the houses and apartment buildings. Most people were at work, or—in the case of her mother—at job interviews.

It didn't matter anyway. It was only a dream.

While she walked—just as quickly as she could while hiding tentacles under her skirt—she devised a way to be rid of this nightmare and wake herself up. She hurried along, all too eager to get it done and over with so she could wake up and tell her mom that she was scared, too.

She unlocked the door to the apartment frantically, then locked it again behind her while the tentacles relaxed and let themselves down. They were still playing with her legs as she made her way to the kitchen, walking bow-legged and awkward to the knife block. The tentacles were blissfully unaware as she pulled out the largest knife she could find and set it on the counter. She pulled off Lucy's skirt and tossed it in the sink.

Amy lowered herself carefully to the floor. She sat against the cupboards with her legs splayed in front of her and for a moment she watched her tentacles explore the cool tile, leaving smears of blood in their wake. They unfurled from the space between her labia minora and labia majora, roughened by little bumps and ridges like the skin of her genitals—or the skin of an octopus. There were four of them on each side. They seemed curious about the world they had erupted into, bloody and vindictive. They seemed happy, if tentacles could be happy.

She picked one and stretched it out along the tile. She pulled her legs wide, and she brought the knife up above her head, with tears streaking down her cheeks, steeling herself to bring the blade down. But, as the tentacle coiled around her wrist, its touch kind, she hesitated, the blade hanging in the air.

# MAKING A MONSTER

by
E. F. Schraeder

## 1. INGREDIENTS

There were body parts to stitch together, but also bones, lots of bones. Blood too. Vats of it! But a recipe? How dare anyone plan to repeat such a gruesome catastrophe!

These days, everyone wants to know about the monster. What makes him tick. How to stop him. What tradeoffs will inspire him to compromise, to shut up. What he's afraid of.

But hardly anyone asks about the details. What nasty bits went where. And no one ever enquires about the skilled surgeon who put him together. No one wants to know about the process. That's my job, assembling a narrative arc. Call it a warning or a how-to guide.

There was no recipe to follow. No one had ever done it before. Not quite like this. To be honest, I didn't write much down while I worked, which hindsight suggests may be for the best. But I'll go back and tell this story as best I can. How to make a monster.

All told, the face, body, and look of the beast took quite a while. Acquiring that number of bones from the dirt of generations was no small undertaking. Simply gathering all the pieces took years—but I'm getting ahead of myself. Let's start with the foundation. Think about the base of this thing—the core. Assembling someone larger than life required help. And I had plenty of help, though it's my name they'll call when they come running with the pitchforks. But trust me, I didn't do it alone.

In the beginning, the work required that I recruit outside of traditional prospects for laborers to do the messiest work: digging. I couldn't have union men asking questions, yet convincing a crew to dig up decaying remnants would be hard, so I paid my workers well. I counted on their labor, and mine, to give the whole project momentum. And it did.

Some parts of the creature could be made of filler, so I advised the crew to bring along the entire corpse of each designated subject. Once I had a small team of people who agreed to do the digging, I assigned each trusted worker a specific component to retrieve, assuring them of their privacy and my gratitude. To my delight, they complied.

Some of the bodies were so ancient they were practically embedded in the soil, falling apart when the shovel struck the splintering wood of their coffins. It may seem odd to use such old components, but a monster needs a history, a backstory. So I allotted extra time for those specific parts of the creature that needed special planning.

I started with the heart. Where to go for an emboldened heart that keeps beating even when it's long dead?

There's no more fertile land than beneath the blood-soaked grounds of yesteryear's mansions and plantations, full of Klansmen and slave owners. I'd be lying if I ignored what came from the Deep South of the U.S. and the segregated north: it's one nasty, brutal legacy that lives on in the dirt with a hatred that brews on. Centuries after the Civil War, the hate is alive as ever. Deep in that rusty soil I located a bigot's heart I knew could be resuscitated.

Then I considered the mouth. No genteel attitudes or pinched lips would work for the kind of mouth I needed. For the creature to gain any attention, it needed a loudspeaker. A brash, bold, grating, big mouth to drown out the competition.

I studied the obituaries, looking for the ugliest caricatures I could find. Anyone capable of badmouthing a respectable gent would do nicely, but it required a bit of patience. Finally, the fates delivered a real tycoon. A city-slicker salesman who simply shouted until he was heard and interrupted when he didn't want to listen. The best the obit could drum up seemed to be that this conman was used to getting his way by sheer force.

I knew at once from the carefully construed portrait in the obituary that no one liked him. That was my man! I sent out a team to dig him up the day after he went into the ground. Such a mouth would do nicely, indeed.

Next, a pair of hands. I knew a few things straight away. They were an upper-class set; they definitely weren't working hands. So, for starters, they were manicured and smooth. Statistics told me they were most likely going to be creamy milk white. The hands couldn't be worn, rough-edged, or seasoned by any kind of labor. They were not the hands of an average man, and certainly not the hands of a woman.

These plump hands only needed to do a few basic things. Waving, shaking hands—no special dexterity was needed for a showman's handshake—slapstick gestures, finger wagging, and the occasional ability to jab or poke would suffice.

Who knows if we got it right with the brain. I knew I needed to construct a live brain, but decided that, for my own protection, the original sources were never to be revealed. Suffice it to say, the process lacked any sort of finesse. But the project demanded more to be conjured than history, so some of the components needed to be fresh. The diggers gathered a few clueless volunteers who agreed to participate in "research" in hopes of a stipend. These poor souls were skewered into place at first, held tight to their posts with a sharp, long stake. Once they were pinned down, it became easy to dismantle them. Especially after the first one. The extra components and leftovers this sloppy process produced were a bonus. A real coup.

The face was tricky. I couldn't have a recognizable man, someone who'd been recently missed. So I decided to assemble bits from the dregs of half-used corpses. The lecherous, leering eyes of a pimp, the perpetually upturned nose of a snob, the teeth of a biting child. The creature was quite a patchwork, a monstrous collage. Some of the selections were symbolic, sure, but they added to the creature's overall impression: This was a construct of epic proportion. He wouldn't be pretty, but he didn't need to be.

There were other pieces, obviously, to constructing his physique, but those features described herein required the most reflection. I assembled him over the course of a few months. Stitching and restitching, testing for tensile strength and resistance until I was satisfied he could withstand basic prodding and poking. But I found this surgeon's work was less provocative than the philosopher's. I never questioned my authority to create him. Not once. Though I carefully weighed the balance of elements that'd be required for his awful success.

I had my most challenging work in creating a mold somewhere safe and undisturbed where the handiwork could set. Of course, laying a proper base was quite an elaborate undertaking. I saw that groundwork as an all-out act of contrition, wading waist-deep in soil thick with black, fertilizing blood. Composed from stones and soil from the center of the earth, the mold was as heavy as it was rank. In a way, it took centuries to form the mold from which my creature would rise!

I knew that in order to get it right there had to be an acidic balance among the components. It wasn't blood type, but blood itself that mattered. And there was plenty of blood, to be sure. To this day, I'm certain that this fecund soak gave my creature life.

To my surprise, I didn't have to search or outsource to supply an adequate quantity of blood or plasma. Those fertile liquids came from the few onlookers and teams of diggers, who were all too eager to provide an ounce or two of their own life-source to continue to advance the project.

I couldn't believe it at first, but the laborers lined up after their shifts, donating by the bag. Who was I to deny them? I eagerly siphoned their lives, pouring the fluids back into the creature's cast. I reserved several portions of the fluids for nutrients, as well.

My pride swelled as I eyed the hidden wall behind my lab where the cutout form awaited. Once he was sewn and sealed, I lowered the creature into the cast to set the stitches and finish him. I waited for him to awaken, like a golem. And when the time came, like a hungry, whining baby, the creature drank every drop until he belched, fat and full of the energy forces that'd been sacrificed to make him.

## 2. TEST RUN

In the early stages of his development, while the creature was staggering around building momentum, onlookers caught notice. Some could tell that the whole project was made up as it went along. I didn't even know where it was headed.

Some later asked if I anticipated the outcome. In truth, it was no surprise, no big reveal: I created something, someone gigantic enough to become a walking, talking train wreck—a powerful spectacle of a beast so horrible he couldn't be stopped.

When I encouraged him to tour, to make himself known to the public, I expected outright condemnation. I joked that he should run for office, calling attention to the monstrosity of government. I said it'd bring focus to the lab's work. I never expected the half-wit would take it seriously.

His mere appearance seemed a hostile takeover of the race. Yet, despite his squealing lies and the dribble from his mouth, people listened. No matter the awful screech his bellowing tongue made every time he spoke, there was a brash honesty to it all. He was welcomed!

The monster never said anything about being nice. He was nothing but cruelty, bluster, and bluff personified. No one had to read between the lines. And the multitudes applauded.

To be honest, even midway through the tour he needed touch-ups. By then, the stench in the lab was nearly enough to ward me off. But I persisted.

With hindsight, if I had to account for it, I'd say time, space, and a lot of unexamined privacy were the obvious, the most basic needs of his travels. Without massive concealment of where he'd come from, how many corpses I'd exhumed to put him together, perhaps he would never have been such a hit.

For a time, I expected him to falter and retreat to the lab halfway through the tour. But gaffes and all, he carried on.

If I had it to do all over again? Who knows. Convincing yourself you did the right thing, in retrospect, that's almost as brutal as the aftermath the beast left in its wake. Once I started to see the following he'd developed, even I grew leery. But by then it was too late.

The end result was a massive disaster, an epic so ugly even I couldn't stand to look. But I continued to work with what I had. The creature needed a spit shine here and there. After his performances, I began to take the liberty of spraying a glossy sheen over the whole creature. I hoped a vapor barrier might help control the odor. The effort also covered up more than a few elemental imperfections.

But surely, I thought, not to worry. His mistakes would be his undoing. Lurking behind the strutting confident freak show and the ever-skulking threat of escalating violence, there were the groaning, gasping hordes waiting to be lulled into submission. And at some point, I resigned myself to taking their money and letting them enjoy the show. What a ride!

I'll admit, most of the upkeep at that point was thankless and brutal. If anyone had thought about it, they might have discovered me, elbow deep in guts, and accused me of heresy. But for the most part I had the privacy of my lab, a small paid staff of loyalists, and absolute freedom to create.

No one could've imagined the decay. Oh, the smell of all that living, breathing death and garbage! By then I knew I'd created something terrible. A greenish, thin-skinned monstrosity with an appetite for cruelty and the absurd. Who cared about the right thing? So passé. I lied to myself more than a little, selling the whole deed as a satire, but he was real. He was alive. And he was gaining a power all his own.

The monster only cares what it wants.

Throughout the tour, he required a lot of stitches. A huge amount. And at times, the whole thing was a mess. Blood and remains of more than a dozen men scattered everywhere. The construction left a wreckage of bodies, nearly sixteen people slaughtered in a vulgar massacre. Gobs of human remains spilled everywhere that crowds gathered to see him, and he feasted on the unleashed violence of the moods and grew hungry for more.

Each time the creature roamed the countryside, he picked up headlines and stragglers like so much bad weather rolling in to tear apart the fields. Everyone wanted a glimpse of the Thing that had been made.

Despite his merely rudimentary grasp of language, his utterances advanced. He became a master of sounding like he had something to say. And with each speech, something new fell apart.

The deconstruction was simple. Take out an eye after a jab to the gut. Rip off the limbs and let the carnage fall. Just press forward.

A strange thing happened on this first tour. The uglier he became, the more popular he got.

"Even when I lose, I win! I could eat one of you right now and still the rest of you idiots would love me!" he bellowed.

I cringed.

But the crowds cheered.

At first only a few had cheered him on, but soon enough a clamoring bandwagon chugged along and drew thousands more. Millions. Did they stare because they were shocked, like villagers at a hanging? Or were they attracted to the exposure of base brutal force?

Who knows if the vision I started out with held throughout the creature's growing success, but the villagers kept going along for the ride.

## 3. NO PITCHFORKS

Soon enough, I tried to back away. I no longer wanted to be associated with the creature's mess.

To my horror, his followers became most loyal servants. If a limb fell off, they simply stitched another on. In that way, they were putting him together all along, one bloody, mismatched leg at a time. The patrols carted him from village to village, adding and subtracting bits of raw skin, as needed. Eventually at their insistence, I returned.

Damn the tongue! I swear that one piece must've been replaced at least a dozen times after flapping out and making a mockery of the whole endeavor. In one brief interval, I had used a venomous snake's tongue, but it proved unreliable and had to be replaced.

But that's only half the picture. That's what I tell myself now. It wasn't me. It took hundreds of thousands of people, dozens from every village they visited, to make him. After all, he had to be pieced together one nerve at a time. Some sources say his initial strength came from a single stinking carcass they dug up and revived. But they weren't there.

It's easy to imagine it that way, a team of psychopaths with shovels, working through the night in a fever dream, leveraging a decaying body from an old grave beneath a tired old flag. But what they found was still very much alive, so maybe it wasn't quite a corpse yet.

Perhaps his unlikely revival was more like awakening from a coma as someone else. Blink once and discover some lingering unconscious urge to dominate. An urge to devour had taken over where reason once prevailed.

"Rare. That's how I'd describe this opportunity." The creature smiled his broad-toothed, winning smile at the crowd. Journalists tapped his words into their steno pads and bloggers snapped pictures with their phones, eagerly uploading stories of his latest pitch. He posed with his usual expression, those small, dark, drooping eyes narrowed.

"We have a chance to really pull this off in a whole different direction. That's my agenda. To mix it up." The creature waved at the crowd and then glanced to the photographers. "See this? They love me!" he said. He clapped his puffy pink sausage-fingered hands together, clapping for himself.

The small crowd cheered. Maybe they were slightly alarmed at first by some of what the creature claimed. He was so mean-spirited, so plainspoken. Half of what came out didn't make much sense. Then the praise trickled in.

"He's on fire," reported The Port. "The Creature came out of nowhere," they said. At the next stop, the curious crowds grew.

"The Creature voices a silent rage," The Daily Rambler wrote.

"The Creature gains ground," a blog in The Recorder opined.

Thus, innuendo became advantage.

"I'm going to change everything. Everything!" the Creature said.

He repeated himself a lot, for lack of much to say. It was true he didn't have a gift for oration, but how could he? Assembled as he was from spare parts. Most of what spewed out only worked half of the time.

But curious, tired, forgotten, and most of all angry people swelled to greet the ugly creature as he toured the countryside, waving and blustering. There comes a moment for every soul to reconcile with what lies within.

Parody. Parade. The words are so close. Feet marching in unison. Saluting an icon. Was it so long ago? The chilling black-and-white footage horrifies.

New footage revealed violence on par with revolt at some of the creature's rallies.

"Subdue the dissidents!" they cried.

"Jail the protestors!" more raged.

"Shoot them all!" the crowd screamed.

Effigies were burned.

And those chants, no matter how vile, were only the voices that were recorded. Meanwhile, some people became terrified as the monster drew nearer their doors. The weather grew cold and the days short. Vandals and violence erupted everywhere.

More headlines followed. "The Creature, Everyman," "Creature Outsider," "Creature Is the Future," "Creature, Change Maker." Labels like this clung to him at first. He'd amassed a wealth of favors from those who'd made him.

A crowd of people cheered, their faces pink with enthusiasm.

## 4. SELF-MADE MESS

Each gross, inept fumble exacerbated the obvious weaknesses. Look up—see the circling vultures overhead? They're attracted to death. Here they come, eyeing his bits and pieces like yummy snacks. Once the seams between the limbs became clear, it was only a matter of time. Pick at one stitch, and two fall apart. The Creature found that his seams unraveled at the slightest tension.

"He just keeps falling apart," the newspapers said.

Soon, no matter what the Creature said, people laughed.

"His own worst enemy," The Port said.

"A Monster," they continued. "Has to be stopped..."

"The Creature's Mess," The Recorder announced.

"Less Mess, Please," The Daily Rambler pleaded.

Vultures swooped as quickly as they'd flocked, to pick him apart. No one really knew if it was too late. Only time would tell.

In a way, he needed those angry villagers, those fearful buffoons, to succeed. Otherwise he was just a word-choked moron stumbling around the field. Even if I'd tried to dismantle him, it would've been too late. He'd been born, and now he'd have his day. I hoped for honest appraisal.

But this was what happened: caught in the frenzy, a lot of journalists skipped the trouble of citing sources. They shrugged. Momentum.

This was what happened when so many people ignored reality. They got a creature willing to devour them and villages willing to offer up their own limbs to feed a blood-soaked savior.

This is what you get.

What's next for me? Mission to the moon. A new land to colonize. A new source to exploit. Probably oblivion.

One thing the Monster didn't have was a soul. No one could've given it that. Not even me. I see it in your eyes, the worry. The one tickling irritation. One more question.

What gave it legs? Why you did, friends. You did.

# HEAL

by
Rider Sullivan

CASE: ND626R-AP3621101

Re: personal mindlink journal chip/State Photographer/Ellison, Hannah
Location of Human Remains Unknown

July 18, 2050

In the year 2026, the People's Coalition rescued the last of the prisoners still held in the Medical Camps. Peace had been declared, signifying a truce between the two economic classes of the world: the State Alliance and the People's Coalition.

In my estimation, the People's Coalition may survive another 50 years. I bring this up now because I want to explain my actions. I don't want there to be any misreading into what I am doing, no misunderstandings.

I can cross both worlds. There aren't any boundaries for me. I am a State Photographer. My job outlines the photographing of State Society and Celebrity, but my off hours may contain whatever I choose. I choose to photograph Disease. I want the State Alliance to see firsthand the effects of their selfishness, of their carelessness, of their greed. I refuse to believe they are entirely blind. They made me an Eye for the State. I will show them everything.

July 22, 2050

I am recording.

The family is surprised that I am black and female and can work for the State. We laugh over this. There is a little confusion over my reasons. I inform them of my purpose: to show the State the fallout from their laws, their decisions, regarding people outside the safe walls of the State.

Jonah is melting, disease liquidating his skin. Gemorah rots and shakes. She vomits in the morning, every morning, and sometimes throughout the night. Light, sound give her severe migraines. She has lost the ability to use the left side of her body with any skill. She needs help to dress, to eat. Ruthie will never see me past the scales covering her eyes. I tell her she's beautiful. The twins have boneless tentacles for arms.

There isn't any running water. There isn't any waste pickup. There aren't any lights once the sun sets.

Welcome to the Quarter.

August 3, 2050

Jonah took me to a funeral. The man being burned died from the Rampage. Once it has been diagnosed by Healers, the disease can take up to twenty years to fully mature. Or it can take three days. Basically, the blood cells turn on each other. They see everything as an enemy. The Quarter is filled with various diseases from Tullah's Ecstasy to the Blue Ridges. Along the walk to the Burning Place, I recorded one woman vomiting blood like water gushing from a fountain. When she doubled up, screaming, no one came to comfort her. I made a motion—a gesture, really—and Jonah grabbed my arm, his eyes wide, his head shaking no. I also saw some who suffered from the Fringe, their heads swollen until their eyes popped out alarmingly, their necks unable to support the weight.

After the funeral, the ashes were swept up into chemical contamination containers by the robotic Guardians from the State Alliance for Disposal.

August 10, 2050

The twins stopped breathing. Gemorah called a Healer. The Healer said, "It's the blood. It's boiling. The poisons must be released." The Healer pushed her hand into one twin. The baby screamed. The other twin screamed. "Cool blood," the Healer whispered. "Cool down now."

I forgot my objectiveness. "She's going to kill him," I shrieked. "Gemorah, make her stop."

The baby shuddered, died whimpering. The twin cried on.

The Healer shook her head sadly. "It was the blood," she said. "It had already turned bad." The Healer looked accusingly at me. I glared back. She told me then, in an angry whisper, "There are other children who want to live."

August 18, 2050

There are bodies in the streets of the Quarter. Bloated, gaseous. Some of them reach up, call out. I have to pull free when one touches me. I can still feel bits of them clinging to me, to my clothing. I can feel it slipping in and then finding its way to my skin, then deeper, into my blood. For one moment, I can imagine disease clogging my veins, riding within my blood and swimming toward my heart, into my brain. I lean against a wall and breathe shallowly. I no longer want to see where I walk. I don't want to care where I go. But I am faithful. I record everything I see.

August 27, 2050

I have a collection of paper visuals. Paper, liquid and light methods. Antique but satisfactory. No one uses paper anymore. I learned the method from history vids. I had to order the materials from merchants on the Netrealm. I was lucky to find a seller. Not much desire for paper items now. The pictures cover my living cubicle. I open my eyes to pictures of blood and limbs and bone. Everywhere I look I find decay and disease. I have caught a recording of Gemorah mourning the loss of her arm. She cradles it like a baby, has wrapped it in a filthy shirt. The way the shadows fall across her face makes her look sacred and hollow.

I have Ruthie posing with her fingers spread across her face, her scaled-shut eyes. Now, there are small strange water-droplet tumors forming on her face, across the soft skin of her hands. I was there when they first came. I remember I could no longer touch her after that. I was afraid of her then.

Jonas has begun to lose his nose; bone peeks out from curling skin. And the others, the others. Here, Tullah's Ecstasy dances a man to death, jittering and shaking so that my recorder slowed the minutes and he dances with echoes of self. Here, the Blue Ridge carves into flesh and bone and makes a child a monster, inhumane, unrecognizable. He curls into himself, his arms and legs bending at impossible angles and then the skin grafting the limbs into those foreign ways. His mouth screams and will never close. When his eyes freeze into place and he can no longer shut them, he will lose his sight. He will still be alive when he is taken to the Burning Place. But there is nothing else to do for him. It is a mercy.

I walk over the paper copies. I drink my substance and replay voices from my chip. They echo hollowly in my head. I drink my nutrients and think of People.

I will have my show in September.

September 6, 2050

My show on Disease and People has ended. I let the State in on the state of the people of the Quarter. I took them from their secure Homes and Work, from their Private Schools and Holidays. I showed them Poverty, Disease and Death.

The State is threatening to revoke my License for misappropriation and misuse of funds. The Newspapers are calling me a political radical. The people at my show drank and laughed and talked. But none of them really saw. I have failed.

September 13, 2050

I missed the Wholesome Jenny Southgate Party. I was supposed to cover it for Work. In her new release, a computer-generated comedy where Wholesome Jenny is the only genetic actress, she gets involved with a cyborg clone in a State Alliance—run Amusement Park in New Japan. When Wholesome Jenny falls in love with the cyborg clone, she wisely undergoes voluntary sterilization.

It is not the fact that Wholesome Jenny cannot logically get impregnated by the cyborg clone, it is the idea that she would chose a different species to mate with. That is why the movie is a comedy. Silly Wholesome Jenny, she always comes to her senses in the last few minutes. Thank the State for being aware of our needs and addressing our desires.

Mathew was pulled in at the last minute to cover the Opening Party. He let me in on the plot from the Party, using his private televid. Days later at Work, Mathew made a crack about how the movie was really about missed opportunity in the face of fantastical ideals. Everyone at Work laughed. Some of them didn't even turn away. They looked me dead in the face and laughed.

September 28, 2050

There are men following me. I've seen them. They broke into the Warehouse darkroom where I make the paper visuals. Then, They came to my living cubicle and They banked my computer. The paper visuals I took last week are gone from my walls. I'm afraid They'll look in my medifiles and discover how to locate and remove my vidieye. I'm afraid I'll wake up tomorrow and find it taken. I'm afraid I'll wake up tomorrow and They'll have cut out my recording chip.

November 10, 2050

I think I'm obsessed. I want to stop, but I can't. I think I will be okay if I just leave my living cubicle, just leave it all forever. I think I could live with Jonah and Gemorah. I think I could live on the streets of the Quarter if they will not take me in. Then, I want to just go to Work and forget about all this. But I can't sleep at night and then I can't tell if I am awake during the day.

November 16, 2050

In the Quarter, a rebellion started. I was not allowed past the Wall. I could not go in the Quarter. I watched it all on public televid. In the past year, twenty thousand babies were born deformed, most dying a few days after birth. State News said it was due to the Healers. During the entire report, the State News Girl never lost her smile. Quarter People rushed the Gate. The Guardians shot them down. No one attacks the State. State News played the footage over and over and over again, thereby neglecting to run *Family Time with the Hendersons* or even the Global prize-winning real-life series *Work Makes the State Good.*


November 26, 2050

The Guardians almost didn't let me cross the Wall. The State has put a mark on my pass. I waited hours until the matter was resolved. I guess I'm allowed to cross the boundaries for a little while longer. I better make it worth it.

I can't find Jonah. Gemorah has lost her teeth, her tongue. I asked her to write. She shook her head, her hands waving helplessly, her mouth an open wound. Of course she can't write. There haven't been Public Schools since the riots of 2030. Ruthie keeps howling, no words, just sounds. The leftover twin is missing also. I hope she died and was given to the Burning Place. But there is always the possibility that Ruthie had to sell the baby for food.


December 3, 2050

The Men following me are no longer discrete. The Pretty One smiled at me when I came home to my living cubicle yesterday.

I am under Investigation at Work. I received a Notice. I can be dissimilated at any time.


December 10, 2050

The Pretty One ... the Pretty One sat on top of me and backhanded me awake. He laughed while the Other tore up my living cubicle. Work Clothing was shredded into plastifiber pieces and then balled up in the Other's fist. The pieces clung together, the plastifiber instantly regenerating into the tight form. The Men didn't even bother to close the door to my living cubicle. My neighbors came out and stood in the hall. The Pretty One screamed, "State Business," and my neighbors scattered, their doors slamming shut behind them. The Pretty One licked my face and bit my nipple, bruising me. The Other shoved my spare recorder chip into my mouth and closed my nose.

Things went red. Things went black.

The Pretty One grinned at me. I saw his face before the rest of the world flooded into sight. He whispered, "Nothing personal."

The Other said, "Your eyes are the eyes of the State. This is a suggestion: Close your eyes."


December 16, 2050

I can't leave the Home. I don't have to leave the Home. I will be good.


December 20, 2050

There are eyes in the walls. They have me on vidieye camera. They are recording my voice. I look out the window of my living cubicle and the Pretty One looks up at me and touches himself. I found a vidieye in the bathroom. I found techwires in the wall next to my bed. I traced them with my fingers, then I tore them out. My dreams are my own. My emotions are my own. They cannot have those, too.

I can see everything most clearly now.

They can't hide anything from me now.

I am the Eyes of the State.


December 25, 2050

Don't have to eat. Don't have to sleep. I 'm open wide. I'm receiving.

I had a vision.
I know what I have to do now.
I must be ready.


December 27, 2050

I have seen the Faces of Gods. In a Retrochurch Chamber on the Netrealm, one face spoke of redemption through sacrifice. From an amulet button there, one face promised creation after destruction. According to the Retrochurch, the saints of the Medieval Ages drank the pus of lepers to purify them.

If my Netrealm account is recorded—and it is, it is, I know I am recorded everywhere by their eyes in here—they must know I have tapped into forbidden venues. They must be viewing the Retrochurch Chamber with me. I no longer can find the hunger to care. Retrochurches know the danger when they post. If they are good at what they do—and they must be, to play in Netrealm—they will have already moved and left dead space for the State to find.

It is already too late.

I have seen the faces of Hope.

I have seen Light.

I have it burning deep within my belly, like embers caught in soft flesh, blurring and charring, and I should be afraid and I should feel pain but I only feel a coolness, a coolness spreading. It is fascinating. A supernova is forming. An implosion of stars is collecting, gathering within the folds of my skin. There is some pain. Now, there is some pain. It grows.

I went to the place they told me about, public, but at night. I waited for the priest. Then, together, as one, we walked quickly toward each other. When we passed, he injected me. I now carry a fine mix of every disease the ghetto has. I'm a carrier. I'm patient zero.

This could scar me.

January 4, 2051

Such light. I no longer breathe. I cannot move. I'm in awe. I'm in wonder. I am filled and shattering. I would cry at the beauty of it if the light had not dried and withered my tear ducts.

I must glow outside. I must shine. I can barely contain so much. I am full to bursting. I am hardly held together. Can skin stretch, can flesh take all of this?

Let them follow me.

I shall burn. The Pretty One, the Other, they can burn with me.


January 12, 2051

I radiate as I leave my living cubicle. My footsteps burn streets. I touch as many people as I can. I have sex with random strangers. I scratch backs. I bite flesh. I enter and am entered without protection. I pass disease. I give death new homes to root and spread. I spread my liquids, my touch everywhere I can. I kiss babies. I sneeze in public. I spit. I cut myself and leave handprints. Everywhere. I travel every street, every center of the State. I spread myself thick and thin. Soon, I will be everywhere. Soon, all the State will feel what the People feel. Know what the People Know. Suffer and Die as the People do.

I take and I give.

It is good.


January 22, 2051

My hair has fallen out. My teeth are gone. There are streaks of light escaping, here from the crack where my arm bends, here from the sores on my legs. My stomach is bloated, extended with the light. I'm pregnant with light. It could just be fever hallucinations. But what wonderful illusions! Light everywhere. I'm light and light explodes from me!

I wake up in blood. I wake up in excrement. I don't remember sleeping. I just remember the pain of a few minutes ago, because now there is more. It keeps gaining on me, the pain. It rides me. Once the pain was waves, ocean tides of pain and release, pain, release. But now ... now, there is only this drowning of pain.

I could laugh. I have never seen an ocean. There are only recordings of oceans. And now, there is just me.

Are they recording me?


January 29, 2051

I'm afraid of dying. Maybe I was wrong. Maybe what I've done is evil. Maybe my mind betrayed me, my ideals betrayed me as now my flesh betrays me. Everything keeps changing. I'm no longer in control. What if I've been blind all this time?

I don't want to die like this.

I don't want to disintegrate.

I thought I'd burn out long before this.

I thought I'd explode. I had hoped I would at least have meaning.


February 3, 2051

My collection of Disease. Jars and bottles. Pus, urine, blood, and tears. I was going to be so brave. This is all that is left of me. I'm buried in this fading flesh, this skin shroud. But, my liquids can live on in those jars. I think of all the others I've infected. They must all be liquidating, too, by now. Watching their parents, their children, their lovers die.

I must be evil. I should suffer for what I've done. I just don't remember having a choice. Did I? Could I have just not cared? Could I have just closed my eyes? I live in the State. The State takes care of its own. I could've just let the people in the ghettos live and die . . . and I would be healthy and well now. And I wouldn't be the death of so many people. It's not like the people of the State have natural antibodies. Why would we need them? It's not like we have any immunity to disease.

I've not simply infected many people within the State. I've killed everyone here.

Are you watching me, Pretty One and Other?

Don't blink. You should record this. Vidieye this.

I shall no longer fight it. I shall no longer refuse it. I'm lost. I'm fallen.

I belong to the ancient Gods of Death and Pestilence. I ride the white horse.

# PRESIDENTIAL PAUCITY

# GREATEST ART OF THE DEAL

by
Gregg Chamberlain

Tribute Day. Today was Tribute Day. Today.

*No denying it now*, thought the president of the United States. No way, no how. No "alternative facts" that he or any of his people could possibly disseminate to demonstrate that today was anything else but...Tribute Day.

POTUS45 stood on the South Lawn behind the White House. Behind him, and surrounding him on either side, stood a phalanx of black-suited, sunglasses-shaded, grim-visaged Secret Service guards. Farther behind the presidential advance group, gathered within the protective circle of their own stone-faced Secret Service chaperones, was the entire First Family. Minus, of course, his idiot namesake. The president's fat features frowned for a moment.

*Lousy punk's probably hiding out,* he thought, *pissing his pants with his pals at the Russian embassy. Well, they can have him. For now. But next year...*

The president fumbled in the pocket of his suit jacket, took out a tiny personal digital recorder. "Note to self," he whispered, holding the 'corder close to his fleshy lips, "later, after this shitfarce is over, revise the selection process for the Tribute list. Add 'President's Choice' to the candidate options."

He thumbed off the recorder and slipped it back in his pocket. Glanced around to see if anyone was watching. Then he quickly and carefully rubbed the pudgy palms of his small hands up and down the sides of his jacket, wiping the thin sheen of sweat away. Hands folded once more in front of him, the president resumed his impatient vigil for the arrival of the Squirym.

Just like other world leaders all around the globe, he knew. Just like them, he waited for the second official arrival, on record, of the first alien race to visit the Earth. As conquerors now, the Squirym were coming to collect the first tribute offering from the latest vassal world addition to their star-spanning empire.

*So much for my American Dream*, thought the president, muttering sotto voce, "Make America Great Again. Pffffbbbbtttt!"

He looked past the scorched southern edge of the White House lawn, over the shattered stump of the Washington Monument, at the partial view of the scattered ruins of the District of Columbia, still smouldering in some places two years after the first visit of the Squirym.

"Yeah, that worked out well," he scoffed, with a bitter smile.

Things could have gone worse for Washington, D.C., he knew, dredging up the reluctant memory of an aerial photograph of the cavernous crater that had replaced Times Square in the heart of New York City.

Biggest hole ever! He snorted, suppressing an inappropriate giggle, yet still he could not resist thinking about the Big Apple Hole's macabre and morbid tourism potential. A phantom trace of his famous sneering smirk tugged at his mouth.

The Squirym advance fleet had appeared without warning at the very edge of the solar system. It was just by chance that the Hubble Telescope had been in the right position at the time, pointed in the right direction at that moment, and doing an automatic sweep just in the very nick to catch the sudden flaring eruption that signaled the arrival of half a dozen alien vessels. As they had made their steady advance inwards, passing the outer planets within a matter of days, the reaction on Earth to the sudden presence of actual extraterrestrial arrivals was pretty much as expected.

Mass panic, alternating with ecstatic New Age welcome preparations, and capped with scornful skeptical editorial opinions and speculative blogosphere commentaries and conspiracy conversations, all covered by and through the regular and social media. Every government around the world that possessed the available academic resources—along with more than a few multinational megacorporations—had assembled emergency "think tank" committees which spewed out instant and massive reports in triplicate in the most obtuse language possible, with "easy-to-understand" summaries attached for the benefit of the average politician and boardroom executive.

The military minds among the major powers had taken the unprecedented action of actually conferring with each other and, even more surprisingly, announced to a public eager for reassurance their agreement on a combined strategy for dealing with the extraterrestrial armada. Should there be hostilities, of course.

While all this was still in progress, the alien ships had crossed the moon's orbit and taken up positions around the Earth, without once making a single attempt at advance contact. For one hour the world had waited with bated breath.

Then a message had come through every orbiting communications satellite, interrupting television and radio broadcasts all around the globe. It had invaded the Internet also, appearing on YouTube, Skype, LookAtMe!, and CanYouSeeMeNow? with automatic links to everyone's Facebook, Twitter, and other social media and email accounts. On television screens and computer monitors everyone saw what looked like a garden-variety black slug—albeit one with definite eyes on its head stalks—standing upright, with a pair of what looked like pseudopod-tipped tentacles clasped together in front of its glistening chest area.

"Greetings!" boomed an obviously artificial voice. "We are the Squirym. We are your new masters. You will serve us or die. Please respond in whatever appropriate subservient manner is your custom."

The president of the United States shuffled his feet and allowed himself a quick look around the blocky black-suited barrier of his bodyguards. Gathered together in a huddle at the back porch of the White House were his advisors, cronies, and sycophants, along with a few Secret Service agents assigned to "Cabinet protection" duty. POTUS45 snorted.

*I should put them on the tribute options list too*, thought the president, *along with all those Fake News fucks!* He glowered as his gaze swept sideways and fastened on the knot of media off to the side, cameras poised to record every second of his latest, greatest humiliation.

Sighing, he turned around and faced forward again. Stared out across the White House lawn at the ruins, and remembered.

The United Nations had held special sessions for both the Security Council and the General Assembly. The G20 leaders had also met for their own secret session. The president had made certain, both in person while meeting with his G20 counterparts, and through his proxy puppet voice at the U.N., exactly what the position on the situation was for the United States, the greatest nation of them all on this planet Earth. He had also included his thought on the matter in his continuing Twitter commentary: *E.T. can play nice or go home!*

In typical rogue fashion, North Korea had responded first to the alien arrivals and their threat, with the launch of its latest attempt in

ICBM technology. The missile had risen just high enough before exploding that a rain of radioactive debris showered all over that politically beleaguered nation. A few of the smaller fragments had also crashed down in neighbouring South Korea and China, resulting in immediate military mobilization in those two countries, just in case any irradiated survivors from Pyongyang managed to make their way to the borders.

Above the Earth the response of the Squirym had surprised everyone. Five of their ships broke orbit and rose above the ecliptic. At which point observers on the International Space Station had reported to both NASA at Cape Canaveral and launch control at Baikonur the sighting of a colourful coruscating flare and the complete disappearance of five of the alien ships. Both military and government minds had pondered the meaning of this. They didn't have long to wonder.

"Damn slugs didn't think we were worth a whole invasion force," muttered the president, kicking the heel of one immaculate and expensive shoe at the ground in childish irritation at the memory. Without a word, one Secret Service agent bent down and replaced the divot of White House lawn.

The remaining ship had allowed one rotation of the Earth to take place before launching a flight of attack flyers. The small disk-shaped craft had swarmed all over the world, blasting away at various cities, military bases, airfields, and shipyards, leaving behind dead bodies, shattered paving, burning buildings, and sunken ships. Cape Canaveral and Baikonur Cosmodrome had received their share of destructive attention. The Squirym flyers had also shot down any and all fighter jets which managed to catch up with them.

The alien pilots also had taken some time out from blowing the world's armed forces to bits to wreak ruin on several of the more high-profile landmarks around the globe. They had reduced the Great Sphinx of Giza to rubble, blasted a hole in the dome at the Taj Mahal, melted the Eiffel Tower to slag, obliterated Stonehenge, decapitated the CN Tower, and given the presidential sculptures on Mount Rushmore a severe makeover. In between attacks on military targets and tourist sites, they had also downed the odd passenger jet and sunk the occasional cruise ship.

A few of the flyers headed straight for the International Space Station. Several well-placed shots had sliced and diced the ISS like a carrot stick. Then, using what several scientists and many knowledgeable science fiction writers and fans speculated were force fields or tractor/pressor beams, the Squirym had sent all of the larger chunks of the demolished station hurtling earthward to wreak further havoc wherever they landed.

"A mass-driver effect," the president muttered, recalling a post-invasion meeting he and his Cabinet had with various military and scientific know-it-alls. He'd actually paid attention to what the geeks were saying, although he did insist on "plain American English, not some techno buzzword doublespeak" when the eggheads explained things to him.

After spending half a day creating global catastrophe, all of the flyers had returned to the Squirym mothership. Soon after had come another message.

"Greetings! Resistance, while expected, is useless. We are the Squirym and we are superior to you and your technology. Surrender now and prepare for servitude."

POTUS45 massaged his forehead with one pudgy palm as he remembered.

*And I had to answer back, didn't I?* he thought. *Be the big strong boss man and inspire everyone, that was the plan, wasn't it? Just couldn't resist getting in the last word, could I? Dammit to hell, everyone knows about my Twitter addiction!*

Soon after the Squirym's second message, the president had texted his reply out to one and all in the Twitterverse.

*This is the President of the United States, greatest country in the world. Shame on you disrespecting our hysterical monuments! Drop dead, slugshit!*

Half an hour after the Tweet Seen 'Round the World, the Squirym mothership had broken orbit and headed away from Earth, past the moon and Mars, straight to the asteroid belt. It had returned an hour later, towing a number of large asteroids. The ship had resumed a parking orbit, the huge hunks of rock strung out alongside of it like a chain of space debris. All except for the last and largest one of them.

The Squirym mothership had singled out that massive hunk of pitted stone from its collection of orbital ammunition and sent it, mass driver—style, plunging down into the atmosphere. The cosmic chunk had landed dead-centre in the middle of Times Square, vaporizing itself and everything else within a radius of several blocks and leaving behind a crater several hundred feet deep. Even now, the death toll for the Big Apple Hole was an approximation. No one really knew who or how many people had been in Times Square and the surrounding buildings at the time, never mind those extinguished without warning in the sections of subway, gas, electric, sewer, and water maintenance tunnels beneath.

Soon after the mind-numbing catastrophe in New York City had come another brief message from the Squirym.

"Serve or die."

The president of the United States shuffled his feet again with growing impatience. Behind and beside him, the Secret Service suits stood silent and stoic.

*First president to reunite the country and bring it back on the road to riches*, he told himself. *I was right, I know I was right, because I am never wrong, I'm always the rightest one around. Biggest popular vote ever!*

He grimaced. *First president ever to meet E.T.s too, and look how that went. First president to lead the country into interplanetary war. And lose! First president to sign an executive order for absolute surrender to alien overlords. Worst day ever!*

*I'd be the first president ever to actually get impeached too*, he thought with a rueful scowl, *except no one else wants this job now, not even the Veep. And they won't let me quit! Damn special congressional bill! And the Senate bastards who supported it!*

He'd had one last chance to turn things around and save his public persona. He'd blustered and bullied himself onto the U.N.-sanctioned negotiating team for the first face-to-face meeting with the Squirym. After all, he had written THE BOOK on negotiation, hadn't he? Who had the best record for making and breaking deals than anyone? Who better to take the lead, then? Be the Face of the World

## GREATEST ART OF THE DEAL

for the first actual meeting with aliens? But, in spite of all his efforts otherwise, everyone else had believed that the U.N. secretary-general herself should be in charge of the discussions.

The meeting between Humanity and Squirym had taken place out in the open, in New York City, at the United Nations plaza, not far from the Big Apple Hole. The Squirym had insisted. Which was a nice tactical touch on the part of the aliens, the president had to admit. Good strategy to discourage any attempts at hardball from the human negotiators. A blatant, and obvious, reminder to everyone about what could happen if there were any more cockups.

The Squirym slid out of their shuttle soon after it had landed, and oozed over to the collection of folding tables and chairs set up in the middle of the plaza. The president of the United States, the United Nations secretary-general and the rest of the negotiating team were positioned on their side of the tables, ready to talk terms, all of them—even him, he'd admitted—hoping to work out some arrangement that humanity could accept, or at least live with. A handful of selected international media were positioned to one side to record and broadcast the historic and heartbreaking moment.

The Squirym pushed aside the chairs on their side of the tables. Huge slug-shaped bodies loomed over the seated humans. One Squirym held up a pseudopod wrapped about a small mechanical device. It placed the machine on the table.

"Greetings!" boomed the device. "We are the Squirym. We are here to accept your surrender."

The secretary-general cleared her throat and leaned forward, hands folded in front of her on the table. "Greetings on behalf of the people of Earth," she had said, gesturing to the rest of her delegation, "We here are appointed to—"

"These are the terms of your surrender!" boomed the translator.

Surprised at the interruption, all of the humans, both delegates and media, had listened, horrified, to the conditions for humanity's subjugation.

All except the president of the United States. He remembered how he'd smiled at the time. When the translator device had ceased speaking, but before the secretary-general could reply, POTUS45 had leaned forward over the table and, his normal and natural smirk in place, had spoken in a loud, clear voice.

"Let's deal!"

The president sighed. His eyes squeezed shut. *Yeah*, he thought, *that went well. Fuck.*

He had argued and admonished. He had blustered and bluffed. He had cozened and cajoled. He had demanded and dismissed. He had exaggerated and expounded. Until, in the end, after several hours of an exchanging of words and offers, most of them his, the president of the United States of America had convinced the representatives for the Squirym to modify the surrender terms for their latest imperial acquisition.

The Earth's new overlords would not swallow the world whole. Instead they would just nibble away at it, slow and steady. Before reboarding their shuttle, the Squirym delegation had left behind a list of items—various transuranic elements, heavy metals, valuable gemstones, and common varieties of mineral crystals—for an imperial collection transport to pick up at a later date. The nearest collection route was several parsecs from the Sol system, which, the Squirym spokesperson had observed, would give the leaders of humanity sufficient time to both explain the terms of surrender to their peoples and arrange for gathering the tribute together.

"Be sure to also include," the booming voice of the translator had said, "a large and varied selection of your species."

"Why?" came the immediate demand from the president, attempting to appear as if he hadn't come out on the deficit side of the negotiations.

The strange black eyestalks of the Squirym leader had inclined downwards as if taking a closer view of the human.

"Scientific experimentation," was the translator's answer, "and also investigation of the culinary potential of the human species. We are very fond of exotic foods."

"They're coming, sir."

The president of the United States wasn't sure which one of his Secret Service bodyguards had spoken. But he himself could also see the disk-shaped Squirym shuttle silently drop down out of the sky.

He straightened up, adjusted his tie with one hand while smoothing over the thinning orange wave of his hair with the other. Maybe he could still get a win out of this. Special concessions for America on the tribute demands. Anything to show that he wasn't a loser, that he was the president that his country deserved.

The shuttle came to rest at the end of the lawn. A portion of the razor-wire-topped concrete anti-riot barricade crumbled beneath one of the craft's landing jacks. A section of the ship's underside slid open and a ramp extended. Half a dozen Squirym slithered down the ramp and across the White House lawn, leaving a glistening trail behind them.

The aliens slid up to within a few feet of the president and his bodyguards.

The Secret Service agents closed in tighter around their assigned subject, but he pushed past them and stepped to within almost arm's reach of the lead Squirym. The alien inclined its eyestalks downwards. Another Squirym slid up, carrying one of the translation devices in its pseudopod tentacles.

*They travel through space from who-the-hell-knows-how-far with WMDs that make our nukes look like shit,* thought POTUS45, snorting, *and they don't know squat about fanny packs? Some superior civilization!*

"We are the Squirym!" boomed the translator. "We are here to collect the tribute!"

"We are the President of the United States of America!" retorted POTUS45 in mocking imitation. "We have our share of your tribute!"

"Including a selection of your species?"

The president looked back at his Secret Service escort and nodded. One of them turned and signaled towards the White House. A back door opened and several soldiers emerged, assault rifles cradled across their chests. Following the soldiers, lurching in lock-step, were a dozen men dressed in orange prison coveralls. Behind them were several more soldiers, using their rifles as prods to keep the orange-suited men moving.

Soldiers marching, convicts shuffling, the group circled around the cowering White House staff and sycophants, passed by the huddled First Family, and halted on the right-hand side of the president and his bodyguards. The "tribute" came to a stumbling stop, leg-and-wrist chains clashing, several of them colliding against the stiffened backs of the forward portion of their military escort. The soldier leading the escort detail turned towards the president and snapped a salute.

With barely a glance, POTUS45 sketched a lazy two-finger wave in acknowledgement. He looked up at the lead Squirym's eyestalks and jerked a thumb towards the group of soldiers and prisoners.

"Here's your Happy Meal." He smirked. "You want fries with that?"

One of the Squirym's eyestalks turned towards the soldiers and prisoners. The other remained fixed on the president. A moment passed.

"They are not the same!"

POTUS45 sneered. "You wanted a 'large and varied selection' of humans, remember? These," he gestured, pointing a fat index finger at the orange-clad assembly, "are U.S. Grade-A Prime examples of the best America has to offer to the Squee-rim!"

Both eyestalks now regarded the president. "Their movements are not the same as the others. Why?"

POTUS45 snorted. "Those ones," he explained, waving a hand towards the prisoners, "are, uh, 'pacified' so they won't make any trouble for you when you take them with you."

"Pacified?"

"Drugged! Tranked! Doped to the gills!" With familiar arrogance, the president snorted and sneered at the same time. "How the hell else do you think we could get anyone to cooperate and 'volunteer' as tribute? No red-blooded American dreams of growing up and becoming a Spam sandwich for space slugs!"

The Squirym's eyestalks swiveled towards the group of prisoners, then turned back towards the president. Another moment passed.

"This is not acceptable. This tribute is...tainted."

POTUS45 smiled. *Gotcha!* "Well, then, if that is the case," he began, "let's deal. I'm sure we can work out some new terms to the agreement."

One eyestalk swiveled around to look back at the other Squirym. At some unspoken command, they slithered forward. In response, the soldiers brought up their rifles while the Secret Service agents advanced to retrieve their charge.

One Squirym produced and levelled a tube at the soldiers. A beam of light flared and they all collapsed without a firing a shot. The prisoners also dropped to the ground.

Another Squirym aimed a tube at the president of the United States and his bodyguards. Another light flash. They all fell to the ground. POTUS45, lying on his back, stared up at the lowered eyestalks of the lead Squirym. He could hear screams and shouts from far away, followed by the sounds of running feet and slamming doors.

*I'm not dead,* he thought. *Why am I not dead?*

He tried to sit up. Couldn't. A bit of science-fiction show trivia came to mind. Some kind of stun gun? He tried to turn his head but could only just manage to shift it far enough that he could see the soles of a pair of shoes. *Secret Service,* he thought, *fucking good they were!*

The lead Squirym still loomed over him. Or was it another Squirym? *All these damn aliens look alike!*

"The tribute is tainted!" boomed the voice of the translator. "The agreement is in default. Penalty clause now applies."

*We can still deal,* POTUS45 thought frantically. *Just let me move, just a little bit, even if I can just speak. We can still deal!*

"Responsibility for reparation for default in quality of designated portion of tribute falls on primary signatory to surrender agreement."

The president watched as an orifice opened up in the "head" of the Squirym. Within it, circles of tiny, sharp-pointed teeth flexed back and forth.

"n…n…n…n…nnnnn…" The president of the United States struggled to speak.

"Reparation will wait while the Squirym retrieve items from the culinary quarters within your building."

"nnnnn…wh…wha…what?" POTUS45 wheezed with the effort. "what…do…you…want?"

The Squirym bent down. "We require the meat substance you call 'bacon'."

"w…wh…why?"

The circles of teeth flexed in and out, in and out.

"The Squirym are always interested in sampling local culinary traditions."

"Iiiiii…donnnn…unnn…der…sssstand!"

The rasp-like mouth of the Squirym loomed large in the eyes of POTUS45.

"Everything tastes better with bacon."

# IN MY MIND

by
Leadie Jo Flowers

"I want you to find connections to terrorists in Venezuela." The president leaned back in his chair, clasping his hands across his expanding belly.

"Excuse me," the Director of National Intelligence broke in from his *at ease* stance, "why would you want to get involved with Venezuela? What they have there is hearsay from a dictator president who is destroying that country."

"Right, and we are going to fix it." The president sat up, moving closer to the director. "Understand that if there are terrorists there we have to flush them out. Get rid of them. Then we can help get those people straightened out. For a 'fee,' of course."

The director approached the desk. "What type of 'fee' are you referring to?"

"Well, they do have lots of oil. We can help them, ah, distribute it." The president sat back.

"I don't believe we have enough evidence to warrant going to war with or for them."

"But you will find it, and that's an order. Dismissed." The president raised his hand towards the door.

As soon as the door closed, the president pulled a second phone from his jacket pocket. After hitting a number, he sat back with a Cheshire cat smile stretching across his face. "Hi, honey, remember when we were talking about doing business in Venezuela? You need to start getting things set up. There will be areas to avoid, but I will keep you posted on that." He listened to her and started laughing. "No one is going to stop us. We will be getting into the oil business and expanding all the others as well. Trust me."

After he disconnected, he pushed the button for his personal assistant, requesting he come to the office. The president played a game on the phone while he waited, shoving the phone in his pocket when the door handle turned.

"Thank you for coming so promptly. I want you to set up a press conference for an announcement this afternoon."

"Mr. President, it will be difficult to pull this off so quickly, is late afternoon acceptable? And do you want any guidelines with regards to questions they can ask?"

The president sat back, staring at his assistant. "That will be fine I need time to prepare my speech. As for the questions, we will just go with my usual signal if I don't want to answer it."

"Would you like me to send your speechwriter in?"

"No, I will do this one on my own."

"What shall I say the announcement is about?"

"About us helping a devastated country in South America."

"But we don't have anything going on in South America. And there are many countries. I need more information to pull this off."

"That will be good. I will explain everything then."

"But, Mr. President, what am I supposed to tell the media? Can you please elaborate a bit more?"

The president smiled. "You will have to trust me on this one. We need U.S. media, the ones who favor the right would be best. Stash the others in the back or in the hallway. That's all."

"Thank you all for coming. I will make this announcement brief and there will be no questions today. At this time, I am ordering troops to be sent into Venezuela to help the situation there. These people are suffering and dying every day. We must stop this travesty! As things progress we will keep you updated." The president turned and walked away under a barrage of questions flying about the room.

Congress called for an immediate session requesting a meeting with the president. There were no talks engaged with Venezuela and no agreements made as to why the USA would be helping the situation there. The Venezuelan president demanded a meeting with the U.S. president. Even the military heads weren't sure what they were supposed to be doing. No military operations had been reviewed or established. The FBI and CIA were called in to give reports on the situation in Venezuela. The president was asked what information his actions were based on. But no answers came forth. Nothing revealed why the USA would move its military into Venezuela.

"We can't find enough verifiable information to support your military request." The Director of National Intelligence stood at attention. "You should have waited for my report before making an announcement."

"You will find the information we need, and we will be moving in there. Do you realize that they have the largest oil reserves in the world? Do you know how devastating it would be if that got into the wrong hands? The hands of terrorists? We have to do this! Find those terrorists so we can get our military in there to deal with this!"

The media were bouncing back and forth about a new war in Venezuela. People objected, and no one had answers. The president just kept making appearances to speak about the atrocities happening there and hinting that terrorists were involved. That he would produce the evidence and the USA would stop these murderers.

Sitting on his bed, the president tweeted another story about killings in Venezuela. He hadn't received any reports about it. He just wrote about it, without proof. Were there any killings? He couldn't remember, but he believed it.

There was a knock at the door and his wife pushed it open. "You wanted to see me?"

"Of course, my dear." He patted the mattress. "Please sit with me and let's talk."

Stepping inside, she turned to close the door connecting their rooms, but paused and left it open. She sat on the corner farthest from him. "What is going on? Are you all right?"

He laughed. "Of course, I'm all right! Why wouldn't I be? Are you accusing me of something?"

She smiled. "No, of course not. I just saw your tweet. There isn't anything in the news about this. What happened?"

"Nothing for you to worry your little head about. Come over here." He touched himself as she walked around the bed, her head down. He grabbed her hand, putting it in his crotch. "You know what I like. Do it."

"But it ..." she squealed when he grabbed her hair and shoved her head down. A few minutes later she ran to the bathroom.

"That's what I like about you, dear. You always do what I tell you, you listen. Now if only these other people could understand that and do the same." He threw the phone he was still holding down. "Has anyone been talking to you about me?"

"No, no one talks to me unless you tell them to. And then I'm sure they just say what you want them to say." She stood with her head held high.

"Why do you look at me like that?"

"I'm looking at a person who is slowly losing his mind and doesn't realize it."

"Bitch, get the hell out of here."

He picked the phone back up and checked his messages. *Phone call with Venezuelan President scheduled tomorrow at 14:00 in the Oval Office.* Great, he thought, now I have to convince this pissant that he needs our help and he doesn't even know it. He typed a message to the FBI, CIA, and military heads demanding to know the status of the Venezuelan terrorists.

The president slammed the phone down. "Why the hell don't these people realize we are their god coming in to save them? Who the hell does he think he is?"

"The president of Venezuela." The Director of National Intelligence appeared to be smiling. "What did you expect when we have no intelligence to support your claims? The normal procedure in these situations is to request an investigation and then make claims on the data accumulated. Not to make unmitigated claims and then try to prove them."

The president stood. He thudded his fists against the desk. "Do you know who you're talking to? I can fire you right now! You need to get out there and do your job. Get that information so we can have our troops in Venezuela this month! Do you understand me?"

"Yes, Mr. President. But let it go on record that I will not falsify information for you."

DIRECTOR OF NATIONAL INTELLIGENCE FIRED blazed across the headlines. *He's not the first and won't be the last.* The president set his phone down. Now he needed someone in there that could get the work done he wanted, needed to continue with his plans. These people didn't understand that he was their supreme ruler, that he was the one that would make the USA great, the perfect leader and the leader of the world. They really needed a new title for someone like him. A title that no one had ever had before, since there was no one else like him.

The CIA director knocked and stepped into the Oval Office. "You requested a meeting, sir?"

"Yes, please take a seat. I wanted to discuss the ongoing investigation in Venezuela. What is the status? Have you found these terrorists?"

"Sir, I'm sorry but we have no solid information about terrorists there. This isn't something where you can look in the Yellow Pages for terrorists and call them up. If there are any there they aren't causing any problems, such as breaking laws, killing people, etcetera. Without some type of activity, it's near impossible to track an unknown down."

"Look, I understand you have a difficult job. But it's obvious with everything going on there that someone has to be behind the decline of this wonderful country. We just need to track down who it is."

"We have tracked that person down, and it's the government themselves, not terrorists."

"No!" The president leaned forward. "It's not the government, or if it is they are working with the terrorists. We need to find the groups behind this atrocity and stop it!" Spittle flew from his mouth. "We have to get in there!"

"Perhaps one of the other agencies can find this information for you. This is something that could take months, maybe even years. Venezuela hasn't been our focus, we've been working in the Middle East."

"Then change your strategy. These people are everywhere, and we must stop them!"

Silence filled the room. Both men staring at one another, neither speaking or moving. *How do I get this idiot to find the information I need?* The president sat in his chair. "If you can't find the information we need, I will find someone else to do it. Do you understand me?"

"Yes, sir. If I don't get your information I will be fired."

The president lowered his voice to a near whisper. "That's right," he said, "you may leave now." After the door closed, he stroked his forehead as he began pacing in circles. "I have to find a way to get these idiots to find these terrorists. Then we can gain control over their oil reserves. We will protect them, and they will pay." He ran through the list of people he knew that he might be able to fill the newly vacated positions with. People who were loyal to him. Ones that would make sure he received the information he needed. Information that was his free ticket to fast-track more business in this untapped country.

Realizing he was spending too much time on this new venture, he called his assistant to get updates on what was happening. Running an international business meant knowing what was going on everywhere. He had to protect his assets and needed to expand more.

After two hours of discussion he understood the need to attend the G-20, to meet with another dictator about nuclear weapons, that he needed to meet the bodies of dead soldiers arriving in three days who died during an attack he ordered, and on and on. They could come up with more bullshit for him to attend when he could be out on the golf course enjoying life. *Isn't that what being the president is about?* He laughed at himself as he sat alone.

The president sat with some of his cabinet. "How do we stop all these imports and start making goods only in the USA?"

Silence filled the room, soon replaced by the sounds of people shifting in their seats. One man cleared his throat. "Sir, we can't just stop imports. First, we would have to start producing these products in the USA, and if these companies can sell their products cheaper than the imports, then the imports will decrease on their own."

"Well, let's do it then! Let's get these businesses going in the USA!"

"Excuse me, Mr. President, but it's not that easy. We also have agreements with other countries allowing us to export to their countries. If we try to stop their imports then they will stop our exports and … well, you can see how that would be a problem. The number of products we can sell will also decline."

"What are you talking about? Everyone in the world wants things from the USA! We make the best of everything! I say we start with China. Everything they sell is garbage. Let's put a tax on their goods that makes it impossible to sell that garbage here!"

The president smiled.

"Mr. President, may I speak freely?" a middle-aged man serenely asked as he stood.

"Of course."

"Are you aware of all the agreements the USA is involved in? I mean, that just deal with imports and exports. Agreements that we worked hard for decades to create and get signed to increase our business dealings. Agreements that we are bound to. Do you understand that revoking or cancelling these agreements, without good reason, will destroy standing relationships, not only with our allies but with countries where we are attempting to better our relationships? Countries where our relationship with them can mean the difference between peace and war?"

The president stopped smiling. "Bullshit! Any contract or agreement can be cancelled, revoked, or rewritten! You just have to make a deal with them. Besides, war is good for the economy." He smiled and folded his hands together. "Yes, war is a good thing, so maybe this is how we should approach it. Get back with me the beginning of next week with your suggestions how to best go about this and where we should start. Thank you for your attention."

The president stood and walked out of the room in silence.

The government was in another shutdown due to the budget not getting approval. Trying to get anything done now was impossible, but the president decided this was the time to try and change things in favor of the government, not the people. He took time to prepare for his meeting with the House Ways and Means Committee. This was key for getting the budget approved and increasing the coffers.

He checked his tie in the mirror, touched up his hair, and practiced his smiling and serious faces. *Hello, Supreme President—or maybe World President?* He had to do this one right to get things moving. The pieces were starting to come together. He received information that they might have found a possible terrorist group in Venezuela. The meeting with Dictator Nuke wasn't a big success, but the media ate it up as they both indicated the talks would be continuing. *Yeah me!* He wanted to jump up and down to cheer himself, but it would mess up the hair.

"I would like to thank you all for coming today," the president said. "As you know, with the challenges we are facing with getting the budget passed, or even a temporary budget, it seems we need to come up with more money. What I am proposing today should help us close the gap with this problem. First, we need more money, and we get our money from taxes. So, I say raise the income tax. Not a lot, but enough to help us through this situation."

"Sir, are you talking about increasing the taxes on the rich, the corporations ... please, give us specific details as to how you propose we do this."

"It's simple, start at the bottom. The corporations and rich are creating more jobs and feeding the economy already. We need to get the money from the, shall we say, lower levels?"

The only woman picked up her bag and turned to leave.

"Where do you think you're going?" the president asked.

"Sir, no disrespect, but there is no way you are going to get Congress to pass a bill increasing the taxes on those who are barely making ends meet when the rich are not going to be taxed anymore."

The president laughed. "You can't be serious. Congress will do what I want. They have to, so they can get this government running again. We can tax the rich, but we wipe it out with more tax breaks, that's all."

Her hand on the door, she turned. "You, sir, have lost your mind." The door quietly closed.

"Gentlemen, now that we have gotten rid of that problem, what do you think?"

The men chatted, laughed, and agreed it could work. They would try but it would require tricky wording and possibly two bills or adding another bill as an addendum to get the tax cuts through. They wouldn't guarantee that Congress would pass it, but they had nothing to lose at this point.

The president picked up the pace back to his office. Rubbing his hands in glee. *It's working! They're listening and finally following my orders. Now to get Nuke Head in line and have him get rid of the nukes. I'll just promise him we will protect them. He will never know what hit him.* He closed the door with a snick, pulled out his phone, and began scrolling through the usual programs and news. It was time to figure out which news reporters would be best for supporting each of the individual programs.

He was now on his second Director of National Intelligence. The guy was almost too easy to sway. A people-pleaser, which was unusual for someone in this type of militaristic position. *But then again, it's my ass he's kissing!* The guy was putting together a dossier on the terrorists. One that would help him get the military into Venezuela. *Once we're in there, taking over will be easy. They'll never know what hit them.* But he still needed to schmooze the president there with his empty promises.

It was time to celebrate, a little treat for himself. He called his assistant and asked him to track down his wife and have her meet him in his room at eight that evening. And told him if she can't make it then find someone else for him.

"Sir, I'm sorry, could you repeat that last part?"

The president started laughing. "It's a joke, don't you get it? A joke!"

He hung up the phone and huffed around the room. *The bastard had to go and screw up my good mood.* He called his daughter to see how business was going. *Fuck those idiots who want me to give up a business because I'm president. I kept it going all these years, they aren't going to stop me now. She will put me in a better mood.*

"Why such a sad face, Mrs. President?"

"Probably the fact that I was ordered to come here."

"Now, is that a way to talk to the president? Come and sit with me. Come on."

"This better be quick, I have things to do."

"That will depend on you. How fast can you do me?"

The president savored the sensations as the door slammed behind his wife.

The announcement on taxing Chinese goods went over like a lead balloon, and the president smiled to himself. The phones were ringing off the hook from CEOs all over the country. He knew better, he had already informed his assistant to field the calls and take messages. He would call them back, even though he had no intention of doing it. He offered them the opportunity to make their own garbage in the USA.

That was good enough. But the headlines were turning into a headache for him. *Once those idiots realize they can make more money here they'll understand. They don't know how to run a business like I do. I'm a god in the business world, they should be listening to me and worshipping me!*

His assistant sat with pages of notes and messages. The president wanted to walk out, but he had postponed all this for a week already. *Maybe I can charge those CEOs for consultation services by telling them how to run their companies. Not yet, must wait till I'm no longer president, unless I can change things around. Maybe I can set up meetings and they can make "donations" to one of my companies. That might work.*

"Sir, sir, did you hear me?"

*No, you fucking idiot!* "Sorry, had my mind on other things. What's at the top of the list today?"

"The Chinese president wants to hold a call with you. He says it's urgent. I have a list of people demanding explanations and meetings with you regarding the new tariffs on China. Heads of many foreign states are wanting to discuss the current situation with you and the agreements that they have with us. Oh, and half of Congress is trying to get in touch with you to find out what the hell is going on."

"That's what I like about you, no bullshit, straight to the point. Tell all the CEOs to open their own factories here. We're giving them tax cuts to benefit them, they should be using them. Arrange a meeting with the Chinese president. Tell the heads of state that if anything changes we will let them know. As of now, everything stays the same. Let's deal with one country at a time, unless they're small ones." He smiled, then started laughing, laughing so hard a coughing fit started. It took a couple of minutes to calm down. Then he saw his assistant's horrified face as he backed away from the president.

"What the hell is wrong with you, don't you know a joke when you hear one?" The president shrugged and smirked. "Come on, sit back down and let's finish this mess."

His assistant slowly took his seat. "Sir, I don't think you understand the seriousness of this situation. Haven't you seen the headlines? I know you read the news. These people are furious and want to know what you are trying to do. I can hold them off for a few days, but they want answers and they want them now, and about the nuclear disarmament talks with President . . . "

"Oh, President Nukehead again? What doesn't that guy get?"

"Sir, you did say that you would continue the talks. It's been two months and you haven't done anything. If you can at least give me some information to relay I . . . "

"Yes, tell the bastard to go to hell or I'll personally drop a nuke on him!"

Silence echoed off the walls.

"Sir, I'll get started on this. You can get back to me on that one later."

The president sat fidgeting with his tie. *Can't these people see that I'm trying to make things better for them? Making things great? Easier? Cheaper? They just need to listen to their Supreme President. I need to call my daughter.*

The phone rang, stopped. A message popped up. *In a meeting.*

The president ordered his troops to Venezuela. He had enough terrorist information, that was all he needed. He didn't need Congress's approval. The Venezuelan president agreed to let them move in silently. That was fine with the Supreme President. *Once they are caught I will tell the whole world how much they all need me. They need my protection, and there is a price for protection. A price that would keep the*

*USA going for a long time. And maybe I need to get that law changed saying I can't run for president again. They should just permanently keep me as their Supreme President without the bullshit elections.*

All this excitement and no one to tell. *They will know soon enough.* He tried his daughter again. Straight to voicemail. *What the fuck meeting is more important than me?* The phone thudded on the bed. Then the lamp went flying off the nightstand. *I can't stay in this pigsty. I need to go somewhere, to golf.* He called the driver, ordering him to take him to the airport. Then he called his assistant to order his plane. All of them telling him that security wasn't prepared to escort him, he would have to wait. He drew his arm back to send the phone sailing when it rang.

"Daddy, sorry I couldn't answer. We were trying to make plans for our new venture in Venezuela. Sounds good, doesn't it?"

"What the hell is going on? I told you to let me know. I have troops going in there. I don't want any screwups!"

"Not a problem. We're taking care of everything. Oh, our broker is buying up the stocks you told me to get, a little here and a little there so no one is tipped off. Once he hits the quota they will be transferred in the company name. Too late for anyone to do anything about it. Perfectly legal."

"Good girl. Now we need to get rid of this Venezuelan president and take over their oil industry. That way the States won't have to buy it from them anymore."

"Oh, Daddy, you're so smart!"

"Yes, I know, I know. Keep up the good work."

"Sir, you are scheduled for a conference call with—"

"Yeah, yeah, I know, President Nukehead. Can you delay the call for thirty minutes? I need to take care of a couple of things."

"I'm sorry, sir. But due to the time difference it really isn't possible. Is there something I can do for you?"

"Yes, tell the Director of National Intelligence I want to meet with him after this call."

"Yes, sir. I'll try to reach him."

As the assistant closed the door, the president started making faces at it. *"Fuckhead, you'll try to reach him. Tell him to get his damned ass in here!"* He rocked his head from side to side. "Blah, blah, blah blah. I'm sick of this shit. Now I have to coddle this idiot when all I want to do is drop a fucking nuke on his head!"

Congress managed to slip the new income tax law through with the budget. No one even realized what was happening. The Supreme President smiled at his image. *I'm so good. They have no idea how good I am.* Now came time for the slick part with President Nukehead, getting him to believe they were allies. None of the other countries believed it, but he kept posting and saying it. Eventually they would come around. *Yeah, I'll have to sign an agreement, but that's what good lawyers are for, to break those agreements. Besides, when you're dead, President Nukehead, it won't matter!* The president started laughing and couldn't stop.

The Director of National Intelligence didn't show up until afternoon. His Supreme President was in a bad mood from his session with President Nukehead. *Why can't these fuckwads put their play*

*toys away and listen?* Now he had to get the ball rolling. The director took a seat.

"Thank you for coming," the Supreme President said. "I really appreciate the help you gave me with those terrorists. Snuffing them is going to be easy. Now, I need to talk with you about something a bit more private. Can I trust you to keep this between us?"

"Of course, sir. I'm here to serve you. What can I do?"

"If there's a nuclear attack—now, I'm not saying there is, but if—where would the president go?"

"Well, if we are being attacked, there are a number of places you can go. The first being the underground bunker right here at the White House. Everything else depends on where the attack is happening and where you can be taken to."

"But what if the attack happens in another part of the world?"

"Much easier. That would give us more time and we could move you to one of our other underground locations where you would stay until it's deemed safe for you to come out. So you aren't exposed to radiation."

The president thought for a minute. "How many people can fit in one of these locations?"

"Many people. Each varies and since it's classified information it might take me a day or two to get it together. I can get it for you but there are a lot of possibilities as to the levels of people required in each facility."

"Um-hm. What do you think of the women in my modeling agency?"

"Excuse me, sir, your modeling agency?"

"Yes, you know, the one where I find all my beautiful women."

"Yes, sir. It's just that I don't get the connection with nuclear attacks."

"You do like women, don't you?"

"Of course, sir."

"If there were a nuclear attack, hypothetically speaking, would we be able to take some of these beautiful creatures to one of our bunkers?"

"I'm afraid not, sir. Anyone there has to have top security clearance."

"But, let's say that one of those bunkers had a few extra places, couldn't we slip a few of them in? I mean, if we have to repopulate the world, wouldn't it be best to have the perfect women?"

The director smiled. "Yes, sir. It would be a good thing. But it takes some time to get the proper clearance. In a situation like a nuclear attack there wouldn't be enough time."

"Exactly! That's why I need you, we need to make sure that no matter what happens, we are prepared to repopulate with the best and most beautiful. So, is there a way you could get clearance ahead of time and should something happen, then we could have a number of these beautiful creatures stashed in a bunker for our pleasure?"

The director looked down at the floor, his face flushed. "Sir, I would love to do that. I'm just not sure I can find a way to do it."

"Let's run a test. You know, just in case. Here is the manager's card for my agency. Call him and see if you can get some these ladies up for clearance. You know, maybe twenty or thirty of them? Let me know how it goes."

"Sir, pardon me for asking, but do you really think there will be a nuclear war?"

The president sat back and smiled. "No, of course not. But you know Murphy's law, be prepared so that it won't happen."

"Of course. I will let you know."

The people were protesting on his front lawn. *Shit! Why can't they understand it is their responsibility to support this country! I wish I had a mini nuke I could drop on them! Now they're pissed because they need to pay a little more in taxes.* He tried to order the police to remove them, but they had permission to march and the police could do nothing unless the protestors broke the law. *Fuck! Fucking idiots! Break the law! Get your asses out of here!*

The Director of National Intelligence sat in the chair, grinning like a sixteen-year-old. "I found a way to do it. There are twenty-seven of your models who can get clearance. It wasn't easy, but I ordered an agent to tap into the system to clear it. Everything should be ready by next month."

"You are amazing. You are going to rise into the stars. Did you like what you saw?"

"Yes, sir. They are very beautiful women, just like your wife."

The president waived his hand. "Pff, she's nothing now. She used to be, but you wouldn't believe how much her doctor injects in her face to keep it looking like it does. And when she takes her clothes of . . . I just keep her around for the kids, you know."

The director's face burned with flush. "Sir, she's still beautiful, and your wife."

"She is the fourth one, I think. Anyway, it doesn't matter. If something happens I want you to make sure she doesn't make it to the same bunker we go to. And I want the women there. This repopulating thing is serious, and we need to make sure it's us smart, rich ones that do that. Not these idiots that protest on my lawn and want everything handed to them. You know what I mean?"

"Yes, sir. I do. I will do my best, should this occasion arise, to follow your orders. By the way, our troops are still working in Venezuela. We haven't found the terrorists, but we will. Those jungles are difficult to traverse. Is there anything else?"

"Actually, there is. This guy that I've been having the talks with, what's his name?"

"Yeah, I know who you mean."

"What is the status on their nuclear arsenal?"

"They only have a few nuclear warheads. But they do have missiles with good range."

"Would you be able to tell me if they are preparing to fire?"

"Of course, sir. We are keeping them under constant watch."

"If they are going to fire a weapon, wouldn't you agree that would be grounds for attacking them?"

"Of course, sir. But at this time—"

The president waived his hand, "No, not about time. If it happens and I give the order, you will make sure the nukes go, right?"

"Of course, sir."

"Thank you. That will be all."

Some of the companies began to produce their own goods or transferred from China to other countries. China was trying to work with President Nukehead, since many of President Nukehead's people were escaping to China. The protests were dying down. The European countries were questioning him, and he continued to ignore them. Mainly because he didn't want to deal with people anymore. They didn't have enough respect for the Supreme President. They couldn't see his side of things. No matter how well he did with his business, it wasn't good enough for them to believe he was doing as well with his presidency. There was talk that another investigation was taking place against him, but they couldn't do anything. He wouldn't let them.

The Director of National Intelligence had said it was urgent they speak. "Sir," he said, "we believe that they may be preparing to fire a nuclear device."

"But they just signed the agreement to dismantle their weapons."

"Yes, sir. But there is evidence they are preparing to fire."

"How much time do we have?"

"A couple of days, maybe."

"Can you get the women moved?"

"Yes, within twenty-four hours."

"Do it. When it looks like they're going to attack, I will give the order. Do we have ships in the area that can drop a bomb?"

"Yes, ready and waiting."

Silence embraced them.

The president stood in the press room. "Dear friends, thank you for coming. I'm here to announce that we have succeeded in capturing a group of terrorists in Venezuela. We are there to help our friends rid themselves of this scourge. Just like we will throughout the rest of the world." Short and to the point, no questions. He walked out.

*Yes, I did it! Now that president will be kissing my ass! And we are going to be rich in oil! Woohoo! I am the most Supreme President!*

They had been requesting him at fewer events, which was fine with him. It gave him more time to practice his golf. He hadn't seen his wife in weeks, but that didn't really bother him either.

The president sat in his chair, cackling. *He did just what I expected. This is my time to prove things.*

The Director of National Security had called an emergency meeting with him. *Now I will prove them all wrong and show them how you deal with idiots who think they know what they are doing.* He rocked back and forth laughing until he heard a sound outside the door.

"Who's there?"

"Excuse me, sir." The director stepped in. "I was on another call and thought it rude to enter when I was on the phone."

"No problem. You said this was an emergency. What is it?"

"They're getting ready to fire a nuke. I have verification they have been preparing. What do you want to do?"

"Are the women in place?"

"Yes, sir."

"Then I am officially giving the order. We will nuke them. And the Venezuelan and Chinese capitals. We will blame it all on them. And have ourselves a fine time in the bunker."

No sooner had the door closed when the laughter started, and he rocked, back and forth.

# RUN!

by
Thomas Logan

*A*nyone making 100x their average worker is not safe.

The Nassir-Ford Range Estate provides a 360-degree clear view deep into the flat desert beyond its private road. The pattern of concentric circles initiated by the property's double perimeter fence continues inwards to an orange grove, a halo of trees around the home planted for shade, for fruit, and for the defiance of environment. At the epicenter, a spacious house of twenty-six rooms with indoor carp pool, helipad, and terrarium holding his private collection of indigenous scorpions and snakes, as well as other venomous desert specimens from around the globe. The domicile is secure. He need not worry.

Inside, the soft bottom of his Jimmy Choo double monk-strap boot's right heel turns on the imported wenge wood flooring as Kip Richards sets his Croma Haiku knife on the freestanding butcher's block. He doesn't care much about such expensive things, but they are a comfort and give others a chance to comment and for Kip to dismiss. The chatter of birds in the trees swells with the morning sun as Kip returns the genuine Kobe roast beef to the commercial-grade fridge. A contemplative moment captures this sleep-deprived man some say is more powerful than the president of the United States with its door open, staring within. The three seated silently behind him can wait. They can continue once he's finished his thoughts and his sandwich.

Kip knows, wiping mayonnaise from the corner of his mouth, this "more powerful than the president" is a dangerous comparison and unfair to the commander-in-chief, who, while leading the free world, is limited by election to a maximum eight-year term. Often Kip wonders about it all, his company's rapid ascent, the opportunities he's seized. His life is now full of riches: a private jet, a boat, a second home where Kip sleeps beside and shares his life with one of the most amazing human beings he's met—his wife—who has an amazing career (though significantly less lucrative) of her own. He has been working half-days (twelve-hour days) for the past few years, but eventually he'll be ready to start up a family again, adopt a foreign baby or two, fill the empty nest, take life a little easier than the roller coaster it's been since Iraq.

Nearly two decades ago, Kip Richards had written a white paper that literally (as he's heard others, shaking his hand or introducing him, say) changed the world, a thirty-page memo addressed to a former company consultant then serving as chairman of the Senate Armed Services Committee. Its subject: how private industry can scale, upsizing and downsizing to escape the present, destructive, bureaucratic typology that annihilated the Soviet Union. He was proposing the U.S. become the FedEx of military action with a just-in-time approach to noncombat security operations. Tragically, but fortunate for the long-term continuance of the homeland, opportunity struck, destroying two Manhattan towers, a wing of the nation's military HQ, and numerous lives. Now Kip had at his disposal the best-trained military force in the history of the planet. He's a proven patriot and a visionary. Kip Richards, by every measure, is a success. Which is why they're coming for him now.

*The good of the many is worth more than the lives of a few.*

Napoleon Bonaparte shared a talent with Kip Richards: He never worried. Faced with dozens of problems each requiring command decisions, General Bonaparte would select one to work on, contemplate, and, if no immediate solution were needed, set aside for future consideration. They say the French nation-builder had mental drawers where he'd file various in-progress solutions, forgetting about them until time permitted or they required his attention. He was a man who could sleep during major battles, confident in his orders, issuing his subordinates an exact time to wake him to decide his next move.

So, Kip does not fret. Kip Richards never loses his cool. Let them keep their appointment. Let 'em come try to kill him. Kip had foresight. His business started as security, protecting the important and the wealthy, people like himself now. He tells himself he will be all right. And so convinces himself. *Say. Believe. Do.* He looks over his shoulder at his security chief, Alexander Morales, releases the fridge door, puts on a grin. Yeah, let those motherfuckers come.

"Cards," Kip demands, rejoining the three with a half-eaten sandwich, an extended palm held open for the deck as he resumes his seat.

He shows his pilot, low on chips, the top card—the king of Diamonds—cuts into the middle of the stack, riffles in midair, cuts again with a certain youthful, impish vigor, and smirks when he reveals to her the king still on top. "You sure you want to continue?"

*The death you are about to witness you may find excessive and unnecessarily brutal. Citizen, this is a cautionary tale. Each of the following Croesuses was provided a choice; they decided their fate, as you shall see.*

*You, too, must choose. That is the law. The good of the many is worth more than the lives of a few.*

*Now let the show begin. <Click Play> to continue.*

Kip Richards grimaces, dealing clockwise. If there was going to be a corporate coup, this is how it would occur. Piggybacking on a real crisis. Limited communication with the outside world. Preying on his fears.

Kip knows how thinly power's held. Money is not security (as his pitch often goes); security is security. Money can turn to paper and electronic accounts can be locked. With the stroke of a pen, a country can nationalize your resources. But what executive orders cannot hocus-pocus out of existence are real weapons in trained hands.

Carved in tight cursive into the mahogany dash of his company car, a Rolls-Royce Phantom, this verse from Revelation 3:17:

*Thou sayest, I am rich and increased with goods, and have need of nothing: and knowest not that thou art wretched, and miserable, and poor, and blind, and naked.*

Kip never dreamt about becoming the president of a private military company (PMC), much less an international business dominating market share with billions in assets. It wasn't what he started out to do, though after a few years it became evident that's where he and Coldwater were headed. Kip Richards believes in fate. And destiny. Follow the right formula for your life and introduce the right catalyst at the right times, and there is no stopping you. You've just got to be aware of your surroundings.

*Communiqué #7.*
*We are everywhere, Corporate America. We are your countrymyn. We are your families, childhood friends, coworkers. We are everywhere because you have made us there. We are Ubiquitous.*
*Remember: No Afghani ever foreclosed on an American home.*
*Remember: No Iranian died to deny health coverage.*

*Remember: The good of the majority is still the greatest good.*
*It is time to bring the war home.*
*End communiqué.*

Kip checks his pager. All guards and systems check.

These men surrounding him are the finer things in life. The strongest, the deadliest, the best in the world at what they do. Talented. There are few Kip Richards's influence cannot reach. He pays well. He invests in his people. Coldwater Global Solutions is the best. He keeps it that way by reinvesting, marketing, maintaining the brand. He dominates through success.

"I'm on," Kaledin says, folds, and stands to adjust his body armor. A steady, dim glow of an LED shows he's activated the personnel switch on his lapel.

Alexander nods, more quiet than usual.

"Invite Johns to sit in if he wants," Kip offers, meanwhile not breaking his stare at the pilot, watching her for a tic or a tell. The closeness in appearance and temperament between her and her sister (his former executive assistant, settlement pending) is uncanny. He just wishes he could make her look different. She's too easy to touch and too goddamn easy on the eyes. "We could use a fourth, or a fifth if you can find one."

"Aye-aye, jefe."

"Tell him," Alexander says, "we're playing for keeps."

*The tree of liberty must be refreshed from time to time with the blood of patriots and tyrants. It is its natural manure.—Thomas Jefferson*

These people who've been playing poker with him, acting familiar, calling him "jefe," they don't have to worry about the survival of the company, being the big swinging dick. They're like these migratory birds chirping their songs safely harbored in his trees; they go wherever there's someone to take care of their needs. They live their simple jobs, surviving off the decisions Kip Richards makes. This he pays them for. There's something inverted to that, Kip knows. They could not survive without him; why then should *he* have to pay *them* when they wouldn't exist without *his* ideas, *his* make-or-break decisions?

But it's the society we live in. They'll never understand the pressures. These Ubiquitous anarchists who've hacked his assistant's computer and set appointments this afternoon for his death want to destroy what they can't envision building themselves. They want to flip the card table over because they can't handle the stakes of the game, play the hands they've been dealt. And after the past seven-plus hours of cross-country emergency travel aggravated by lack of sleep, Kip's beginning to think, Let 'em. Yeah, let 'em, and then let the 99% deal with the fallout.

Kip's good government friends were keeping reports of the eleven confirmed deaths purposely vague, conducting investigations behind the scenes to avoid panic.

The first victim, an oil exec (name withheld but a real douchebag diva behind closed doors, Kip knew, bitching and yelling and throwing his company's weight around), was waterboarded with gasoline Thursday night. He didn't drown. What killed the loudmouth limey S.O.B. happened after his torturers dropped a lit match between his sobbing, sorry lips.

On Friday, a power company exec notorious for coal exports and fracking was introduced to bare wires at 110V. His pacemaker quit. Video seemed to relish his flopping around, turning purple.

The mantra, a title card opening and closing each ad-length moment of grainy horror: *Anyone making 100x their average worker is not safe.*

Network providers pulled the posted clips from servers, began traces that led nowhere. No leads beyond the usual suspects, most of whom were already serving time or converted to work top secret projects for NSA or elsewhere.

To add insult, witness the vandalism of a billboard across the street from Coldwater's corporate offices. Or the same message on hacked business and homeland security pages, the clunky Web 1.0 banners hovering over and scrolling across the middle of secure pages blaring another of Ubiquitous's corrupted slogans: *The good of the many is worth more than the lives of a few.*

Whoever these Ubiquitous were originally, whatever monster they started out as, they're now a hydra. They've spawned copycats. Opportunists. Which means the idea's gone viral.

On Monday, parcels began arriving, stacking up outside Goldman Sachs, CitiCorp, BofA, Barclays, and other 2B2F (too big to fail) types, each parcel delivered within seconds of one another by bike messengers who—Kip's and government professionals reviewing the surveillance tapes suggest—knew the precise positioning of security cameras. The contents of each parcel weighing an exact pound. Each sixteen ounces of skin taken (DNA testing confirmed) from missing persons on each company's respective board.

The most upsetting part: no profit; there's no direct self-interest. Nothing is built. It's only done because ungrateful people are upset with where their average (at best) intelligence and ambition leave them. A dangerous element in our society has been indoctrinating the masses that they are entitled to a certain lifestyle, a certain level of job security after paying for A's at their public college diploma mills or working the same job somewhere for thirty years. It's an Ayn Randian nightmare come true.

*The Eskimo hunter buries his knife fresh from butchering hilt down, blade up, letting the blood freeze. Then he adds a thicker coat of animal blood. It freezes. This repeats until the blade's edge is concealed by frozen blood, sticking up from the tundra.*

*This is how he protects his kill from the wolf.*

*The wolf's sensitive nose detects the fresh blood of the knife, more pungent than the Eskimo's kill. She licks the blood away. As she gets to the blade, she begins adding her own blood, which is fresher. So, the wolf licks faster. And continues to lap. She is numb to the many cuts on her tongue. Blood hunger takes over. And in the morning the hunter finds her bled out upon the ice.*

*Money is the blood. Capitalism is the knife. We are Ubiquitous.*

Kip's not bothered by his pilot taking her sweet time to decide. (It's poker, after all.) Nor is Alexander's quiet looming what's bothering him. Just the opposite.

Kip doesn't need to look over to the towering block of half-Mexican muscle compressed in tight, anti-reflective black casual combat wear; Kip can feel Alexander's loyal, canine-like concern. Forget pound-for-pound and how much meat there is on that body, how he took a bullet and didn't realize it until two days later when he escaped back to base camp: by any metric Alexander Morales is the best money can buy, period. An abusive addict mother who worked the streets, foster care, a junkie brother, an ugly divorce, not seeing his daughters, and other sob story setbacks had—instead of a prisonbird or welfare recipient—pounded Alexander Morales into a weapon. The best in Kip's arsenal.

When Alexander trails Kip into a meeting, all eyes swing to him. It's in how the ex-SEAL moves, how he reconnoiters a room. Kip likes to ask those envious Harvard and Princeton sonsabitches while Alexander, silent and obedient, stands guard: "What, you think the president of Mercedes-Benz drives an A-Class?" If Kip didn't think it was beyond Alexander's faintly Catholic morals, he'd put the spic superman out to stud, build himself a super army. The Morales Boys from Brazil.

No, what's annoying Kip is that one of his pager's bulbs isn't lit. One of the guards hasn't checked in. Alexander still studies him, standing cross-armed (no small feat), the large, stuffed black bear in the corner dwarfed by the Mex merc's muscled body. The pilot also studies Kip before slowly sliding chips into the pot, easily a month's pay in re-raise. But Alexander owns the second pager.

Each light corresponds to a different threat. As long as each is lit, all is good. If an LED goes out, that's cause for caution. If the pager vibrates, time for the panic room.

"Kaledin didn't check in," Kip states, clicking his clay poker chips.

Alexander nods in Kip's peripheral. So not just a bad LED. Kip'll file this away, trusting his security chief's instinct. Meanwhile, he continues studying his pilot, who has a jack showing to Kip's exposed ace. It is all up to pocket cards. Kip calls.

As the pot's gathered and cards pass now to Alexander for his turn to deal, his security chief asks the pilot, "Want to cut to see who stays?"

"I'll go check on Kaledin," she volunteers.

They are just two now. As Kip stacks his chips. As another LED goes out. As Kaledin doesn't return. The plan is in motion. Kip Richards will die. The beeper vibrates.

*Violence is a language. Shall we continue shouting? Are our words clear?*

Kip's yelling:

"I want them to come. I want these assholes to show their faces so we can decapitate them, shit down their throats, and fill their heads with literal shit."

He's in the panic room. And he is panicking. It's like his insides are far out at sea, on four or five different yachts, each lurching in ways Kip can't go all at once. Kip's lost his cool. He thinks he heard shots fired. The camera monitors have been snowing out—one, two at a time—until now only one remains, the camera inside the panic room.

Alexander was the voice of reason. "Granger, Galleani, check in. Over."

The pilot hadn't confirmed in, and now there is a third missing, perhaps all five if Granger and Galleani don't respond. This, whatever it is that's happening, just isn't possible. The place is a fortress.

"Sir, if you'd please stand still."

"I beg your—what?"

Alexander unholsters and hands Kip a sidearm; his other hand draws a long blade from its sheath strapped behind boulderous shoulder blades.

"If you'd stay standing, Kip Richards, I have something very simple to say."

Before Kip can respond, he's distracted by the clinks of the vault's reinforced door unlocking. Which is unthinkable. As the panic room door can only be opened from a coded command from the inside once the locks are set. Yet standing at the opened door with weapons drawn, it's the pilot, Granger, Galleani, and the rest.

"Please place the pistol's muzzle upwards beneath your chin, sir."

"What? Alexander, who's watching the goddamn—" Kip stops. The words of the man he trusts most register. Kip wishes he'd realized sooner, been able to say something less petty or better worded. These could be his last. As his wife reminded him regularly, he has a legacy to consider. And he knows he might not be seeing her again.

"We need him to step forward about four inches," one of his security details tells Alexander; he's studying a tablet screen.

Kip sees what this is about. About four inches forward, and he'll be better framed inside the panic room's remaining camera. Alexander, meanwhile, helps Kip's numb gun hand find the underside of his chin.

*Title card: Anyone making 100x their average worker is not safe.*

*"Kip Richards, you face the future, sir. For too long, you have felt safe. Your clients have lived free of consequences in a world walled*

*off from reality. And have not taken responsibility for the other worlds your actions helped create.*

"Today, now, at this moment, the burden of your decisions returns. You have a very simple choice, sir: Walk away. Walk away from this life you've inherited. Or take it."

"You backstabbing son of a whore," *the short, overwrought, middle-aged man in the video yells wildly as his gun arm swings up over his shoulder and blindly points the pistol behind him toward the block of muscle.*

*The pistol dry fires. Then two more clicks in disbelief.*

*Empty.*

*The knife is too fast for the camera. It glints as the gun drops. The man follows it to the floor, gripping his wrist.*

*Black.*

Kip is jostled awake, a lunging motion through the dark. He cannot see. Blinded permanently? He reaches to put a hand in front of his numb face, but his wrists are bound behind him.

There is movement within the stopped vehicle, and he senses beyond the coarse material over his eyes the closeness of other bodies seated near him. Whatever drugs he's been given are substantial; his mind feels like a pool of water. It brims and occasionally seeps down through fissures along the margins beyond his skull, a Teflon sensation like fountain water pooling over polished steel at a restaurant whose name he cannot recall.

Just as he's understanding the repeated words to get up, he's grabbed, yanked forward, and then down out of a large, high-bed vehicle. He might have injured his ankle—it hurts—and the blindfold slips, showing trees and then the leafy forest ground. This ground comes quickly into view as Kip approaches face first, no hands to break his fall. He's been tripped. His leg swept out from under him.

A man in combat boots kicks him in the side, not too hard. The pain in Kip's skull is becoming more real as he tries lifting himself back up using his shoulder for leverage. Dirt and small sticks stay stuck to his face. Someone beside him helps. The blindfold slips further. Not tripped: He's leg-ironed to another person. The afternoon weather is humid. Birds sing loudly, obnoxiously from the brush.

The barked orders to move are clearer now, fogginess in Kip's head draining like after a night of heavy drinking. The methodical walking in sync with his partner is working the poison loose, which is not good for the gash in his unnumbing head or his swelling ankle tight against his Jimmy Choo boot or his bandaged wrist.

He does not tell Kaledin or the two other guards that he can see. They've journeyed out into a clearing with a kind of lookout tower. There are a half-a-dozen other pairs already present. These blindfolded men and women hold their heads at obtuse angles, ears pointing out, scanning and collecting sounds like a field of radar dishes. Men and at least two women armed with AR-15s and M4s circle this staggered row of people as the birds grow louder. It looks almost like a ceremony, the paired prisoners so stoic and still, the passing paramilitary personnel so precise in their movements as the blindfolds come off.

They look about the world that's returned, blink in recognition of their fellow prisoners. Kip looks to the person he's partnered to, the senator from Kentucky. She frowns, seeing their situation. Kip watches the other military and security contractors, all familiar faces likewise paired to politicians, tries gauging their response. Some are looking over his head, upwards towards mid-sky. More follow these persons' uneasy gaze. Kip Richards understands how Ubiquitous plays their ironic death games. He doesn't have to look to know what death circles above.

It's a talk show pundit who speaks first, tries words on the situation. A large-bore pistol's report stops him short. The people and birds are silent. The gunshot echoes, then all is quiet.

"Now here's something we like to call 'Trickle-Down Terronomics,'" shouts a soldier of fortune at the controls of a drone, smugly and seemingly for the benefit of the many cameras recording.

"You've had your second chances," comes a voice from on high. "Now it's fun and games. On your marks, profiteers. Get set."

Alexander nearly blocks the setting sun from his post in the guard tower, his massive arm tapering up to a pistol pointed like a starter's gun. Around the manacled pairs below, the soldiers' knives come out when the gun fires a second time, and Alexander yells, growling with rage:

"Run!"

# APPLICATION TO TEACH FUTURE PATRIOTS IN HIS GLORIOUS WORLD

by
Donna J. W. Munro

*I, Katarine Smythe, submit that the following essay is true.*

*Why would I consider myself loyal enough to be trusted with the minds of our most precious resource? Though I've known ever since the Leader began his climb that he would remake the world, mold it for the better, that I wanted to serve His will in the best ways, I didn't know where my talents would lead. I did prove myself loyal from the beginning.*

*A proof of my loyalty: The attached photo is me at one of the earliest of His rallies, before the first election, even before He shocked the old nation by winning the nomination for His party. Note my hat and shirt. I still bring those out each election day, wearing them proudly to show the world how my devotion started in the very earliest days.*

Private journals of Kat Smythe, found in her apartment, under the floorboards in her closet.

Dear Diary,

It's Mother's birthday today and my sister, Josie, and I planned to get a cake from Dom's. Best damn cakes between home and the university. Perfect because I don't have much time today. Run home, celebrate with the fam, then a campaign event tonight.

"How can you support him, Kat? Seriously?" Josie doesn't understand how deep my hatred of our President and his party is. How different my view of our options is. She wants more of the same. More of the boring same that doesn't care about our past being disrespected by these progressive idiots. She's a progressive idiot. Why can't she see the forces of evil, just like he says, gathering to crush us? To take our greatness and wealth?

They flood through our open gates every day. They don't bother to speak our language or try to fit in. Why would they? They will just overwhelm us in the end.

Journal part 1 checks out. Submitting journal part 2.

*ESSAY CONTINUES. SUBMIT FOR ANALYSIS.*

*Since His ascension, first to President and then to Lord, those years ago, the world is remade just as he promised. They accuse him of lies, but the loyal, like me, know that those weren't lies. They were diversions. The meat of his promises, the big ideas that the party dismissed as rhetoric, those were the truth waiting for him to shed light. Bring them into the real.*

*No more immigrants.*

*No more unemployment.*

*No more assault on our traditions, religion, and values.*

*A true patriotism not seen in our nation since grandpa stormed the Norman shores in WWII.*

*I believe in His greatness. That His rise is our rise. That His rise is the culmination of history, religion, and social strength granted us through our blood and soil. His rise was ordained by God and history.*

Journal part two of Katarine Smythe, analysis complete on 12.18.12 Year of the Lord.

"It's all a sham, don't you see?" Josie whispered to me as we walked together to the university. Few of us still bothered to go anymore. The culling of leftist traitors meant too few professors to offer much of a program anyway. Not that I blamed the school administration. The professors had been leading kids to rebellion with socialist rhetoric promising free college and health care, as if their needs were greater than the needs of us all.

The streets rang with our footsteps, safer than ever they'd been in my life since the new patrols and the employment initiatives took effect. If you didn't join the police force (most did), then you reported to the job the administration assigned you. Daddy, for example, worked on weapons design at the plant. Not a big change from what he'd done before, engineering passenger planes, but more useful to our efforts as a nation. Other people, less skilled, worked menial jobs to feed their families, pay their flat tax, and make donations to Administration campaigns.

"A sham? How can you say that?" I asked. Her words bordered on treason, but I was sure I could get her to see reason eventually. History will not be denied, as the leader says. "I'm working at campaign headquarters tonight. Come with me. You'll see how important the work is. How much difference we can make."

She scoffed, but kept her mouth shut. It was not a conversation to have in the open.

Later that night, right before I left for headquarters, she picked it back up.

"Kat, he's already President for Life, why do you need to go work at headquarters? Mom and Dad are . . . "

"I know, worried. They should worry about you, not me. You don't do the things you are supposed to, Josie. You don't go to the mixers to meet a nice party boy. You keep trying to get a degree that won't help you in the new world. I mean, sociology is close to being named a heretical subject now. Switch to party history or even psychology like me. Something useful."

"What He says is useful, you mean?"

I didn't bother to answer. She needed to chew on her own words for a while.

Josie huffed, sitting next to me on my bed, whispering so our parents couldn't hear. "We aren't like you, Kat. We don't know how to be what they want us to be."

She leaned in, her eyes full of something she wanted to say, but next to it sat fear. Whatever secrets she kept bothered her. Rattled her, from the look in her eyes. I waited, hoping it wouldn't be something that I'd need to report. Something heretical to the party. She kept it to herself.

That night she came with me to headquarters. I told her it would be good to be seen there. That expectations wouldn't be so heavy for someone new at the local level. That I would be able to protect her. I wish I'd've known what would happen.

Journal part 2 checks out. Submitting part 3 for analysis.

*Essay continues, submit for analysis.*

*Working with the local and state party headquarters, I am proud to have seen and in some small way helped the rise of the party, the elimination of the stain of old Federalism, and the Administration's master stroke in replacing all governors with men of the party, sworn to carry out the goals of the party and our President, who became the Lord when the rebels fell.*

*No nations. No separation. All under the firm loving hand that the Lord applies.*

*Kind with kind, level with level, though the Lord sometimes raises us if we work in our places well.*

*Children, the precious reflections of our Lord's power and His intent for us to overspread the Earth, must be raised by those most qualified. Those with ideas grown in the hothouse of the Lord's own garden. Tended by his hands.*

*In his wisdom, he eliminated the guarantee of parent relationships and procreation. I would be the mother, sanitized of the past and a font of the Lord's love for the children of those deemed unqualified for parenthood.*

Journal part 3 of Katarine Smythe, analysis complete on 12.22.12 Year of Lord.

At headquarters, Josie smiled shyly at the handsome boys that pulled out chairs so she could answer calls, sort papers, roll the handbills the boys took in side-slung sacks from door to door. They flirted with her mercilessly, though I could have told them that Josie had no tolerance for silly talk. She'd always been short with boys.

"Who is this, Kat?" Jack Voilette asked, sliding in between us without waiting for an invitation. A little forward, sure, but he was running for governor.

"My sister," I told him, tapping away at the computer, constructing the next local email solicitation for campaign funds.

"How are you, beautiful girl?" he said, reaching for her hand. He was unmarried, after all, and a directive of the President was that we should embrace traditional family life with the hopes of being qualified to breed the next generation of patriots. Marriage, pregnancy—party loyal to build on party loyalty with their blood. I was jealous. Josie always seemed to attract the best of them with her big doe eyes and shiny hair. My own kinky waves and muddy brown eyes never shone quite as beautifully.

Josie made up for her beauty by being standoffish, never allowing people to touch her, though I thought she jerked her hand dramatically away from his, teeth gritted together in a blank smile I knew wasn't real. Good thing he didn't. He just chuckled and pulled his hand back.

"All right, just a name then, lovely. I would like your name to keep, m'lady." He leaned in, his patented Voilette charm vibrating out in petals of warmth.

"Josie." She continued her work, not returning any of his interest, face set in polite pleasantry.

Damn that Josie, always manages to attract the men I'm interested in. My hopes for a connection with our future governor deflated by the second. Each time I looked up from my data entry, his eyes were on her slim hands, her bright red hair, her pale skin. Why had I brought her to the campaign? To win her over to our cause? Watching her work, others would think her heart was in it. But I knew she didn't really care about the leader, our administration, the governors' future. No matter how much she irked me, I wanted her on our side. So maybe she would fake it next to me until she found the truth in the words and promises of our President.

Still, Jack kept watching her.

Journal part 3 pass. Submitting part 4 for analysis.

*Essay continues, submit for analysis.*

*I submit my parents' intellect—they were an engineer and a museum curator—as evidence for my own. Intelligence is a thing bred in us, as the Lord says.*

*Loyalty is the next great necessity in being qualified to teach the future patriots. I have proven my loyalty, something the Lord says we must show in every action and every step.*

*Proof two of my loyalty: Attached is the document I submitted to the central enforcers office about my own sister's deviant activity, as outlined by the Leader's twelfth declaration of legal and pure traditions. All sex is to be for the glory of the Leader and to produce future patriots. Any sex that doesn't meet that goal is deviant and punishable by isolation in camps for retraining therapy.*

Journal part 4 of Katarine Smythe, analysis complete on 12.23.12 Year of Lord.

Jack asked me to help him court my sister. Dates and swiping left were things of the old world, a sign of the decay of traditional values and the lack of vision that our former leaders had. I nodded sadly, wishing he'd asked Josie about me instead, but one does what one is called to do for the strong men of the state.

On our way home, I shuffled my feet, slowing us. Josie didn't seem to be in any great hurry either. Between us there was only a foot or two, but the air felt as thick as the soupy Milky Way must feel when it spins. We had so many words, we didn't say them. They clogged us up with chunks of silence.

As we walked, we passed a house being searched by the police. The lights burned bright and the windows stood open, airing the shouted denials of heresy and the splintering crashes of the search for deviant materials. Sounds were good. Sounds meant that the police hadn't found anything. Perhaps they'd find nothing. It happened. Sometimes. But more often such a search ended with a—

BANG. One shot.

BANG BANG. Two more.

Then silence too perfect to exist in this world. Like even the clouds froze to witness the execution of the Jacob family, traitors every one.

Josie reached out and grabbed my hand in that moment, clutching me like she was the one who'd been shot. And I couldn't help it. I clawed her right back. They never wasted bullets. Three shots meant they'd all died up there. I'd babysat their young boy when I was twelve. They'd shot him, so he must've been part of the heresy, but all I could think of was his beautiful eyelids that slouched over his lashes. His skin not tan, but not white either. His black hair so inky. His parents' words, tangled from their origin in Vietnam, sliding from his tiny, bowtie lips when I rocked him. Duc. My little ducky, I'd said to him.

"What if they come for us that way," Josie whispered in my ear, pulling me forward for the last block to home. "What if they come for me? Will you stop them?"

The question snaked like ice in my mind. Of course I wouldn't stop them. Of course I would. Who was I? "They won't. We"e all clean. I mean, sometimes you all talk a little . . . loose, but your blood is good and you . . . "

Josie's eyes had shifted to me, locked on me in a way that told me she had secrets. Things she didn't know if she could share.

"What?" I asked, blood racing.

She measured me with her gaze, and for a long second I thought she'd tell me the thing behind her eyes that made her so frightened. Instead, she gave me a side hug.

"I'm just glad we have you to take care of us, little sister."

I should have told her about Jack then. If I had, maybe then . . . If only I could go back to that moment.

Journal part 4, questionable content. Flagged for later analysis by Lord's Minister of Education and Reeducation. Submitting part 5 for analysis.

*Essay continues, submit for analysis.*

*My sister's deviance is attributable to the degradation of society before the Leader remade us in the image of His own vision. Her deviance is not my failure, though I would, if offered the chance, use my knowledge of deviance to watch the future patriots' development, to make sure that none of them cultivated unhealthy, unwholesome love partners as she did.*

Journal part 5 of Katarine Smythe, analysis complete on 12.25.12 Year of Lord.

That night, we ate slowly at the table, dipping our bread into the stew Mom had bought on the way home. None of us were cooks. We could hire one of the rejected people to come cook for us, but Mom wouldn't have it. She'd come up in a confused time when the races and the levels had mixed and called each other equal. Before the Leader's science team had proven that there is a degradation among the rejected. Before the Leader and his Administration there had been a time of speeches and marches, confusion and riots. I learned about it back in elementary school, before the Leader came into power. They taught us to be proud of the chaos. That somehow the mixing of people led us to betterment.

The Leader ended that mode of education before I'd even moved into middle school. The teachers disappeared, and for a while there was nothing. Then the Administration opened the reeducation centers. The younger kids went first, because they needed less prequalification or grooming. I passed with flying colors. Josie struggled. By the time we graduated, all the rejected kids had been removed to other schools and the kids who wouldn't learn were taken to camps for a deeper training.

When we slurped down the thin, salty stew in quiet, I saw their worries written in every line of their faces. I knew how little they trusted the Leader. The older you are, the harder it is to forget the chaotic freedom of the old world. Father didn't say it often, but sometimes he muttered about missing ice cream and supermarkets. Mother whispered about her fears. About how she guarded the art in the basement of the old museum, renamed the People's Celebration of the Lord Pavilion. So far none of it had been heretical, but if it were called heretical, I think she'd still have done it. They were so set in their ways. I just did my best to correct them and remind them what the limits were on their speech and actions.

"Mom," Josie started, stirring the gray meat hunks in her bowl slowly. Her eyes slid to the left as she gathered her words. "I'd like to go to a study group at the college tonight. Can I?"

Mom took a breath, but in that moment I said, "Josie, walking alone isn't allowed. You know that."

"I'll take a cab. I have credits."

For her to spend the few credits she had from her work at the university on a study period seemed wasteful, but mother nodded. She didn't ever suspect Josie of anything, but I knew she was lying. My classes in Intelligence for the Administration had taught me all about tells and shifting eyes. Josie's voice broke as she prattled on nonsensically through the rest of dinner. Dad and Mom both nodded and tried to be interested, but the day's work wore on them. They seemed so much older now. Even in the last ten years of the Leader's rule, they had become like gray grandparents. Their skin stretched thinner on their bones and I wondered why they didn't just embrace this life. There was nothing they could change, so why not accept the fact that they were on the winning side of history?

A horn sounded outside and Josie jumped up, pecking Dad on his cheek and giving Mom a hug. She even leaned in and put her lips against my ear.

"Love you, little sis."

I grabbed her and pulled her into a hug, whispering back. "I wanted to tell you something earlier, but I was a little jealous. You are my sister and I just can't keep good news from you."

She pulled me up, smiling at the parents and toward the door, where she put on her coat on and her overshoes.

"What, Kat?" The roses in her cheeks bloomed, I thought from the promise of a secret between us.

"Remember Jack Voilette?"

She nodded, glancing up at me through the curtain of red hair that had fallen across her eyes.

"He is taken with you, Josie. He wants to court you for wife."

She straightened up and grabbed me by the shoulders. "But what if I don't want him for husband?"

She had to be kidding, right? The up-and-coming governor, confidante of the Leader, and handsome besides? What beautiful future patriots they'd make. And the ice cream for Dad. And Mom's position at the People's Celebration of the Lord Pavilion protected for life. So many perks. Perks that would be in addition to having a Leader-approved marriage. She'd be guaranteed children of her own.

"Just think about it," I said. "About the good that comes from a marriage. For us all."

Her eyes clouded. Slid away from my gaze like they were buttered.

"Let's talk about this when I get back, okay? I'll think about it until then."

And she walked out without another word.

*Think about what*, is all I had in my head. What was there to consider?

I followed, once I heard the door of the cab open.

Cab #842.

One phone call and I'd know where she'd gone.

Journal part 5, pass. Submitting part 6 for analysis.

*Essay continues, submit for analysis.*

*There is no future without the training. There is no way forward without our future patriots. The loss of bright people, people like my Josie, is a wound we can stanch with teachers. This is why I want to be a part of the future.*

Journal part 6 of Katarine Smythe, analysis complete on 12.27.12 Year of Lord.

At least she didn't lie about going to the university. It cost me credits, but my cab kept pace with hers, spilling me out at the iron-gated entrance. She wasn't hard to follow, with her clunking footsteps echoing off the slick bricks of the sidewalk. She turned toward the barracks that the kids without parents lived in. Kids with big talent and little money. They lived there, cooked food for the party professors, and cleaned up, working hours beyond the eight hours of school per day. The Lord said it would toughen them. That if they made it through, they'd be his elite.

Sometimes I wished I had such a promise.

But that would mean . . . I didn't really wish that. I just longed for the romance of it.

Josie turned up the open stair on the outside of a concrete building, a squat rectangle. Education for the masses didn't warrant beautiful buildings. Beautiful minds, honed against stone and pain, grew in the harsh light of truth.

She glanced back once, but I'd hidden myself in the shadow. Her eyes slid back and forth, looking for someone to catch her. Suspicious. Then she bent, picked little stones from between the bricks and threw them at a dimly lit second story window. The sputtering light winked out as the third stone ticked off of the glass. The window slid up and two legs swung out of the window, connecting with the trellis outside, hooking into the ivy growing thick and unkempt against the wall. Foot by foot, the figure scuttled down until its feet hit the stones below. Josie waited there, arms reaching out desperately, clutching the figure to her. Their lips crushed together in a passion I didn't know existed in my sister, my dull old sister, Josie.

I moved in closer, needing to see, but not wanting to. I couldn't help my doubts, my worries. I couldn't let this unsanctioned, secret relationship go on, could I? But she wasn't officially with Mr. Voilette yet. Still . . .

Whispers. The voices reached me. My sister, voice low and sweet. Giggles filling the spaces between her words. And the other voice? Higher. Almost like a child's lilt. The body, encased in black pants and a heavy overcoat, could pass for a young boy's. But that voice wouldn't. Not even a little.

They ran off behind the building, hand in hand, stopping every few feet to kiss, lips so deep in one another that they seemed to become one. Duty told me to follow. To learn the name of her lover. But the tears stung my eyes until I couldn't see the way they ran.

Degenerates. My own sister, a heretic. I took a cab to the police before my nerve gave out, filled out the report form, and told them where to find the lovers. I swallowed the bile climbing up my throat and accepted their thanks, their smiles and compliments, their hands full of credits for me and my family. I rode home in an administration car with a basket of extra food and even a tin of ice cream for Dad.

Journal part 6, pass. Submitting part 7 for analysis.

*Essay continues, submit for analysis.*

*I may be a party regular, Jack Voilette's fiancée, and a certified member of the Administration, but I feel my true calling is with the future patriots. I've given my all for the Lord. My every breath and my every love lie within the progress of our empire. There is no job more important than this one.*

Journal part 7 of Katarine Smythe, analysis complete on 12.27.12 Year of Lord.

"Why hasn't she come home yet?" they asked each other, but I knew they were asking me. When I showed up with the ice cream, Dad took it with shaking hands, put it in the freezer, and shut the door slowly. I took my place in front of the wall screen, tuning into the Leader's nightly address, my back to them, but I still heard the whispers.

I couldn't face them. Not yet. Not with the sting of doing my duty still burning my eyes.

I thought they'd bring Josie home fixed. Reprogrammed.

Weeks went by and there were no words. There were opportunities. Dad's promotion came through. I advanced to the next level in party hierarchy. Mom's collection found a secure resting place in the Leader's own vaults, where she could restore, catalog, and build up the collection in perfect safety. But still no Josie.

Mom and Dad stopped asking me what happened.

They stopped talking to me all together.

Jack visited frequently, bringing sweets for them and clucking at the threadbare furnishings. He offered to set us up in a new apartment, one recently vacated in a sweep.

"No!" Mom shouted, though Dad shushed her.

He stepped in front of her and replied, "No, thank you, Jack. It's too kind. Besides, what if Josie came home and we were gone?"

That's when I saw the grim set of Jack's mouth.

He took me to party headquarters that night for a performance of the newest Lord production of party-approved music and entertainments. Jack held my hand and smiled brightly as Administration officials asked him who his lovely young lady was. The night swirled with excitement and color, leaving me drunk on sips of wine and freedom, clinging to his strong arm. Still, in the back of my mind, Josie whimpered.

Sobbed.

"Jack," I whispered between kisses in the coach on the way home so late it might as well have been the morning, "what do you know about Josie?"

He pursed his lips, pulling away from me and straightening his tie. "Are you so interested in a party traitor?" His voice echoed across a vast gulf suddenly between us. To bridge it, I had to be careful.

"Darling Jack, she's my sister. My poor old parents need to know how she's faring in her reeducation." I twirled my fingers in his lush black hair, falling in a swath across his forehead. I couldn't resist his beauty. The Lord did well in choosing him. Such a specimen.

"She . . . " His eyes searched my face. Lighted on my lips and my own dewy gaze. "She progresses. She is at the South City Camp. Perhaps she'll be home for Christmas."

The coach pulled up at my door and he helped me out. Then, there on the steps, he said, "I would have you as my wife, Kat. Your loyalty is second to none. You are growing into quite a woman. Will you consent?"

Even if it was possible to say no, why would I?

"Yes!" I kissed him breathlessly, though my Josie still sat in my thoughts, crying softly.

"Let your parents know we will be married by the Lord himself next inaugural. Let them prepare." He turned and walked back to the coach, pausing at the door. He turned back and said, "Maybe Josie will be well by then."

I know my smile stretched wide enough to dimple my cheek, my most charming affectation. "She'll be my maid of honor."

He nodded, mouth falling into that grim set, then slid into the coach.

I ran inside as it motored off down the street and found my parents at the table, weeping.

"What's this?" I said, my smile crashing in on itself.

"Where is Josie? Do you know, Kat? Tell us," Dad begged, voice creaking like an angry floor.

In that moment, I lost my reserve. My respect. I treated them to all of my jealousy and my bitterness, because they should have been overjoyed at my match with Jack. I had news. A wedding. All they could think of was their deviant daughter.

"Damn you both! She's in a camp being altered. She's a sex traitor."

Mom's choked gasp sucked the warmth from the room. The air thickened as if with ice as they measured me and my nasty words.

"I'm sorry, but it's true. They caught her in a lesbian's arms. But Jack says she might be back in time for . . . for our wedding." I smiled at them, hoping the news bought my forgiveness. It didn't. It was as if they didn't hear me.

"Where is she?" Dad shouted, thumping his fist on the table. "Where did they take her?"

"Didn't you hear me? I'm getting married."

"We heard you. You are marrying that . . . man."

Dad spat the word, the taste of it sour enough that he coated it with his hate. Might as well have called him a monster.

"Where is your sister?" Mom came to me and drew me into a hug, though it felt less like a celebration, more like a beggar's clinging embrace.

I jerked out of her grasp and stomped off toward my room, too angry to breathe the same air as them. I told them, "The South City Camp," as I slammed my door and fell onto my bed, biting back my hot, teary embarrassment.

The next morning, I got up and they were gone.

Journal part 7, pass. Submitting part 8 for analysis.

*Essay continues, submit for analysis.*

*Each child is a brick in the palace of the Lord. Each future patriot is a muscle fiber bound to lift the Leader's banner and carry it across the world. Nothing is more important than the thoughts that they think and the lessons that they learn. To help them become perfect reflections of the Lord's message is the greatest calling. Creating the new people we are molded to be.*

Journal part 8 of Katarine Smythe, analysis complete on 12.28.12 Year of Lord.

Mom and Dad never came back. Day after day, as I went on without them, every sound outside the door brought me running. They had to come home, I thought. They'd taken nothing with them. Nothing. So every day I counted their shoes and touched their suits, hoping I'd find that some had gone. I found myself wishing that they'd fled. That they'd become renouncers and run to the Canadian wastes. That's a heretical thought, I know, but for them to disappear without a word hurt. The last things I said to them burnt like a brand on my bones.

Jack took me to a state dinner one night, giving me a glittering dress to wear. Something that Mom would have given me in the old days for what she called prom. Something that probably cost more than Mom and Dad made together in a month, maybe more. I spun in it for him, letting the firelight in my sitting room twinkle across the sheen of the skirt.

"Why won't you move into one of the new apartments?" Jack asked. "It's not right for my fiancée to be living in squalor."

I hated when he talked that way. It was his right. He was governor after all, party loyal and part of the close administration. His words protected the Lord's will. But to look down on us for what we had, like it was our fault, when we lived as we were told, seemed cruel.

"I can't move," I mumbled. "My parents . . ."

Jack's mouth hardened again. I'd come to know that gesture. It meant a truth trapped behind his lips. Something I'd be better off not knowing. My loyalty and works didn't matter, in his view. Some things weren't meant for women. Even fine party patriots like me.

"What, Jack? Do you know something about my parents?" I couldn't help but beg for the crumbs. My loneliness, my shame, sat on my shoulders each day, slumping me like a granny.

He swept me out of the room and into his car, refusing to speak further of it. In the coach, we sat side by side, though a wall might've sprouted between us there. My heart ached, even if I let my smile shine for him. Mom. Dad. Josie. All their voices whispered in muted notes in the back of my mind. I almost heard their words, their warmth, but the wall between us echoed them back into the oblivion they'd chosen.

At the party, he swept me from conversation to conversation. His pretty little patriot, decorating his arm and spouting the Leader's philosophy like the Administration heads. The others cooed, hugged me tight. Other governors with brides less impressive swept forward, forgetting their own ladies to hear me sing and warble for my dinner. The words were all I had left.

That night, he'd softened his resolve. Pride or drink made him more receptive to my questions.

"Where are my parents, Jack?"

"Sweet little Kat. I'm glad you rose above the others. None of them would be such a glittering jewel as you." He pressed me against him and smothered me with his rum-soaked kisses.

"Jack, I need to know, please." I didn't push away. That would enrage him. No, instead I tipped the words into his questing mouth, letting him do as he would in between.

When he withdrew from me, finally satisfied, he stroked my hair. "I will take you to them, yes? Then this will end and I will move you into the apartments I want for us and you will take a position in the administration. Something ladylike, but important just the same."

Plans for me. Planned for me. That's the way of things. Like the Leader was father to us all, Jack was the paterfamilias of my life.

He ordered the driver to South City Camp. I hadn't been to South City since before the Leader came to power—I might have been five or six years old then. Once it had been a place of neat brick houses and flat yards. Nothing fancy, but well-tended and loved. Now . . .

The brick houses stood bare and stark behind double fences topped by razor wire. Sentry towers sprouted in old cul-de-sacs. Lights swung, sending bright pools to probe the fences and the alleyways between each line of brick. Men in black barked orders through microphone headsets and people poured out of each dwelling. So many in each of the little houses. So many.

The car slowed next to a larger building, brick and much fancier than any of the others. The letters across the facade had been pried off by the party as a leftover of the old world, but the faded shadows told me this had once been a school.

"This is the camp commander's headquarters. Your parents sleep in here," Jack said, cheeks still red from the fumbling we'd done in the car. He pulled me close, protective and possessive arms wrapped one around me, one anchoring me to his side.

My mind filled with thoughts screaming to get out. *Why were they here? What do you mean, sleep here? Where is Josie?* None of them seemed safe to ask. So I let myself be led to them, stomach churning with battery acid and poison. We passed the guards, all at attention for the governor and his fiancée, maybe all knowing that my parents and my sister were party traitors. Traitors to the Lord.

My shoes seemed tight suddenly and my feet stupid, but I let him lead me up the stairs into the building, slick floor echoing my clicking heels. At least it was warmer than the bitter night outside. Jack pushed his way into a room to the left, a library set up as an office for the camp commander. Behind the desk, a gaunt man leaned over a pile of paperwork, glasses flaring in the florescent overhead lamps. There in the corner, Dad picked books from the shelves and, sheet by sheet, pulled them apart. I watched him work, his face drawn in pain with each rip and hands crisscrossed with cuts. After one book was stripped he pulled down another and begin the process again, never looking up from his work. I pulled from Jack, but he held me against him.

"Commander."

The man looked up, skeptical of Jack's tone of authority, but he stood at attention when he recognized the governor standing before him.

"My fiancée needs time with her parents. May we use your parlor?"

Jack didn't wait for an answer. Instead, he spun me and marched me back out of the room into a converted classroom, walls hung with maps and banners of the party. The center was furnished with overstuffed chairs and a long couch. He deposited me there, gently, then put his hand on my shoulder, a weight so heavy it felt like the irons of a dungeon.

He squeezed and then drew back, the lifting of a pall. Behind me I heard the tell-tale spinning clink of an ice cube and the warm glug of liquor pouring over the crackling ice.

Dad pushed the door open and tugged in Mom, both of them a color I'd never seen. So white they looked blue. Pale and ghostly in the reflections of the lamps. Mom saw me and sobbed. She rushed over, throwing herself next to me onto the couch and clinging to me for all she was worth. Clutching desperately to me.

"Kat, oh my Kat," she whispered, rocking against me.

Dad sat on the side of the couch, so much smaller than I remembered. Stooped and pained. The months looked like years in his lined face. Something broke in me as I looked at them. My tears silently wet Mom's face as she sobbed, but it was Dad who spoke into my ear, the barest whisper.

"Save your sister," he said. "Use all of your power to get her out. She'll die in there, baby."

I turned toward Jack to ask him about her, but Dad grabbed my hands, clutched them tight. Then he spoke to Jack.

"I'd be willing to do anything to get my daughter out of here, Mr. Voilette."

Jack smiled wide as the dawn on a clear, fall morning. But in that smile, tightness. What I knew to be a lie waited inside the gates.

"Sure, Smythe. We'll get you all set up in a new place. Of course, Kat will need to live by the city center. Away from you."

Mom nodded, her eyes red and scratched from so many tears. Tears I didn't know she'd been crying. Something had to be wrong with my Josie. Something terrible.

"Can I see Josie?" I asked him.

He and my father answered, "No!" at the same time. Something really terrible.

I stood, pulling myself out of my Mom's embrace. "Jack, take me to Josie."

Often, Jack would ask my opinion, revel in the quickness of my mind and the complete knowledge of the party and the Leader that I possessed. The habit of respecting my words hadn't diminished with the drinking. He blinked and nodded. He took his phone from his pocket and spoke softly into it.

Then he said to me, "They will be here in a moment. I'll let you see her for a few minutes. Your parents and I have things to discuss about our future."

Then he pecked me on the forehead and steered me toward the door. It opened and a blank-faced guard met me, escorted me out the warm entry hall, back into the dark bitterness of night. We passed gate after gate, brick hovels in rows. My fine shoes sunk into the cracks between broken bricks and piles of waste dumped in muddy, stinking rivulets. Faces pressed against windows, some with broken glass, rag curtains fluttering through.

The guard stopped and pointed. The door hung half open, wind catching and rocking it gently. I pushed against it, not slowing for the stink of shit and blood that hit me in the face. My stomach climbed up my throat, but I swallowed it down. I'd see her if she was here. I had to.

I pushed past bodies, more like bulbous heads on sticks. Brown people, people without hair, the rejected.

"Josie," I yelled.

The walking dead, scabby and weak, shambled back from me, like I would burn them with a touch. They made a perfect alley in the crowd of people pressed together in the room. I stumbled over legs of people sprawled out, too weak to move out of the way. Shuffled to the corner they all pointed to. A red flag of hair peeked out of a drab olive blanket. My hands shook but I clutched the rough blanket and jerked it back.

Poor Josie's skin poked with black divots and white peaks of puss. Her face turned toward me, drool slipping through her ragged lips. Her eyes were unfocused, wandering in space like the walls didn't contain her.

"Josie. Josie?" I pulled her onto my lap. She only weighed as much as a child, bones with skin. Her hair weighed more than her, I bet. "Sis, my poor sissy."

Her eyes found me, though it felt like they traveled around the world and back to connect with me.

"Kat?"

She smiled. Gums pulled back from teeth yellowed in the months past. Eyes swimming in a rheumy swamp. She clutched me weakly with fingers made of dough.

"My Josie. My poor Josie."

I pulled her into a hug, thin skin rubbing against mine like paper, tearing with the pressing.

"Kat?" she whispered. "Kat? You came? Mom said you would. Mom said you'd come."

I had no words. What could I say to the sister I'd doomed? I'd brought her here. I'd turned her in.

She coughed, startling barks that shook her bones and mine. Uncovered, she looked like a piece of jerky, dried out and gray. I gathered her up, but there weren't enough hands to cover everything that looked hurt. Everything that looked bad. My poor Josie.

"I'll get you out of here," I whispered in her ear.

She shook her head, slowly, struggling to do it. She clutched at me with her skeleton fingers.

"She's dead, Kat. They killed her. Dragged her behind a truck and made me bury her. I'm ... I'm nothing anymore."

"No!" I shouted it, right in her ear. "You are Josie. This isn't what was supposed to happen!"

She struggled up, clinging to my neck even though it cost her breath. "It isn't your fault, Kat."

Her words slapped me. Things in my life stitched together and I realized that I had caused this.

"Don't let Mom and Dad suffer," she said. "And ... and I love you."

I buried my face in her hair and let myself weep. Clung to her bones until they were cold. Kissed her face until the frost made it glassy. My Josie died in my arms that night. In my arms.

Journal part 8, questionable content. Flagged for later analysis by Lord's Minister of Education and Reeducation.

*12.30.12*
*From: Minister of Education and Reeducation*
*To: Lord*

*In the case of Katarine Smythe, the minor platform inconsistencies displayed in Katarine's personal diary do not outweigh the acts and history built for many years of her life. Additionally, moving her parents from the South City Camp to a dotard community in the party limits, with twenty-four-hour care, must have eased her worries over the loboto-raisure of both of her parents. Additionally, her position as Governor Jack Voilette's fiancée cements her position in Administration society. I recommend she be appointed head of Early Party Education, where she can choose the content of lessons and hire the teachers best suited to mold our future patriots.*

1.5.13   New Journal: Day 1

Dear Diary,

This is my Declaration of Independence. I will bow to the Leader, his Administration and his puppets. My beloved Jack, so disdainful of the people. So willing to hurt my parents and my sister without a thought about what it meant to me. And me. I want to be independent of the me they made me.

It starts with children.

I will hire teachers with a sparkle of self. The curriculum will build thought. Creative problem-solving. We will tell them about what freedom used to mean.

In the end, I may be caught. Some of my teachers might be caught giving children heretical ideas. But, in the end, we will overthrow.

My teachers are all called Josie. They are all her disciples. And I, her Judas, will atone.

This I swear.
Kat Smythe

# SEEDS

by
John Palisano

Those sons of bitches just won't stop, will they? They say we are in Satan's realm here on Earth, and that this is the Devil's Playground, and that the States have turned into a modern-day Sodom and Gomorrah. Well, I sure don't know much about that kind of thing—because after what I've seen over the three and half decades of my life . . . I think it's something a lot more sinister.

Ross campaigns left and right, up and down. His salt-and-pepper hair seems everywhere: The Internet news sites have nonstop stories about every little place he goes. The guy can't wipe his brow without something being read into it.

*Ross! The Right Boss! The Right Time!*

Everything seems right about him, but I know better.

He's not going to end the world like some giant eye in the sky from another planet. His platform skews right down the middle. Seems the guy's got that rare personality that appeals to the conservatives and the leftists. Okay. So, the extremists on both sides have found plenty of dirt. Don't they always?

Ross spun that, too.

"They can find as much dirt as they want on me," he proclaimed, in a widely spread meme. "We'll use their dirt to plant new seeds."

There's the rub. Right there, out in the open.

And no one seems to see it.

Or notice.

Or care.

Well. Not no one.

I do.

We do.

Me and Penelope. Yeah. She's our cockatoo. Lots going on with her. She's a conduit. So am I. Some of us can travel.

*Travel.*

If the circumstances are just right, our thoughts can inch outward, rushing toward other thoughts, finding them in the great noise of the ocean of collective unconsciousness, and maybe putting seeds in there.

Just like Ross.

Yup.

There's a reason he's got folks behind him. Sure, he's a good-looking, middle-aged, apple pie son of a bitch, but there's more.

Ross can travel, too.

When he does?

Seeds.

Everywhere.

He's like a cranberry shrub in fall, spewing thousands of the little red berries, many half-ripe and rotted, into the bogs of our semiconscious, plugged-in minds.

Ross makes people think of him. Longtime couples think of him during their clumsy lovemaking. Hipsters think of him when they put on their Florence and the Machine re-issues. The news loves him. The other candidates—Dioses, Morton, Harris—they seem to always need to mention him in their interviews. Ross never mentions them. Ever. Not by name. He just acts like they don't even exist. It's impressive. He doesn't sling mud. Which infuriates his opponents.

He knows he doesn't have to resort to anything.

He's got this.

It won't be a landslide, by design, but it'll be a win by a comfortable lead.

That's what I've figured, from hearing the echoes.

They bounce. They're hard to hear, but they're there.

Penelope hears them, too. She can repeat them. Just like when she repeats the live speak, she deduces them in just a way that makes the distortion and echo go away . . . makes them clear . . . something about the way she processes language.

What does he want? Change. They all want change. That's what we have found out. Inside the echoes.

*We only want to take out the New Ones. The people . . . if we can call them that . . . who've got the pieces inside them.*

There was a growing amount of a kind of person—the type who had to be very prominently of mixed heritage—that'd grown in popularity. Many had even gone through the gender mods to get there. They could buy race off a shelf. They put the small cartridges inside a device that would send its signal using a kind of osmosis through the skin of the top of the hand, and within days they'd take on some of the characteristics of whatever race that held their fancy. People were mixing ethnicities like cocktails. And other people were getting pissed.

The arguments came.

*They aren't of God. They're not pure. They're messing with things they shouldn't be messing with.*

*Not.*

*Pure.*

That's where Ross came in. He was pure. Oh, hell, yes, was he ever. Growing up in Pine Valley Project, where they check your DNA at the gate, Ross was a rare bird. Caucasian, with a pure European bloodline. It didn't make sense. How could someone even be that anymore? Everyone in the States was mixed with other continents. Everyone. Those that weren't were freaks. On top of that? He grew up poor. He wasn't from one of those double-gated communities, swimming against the tide of change, trying to protect their "kind" or whatever. No. Ross was one of us and had a very diverse, working-class upbringing. Which was another big reason he seemed to be able to talk out of both sides of his mouth and please folks on both sides. The conservatives liked him because he was a throwback to a long-gone era, and the leftists liked him because he truly seemed to be nonpartisan when it came to race.

For a time, Ross was nonpartisan.

Until the Looming Good got to him. We all sensed the pushes toward him from the Good. He had grown too large not to become a target. Over many weeks, there were ripples in the echoes as the Good coordinated attacks on his psyche.

But Ross was a Traveler, like us, and Travelers are strong. Or supposed to be.

Are you ready? We're going to go inside the echoes now.

Shut your eyes. Lie back.

Yeah. It sounds like a hiss at first.

So, focus.

There. There. Settle in.

Do you hear Penelope? That high-pitched chirp. It's very distinctive. Follow her sound.

Got it?

Good.

Relax. Don't shut your eyes so tight.

Okay?

Do you hear the echoes? Their voices are all mixed together. So, listen for Penelope's chirps. That should help your brain to focus. Her sounds act like an antenna. If you are able to focus you can . . .

You hear them? Getting more distinct? Right. Morgan will separate them. She knows how to hone in on him. On them. He is open and doesn't realize anyone here is listening.

*The*
*Grassy*
*Knoll*
*Grows*
*Inside*
*My*
*Mind*
*Can you feel it?*
*Can you sense it?*
*You can.*
*I can.*
*We can.*
*We*
*Can.*
She's a conduit. The bird. The damn cockatoo. Penelope.
What does he want? Ross? What is he hiding?
The voice, familiar from so many clips, yet different in its casualness. A little less sure. A little less likable. A little less on stage. Sounds like he's talking to someone.
Who?
We know, don't we?
Ross's voice, then, loud and clear.
*We can't have them. These New Ones. Erasing humanity. Changing their race. They're making fun of everyone. They have no respect. They don't want anyone to be unique. America was made on people being unique. You know this.*
But it isn't Ross's voice, is it? Feel that chill in your gut and inside your marrow? That's the Looming Good. Another collective of Travelers. They all speak as one, unlike us. Isn't that funny? They speak as one just as they spout on about being unique and special?
There's Ross, lying down somewhere, hearing all this—being programmed with this—their seeds deep in the soil of his thoughts, growing, sprouting, with strong roots, with flowers about to bloom.
Bloom they will. Gunshots like a million flower-shaped bursts of fire. Once he's inside. Once he's rooted. Once it's too late to turn

back. First, it will be the New Ones. Then it will be anyone not like them—anyone not like him or them.

You're asking if there's any other way to stop him? Call off the election? Make this public?

We can't make the Travelers public. There would be a slaughter unlike any other. We need to keep this hidden. The risks of discovery will lead to our demise.

How, you ask?

The same way we're going to take out Ross.

Ross the Boss.

Elect him or pay the cost!

Or should we rewrite his pitch as . . .

Elect him

And . . .

Pay the cost?

*The grassy knoll grows inside your mind.*

In this era, there's no way to kill someone and get away with it. Cameras are everywhere. Every spoken and written word is recorded and backed up somewhere. Everyone is a detective. Everyone knows everything now. Secrets are hard to keep. There is a place, though. You know where. Inside the echoes. No one's figured out a way to record thoughts. Maybe one day, but not yet.

So, let's take our chance.

We'll each zero in on Ross. Make him do it. Make him take himself out.

Each of us will be like Oswald aiming a rifle. Wherever he goes, we will see, and we'll all have him in our sights. Oswald didn't act alone. Or so they say. Whatever happened then, doesn't matter. It'll be the same, in that Ross will be driving right into our sights, unknowing until it's too late.

There are others. Several. I hear their voices. They speak in unison, men and women. Some speak different languages or a mixture of two.

We have met inside the echoes. Penelope has guided us to Ross. His head is in his hands.

There is no time like now. Nothing gained by waiting.

*Pull the trigger*, someone says. Someone else laughs.

*Pull the trigger, Ross. Do it, fucker. Better now than later when everyone finds out. They will. It's the way of the world now. There are no secrets. They'll find out who's pulling your strings. The Looming Good. Yeah. They're going to be found out, too. No genocide on our watch. The New Ones will be fine. The ones who have harvested everything. The ones who have evolved won't be stopped. Not now. Not by you. Not by the people pulling your strings. You're a Traveler, like us. But we are going to fuck your shit up. This isn't happening. You've disgraced our kind. And you know you have. There's no turning back. We won't stand for it. No turning back now. Unless you pull the trigger. Unless you do it. Then you will have redemption. We know you don't want to do this, anyway. We know it sounded good until it became too real. So let yourself off easy. Before there's too much damage done, okay? It'll only take a few seconds and then you'll be released. Into the great Nothing. Maybe we'll see you here . . . somewhere inside the echoes.*

We don't hear the gunshot, but we feel it as millions of seeds that once made up Ross's head spread far and wide, painting his hotel room, each seed vibrant and alive for a split second before dying.

Then we pull back and out of the echoes, before it's too late, before the Looming Good go searching. We're gone without a trace, his memories evaporated like steam.

The news is breaking.

Ross the Boss!

Lost. Lost. Lost.

We lost him.

Their story begins.

Dallas, TX November 22—Popular presidential candidate Tom Ross has been found dead from what appears to be a gunshot to the head in an apparent suicide. Authorities are scheduled to make a statement any minute now . . .

The echoes are quiet for a time. Then we are summoned. A fair-haired child, drawing on a large piece of construction paper, black circles, deeper, again and again, angrier and angrier, until the paper rips.

We hear her when she travels. We hear her when she says, "I want to do this to people. A whole lot of people."

And thus, we know her first seed has sown.

*This story was previously published in the Dread State anthology by Thunderdome Press on December 7, 2016

# SOCIAL DISTORTION

# STONE IN STREAM

by
Broos Campbell

Gil kept his eyes moving between the smoke and the mirrors and the mountain ahead. Nobody'd ever know what he was going to do up there. He'd bet his life on it.

The peak had been taking shape through the murk for half an hour, an eight-thousand-foot pile of rocks with a bald spot on top. Its year-round snowcap had evaporated in the hot dry wind of Inauguration Day and had never come back. Wasn't like the mountain had ever been worth much to anybody anyway. People used to come out here to shoot jackrabbits. And each other, probably.

He hoped there were still jackrabbits. There'd still be some shooting, at any rate.

He plucked his sweaty T-shirt away from his back and settled again into the man-shaped hollow in the cracked upholstery. The old pickup would get him there when it got him there.

*Rearview.*

Nothing moving but smoke and dust. But the Greenies were out there. They'd been oozing out of the city in ones and twos since the election, like the first few warning drops from a bulging bag of pus. A vote was an amazing and powerful thing.

He fished a Kool out of the pack on the dash and struck a light on his Navy Zippo, sucking in a lungful of lighter fluid and mentholated smoke. There were faster ways to die.

One more kill. It was his own stupidity that made it necessary, but that didn't mean he had to like it.

*Rearview. Driver's side. Passenger side.*

The Apache's little round side mirrors were about as useful as an empty gun.

*Road ahead. Mountain. Rearview.*

He stubbed out his smoke and reached for another.

*Something.*

He grabbed the rearview to stop it from vibrating. Far back on the interstate, stretched tall by a heat mirage, something moved in the smoke.

He drummed on the wheel of the old pickup, maintaining speed in case there were still cops out here, playing with the radio dial, trying to figure out if the noise sputtering through the static in his head was Skynyrd or Marshall Tucker, music as old as the station that was broadcasting it, until a long bend in the road put a hill between him and the hell behind him. Silence, inside and out.

Slowly the normal noises came back—engine chattering, tires humming on pavement, wind shrilling in the gap in the passenger-side window that persisted no matter how hard he turned the damn crank. He leaned over and gave it another tug anyway.

The shrilling stopped.

That was a mistake. Now he could hear himself think.

The radio had cut out but he kept chanting the song in his head. *Nobody gonna know.* He knew the words but he couldn't find the damn tune.

No cops in sight. He stomped the pedal to the floor, trying to squeeze some speed out of the wheezing bastard to get away from whatever was behind him.

At the next exit, he pulled the Apache off the interstate in a rattling swerve down into a sunken two-lane and in the shade of the overpass. He got out and climbed the embankment and squatted in a mesquite thicket by the road, staring straight ahead at nothing. He counted to three minutes and forty-seven seconds before he heard the car rumbling down the interstate. Mindless chatter cut through the whine of rubber on asphalt, and over it all hung a shriek of brainless laughter.

He boiled out of the brush with the .45 in his hand, yelling as he emptied it into the car.

He changed clips and chambered a round, watching the car bumping and lurching as its momentum carried it out into the Mojave. He hadn't hit anybody as far as he could tell, not that they'd even noticed what was happening. But reality always set in sooner or later, even for Greenies. The desert doesn't care if you believe in it or not.

He'd feel better for a while. Matter of fact, he felt goddamn-fucking-tastic. Couldn't hear a damn thing but the ringing in his ears.

Then the static came back.

The state route Gil had stumbled onto was taking him up a spur called Condor Ridge, according to the sign. You'd think you'd be able to shoot one lousy bird in a place named after them, but you can't shoot ghosts. He'd tried.

He touched the greasy cardboard box on the seat beside him. Way more ammo than he needed.

*Mirrors.* Nothing.

He got the box open one-handed and pulled out a cartridge.

*Rearview.* Nothing.

He flicked the shell out the window and watched for its glint in the mirror.

Nothing.

He tossed out another. A glitter of brass tumbled along the asphalt. Breadcrumbs for finding his way back if he failed.

He tossed out the rest of the box a cartridge at a time, no longer watching where they went. Then he ejected the clip of the Colt and thumbed all the shells but one into the box. Those he flung in a single handful across the road into the brush. Let someone else follow that trail. Nothing else out there but sun-dyed bottles and rusted cans all the way to that damn mountain.

Check the mirrors.
*Nothing.*
*Nothing.*
*Nothing.*
Eyes on the road.
Mirrors.
*Something.*

He ditched the two-lane for some county blacktop that wound along a dry creek. Bare branches of cottonwood and willow whispered in the streambed. Sometimes there were skeletons of orchards with whitewashed trunks. Once he saw a barn, scoured gray by sand and wind, with sky leaking through the rafters. Then he was climbing into a forest of dying oak and pine, one kind after another, sunlight and shadow flickering on his retinas as the truck labored up the road.

He became aware that the Boogerman himself had broken through the static, yowling on the radio about hellfire and salvation. This was a new wrinkle. The Boogerman had shown no interest in religion before, and you'd think even Greenies would get tired of being led around by the nose, but no, they had the spirit in them. You can't fight ghosts that vote and will not die.

And then the Boogerman was more static than yowl. Always had been, if only Gil had seen it in time.

He thumped his hands on the steering wheel, sun-shadow-sun-shadow in his eyes as he rounded a curve. Gravel rattled in the wheel wells as he braked for a bullet-riddled stop sign where the blacktop ended.

Brush-grown ruts ran left and right. No fresh tire tracks. No dust hanging in the air but his own.

A yellow road sign with a double-headed arrow on it leaned against a rusted metal fencepost across the way, like somebody had shot hell out of it and left it for dead, with the mountain rising beyond it across a wide rangeland of hardpan and creosote bush. Strands of barbed wire coiled off the fencepost. Fences meant cows. Cows meant people. People meant he hadn't come far enough.

He glanced toward the sun, measuring its height with his hand. A couple hours to go.

The motor pinged as he idled. *Left, right—just choose.* He smelled burnt metal. Probably the clutch, fuck he cared as long as he had one forward gear to get him where he needed to go. The static came back in hissing waves. Left, right—*sweet fucking Christ*. He clutched the steering wheel in an agony of indecision. The bullet holes in the stop sign were rusted around the edges. Puny shit from bored kids plinking with a .22. He wished he hadn't tossed away all his cartridges but one. He'd freshen the sign up a little, show folks how to make some holes.

The Boogerman's nasal yowl broke through the static loud and clear: "—Goin' *right* to hell!"

Right, then. Gil flicked the turn signal out of habit and realized it was already on. He yanked at the lever, jerking it around until the plastic tip came off in his hand. He threw it out the window. Another breadcrumb.

Nobody cares if you light fires in hell, but a man has to be better than somebody.

He got out of the truck and picked it back up.

The oaks gave way to aspen and pine. Trees were still green up here on the mountain, and the shadows carried a chill. One way or the other, it'd be cold tonight. That was a marvel. He couldn't remember the last time he'd been cold.

He held his hand against the light filtering through the trees, estimating how many hands remained between sun and horizon.

One.

An hour left, give or take. Then he could rest.

And then the trees gave way to sky, with puffs of cloud in ordered rows to the horizon. He stuck his head out the window to glory in it. Halla-fucking-luya, he was running out of mountain. Out of road, anyway. He braked as a brown and yellow campground sign loomed out of the long shadows on the left: *Owl Creek Loop. Fee Required.*

This was the place. A padlocked chain hung across the entrance. Tire tracks in dried mud led around the gate. In the shade of a twisted pine sat an SUV, gray with dust.

He killed the engine and got out. Dead silence descended on him. No static. No yowl. He listened harder. Blood in his ears. The ticking of the hot engine. Whispers in the shadows behind him.

No point in turning to look. The voices always came from behind.

He stepped around the truck and looked down. The mountain fell away maybe eight, nine hundred feet into a gorge with a tangle of junipers at the bottom. He could hear ravens croaking down there. The sides were lined with decomposed quartz that looked ready to roll halfway to Mexico if it got a good enough shove. No road down there, no sign of a trail.

*Time to burn the boats.*

He climbed back in the truck and slewed it around. Then he put it in neutral, got out again, tucking the .45 into the rear of his Levi's, and walked the old Apache over the edge.

He heard the first impact, a pop followed by an ominous silence, like a firecracker tossed into a bucket of bees. But then the static hissed in his head again and the truck leaped in silence like a hooked trout until it disappeared into the thicket. Through the soles of his boots, he felt the rumble of the boulders that poured after it. He followed the truck's progress by the sway of junipers and sudden clouds of birds.

Dude knew he was coming. Having a smoke wouldn't give him away at all. He patted his pockets, realizing he'd left his Kools in the truck.

It was as good a time as any to quit.

He walked past the SUV along a trail to the remains of a picnic and a family of three. Papa Bear, Mama Bear, Baby Bear. Who's been sleeping in my bed? Who's been putting bullets in my head?

Papa Bear, that's who. A rusted revolver lay in the grass by the man's feet.

Gil walked on till he came to the creek.

The bridge was out. Water glittered over tumbled stones down in the creek bed, silent in the static. You had a trail going to a creek, you'd think some ranger could hump his fat ass up here and check on the bridge now and then.

Gil wished he'd been a ranger. He'd shot a lot more people lately than he liked.

The ramp on this side of the creek was nice solid WPA stonework. He pictured the men riding up here in open trucks, armed with nothing but picks and shovels. But now the bridge was down and no one was ever coming back to repair it. No profit in a footbridge. Put a tollbooth on a footbridge, people just go around.

He breathed in. Moss. Moving water. The stench of corpses eighty miles away.

He must not be as near the summit as he'd thought, judging by all that water. Springwater, not snowmelt. He wished he could hear it.

Gil stepped through the broken arch of the bridge, moving downstream from stone to stone till he came to a place where the sky poured through the branches and the stream shot past him in a wide white arc that feathered away to nothing as it fell into the gorge below. His eyes sought the horizon and he grabbed at air, swaying. He sat.

Feet dangling like he was sitting in the world's tallest highchair, he tried various ways of holding the gun. It had a grip safety that made firing it awkward unless it was pointed away from the shooter. Which didn't mean there wasn't a way. It just meant he might fuck it up. He either had to cram the barrel against the roof of his mouth, which meant he'd blow his face off if he wasn't careful, or put it to his temple, which could result in a through-and-through instead of a brain blender. He reversed the Colt, squeezing the grip with his left hand and looping his right thumb through the trigger guard.

The barrel stank of sulfur and burnt scalp. Gil closed his eyes and lowered the pistol.

Static shivered around him as the mountain pushed against his back.

*You can do it.*

He forced his eyes open against the tears and put the barrel against the right socket. He wanted to see it coming. His index finger cocked the pistol, his thumb squeezed the trigger, the trigger tripped the hammer, the firing pin struck the primer, and the primer ignited two hundred and thirty grains of powder, sending the flat-tipped unjacketed lead slug spiraling up the barrel at eight hundred and fifty feet per second. It seemed exquisitely slow.

Gil's imagination was getting the best of him. He eased the hammer back and set the pistol in his lap.

And then, like the top of his head lifting, the static suddenly flew away. Birdsong sparkled in the pines and peace lay on him for the first time since his little brother had made the goddamn booger monster. He'd done it to scare Gil, but it hadn't worked.

The thing had been a joke, lurking under Emmet's bed by day and wandering around the house at night, pulling blankets off sleeping people and testing the doors. But Emmet had kept adding to it over the years from the inexhaustible supply of boogers that he dug out of his nose, till the thing discovered how doorknobs work and began lurching around the neighborhood at night. And everybody else thought it was a joke, too. Running it for president, now that was hilarious. Gil had even taken it to rallies, small ones at first from the back of the very pickup that he'd dumped down into the gorge, and then in auditoriums, and then in stadiums. People added their own boogers to it, patting it and shaping it and laughing because nobody ever thought the thing would get past the primaries, until the thing was as huge as its appetite for destruction. It's all good fun until someone loses an eye, as Mom used to say.

And now the entire country was blind.

Light flooded into him. He cradled the pistol in his lap, reveling in the cool air drifting along the water. Long-winged swifts darted through the downy swirl of gnats that drifted out past the edge of the waterfall, and ravens wheeled and croaked down in the gorge.

Gil sat on his stone in the stream, head back, eyes half shut, while the horizon rose up to cover the sun and the stars began to shine. Then he thumbed down the catch and drew the slide back. His last cartridge ejected over his shoulder into the stream. A final breadcrumb for whoever wanted to follow the trail. He didn't need a gun anymore.

He got to his feet and took a pitcher's stance, staring into darkness, jiggling the pistol behind his back until he was satisfied with his grip. Then he drew his knee across his body, pumped his leg and hurled the pistol out into space. Even unloaded it weighed five times what a baseball did, and he hadn't thrown a pitch since Little League. He rubbed his shoulder and shook his arm as the .45 clattered from boulder to boulder down the ravine.

Then he leaped after it.

# THAUMATURGY

by
Michael R. Colangelo

"*Thaumaturgy . . . which giveth certain order to make strange works, of the sense to be perceived and of men greatly to be wondered at.*"
—*Mathematicall Praeface to Euclid's Elements*, John Dee

The airport limousine dropped Kate Fischer at the doorstep of Senator Auberon Marshman III's home in the pleasant Golden Triangle of Greenwich, Connecticut.

She paid the fare, asked for a receipt, and then stepped up to the big double doors of the home. She paused briefly before pressing the buzzer to admire the well-tended gardens of the grounds.

That was the nice part of her job, which was writing quick biography-interviews about various government officials and party members. She got to leave her cramped New York apartment to travel to some of the richest neighborhoods in America. Got to see and experience things only the very privileged normally got to see.

The unpleasant parts were interacting with the very privileged themselves. Some of them were sweethearts, of course. Many were not.

There was a social divide. It was a cultural thing. It wasn't even a liberal versus conservative thing. It was a wealthy versus poor thing. You were either seen as a part of the wealthy or you were the hired help. There was no in-between.

Fischer was largely seen as the help, of course. But when an interview didn't go quite right, if tough questions were asked or criticism was written for public consumption, well, then the help wasn't being very helpful, was it? And that turned the help into the enemy, in these people's minds.

And the enemy—that group would be the drug addicts and ne'er-do-wells that occupied Wall Street. The faggots and terrorists and likely illegal immigrants that resorted to violent street brawling and Internet hacking to get their agendas across. The help that no longer wished to be helpful. Outlaws. Those individuals that chose anarchy over civilization.

Long ago, Kate Fischer understood she needed to be very careful about what she printed and how she acted when handling these people. If she were ever labelled as an enemy, well, then that was the end of her career.

As she waited now at the entrance to Marshman's home, she hoped that the senator fell into the first group of rich people. The ones that were simply happy to have more money than they needed.

She waited so long that she pulled out her cell phone to call Marshman's aide and ask what the hell was going on, but then the doors opened. Auberon Marshman himself stood before her dressed in a beige bathrobe and pool sandals. He blinked at her. His blue eyes were clouded with a slight confusion, like he wasn't sure why exactly she was standing there.

She held out her hand.

"Kate Fischer? With the *Lemming*? For the interview?"

Marshman shook her hand. His mouth gaped. He was still confused. The handshake was well-practiced and mechanical. An immediate reaction.

For a moment after the handshake, the pair stood silent. He didn't invite her in right away.

His eyes cleared, however. His mouth closed and his expression grew serious and stern. His business face.

"Yes, of course. Through the PAC. Come in. Come inside."

He motioned with his hand and she stepped in.

In the lobby of his house, a stone pedestal had tipped over. A broken plant pot littered the floor. Soil and broken shards of pottery spread out across the marble floor in a haphazard pattern.

"Watch your step," he told her. He led her down a big open hallway. "I've sent everybody home for the week. Hopefully I don't ruin this place before they're back."

She laughed. A joke. You laughed at their jokes.

She followed him through the big house to the back. Out here was a large kidney-shaped pool brimming with blue.

Marshman took a seat in a lounge chair and ate some toast off a plate resting on a wicker bench. He gestured for Fischer to sit down. She did so.

He prompted her to ask the questions that she needed to ask, and so Fischer went through the list.

It was pre-prepared by the PAC. At one point in the history of things, journalists would write down their own questions. Things they wanted to ask. But those days were long gone. If the PAC funded the *Lemming*, well, then the PAC got to do what it pleased. They hired writers outside of the staff for these kinds of things. Unknown entities. For all she knew, these questions came from Marshman himself. She wouldn't put it past them.

His answers were basic and neutral. When his answers were too basic and too neutral she prompted him for a little bit more. Carefully, though. If he got frustrated, that would get back to her bosses at the *Lemming*. They wanted their subjects to have positive experiences with their journalists.

When she'd run through the questions and coaxed enough material out of him to put together a piece, she thanked him for his time and stood up to leave. Marshman looked surprised.

"Oh. Will you not stay? I'm having a party."

He gestured beyond the pool to the other side of the big lawn.

Set up next to a hedge maze were a pair of white catering tents, a band stage, and rows of slim white wooden lawn chairs. Red, white and blue ribbon hung from a pair of ancient elms. Clusters of balloons decorated both of the tents.

He smiled at her.

"Oh. Yes," she said. "Of course, I'll stay." She smiled back.

"Very good. Would you like some toast?" Marshman used his fingers to offer her a piece off of his plate.

She shook her head and ask to use the washroom. He gave her brief directions and she left him to his breakfast.

Inside the house, everything was still and quiet. There was nobody else here except for Marshman. And other than the smashed potted plant at the entranceway, nothing seemed out of place. Everything seemed perfectly placed and curated. It reminded her of a museum with no visitors. No staff. Where was the help? Shouldn't he have caterers?

She climbed the big curving stairway and found a washroom that was bigger than her apartment. She sat on the toilet and called into the *Lemming*. Told them she'd be late coming back. That there was a party. Marshman insisted.

And that was fine with them. Whatever kept him happy. Whatever kept them in favor and afloat. The Internet made publishing easy. They could wait a day or two longer to run the article.

She said goodbye and went back downstairs to reconvene with the senator. He was finishing up his toast and she sat down to watch him.

He didn't speak until he was finished eating. Then he pushed the empty plate away a little and asked her a question.

"What do you know about me?"

She ran off what she'd researched. Key points from his Wikipedia article. Bullet-point things, mostly on what bills he'd supported in the recent past.

"Yes. But. Everybody knows those things. What do you really know about me?"

"Um. You have a really nice house?"

He didn't smile at her humor.

"Playing dumb, then. Okay."

He stood up and began walking back inside the house. He beckoned for her to follow him.

"Follow me. I've something to show you. Leave the remnants of my breakfast."

She got up from her lounge chair and followed him into the house. He took her to a side room that was organized like an office den.

Again, she got the sense that she was inside a museum rather than a house. The den felt unused and uninhabited. As if no one had ever stepped foot there before. As if it were staged in a display window at a furniture store inside a shopping mall.

Three photographs hung from a wall. Three men. One in each picture. They were old pictures. Tinged yellow with age. Wide-collared shirts and bell-bottom jeans suggested the pictures had hung there for decades.

"My sons."

Marshman's party began at noon.

She sat among the sea of empty white chairs and watched him struggle to set up a PA system.

He'd changed out of his bathrobe. Now he wore a white suit with a red bolo tie that wrapped around his neck. Shiny black shoes on his feet. A big white Stetson on his head. He looked like Colonel Sanders now.

But that was what happened when you dismissed the help for the weekend.

Once he had the microphone working, he pulled a stack of index cards from the pocket of his trousers. He cleared his throat and he began to speak.

His speech was introductory. Its tone and content very much like an article published by the *Lemming*, it provided the very basics that a host might need to make guests feel welcome.

She'd sat through speeches like this before.

For example, you might be invited to a charity ball or dinner by someone running for office. This would be the speech you would hear upon arrival, before the food was served. The host was very pleased you could join him; hoped you would have a wonderful evening. She'd heard its variant hundreds of times before.

She resisted the urge to look around for some quick exit to take out of the back of his yard.

The hedge maze, maybe. But the house was walled off by a brick perimeter 10 feet high. Kate wasn't sure she'd be able to clear it.

She might lose the old man in the maze and then make a break for the wall. Might. If she hadn't seen the revolver he'd tucked away beneath his suit jacket.

When he was done with his speech, he turned the mic off and left it standing solo upon the stage. He stepped down, came to her side and sat in the chair beside her.

"Aren't you enjoying yourself?"

"Yes, certainly. Uh huh."

"Are you hungry?"

"I'm not."

"Catering tent over there is serving food. Why don't you get us a plate of snacks? Do it before I have to go up for the second presentation of the afternoon. A man needs to keep his vigor up."

He elbowed her ribs. She got up and went into the tent.

The tent was largely empty. The air inside was humid and suffocating. There were three long buffet tables set up around the perimeter.

Two of them were empty, but the third had a plastic cooler filled with stale, melted ice water and cans of beer and soda. Beside it, an old coffee maker and a stack of paper cups and plates. And beside the coffee maker, a sparse number of hors d'oeuvres and an ancient-looking pizza cut into squares.

This certainly wasn't the work of caterers. But it was definitely the work of Marshman.

She put some of the food on a plate and grabbed a can of pop from the cooler. When she went back outside, Marshman was standing over by the second tent.

He had wheeled some kind of contraption onto the lawn. A crudely built thing of hammered-together two-by-fours and rope. A long pole protruded from its base. Marshman had attached a plate-sized lens to its end. Inside the contraption's frame, he'd hung a clock face with too many hands on it.

He was fidgeting with the device. Adjusting the lens into the sky and then moving the hands on the clock face about. She crossed the lawn and presented him with the plate of food.

He ignored her offering and so she took a Nanaimo bar for herself. It tasted like he'd simply re-used whatever had been left over from the last time the caterers had visited him.

Kate Fischer ate it anyway. It had definitely been a mistake to skip breakfast. She wasn't about to try the pizza.

"You are wise to technology, Ms. Fischer," he said. "Tell me, are you familiar with this device?"

"Nope."

"Well I'll tell you about it, then. Often, we take for granted the concepts of science. Don't we? My peers, I mean. When I say *we*. You people have your MTV and whatever else it is you do in your down time. Surfing the Internet, perhaps."

"That's true."

"Religion! Right to life! Abstinence from sex! Some other things to shout! The list goes on and on. Doesn't it, then?"

"It certainly does."

He stood up and brushed bits of grass from his knees. Muttered and cursed the grass stains that streaked across the white fabric. Finally looked up from his ruined pants to address her again.

"Well, you've read my history. Big supporter. Lots of money in that kind of talk. Lots of votes, I'll tell you."

Kate had to go to the bathroom for real now. She didn't dare ask him though.

"I stopped all that after the plane accident. Did you research that? There were some newspaper articles. But they don't like to talk about that very much."

The tone of his voice had changed. For the first time that day, Marshman sounded a little vulnerable. A little bit sad. A little bit broken.

"I didn't."

"A fishing trip. We took one every year. Alaska's such a beautiful state. One of our finest."

She had to ask him. It was unbearable.

"Can I use the bathroom?"

"Again?" He checked the expensive watch strapped to his wrist. "As long as you're back soon. You'll miss the ceremony."

She put the plate and the can of soda down and jogged across the lawn back into the house. From there, she ran back upstairs and peed.

Then, hurriedly, she went back downstairs and out the front door of Marshman's home.

He lived in the suburbs. In the middle of nowhere. It was going to be a long walk back to the airport. At least a long time until she found a taxi cab.

But she started walking anyway. Because that was certainly better than going back in to Marshman.

Of course, there were no charges to press against him. Marshman did have a revolver, but that wasn't illegal. Technically, he hadn't threatened her with it. He hadn't threatened her at all. Not really.

Worse, there was nobody to really tell the story to, either. Reporting it back to the *Lemming* would cost her the job. Reporting it elsewhere would probably cost her the job.

Nope. Nothing to do but grin and bear it and chalk it up to one of the occasionally bizarre situations that the occupation presented her with.

She wrote the article and handed it in. It was published overnight and then collected dust online. No comments, no shares. Just like all the other articles that the *Lemming* ran. Everybody got paid. Nobody cared.

She was alone in the apartment the day after the article had been released, sitting in front of the television with the volume turned way down and reading a book.

Her new telephone buzzed quietly. She picked it up to look at its screen. See who would be calling her so late at night.

The number on the phone was the same. Her old number. Marshman calling her from her lost telephone. She put the phone down and it stopped buzzing soon after.

It made a new sound. A text message. She picked it up again.

The text was from herself.

THE ESSENTIAL SALTES OF ANIMALS MAY BE SO PREPARED AND PRESERVED THAT AN INGENIOUS MAN MAY HAVE THE WHOLE ARK OF NOAH IN HIS OWN STUDIE

She blocked the sender. Marshman losing his mind. It would only be a matter of time before someone checked up on him and put him in some secure retirement home where he couldn't pass votes anymore. It wouldn't be too long until he left her alone.

Relief. As she realized she'd done the right thing in keeping her mouth shut. Someone else would eventually call him on his senility. She'd keep her gig at the *Lemming*.

Life would simply grind onwards. Hopefully upwards, somehow.

A knock on the door. Somebody at the door who'd bypassed the apartment's lobby buzzer. A neighbor maybe. Sometimes they came by to complain about management or complain about her.

Through the peephole. Three men. Well-dressed.

Familiar strangers. She'd seen the men before. Never met them, though. A plane crash in Alaska, Marshman had told her. A beautiful state.

*You'll miss the ceremony.*

She left the door and went back to the couch. Picked up her book and tried to concentrate on the words. She saw the print on the page, but nothing she read made sense. A blur of printed nonsense written down there.

The knocks on her door continued.

Sooner or later Kate was going to answer.

Sooner or later she was going to have to find out what the Marshman boys wanted.

Her mind. A blur of printed nonsense.

# DEFEND ATLANTIS

by
David L. Day

We deployed at four in the morning, battling thick humidity in the city's old infrastructure tunnels, our first hours lost trying to find the last known location of the mud dragons marked by Aleph recon team the night before. In the end, we found the scattered shards of a smashed beacon, oriented ourselves, and marched deeper into the long-forgotten burrows. One of the critical massive rebreathers hummed away miles behind us near the edge of our territory, its stark breath cooling the air, conjuring plump drops of dew on rough walls hewn generations ago.

Rook stopped at a fork, dropped his pack, and shrugged off his portable rebreather. He crouched down, inspected faint traces on the ground. "Fresh footprints. Looks like three mud dragons came up from that way." He wiped a sheen of sweat from his smooth head, chuckled to himself. "Three. Shit, we'll make it home for supper."

Jains joined Rook and sifted a handful of pulverized stone between his fingers. "Small prints. Children?" He glanced up at me, then obliterated the prints with two quick swipes of his bony hand.

I felt flush from the weight of his look, so I tilted my head into shadows, then twirled a finger in the air like we used to do in training. "Round 'em up; reel 'em in."

Rook cocked his semi-toothed smile my way and Compton slapped me on the back. Grunted out, "Our girl's back."

Jains raised an eyebrow, stood, and smacked both palms on his thighs, faint clouds of dust puffing into oblivion. "Rook on point. Single file. They have at least a half-day head start. Poseidon help us if they breach the outer wall."

The tunnel shook in a sudden upset that could only come from down where our great protector Carcinus lay, the very foundation of our world. We cast about like knuckle bones, pressed tight against the walls, and held steady.

The tremors subsided, but my stomach roiled on as Jains motioned us onward through the settling dust. No one spoke; we didn't have to. Any harm to Carcinus or the outer wall and the city would collapse.

We found more signs of mud dragons sometime after mid-day in an area large enough for a dozen burly squads. A portable heating quartz hummed in the center of the chamber, an older model from the first days, judging by the rust and grime and oversize controls, yet still able to cast waves of warmth across a floor covered in a confusion of footprints.

Rook circled the faintly glowing unit, pacing intently, scanning the room, stony and focused. "They've used this as a meeting hall for years, by the looks of it."

Jains turned to Compton. "Set a beacon . . . make it two, one out in the open, one stashed in that alcove over there."

"Sir." Compton set about his work as Rook continued to study the traffic patterns in the dirt.

Jains pulled me aside with a firm but compassionate grip. "You see those prints. This cell attacked a major rebreather. We have to take them out before they can do it again." He paused, looked aside briefly, then sized me with his signature stoic, fatherly stare, making me feel like a first-year cadet. "You sure you can handle this? We've found enough to call this a successful mission, head home, and regroup. We might do well to enlist some backup, anyhow."

I glared back at him, jaw tense, ears burning. He had a good point, but his unwarranted insinuation stung like a slap to the face. "You serious? The Magistrate—"

Rook screamed, Jains and I both twitching at the sudden outburst. I swiveled around, and he staggered back from the alcove like a drunk on payday, hands at his neck. A feral shadow streaked off into the darkness and disappeared down a side tunnel.

I scurried to Rook's side, my med kit out by the time Jains and Compton huddled around. "Okay, big guy. Let me see."

Small crimson drops squeezed out between his fingers, but not enough to unsettle my cool. I peeled his hands away with a mother's touch and found, to my relief, a superficial wound decorating his neck. I pulled supplies from my kit, coated the wound with urchin oil, then wrapped the damage and tied it off with a dry chuckle. "You'll live. Besides, you look good in an ascot."

Jains nudged my arm, gave me a questioning look. I nodded, and he turned to Rook. "Can you speak? What happened?"

Rook cleared his throat, sipped water from a canteen offered by Compton, then shook his head. "It sprang from the alcove. I went to place the second beacon. Didn't see anything but a flurry of rags and hair."

Compton shimmied his awkward bulk into the alcove, fatigues scraping and catching on the jagged opening, then called back a report, his voice eerily distorted. "Sentinel nest. Nasty in here." He backed out dragging a sheet or a bedspread with a jumbled mound of broken paraphernalia piled in the center.

I gave Rook's wound a final check, then handed him over to Jains while I joined Compton. He'd found a blanket, hand-woven in the old-style, spots of faded colors showing through a dingy gray patina. On it huddled a sad assortment of small toys—a tattered rag doll, a chipped quartz projector, other knickknacks—traces of sweat and urine wafting off the whole heap.

"We had her cornered." My heart sank at the thought of her fear. I lifted the doll from the mess, cradling it under the arms like an infant, and held it up for Jains to see. "A kid, of course. Probably could have killed Rook if she'd wanted to."

Jains slipped up behind me, snatched the doll, and chucked it back onto the blanket, acting more disinterested than belligerent. "Pack up. Time to move on."

The others returned to their gear, but I lingered by the detritus of the poor little mud dragon's existence. I plucked the doll from the heap, a frail thing, face smoothed to an oily sheen, one eye missing. I tucked it into my jacket and zipped up, the precious lump pressed against my abdomen, then gathered my own equipment and joined them.

We trekked another five hours, breaking once for a brief meal of grain cakes, jerky, and water. Before my leave I would have devoured the jerky, but I offered it to Rook instead, feeling I could never bring myself to eat the awful carrion again, unable to even watch as the other three tore and chewed.

Two of our quartz torches lost their charges along the way, leaving us to march through a shroud of shadows with nothing but a single beam cutting our path forward. Not long after the second torch died, the tunnels resonated with the soft scuttling of mud dragons, bearable for about the first hour, maddening after the second. They kept their distance, watching us, but for whatever reason did not attack. Whether they feared our annihilators, or whether they led us toward some trap, didn't matter. By then we'd gone too far to back out.

We rounded a sharp curve and the mud dragons fell on us in a tide of limbs, hitting from all sides, a mass of soiled clothes, wild hair, and puckish giggles, grungy boys and girls, none older than nine or ten.

Their sudden, flowing mass clogged the tunnel, constricting it like a swollen throat.

Compton pumped off five or six quick shots of his annihilator, its thin ruby beams severing limbs and scorching chests. Rook joined the firefight, and between the two they slashed a brief opening in the crowd, paving it with stumped and charred bodies. But they couldn't sustain the clearing. As one mud dragon fell in a steaming mess, two others swarmed in to take its place.

The little beasties outnumbered us beyond count, so nimble and quick, swarming us from all sides, sprouting from the walls and floor as if the relentless rock itself opposed our progress.

I didn't fire once. Despite their tattered, ragged, and slimy appearance, I couldn't blast on children. They circled us, leaped on our backs and hung from our arms, their shouts ricocheting off the walls as they called names and cheered each other on. They executed the assault like a well-played game of Capture the Crab or Defend Atlantis, our loss inevitable.

I fell slack, tumbled backwards from their weight, and lay passive as nimble little hands stripped away my rebreather and equipment. I struggled to peer through their teeming bodies until I spied Jains and found him mirroring my reluctant compliance. My love for him rekindled, a small, hot fire in my soul.

Somewhere over the raging sea of mud dragons Rook and Compton shouted, their voices cut short, two heartbeats passing before nimble fingers crammed a rag in my mouth, the cloth pregnant with the taste of salt and mud. Lithe fingers slipped thick cord over my wrists, binding them too tight and cutting off circulation, a jumble of clutching little hands raising me to my feet once more.

A current of mud dragons swept the four of us deeper into the network of tunnels, the heat and humidity steadily rising, our ancient past almost palpable as we descended toward Carcinus.

Another hoary city unfolded before us, twice as large and labyrinthine as the Magistrate's palace complex, shimmering pools of water purified by the bedrock, innumerable quartz lights strung haphazardly about, heaters strewn throughout blasting warmth. The cavern walls, sprinkled with erratic cliff-dwellings and makeshift rope ladders, stretched hundreds of feet upward to a ceiling thick with shadows, an organic refuge toiled upon over decades and then some, a living playground or a massive fort in which children played endless games.

A scattering of men and women circulated throughout as well, those closest giving us wide berth and disdainful looks. Our captors moved without leadership, an amoeba pushing and pulling us onward until we arrived at a small passageway nestled in an obscure alleyway.

The children lined us up before a gaunt entryway smoothed by time and humidity, and then receded like the evening tide.

Before us stood a whisper of childhood stories, an old, withered woman clad in a threadbare mockery of the flowing maroon robes of the high priestess of Poseidon, exiled before my time, faint trident and circuitous claw patterns embroidered in gold around the cuffs and sleeves. She could have faked the swirling tattoos on her face, neck, and hands, but the command filling the cold chips of her eyes said otherwise.

She led us into an antechamber, a delineation between the profane and the sacred, and motioned for us to sit. I refused at first, but the others complied without hesitation, and when I glanced at Jains I saw a certain mixture of awe and confusion, so I settled down on crossed legs next to him.

"The first of us built this place long before your bubble of stone and iron." Her voice, like whale song, thrummed and hypnotized as she raised a quartz light and chased shadows from the wall. Cracks and striations resolved into the delicate, intricate lines of a mural.

"You've heard our history, or some version of it." Her voice lowered with challenge. "Now look upon it for yourselves." She waited, light raised, herself lost in the massive, sprawling pictograms spread before us.

The first section showed a map, continents and oceans cut with territorial lines, followed by a panel of buildings in the open air, collapsing in the next, then people slaughtering one another, mechanisms in the sky and on the surface waters. A new section showed the tale of our island's descent, great Carcinus lowering us with a mother's grace into the safety of her birthing waters.

Then came the chronicle of magistrates, the expulsion of the priestess, a portrayal of the council's saving vote, the first division of children, and a dark and somber portrayal of the Council's Modest Feast. The last panel, incomplete, the colors still crisp and fresh, showed an exodus of some sort, with Carcinus crushed under the weight of a crumpled city. Our city.

The priestess turned her cold, obsidian gaze to us once more, and my blood boiled as I struggled against my bonds. Our great Carcinus raced toward death because of this crazy woman, dragging us along with her, even this witch and her damnable brood.

I became a mother without a child because of her refusal to support the Magistrate, and her continued attacks on the city.

Compton freed himself and hefted his dense fireplug body across the room in a blink, hands at the old woman's neck, face straining with rage and fear and doubt and remorse. None of us chose our ways. Our parents and our parents' parents thrust them onto us, and even though surrendering a firstborn hurt more than a shot to the gut, our tradition, and the Magistrate, mandated doing so in the name of survival.

The old woman scratched at Compton's face, pumped her fists against his chest, and then Rook and Jains both loosed their bonds, scrambling to join their comrade. I managed to loosen my bonds as well, but the cavern tumbled without warning, and the old woman shook free of Compton's clutches in the turmoil, then scampered to the doorway and screeched out a piercing, sickening sound.

The world righted again and I managed to slip free of my bonds, but before any of us could regain our footing, the tunnel opposite us resonated with a harsh low clicking, distracting us from the priestess.

The room filled from both ends, children streaming in around the old woman, shielding her with their scraggly smiles and chipped laughter. Four of them, older than most of the rest yet still bearing looks of naive mischief, leveled our confiscated annihilators squarely at our chests, poised for kill-shots.

A slow march of giant spider crabs emerged from yet another tunnel, thick, spindly legs clacking harshly on the rock floor, each bearing a plump slab of crab meat on its back.

The crabs crossed the room, flowing like water, clicking their way through the children, and the priestess reached down, plucked two thick hunks of meat from the backs of a couple of the shelled beasts. "You think we caused your problems, but the Magistrate corrupted your thinking and ruined your perspective. Trained soldiers? No. More like hoodwinked children. Here. It's much better than that jerky, and it's given freely. No mandates. No rules. Pure sacrifice."

She tossed a hunk of the fresh, pink meat to Jains and another to Compton. Jains tore his in two and handed a piece to me, its bulk thick and cool. Compton tossed a hunk to Rook, but none of us ate, our years of training evoking suspicions of poison. The priestess smirked, as if reading our minds, then dipped her trembling maw in her own piece, tearing off a bite, chewing it, savoring it, swallowing it with eyes closed and lips curled in delight. "See? Not tainted."

The flesh smelled salty and raw, but my stomach gurgled, demanding food, so I bit. That first chunk chewed like butter, wonderful, fresh and fulfilling, and I gobbled down the whole thing before I could stop myself.

Jains also chowed down, but Rook chucked his aside in stern defiance while Compton icily let his slip into the dirt.

The children rippled with a collective giggle, and the priestess smiled as she leaned down and whispered to a little girl decorated with smudges and scars. The child kissed the priestess on her cheek and then sprinted out of the chamber, leaving the old woman's attention on us. "You should have eaten your last meal. Let me show you something."

The crabs vanished into the recesses of the labyrinthine tunnels. The gaunt priestess and the four lank preteens bearing our annihilators escorted us out the far side of the chamber, through a length of downward-spiraling tunnel and into yet another immense cavern far below the city. The rock walls were reinforced with scavenged ironwork, regular grids of lighting and heating quartz placed throughout. We emerged through a great iron portal fashioned over the tunnel, another mirroring it on the far side.

The priestess led us to the opposing portal, through which stood a massive wall of hacked flesh and chipped shell.

Carcinus.

The priestess turned on us, cold and defiant, her voice crisp, full of accusation. "She nears her end, sad and weary, weeping for us. I told the council she would never support their solution, that she'd rather die, but they saw me as nothing more than an apprentice, and even though my matron protested as well, the Magistrate never saw past our femininity. Those pompous bureaucrats wouldn't listen, called her a luddite, an archaic form of societal control. But Carcinus speaks to me, as she has to all priestesses before me. And like any good mother, she knows when to let go."

Behind us the room filled with children, chaperoned by a smattering of subservient adults, clutching small bundles of dingy clothes like precious dolls, settling around the room in little groups.

The spider crabs clicked in behind them, slipped past us, and carved more hunks from Carcinus's open wound. The queen mother shook, and our world trembled with her. When her shelled army finished, they reemerged with fresh lumps of meat and stacked them along one wall.

The last clutch of children streamed into the chamber, their guardian closing the portal behind them, sealing us in.

Rook lunged at the priestess again, teeth bared, testosterone rage coloring his cheeks, but an annihilator blast opened his gut mid stride. His innards spilled in a steaming, squiggly mess, dropping him to his knees in a bloody heap. Across the room a little girl held her weapon steady and stared at the mess with cold and weary eyes.

Compton fled, trying to escape the way we came in, fear getting the better of him. Another child fired, lopping off one of his legs, fired again and sliced off an arm. He tried to take a step with the missing limb, his howls silenced as a final blast erased his head with a sickening pop.

Jains shoved himself between me and the children, his arms raised. "Stop this! We won't tell anyone about you and your mud dragons. Please . . . leave the rebreathers alone. You need them as much as we do."

The priestess tossed her head back and barked a sharp, angry laugh. "You don't understand. Our worlds shudder from Carcinus's death throes, not from our attacks. Once our capsule breaks free we'll rise to the surface and your precious city of cannibals will collapse."

She meant to slaughter our entire society, thousands upon thousands who had little choice in how they lived.

I stepped out from behind Jains, knelt down before the girl who shot Rook, and drew the doll from my jacket. I held it out, cradled in my trembling hands, waited until recognition spread in the girl's eyes. She reached out tentatively, stroked the doll's hair once, and peered up at me with suspicious hesitation. I lowered my gaze, held the doll closer to her, heart pounding out ocean waves. She lifted the doll, and I snatched the annihilator from her, turned, trained it on the priestess, hands quivering with repressed rage and hurt.

"The Magistrate has my child locked up in their stinking, filthy pens, suffering along with countless others." I glanced at Jains. "Imagine our child packed in with the rest of the livestock where she'll breed until . . . until they slaughter her, turn into jerky or roast her up for some gourmet feast." I swallowed back burning tears, focused again on the priestess, summoning my resolve and faith but coming up short on both counts. "I've petitioned the Magistrate. Surely, they'll release her. Tell me why I shouldn't cut you down where you stand."

She studied me, her features cool and unmoving at first, then her expression softened, pity blended with frustration. She shooed the children away and motioned for me to stand.

I rose, stood at attention next to Jains, who leaned in and whispered, "A girl?"

I nodded slightly, cheeks warming at what I took for hope and happiness in his voice.

The priestess sighed. "In all my years, I've never known the Magistrate to grant an exception. Have you? The firstborn belong to the Magistrate." Crabs scuttled by her once more, returned to Carcinus, and slashed more meat from her dwindling bulk. The room shuddered, but not nearly so much as before. "I could let you return, but we leave regardless, and once we do you'll perish. The waters will rush in and the structure will collapse, crushing you along with our dear Carcinus."

Her words captured what I'd not wanted to admit, wrenched free the sinking despair I'd battled over months of leave and swallowed in the end along with a handful of mandated pills. I turned to Jains, chest tight and stomach in knots, knowing we could never go back, wanting him to reach the same conclusion on his own.

He leaned in again, conspiracy in his voice, "We could take them. One well-placed shot at the controls and this portal won't close. Those mud dragons couldn't hit a bull shark from this distance. We use full force to escape, lead a large squadron back down here to round them up, and no way the Magistrate denies our little girl's release."

His hot breath filled my ear as he awaited my response. I stared at the priestess, struggling to keep an even keel. "We have one child above, and if lucky we can have one more, but I believe her. The Magistrate would never release a child from the pens. Look around. We have a chance to help hundreds of children."

Jains kissed me on the cheek, but his voice held cold stubbornness. "We have to. It's our duty. And even if we don't get her back, so what? I'll sit with the Magistrate one day and I can work to find a better way." He screwed his face up, unable to suppress his disgust and misappropriated authority. "They deserve the pens. Their attacks have escalated over the years, they wrecked a rebreather not two days ago, and now? Their next move involves collapsing the whole city." His voice broke. "And you talk about saving these children? We can have more children. We can't build another city."

I had held my daughter long enough for the memory of a weepy bundle of new flesh to etch itself permanently on my mind, and then the midwives took her away forever. She never even opened her eyes. I never gave her a name.

I thrust the annihilator into Jains' gut and pulled the trigger.

# NO SUCH THING AS A FREE LUNCH

by
Kev Harrison

Staying off the grog is hard enough in the summer months, but when a storefront is your bed in January, it's nigh on impossible. That's how I found myself staggering down the street that Thursday afternoon. The suits were breezing by on their way to wherever they had to be. Somewhere warm, no doubt. Somewhere with food and clean water.

I'd ask them—always politely, you understand—if they could spare a little change for a man who was down on his luck. Some of them were polite. Some of them were downright rude. Few of them had a coin for me.

The reason I'd left my sheltered spot in the old bookstore window, in spite of the brutally cold winds that day, was that Eric, another fella who was out on his ass, had told me about a new place for us untouchables. A big businessman turned politico, a local boy made good, had set up a new soup kitchen to help us homeless get a bite to eat. According to Eric it was good food—and no alcohol or drug tests. Just a meal for those that needed it. A good meal at that. The last good meal I had was . . . well, I can't honestly remember. But it was sure to beat the half-finished sandwiches and cold, leftover French fries that I was all too used to digging out of the trash these days.

In what was once a leisure complex, with a couple basketball courts and whatnot, the lights were on for the first time in a while. I pushed at the heavy double door and felt a pleasant wave of warmth wash over me like that longed-for spring sunshine. Right behind the heat was a second wave, this time the delicious fragrance of marinated meat loaf, freshly cooked peas and corn, and roast potatoes. I breathed it in deeply, savored it, and my stomach cramped with hunger. I picked up the pace, ignoring the buzz from the store-brand vodka I'd been hitting since the early hours just to keep warm.

"Good afternoon," I said, surprisingly lucidly. "I've come to see if I can—"

"You've come for a meal, sir?" the woman with the Hollywood smile behind the reception counter interrupted me. "Of course. I just need your name and Social Security number, if you know it, and I'll give you a voucher, right away."

I scrunched my fingers into a fist once, twice, trying to get some feeling back into them. Then I took the pen from the counter and, hands still trembling and somewhat claw-like from the stiffness, scrawled the information she was asking for. She passed me a voucher, a slip of pink paper from a raffle booklet. I thanked her and followed her direction into what had been the main basketball court. There were fifty or so ladies and gents of various ages queuing up. Another thirty or so were seated and tucking in to steaming plates of what looked like great food. Eric waved at me. He was sitting at the end of a table with a woman I didn't know and another guy I recognized from a window spot on the promenade near the railway station. I waved back and joined the line.

After shuffling forward for about seven or eight minutes, it was my turn.

"What would you like, sir?" asked one of the cheerful men behind the serving table.

"Whatever you have, sir, I will gratefully take, thank you."

I felt my facial muscles turning up into a smile as he piled a thick slice of meatloaf, a good scoop of veggies, and golden, crisp potatoes onto the plate, slathering gravy on top of it all. I swallowed, my mouth was watering so greedily, and thanked him as I took the plate and turned to walk over to Eric and his group.

"Orange juice, Jake?" he said as I sat myself at the bench, next to the other guy.

I nodded, that almost painfully wide grin still etched on my face. I greeted the others and picked up the knife and fork at the table setting. I sliced into the meat loaf first. The grain of it was smooth and tender, just a little underdone in the middle, with a dark crispness to the outside. There was even a thin layer of stuffing. I used the knife to brush gravy on to the top and scooped it into my mouth. As my teeth sliced through the meat, I tasted the freshness, the delicate range of herbs used to season it, the occasional lump of sea salt bursting with flavor. None of us really spoke until all four of our plates were clean. I resisted the temptation to lick the last of the gravy from the surface, and suspected the others were fighting the urge to do the same.

"So how the hell did you find out about this place, Eric?" I asked, sipping at my orange juice—freshly squeezed, no less.

"It was on a paper at a newsstand along the street from my spot. You know this guy is running for governor, right? And, well, he said he wants to help the little people, the forgotten people. One of his first actions is this place, for us down-and-outs. That and getting the crime off the streets. I don't give much of a damn about that one, having nothing worth robbing me for. But this is great. Gonna be here five days a week, least till the end of winter."

I gulped down more OJ. "That's the best news I've heard in a long time. Was it this good yesterday?"

Everyone nodded, groaning in approval more than verbalizing. That was good enough for me. Tomorrow was Friday, so I'd still be back to the trash for Saturday and Sunday, but with almost two long months to go before temperatures really started to climb back up, this was a gift from God, or from the governor-to-be, anyway.

"Hey, Eric, has Miguel been down here?"

"Not seen him, man. I thought you might've told him, as he usually holes down in the old shelter in the park at night. That's up your way."

"Sure thing, I will. I'll walk back that way after we're done here. Hey, is that coffee I smell?"

"You bet. Fresh cream, and cookies, too. Let's go."

Every got up from their chairs and clamored to the coffee trolley. Within minutes we were all standing around dunking chocolate chip cookies into creamy coffee like regular folks on a winter's afternoon. Just for that hour or so, I felt like a human being. With dignity.

The place closed around six forty-five, and I said my goodbyes to Eric and his pals, heading straight down to the park, my hands stuffed tightly into my pockets. Thick frost coated the fat blades of grass. I felt it crunch underfoot as I crossed to the rocky overhangs beneath the flower gardens. It's amazing how much easier it is to appreciate winter's beauty with food in your belly. Miguel's makeshift shelter was empty when I arrived. I sat down on his sleeping bag and blankets. I'd wait, he couldn't have gone far in this weather. A few minutes later a body in the next gap in the wall rolled over.

"Lookin' for Miguel, son?"

I nodded.

"Not seen him in three days. He went to pick up some supplies with the coins he'd managed to get together. Poor bastard never came back."

When the mercury is dipping towards minus twenty, no one stays out of their shelter for three days. My mind started flashing with possible fates. Arrested, assaulted, *murdered*? These possibilities became somewhat routine when you were on the street. I thanked the old fella and shuffled back to my own shelter in a daze, a new and different cold eating away at me from inside. I asked a few of the other street folk at my end of town, but no one had seen or heard from him. I got my head down, pulled a blanket over my head, and let myself drift to a place that was sure to be fraught with nightmares.

The following morning was little more than an exercise in trying to stave off the bitter chills until the new lunch spot opened. I'd scavenged one of the newspapers Eric had mentioned the day before from a gutter and, through the grease and oil on the page, I had read the interview. Our local entrepreneur had certainly come up with some good ways to help people like me. He had good ideas about job creation too. But he also had some highly alarming ones about minorities. It had been a long time since I'd seen a would-be elected representative refer to *black* or *Hispanic* problems in so many words. I tried not to dwell on that part as, in this punishingly brutal winter, I didn't see any other way I was going to come by a hot meal.

Not long after one in the afternoon, I was shaking hands with Eric and his friends on the sidewalk outside. Again, the warmth was like a loving embrace as we entered, accompanied by the divine fragrance of stewed meat.

"Come right along, ladies and gentlemen," the smiling lady at the reception desk from the day before urged us. "We have a delicious meat and vegetable stew today with mashed taters. You're gonna love it."

We all filed over, licking our lips as we scribbled our details on the forms and entered the hall, thanking her as we went. After what felt like an eternity of mouth-watering anticipation we were tucking in to our meals. Great heels of cornbread in hand, we dipped them into the rich, meaty gravy between scooping up spoons of tender meat, chunky carrots, and silky-smooth potatoes. Again, there was near silence as we ate, feeling the warmth blooming from our full stomachs. After mopping our dishes clean, we went and stood at one corner of the old sports hall, dunking raisin cookies into our creamy coffee, talking and laughing like ordinary people again.

Just before closing at six, I decided to go to the bathroom. I was directed around the side of the kitchens to a corridor. I walked along, the alluring smell of the food still lingering in the air. I pushed at the third door on the right, as instructed. I used the urinal and washed my hands, embracing the unusual sensation of soap on my skin. I dried them on paper towels and left.

I heard the crashing sound of falling pans behind me from the kitchens and spun around, disorientating myself. I took a few steps forward, then turned too early, walking into the kitchen through a swing door. I was utterly unprepared for what I saw.

On the ground, face-down on their knees, hog-tied, a line of men and women were seemingly unconscious. They were folded, contorted in tight positions, like the lumps of flesh they'd been reduced to, their skin in shades of caramel and ebony. I took a step closer.

Reached out my right hand. Warm. I held it to one man's back. It rose and fell. Breathing. Alive. I looked to my right and saw the line of people continuing, all kneeling, all hog-tied, all naked as the day they were born. I looked to my left, through a doorway, and immediately felt myself retching. I turned back to the door and just managed to empty my stomach away from myself and my shabby clothing. There was blood. So much blood.

Then I heard steps. A man in a suit came from the next room. He had to have heard me.

"What are you doing here?"

I wiped my mouth. "What am *I* doing here? What's *happening* here?" I waved my arms wildly, gesturing at the bodies.

"Did you enjoy your lunch?" The man in front of me smiled. I didn't return it.

He continued, not waiting for me to reply.

"This is the governor's new plan that you and your kind have been singing such high praises about. All-American Joes, down on their luck. Not a bite to eat. That's the first big problem that our man promised to fix. And those bellies are full, aren't they? Not gonna starve, are they?"

I felt myself retch again. "What are you talking about?"

"The second problem"—this was a monologue, not a conversation—"is the crime, the chaos that's taken over our streets. The black crime. The Hispanic crime. How does Governor Punt solve both of these problems in one fell swoop, you might ask?"

"No. No no no. This is not . . . This cannot—"

"Beggars can't be choosers, little man. You need a hot meal. In this weather, you and all your gutter-dwelling buddies do. And if we get this vermin off the street ... These so-called people that have been robbing our stores, bringing drugs and rape to our streets ... well ... we're back on the path to greatness."

"People won't . . . this is . . . people won't allow this."

"People will allow what they're told is necessary. We'll make our case. Fox, the web. And if they really can't stomach it—pun *intended*—we'll make it untrue. Alternative facts."

# NO SUCH THING AS A FREE LUNCH

The man in the suit crouched down to my level. "Would you like me to get you an extra portion, seeing as you threw the first one up? There's plenty meat left, as you can see." He shoved at one of the prone men at his side, and I felt my stomach turn as I saw the flesh crease and fold under the pressure.

I felt the blood rush from my face, faintness overcoming me. I managed to shake my head, scramble to my feet, and stagger out of the room. I heard his voice, taunting me as I left.

"Tell your friends, if you like. They won't believe you. The truth is what *we* say it is now."

Still trembling, I half ran, half staggered down the corridor and pushed open the swing door at the end. Eric and the others were still smiling, talking, waiting for me.

I shouted to them with all my strength, still wiping the vomit from the side of my face, "Meat loaf is . . . is *people*!"

All eyes in the hall fixed on me, everything had fallen silent. Then the first couple of people started laughing. Soon my friends and everyone else had joined in. A cacophony of laughter filled the room. I looked around, incredulous at first, and then I too started laughing. Who would believe me? Only a madman. And how else would I survive this punishing winter?

"See you Monday," I said to the grinning receptionist as we left.

# MEXICO CITY

by
Russell Hemmell

"What's your name?"

"Irrelevant. You're not here for my fascinating self."

"They said you are the best."

"So, the best I am. Sit."

The lady nodded, unconvinced and with a disappointed look in her eyes. But she did sit down in the dimly lit shop, her blank stare wandering around the featureless room. Clemance noticed her appearance—an elegant red dress and expensive makeup contrasting with her messy nails. First-time gamers were always nervous.

"Mexico City, or whatever you call your office. It was difficult to find, you know? I almost gave up."

"Were my indications unclear?" he asked.

"On the contrary. It's just that I was unaware this kind of business even existed in my hometown. Here, in the very centre, under everybody's eyes."

"The best place to hide something is in plain sight. And this is by no means the only one. London is a big city."

"That a foreigner like you seems to know better than I do."

"Since you're here, you should consider yourself lucky," he said. "Have you got what I've asked for?"

"My specs? Yeah, sure. I have them here on a card. You can retrieve all you need from that."

*What an old-fashioned and unsafe way of treating sensitive data. But then, she wouldn't be here if she cared about them in the first place.*

Clemance kept his thoughts to himself as he took the device, inserted it in a long-unused card slot, and started working. His tiny computer was a shining, compact, dark-blue cube—the only bright light in the small room.

"I've already got everything at home. The hardware, and all the rest," she said in a low voice.

"Obviously."

She stared at him for a moment, and then her eyes began wandering. Inquisitive, and yet nervous, almost scared. "This trade. For how long have you been doing it?"

"Long enough."

"So, you're an expert. Tell me something. What's the most common scenario customers want you to prepare?"

"You're one of them. Can't you guess?"

"No. Yes. Sex perversions, maybe?"

"Sweet. You're definitively not my typical client." He couldn't avoid smiling. *Naïve too, and this was not typical of first-timers either. Maybe in this resides her charm, more than in her beauty or her exquisite clothes.* "People are not that normal. Not in these days, no."

"Answer me. Please."

"Death," he said, matter-of-factly.

"You mean killing people?"

"No, even though killer scenarios are quite popular. Nobody kills any longer—rich people like you, at least. That's a poor man's fancy nowadays. Impractical and rude." He shook his head. "But I meant something different. I was referring to their own death."

"I'm not sure I understand."

"Humans are afraid of dying. So, they want to experience what death is. What it feels like." He shrugged. "They think knowing in advance will take part of their pain away. Their fear."

"That's impossible."

"Is it?" He stopped for a moment, staring at her. "Actually, it's rather easy."

"It's a question of logic. If you're dead, how can you feel anything at all?"

"You don't get it. They're interested in experiencing what comes just before. How they would feel at that very moment. What follows afterward, they won't care. That is, most of them don't."

She looked away, and he carried on—working. "Relax," he said. "It will take a while."

"We're searching for hell."

"Reality is not bad enough for you?" Clemance observed the strange duo in front of him. One of them was older, huge and richly clothed; the other, young and handsome, with classical features and a vain expression on them. They had come in without appointment—a few hours after the young lady in red. That alone spoke volumes about how well connected they were—to know where to find him straight away. Not first-timers for sure, these fellows. He knew his joint, Mexico City, could be a place pretty hard to locate without contacting him first, and it was intended to be.

"You're a funny one. I like people with a sense of humour," the older one said. "But no. What we want is the perfect ordeal."

"Perfection is in the mind only and doesn't generally translate well in human artifacts, virtual or not," he replied, noncommittal.

"You're a game dealer. Better than that: You're known to be a fucking genius in this trade—the ethical genius, or so they call you. Well, genius, you will prepare for me the scenario I'm looking for. I want him to scream," the old guy said, indicating his companion. "I want him to bleed to death. A thousand times over."

"And you, what do you want?" Clemance asked the other, who had not yet said a word.

"Me? I only want him to beg mercy for the sins of the flesh. When he's feasting on my body."

He observed the young guy, dressed in black, his hair platinum blond, and with transparent nail polish on his manicured hands. At a pure aesthetical level, they would make best-selling characters. If only they weren't morally so unoriginal. Some hours of hard work on these two.

"I can deliver suffering and anguish, all shades you can dream of. And you'll be able to tweak the scenario afterwards, to suit the mood of the moment," Clemance said, eventually. "I believe I've just received your encrypted specs on my cloud-box. Do you want me to start?"

The two looked at him, nodding.

"It's going to be rather expensive."

"I know your tariffs," the older one said.

"I'm not talking about money."

"Why have you called your shop Mexico City, anyway?" the young asked with a curious regard. "Addicted to Latin American stuff, that's it? But you have nothing of the sort here. Not even a goddamn picture on the wall. Is it just for the exotic vibe of the name?"

"I thought you liked exotic."

"Here." The other ignored his friend altogether and made a couple of quick operations on his tablet. "Stocks are already on your corporate account. You can check it out. Now proceed. We don't have the whole night."

The conversation was over. Clemance patiently unfolded the encoded data and began weaving them in the appropriate scenario, while the two began caressing each other, ignoring his presence. Then the young one produced a shining stiletto, cutting the palm of his hand and letting his companion lick out the blood. His fingers dancing on the virtual keyboard, Clemance remained still, observing with cold detachment the reflection of his green screen on the blade.

"Are you there?" a voice cracked from the speakers a few hours later.

A few moments of silence, then it came again. "Clemance, put your goddamn finger on the goddamn keyboard and open the channel."

He contemplated for a moment an act of rebellion. Consolatory and useless, like the majority of human actions. He did as instructed.

"I'm here. So?"

"Just checking in. Tell me about your daily preys. Make me dream."

"Got three new profiles. Readying them for upload."

"Fire them out."

"I'm not done yet. Still filtering. It will take about thirty minutes."

"Oh yes. I always forget—you're one of the ethicals."

"Don't like to be called in this way."

"But this is what you are, my boy."

"No, this is what you leeches call us," Clemance snapped.

"Whatever. Too bad the others are not geniuses like you."

"Make it one hour. For my coffee break."

"You lazy, touchy bastard." The voice sneered at him, before breaking into laughter. "Leave the full profiles out for now. Give me specs I can use. Anything good?"

"You'll like them. A lusty she-economist; a young, suicidal emo; and a sadistic shotacon."

"Nothing original. You disappoint me, baby."

"Quite common, I'll concede. They look pretty though. Stylish even in the flesh. Almost authentic. And they get better when you load them on."

"I'll trust your judgment. What's your favourite?"

"The economist."

"Why? Because she's lustful?"

"No. Because she's desperate."

"Is she going to be a good sell?"

"Magnificent."

Through the speakers, he could hear the familiar sounds of his handler recording the information, preparing the calls and updates for the market.

"Fine job, my boy. If we're lucky, we might use these ones in a few new scenarios. Or we can let clients bid individually for including them as guest stars in their otherwise fully loaded games. A bit of novelty is always welcome. Especially now that we're getting better customers by the day." A laugh, with a satisfactory note in it. "We're upscaling. Old wealth. That kind of people wants the real thrill, not fake simulations. Their boredom threshold is dangerously low, and we need to beat the competition. The good news is that your brand, Mexico City, is becoming a guarantee of quality. Dystopia on tap, refined and glowing. You might be an ethical smug, but you're a damn good one."

"Glad to have made your day."

"By the by, do you think your newbies will live long? Outside your games, I mean."

"Why do you care? I'm not going to give you their unfiltered data anyway."

"I know you won't. Call it professional curiosity. And now that we talk about it … I've always believed you're a sick fuck, Clemance. You, with your reptile eyes and those delicate white hands of a princess. You look so gentle and polite, and you're the nastiest of all game architects I've ever met in my long and adventurous life. You're a monster, a vampire without all that shine and sparkle." The voice sounded lower now, its tone more confidential. "I have checked your records. A surprisingly high number of your customers remain alive for only a few weeks after they have come to see you. Ethical, my decrepit English ass. If I didn't know better, I would start thinking you hand them something toxic." Another laugh. "Or maybe Mexico City games are simply too amazing for them to come back to reality after they've tasted them. You're too effective for your own good."

"Are you complaining, Neil?"

"With all the money you bring in? I wouldn't dare. But at least you could give me their complete data once they're gone for good. What damage could it possibly do?"

"You already have my answer. It's not going to change. And no, it's not a question of price."

"That's why I never offered you one. But just to let you know, baby, I've come out with a little theory about this too."

"You seem to have a lot of free time these days. Has your mistress dumped you? Your wife did it long ago."

"Smartass. You see, I'm convinced you have your own collection of horrors. For your private entertainment, during all those long nights alone in your cubicle designing nightmares for public consumption. I don't really want to know."

"And you won't."

"No doubt about it. Well, my sensitive, ethical genius, have to go now. Stay cool."

Clemance unplugged the speakers and closed his eyes. His mind went back to the lady in red, the economist. To what had happened after.

It had taken him about one hour before the game and its characters were ready, according to the specs she had provided.

"Have you tried it yourself?" she'd asked him.

"Tried what?"

"The scenario you were talking about. Death, you know."

He had looked at her, into those amber eyes unable to conceal a tormented soul. He never discussed anything but business with customers, and personal questions were not included in the service agreement. The young woman was so new to the market that she ignored even those basic rules.

"Almost every day." He'd paused, searching for words that would not sound too cynical. He didn't want to hurt her. Actually, he didn't know why he was replying either. *Maybe because I could feel sorry for you, gorgeous lady in a fancy dress.* "I'm pretty ordinary, lady, like the guy next door. Each time, I try a slight variation. There are so many ways to die, you do wonder how we keep alive. I came to think it's this very wonder that does the job. It's ... refreshing."

She had shivered, looking at him with her eyes wide open. He could read attraction and revulsion at the same time, but also a bottomless sadness and loneliness.

"You need not to fear me, Coralia," he'd said, gently.

"How do you know my name? Wasn't in the specs."

"As if anybody spending his life in the virtual land could ignore these things," he'd replied, trying to wash any hint of sarcasm from his voice. "Relax, I said. I'm here to serve."

He had retrieved the device from the box and put it down on the table. "Procedure completed. The game has been preloaded with your biometric data and your preferences. New behavioural details will be locally uploaded at each run, to make simulations more accurate. You will get loading instructions and access codes directly into your cloud-box. Identification is by a combination of iris recognition and psychometrics. To make sure only you can access and play it. We care about your privacy. And talking about that…" He tilted his head, hinting at the card. "Don't ever do it again. Encryption on external devices is always insufficient. They're too old, and you don't need them anyway." He'd smiled at her. "Good fun ahead, lady in red. That lithe alien is going to give you a lot of pleasure. It will be exactly like in your dreams, only better. You might decide you don't want to get back to this world, but this is a risk you knew you were taking when crossing this line."

She'd lowered her eyes, suddenly embarrassed. "How much do I owe you?"

"I don't want your money," he had said in a cold voice. "You've already paid me anyway."

"How?"

"Haven't you figured it out yet?" He stared into his screen to avoid meeting her regard. "With your own data. They're now part of my virtual bank. They will be anonymised and used to construct other games. Other scenarios, and characters, for people that pay us real money. Some of them will virtually kill other customers like you, populating our prime clients' unique version of delirious escapism. In a way, you will live forever."

Clemance could see her shaking.

"Privacy and personal data protection are the reason, right? The reason why it's illegal."

"No." He'd lifted his head, looking straight into her eyes. "But it's because it's illegal that you're ready to pay such a high price. Didn't prohibitionism teach you smart people anything? Not even to you, Coralia the economist?"

She'd grabbed the card and collected her bag, in a rush of panic. "Goodbye. I don't think we'll see each other again."

"Not if you can avoid it. Enjoy your game."

She'd left and started walking in a hurry on the Strand toward Waterloo Bridge, dismissing the cabs. Within seconds, he had closed his shop and followed her, for once inexplicably drawn to a customer. He knew by instinct where she was going, and he was not mistaken. After a short stroll on the Thames' desolate bank, she'd stopped, looking at the murky water. He could hear her mind screaming, speaking more loudly than words. And he'd kept watching, waiting, not sure what to expect, feeling her pain.

"Delirious escapism, this is how he called it. Is that what I have bought?" she'd said aloud, almost in reply to his thoughts, turning her head to observe the city. "Yes, escapism—delirious or fucking lucid. It doesn't matter, at the end of the day."

Clemance hadn't been able to avoid looking at the Thames either. Dark waters with a sparkle of lights, futuristic buildings and gargoyles in grapheme, back stages of so many of his games. He'd felt the urge to go and get her, take her into his arms, but he could not force himself to act. After having explored all combinations of lives, created all possible outlandish scenarios, and for such a long time, he found himself surprisingly shy in a three-dimension reality. He'd stood where he was, unable to make a move.

She had smiled at the gargoyles, observing their monstrous heads and their hollow eyes. "I should have populated my game with gargoyles, instead of unlikely aliens," she'd said. "Being one of them. At least I would have the option of coming here and talking to my stony sisters, when losing my mind once for all." Calm and collected, she'd produced a cutter from her bag, plunging it deep into her throat. Then she'd jumped in the water.

He had remained there, like he was watching the scene of a movie or one of his games. Not moving, observing her body in the dark red dress slowly carried away by the river, for minutes that had seemed ice ages. Then he had left the place in silence.

*So sad. She hasn't enjoyed her alien lover—not even for one night. She could have waited.*

It was dawn, and a pale light came through the glassy panels of his ceiling. Mexico City, his shop, the centre of his world. *This would be a weird place in hell, should it exist—which it does not, of course. And I would be the trickster god that shows souls their way, leading them to the fall.* He had almost finished his work—scenarios like exquisite artworks, selling lucid dreams and hallucinations-on-demand. Building perfect places for people to go and stay there, never desiring to come back. Until ready for another outstanding simulation, signed off by the ethical genius that so often claimed their real lives.

*Enough of self-pity, you ethical idiot. Be the monster you're designed to be, and take responsibility.*

He observed his latest creations with the clinical eye of a neuroscientist and the refined taste of a great artist, like the genius game architect he was. Clemance, the best of all. His three new characters were there, slowly moving on the screen, rising from their slumber.

The pretty economist, the sadistic old guy, the depressive teenager. Eternally young, forever smiling.

# VOODOO THAT YOU DO DO

by
Andrew J Lucas

Franklin, not Frankie—never Frankie, perched on the edge of his bed his four hundred pound frame sinking deeply into the mattress pad. The tower advertised a 'most luxurious of true New York experiences'. He supposed this was mostly accurate—his bed back in Hollywood wouldn't support him comfortably either. It didn't matter one way or the other, he wasn't here to enjoy a comfortable sleep, he was here to change the world.

He only had the room for a few more hours, and time always a concern, more so now than ever. He remembered when he'd had plenty of time. A struggling actor, like so many others in Vegas. Frankie wasn't especially talented, ambitious, or handsome. He did however have a gift for mimicry. His act at Treasure Island featured passable imitations of many popular stars. Cher, Celine Dione, Madonna—Liberace was always a crowd favourite and he could handle a passable Elton John. One week he had added Michael Jackson to the routine at the insistence of his yuppie manager, who thought blackface was a good idea. He had actually been booed off the stage that night. Almost lost his booking too.

Vegas was good to him, but his voice began to go because Frankie aging along with the stars he imitated, he just could not keep it up. Something had to give and he was betting on his luck and his body. He tried to salvage the act by cutting back on the throat killing vocals and mixing in more middle-aged impersonations and some comedy for good measure. Michael J Fox, Tom Hanks and Bruce Willis all joined the act and kept it afloat, but it was not until reality TV hit the scene that his fortunes changed. Jeff Probst and a most unflattering rendition of Julie Chen played for comedic effect that really never struck home with the audience. However, it was the host of the business oriented reality show that really took off. When he strutted about the stage spouting inane one-liners and sending members of the stage crew to the unemployment office for staged pratfalls the crowd went wild.

A Hollywood talent scout caught his act and was just as impressed by his uncanny impression of the flamboyant tycoon. According to the contract Franklin—never Frankie, would tour the nation with his show, but also would have the opportunity to play the businessperson as a stand in, or celebrity impersonator. He became the country's premier impersonator of 'Big D'. He made the rounds of all the local morning shows tossing catchphrases at the yokels, cutting ribbons at state fairs and car lots during the day and playing comedy venues and small theatre houses with his act in the evening. Then he was called up to the big time, a couple of roles in comedy movies with b-list stars needing a 'Big D' and not wanting to pay for the real one. Apparently parody laws allowed this and they got away with his second string imitation. He even appeared on all the big name talk shows multiple times. Letterman loved him. The Daily Show brought him in a whopping seven times. He'd even guested on three decades of The Tonight Show, Carson, Leno and Fallon. O'Brien with his own shock of ginger hair schlocked out his one impersonation for the audience. Frankie thought it was ok

Then the calls started to slow and his agent stopped calling. Venues started to cancel on him, and Frankie knew he had to do something—something drastic. He took acting classes.

In class, he learnt about method acting and how to really become a character one had to immerse oneself in the character. To become them not just when you were acting but in your everyday life. Frankie took to wearing a thousand-dollar suit, ridiculously long ties, and neo-pompadour wigs, and ate nothing but porterhouse steaks and brandy. Damned if his shows didn't improve as well; calls started coming in and gigs started lining up again. However, it didn't last more than a month.

Franklin, never Frankie, wasn't one to give up easily, not when he saw his meal ticket going away. He stepped up his method acting, trolled eBay for items the Big D had once owned, and added as much poundage as the man himself had over the years; the red meat diet helped. He even had Brooks Brothers suits tailored in the same style. Each new item or affliction he added to his lifestyle added to the realism and the people knew it. They lapped up his performances as if it was feeding time at the kitsch farm. But it never lasted, the impression faded, became less lifelike—drifted if you will.

The ultimate impression was elusive. Franklin, never Frankie, continued to add affections to his lifestyle, becoming more and more like the 'Big D' each time. One day he woke in his home, sweat soaking his bathrobe pilfered from the set of Home Alone 2, surrounded by furniture he had sprayed gold with paint he'd pick up at Walmart. The fumes had filled the room as he'd painted and he'd passed out. He would have cracked a window but his apartment was now a replica of a New Yok penthouse and those windows didn't open, did they?

His mind was still reeling from the fumes as he picked up his Galaxy S3, scrounged from a curio shop in Greenwich Village that swore the 'Big D' had once owned it, to text his agent to come help him. Who else would he call? He had no friends. He hammered out a text to his agent, but the fumes were still playing havoc with his motor functions and the message he meant to send asking his agent to rush him to detox before he died was garbled—then he passed out.

The next morning, he woke in a pool of his own vomit with a splitting headache and was pretty pissed that his agent didn't care if he was alive or dead. Damn agents almost as bad as politicians. He made a cup of espresso from one of those environment-hating plastic cup things and turned on the TV. The news was blowing up that the 'Big D' was texting that the Russians should hack the DNC. That was some crazy stuff right there and Franklin, never Frankie, forgot how much he hated his agent and rooted about his apartment for his phone to text his agent and laugh about it. The Galaxy had a couple of spray-paint fingerprints on it that he'd have to buff those off, as they threw off the impression. Then he stopped cold. The cell phone displayed a text identical to the one the news had been displaying.

Was the object of his imitation tweeting him directly? But no, this wasn't an incoming tweet; it was a text that he had sent last night. Strange that it was identical to the one the president had sent. Franklin, never Frankie, shrugged. It was a weird coincidence, nothing more. He texted his agent again, asking what the hell is wrong with this country and why didn't he come over? Was there a wall or would he haul his fat Mexican, rapist ass over here and pick him up.

He was waiting for a return text when the TV interrupted the current show—they loved to do that—with breaking news. Probably it was some celebrity coming down with a cold or getting in a fistfight with paparazzi or something. But no, it was news about the 'Big D' himself, who was running election campaign rallies across the country. Apparently, he'd texted again, even though it was something like 3 a.m. at his golf course in Florida.

This time the text was about building a wall to stop Mexican rapists and other bad people coming over. Franklin, never Frankie, looked at the text he'd sent. It wasn't the message he'd sent to his agent at all, but a garbled message of racist fear and impractical border security identical to the one the news was displaying. What was happening? Needing to clear his mind of the lingering fumes, he decided to take a shower. The hot water soothed his troubled spirit and washed away any lingering bile. Refreshed, he dressed himself in his best suit, a second-hand Armani this guy on Vine swore used to be worn by the man himself.

He returned to the news, where Republican hacks were in full damage control mode, even at this late hour. The candidate was misquoted, his text was an allegory, his statements later that day would make everything clear. Franklin, never Frankie, wondered about that. He'd followed and lived as this man had for many years now. His every impression was that the man was a huge tool, with little redeeming characteristics, aside from his inherited money—well that and he'd provided a pretty easy persona to caricature.

He texted his agent and had no problems getting an immediate response, no sympathy but a response nonetheless. None of these crazy tweets or texts from the Republican candidate. He was relieved until he watched the evening news and saw the man doubling down on the Mexican comments and urged Russia to hack his political opponents. What the hell?

It was a mystery and one he didn't really think much about until a few weeks later, when the election was in full swing. He'd just completed a very difficult show, filled with left wing protesters who heckled his showplace performance—very frustrating. Franklin, never Frankie, was on his third bottle of wine—from Martha's Vineyard, of course—and again was texting his agent because what performer had real friends. He was struggling with a bad fish taco he'd picked up from a street vender on the way home. The wine and the ethnic food were not agreeing with him and his texting suffered for it. He wished the damn thing had never made it into the country—then he threw up.

The next morning the news was filled with promises of travel bans and suggestions of deportation of 'undesirables' all tweeted in the early morning and identical to the rambling text he'd sent his agent. Now he was worried. He texted the joke of the day and got a nicely innocuous story about a misplaced goose and a bakery in return. Was his cellphone really somehow mimicking the 'Big D's just as he himself mimicked its owner? He had to be sure.

A month later the Republicans had decided to back a single candidate, and Franklin, never Frankie, had his answer, or at least a working theory. He'd delved deep into the internet, using all the latest cyber to find his answer. He learnt about sympathetic magic, gestalt states, voodoo, posthypnotic suggestions and fetches. His theory was that as two objects became alike, physically, emotionally, even geographically, they began to act alike.

His amassing objects the 'Big D' had owned or touched had created a link between the two. His assuming his mannerisms had cemented it like a program running simultaneously over two identical computers, he thought. It was as good an analogy as any, and explained in a way how his drunken midnight texts affected the mind of a man thousands of miles away.

Of course, it only worked when the man was asleep and when he himself was in a drunken stupor or drugged out of his mind. Maybe the link used the identical Galaxy S3s somehow. All he knew was that the man tweeted whatever he drunkenly texted in the middle of the night—more than that, he believed it. Believed it wholeheartedly and more so defended it and acted upon it. Franklin, never Frankie, did not and vowed to put an end to the man's rise, no matter how much booze, cocaine and hookers it took.

Now deep into the man's presidency, seated on the edge of a Washington hotel that used to be a post office, Frankie, used to be Franklin, realized there wasn't enough drugs or alcohol in the country to make this right. Over the last months his last few attempts had resulted in the cancelation of NAFTA, three new travel bans, nationwide travel IDs, genetic screening of the unborn and perhaps worst of all the nationalization of broadcast TV. He looked over at the clock on the bedside table. Almost 3 a.m. The Russian prostitutes would be here soon. He'd have to try again, God help him. He hoped he had enough cocaine and a full charge on his cell.

# WISH GRANTERS

by
Adrian Ludens

"Come on gang, hustle!" Gada's father stood in their driveway and waved one arm like a traffic cop. "You'll miss your wish if we don't get moving!"

Gada let her mother steer her toward the family's maroon SUV. "Hurry, honey; you know how your father gets."

"I *am* hurrying." If her mother noted the petulance in her tone, she let it pass.

"This will be terrific," her father said as he slid behind the wheel. "Hundreds of like-minded people gathered for a common cause." Gada heard his seat belt latch closed as she hunched her way to the rear bench seat. Her older brother, Colby, had already claimed the front bench and despite her failing health, she knew better than to ask him to move. He still considered himself top dog. Gada dropped onto the rear bench as her mother climbed into the front passenger seat.

"Can we stop for food?" Colby asked. "I'm starving."

In the rearview mirror, Gada saw her father's eyes narrow in irritation. She was hungry too, but felt relieved that her brother had asked the question and drawn her father's ire.

"We'll hit a drive-through on the way," he said and stabbed the key into the ignition. The SUV roared to life. "Gada, you get to pick, since it's your special day."

"Move it, move it!" Missy's dad called up the stairs. "Time's wasting!"

"Are you sure we can't leave Robert at home?" Missy heard her mom ask. "He doesn't have to be part of this."

"Allie, for the last time: no." Sam sounded like he was talking to a puppy that had made a mess on the carpet. "Missy was selected by a classmate to be present for her wish. It would be an insult not to at least pretend to show our support."

"Missy! Robert! Let's go!" Not Dad this time, but Mom calling.

So, she had given in. Missy sighed and slid her feet into a pair of flip-flops. In the hall, her older brother brushed past her, preoccupied with something on his phone.

Out in the driveway, he and Missy played Rock Paper Scissors. Missy lost. She trudged with hunched shoulders to the back of the van. Robert plopped down up front, just behind their folks, and started messing with his phone again.

"You kids are in for a real treat today." Missy recognized an undercurrent of sarcasm in her dad's tone. She watched as he looked at each of them in turn in the van's rearview mirror. "You'll see how delusional most people in this town are. These 'wish granting' ceremonies can be downright creepy; so many people chanting and cheering, but they don't really care about others. After this you'll be proud to be a bleeding-heart liberal."

Five minutes later, with Missy still pondering the elusive but somehow terrifying meaning of 'bleeding-heart,' their gray van merged onto the highway.

"The importance of the Wish Granter ceremonies is almost as important as the Rallies and the Worship Services. Gada, I am sorry you are dying, but I am so proud you were selected as the Kid Wisher for today's ceremony."

Gada's father had not stopped talking since they'd left their driveway. True to his word, he'd ordered lunch at a fast food drive-through she'd picked, but there he'd done all the talking, ordering her a hamburger kid's meal without even asking what she wanted.

Tentacles of boredom dragged down her spirits. This felt even worse than the times her mother forced her to go with her to the fabric store. At least she always got to bring along—

"Donkey Hoaty!" Gada cried. "I left him in my room!"

"Well, it's too late to go back now," her father said. "We've over halfway there."

"But, Daa-ad!" In her dismay, she added a second syllable. "He's gonna be lonely."

Colby's chuckle dripped with the special kind of derision only an older brother can muster. He could afford to laugh; he'd brought along one of his handheld video games.

"No whining, young lady," her father scolded. "I don't want to hear any more about that beat-up doll, you hear me?"

"He's not a doll, he's a stuffed donkey." Gada felt tired, hot, and near tears.

"Either way, no more whining."

Gada folded her arms and slumped against her seat. Outside their SUV, buildings seemed to march past like soldiers in a parade.

"Those lunatics have no one to blame but themselves." Missy's dad kept talking as he drove. His voice was loud and gravelly, and hard for her to ignore. "They blindly follow, shortsighted, never questioning anything."

In truth, Missy couldn't understand why her father was so intent on going to Gada's ceremony. When her classmate, who she didn't even get along with, invited Missy and her family to come see Gada's wish get granted, Missy's father had leapt at the chance to attend, despite his constant claims about how dumb the ceremonies were.

Missy pretended to be stretching, lifted her arms, and crossed them over her head. She pressed her upper arms against her ears. It wasn't enough to drown out her dad's never-ending speech.

She wished she had brought along her pillow, or—

"Dad!" Missy dropped her arms. "We gotta go back home!"

He broke off speaking and frowned over his shoulder at her. "What's the matter?"

"I want to bring Salvador Dolly along to keep me company."

Her dad rolled his eyes and turned his attention back to the highway.

"Salva-*tore* Dolly, more like," Robert scoffed. He swiped a finger across his phone's screen.

"Missy, you'll get along just fine without that old thing," her mom said. "You're getting to be a big enough girl."

"But Dolly's my only friend!" Missy felt a lump in her throat. It hurt and made it hard to swallow. Tears welled. "Can we please turn back?"

"I don't want to hear any more about that old thing." Her dad turned to look at her. "And no tears, am I clear?"

Missy nodded, and a tear spilled from each eye.

"Some people go out of their way to show favoritism to every freak out there! The bigger the freak, the better; that's the way they like it." Gada's father sought them out in the rearview mirror again. "You kids ought to listen up back there."

Gada thought her father sounded angry. Was he mad at them? His words came out sounding higher, his tone tighter.

"No one's disagreeing with you," her mother said, trying to calm him down. For this Gada felt thankful; she didn't like it when her father acted this way.

"I know, but trying to explain to those libtards that things are better this way is like trying to pull wisdom teeth with a plastic spoon. They drag their heels because they're scared of hurting anyone's feelings!"

Gada swept her crumpled-up food wrappers onto the floor, unbuckled her seat belt, and stretched out on the bench. The vehicle stank of fast food grease. The trip seemed to be taking forever.

She hoped seeing her wish granted would be exciting but doubted it. She knew Missy would be there with her family, so she'd finally get her wish, but it also sounded like there was going to be a bunch of people just sitting and listening to a bunch other people make speeches first.

"Hey, not much longer, gang," her father announced. "Only another two miles and we'll be there."

Gada closed her eyes. She twirled a ringlet of her hair with her pointer finger. It relaxed her. Gada's mother told her she used to do the same thing when she was a toddler.

"You're lucky," her mother once said back when life seemed more carefree. "You have such beautiful hair." Treatment would have made her lose her hair. Gada felt glad that treatment had been banned.

Her mother had leaned down to plant a kiss on her daughter's forehead. Gada could almost feel that kiss now, so strong was the memory. She closed her eyes, let her thoughts drift.

Sleep had just taken her when she awoke to her father saying, "Look at all these people, Gada! They're all here to see your wish come true."

"They'll destroy the country if we let them. The Leader is a blithering buffoon and his followers are idiots. We're regressing with each passing day."

Missy shifted in her seat. She needed to pee. She didn't want to say anything, though. Her dad would just tell her to hold it. Her mom murmured in agreement every time her father spoke and Missy wondered if she really felt the same way or just pretended.

"And don't even get me started on all that gerrymandering and voter suppression," he said, and smacked the steering wheel with his hand.

Her eyes moved from her father to her mother, and then to Robert. They all had dark hair, matching brown eyes, and skin that tanned in the sun. She felt self-conscious, with her curly blond hair, light blue eyes, and pale freckled skin. Gada had once asked her if she had been adopted. Missy's face had burned with embarrassment as she stammered her response. Gada had only sneered and turned away.

"The turn-off to the ceremony is half a mile ahead," her dad called. "Now remember: stick close together! I don't want anyone in the family getting separated. We'll hang back and see what this is all about."

Missy had to pee—bad. She took her seat belt off but that only made it worse. She felt like a water balloon filled too full.

"Dad, I really have to use the bathroom," she moaned. "How much longer?"

"Didn't you hear me just now?" Her dad stared at her in the rearview mirror. "I just told you we're almost there."

When they arrived, some of the event staff escorted them to a special room behind the stage to wait for Gada's wish. When Missy saw the structure erected on the stage as they passed, she lost control of her bladder and began to sob.

*The Wish Granters Ceremony Script. These pages were found lying scattered in an adjacent alley following the event:*

(PRE-SHOW MUSIC AND VENUE ANNOUNCEMENTS)

VENUE ANNOUNCER: "Ladies and gentlemen, welcome your host for this morning's ceremony, Mason Crewell from Channel 2!"

(HOST ENTERS TO LECTERN)

MASON CREWEL: "Good morning, everyone, and welcome to the Fifth Annual Wish Granters Ceremony! It is hard to believe this event is celebrating its fifth anniversary already! Channel 2 has been involved since the beginning and we are a proud partner of Wish Granters. Today I am here because, like you, I believe in the power and strength in granting a wish and I want to make sure that every eligible child facing a life-threatening medical condition here in the Black Mountains is able to have their wish granted. Each year, well over six hundred wishes are granted.

"So thank you for being here today and for believing in the Black Mountain Chapter of Wish Granters and its important mission of providing a bit of entertainment to sick kids and their families.

"We need to thank the people and organizations that helped make today's event possible. Please join me in thanking our leading sponsors: Esoteric Order Insurance, Flensman Exterminators, and Bathory Tools & Supply, as well as all of the other sponsors you see listed on banners displayed throughout the town common!

"Let's give them a round of applause!"

(LEAD APPLAUSE, POINT OUT ANY NONPARTICIPANTS TO SECURITY)

"Special thanks to our dedicated volunteer committee and volunteers who handled every detail to make this day perfect for the wish family. In addition, thanks to all of you for being here today! It makes me proud to see all of you lined up in front of me. I feel honored to be here.

"I also want to recognize Agnatha Tetsy, regional director of the Black Mountains Chapter of Wish Granters. Along with the volunteers, Agnatha coordinated today's event. Joining her today from the National Wish Granter Headquarters are Hector Damien, Volunteer and Outreach Director, and Paul Ghast, President and CEO."

(LEAD APPLAUSE, POINT OUT NONPARTICIPANTS)

"As you know, today's event is primarily a fundraiser. While we thank each of you who raised essential funds, we want to recognize a few of you who have exceeded every possible expectation. Leesa Caturia, representing our primary sponsor, Esoteric Order Insurance, is here to help present awards. Thank you Leesa!"

LEESA:
"As we read your names, make your way to the front of the stage to be recognized. Please remain on stage until the last name gets called, then follow Mr. Ghast to the panel truck waiting next to the stage.

"As of 5:00 p.m. yesterday, we want to thank our number five fundraiser, _____ (CLAP, escort to truck) our number four fundraiser, _____ (CLAP, escort) our number three fundraiser _____ (CLAP, escort) our number two fundraiser _____ (CLAP, escort) and the top individual fundraiser for the Black Mountains Chapter of Wish Granters, with more than $_____ raised, is _____!"

(FINAL CHEER, ESCORT)

"We also have some amazing teams out there, and I would like to recognize our top three fundraising teams. Number three is the _____. Number two is _____. And the top fundraising team for Wish Granters, with more than $_____ raised, is _____!" (CHEER, escort all to truck)

"Congratulations everyone! We know many of you are donating today and we want to thank you for your generous support. If you have not yet had the chance to give, gifts can be placed in the designated donation jars, at the merchandise tent, or at the donation table right here by the stage. Credit cards are also accepted at the merchandise tent. Help us reach our goal today of $85,000!"

(MUSICAL FANFARE—LEAD AND ENCOURAGE APPLAUSE)

MASON: "You will find wish kids in nearly every community. Unfortunately, kids everywhere face medical challenges that are sometimes heartbreaking, but unavoidable. We can draw inspiration from their situations. And, as we will witness today, the granting of a wish will provide the rest of us with some wonderful entertainment!

"What all these sick and dying kids share is the unique experience of being a part of the Wish Granters family—one of the fastest-growing organizations on the planet. Since the Black Mountains Chapter of Wish Granters started in 2020, more than 12,657 wishes have been granted—that is more than 12,657 wish kids and thousands upon thousands of family members who have been impacted by the work of Wish Granters.

"During the march, you will have a stop along the way at Gaston's Theatre to watch the powerful story of Sam's wish, which was granted last summer. In addition, following the march today you will have the chance to be part of a wish and see the magic for yourself. So be sure to come back following the march!

"At this time, we would invite ANY KID WISHERS here today to make their way to the front of the stage. If your kid wisher is unable to be here or is no longer with us, we invite a wish parent or wish sibling to come up to represent the strength and bravery of your child. We will recognize all of you shortly!"

(LEAD APPLAUSE)

"Today we celebrate wishes because EVERY child between the ages of three and seventeen with a life-threatening medical condition deserves a granted wish.

"One of my favorite parts of Wish Granters is getting to meet our wish kids and their families. These are our real-life celebrities among us! A good number are here today near the stage. Let's give them a big round of applause."

(APPLAUSE)

"Be sure to say hi to the wish kids and ask them about their wishes. There are so many fun stories!

"As you march today, think about the kids and families standing here now, the 12,657 kids and families across the state who have had wishes granted, and all the kids waiting to have their wishes granted. There is so much more entertainment coming, believe me.

"Join us immediately after the march, as a special wish will be granted here today! Trust me, you are not going to want to miss this. There will also be music, food, and drinks, with all proceeds going back the Black Mountain Chapter of Wish Granters. Also, do take a moment to visit all our sponsor booths. Each one has a creative activity. And if you haven't had a chance to give yet and would like to, be sure to do so at the donation table near the stage, the merchandise tent, or in one of the designated donation jars.

"Now, as I mentioned earlier, we have a special stop today during the march. We will march from here and gather inside Gaston's Theatre to hear the story of Kid Wisher Thaddeus, and his granted wish. Then we will proceed on our normal march route west down Saint Vitus Street. Just a reminder that when we get to Gaston's, it is very important that you fill the front rows first and find your seat quickly.

"It's time to get started, so let's bring up Silas, one of our Kid Wishers who is still with us, to help us count down. Silas faces an autoimmune disease, and he had his wish granted last summer. Boy, that TNT sure was fun, wasn't it Silas?"

(PAUSE FOR CHEERS)

SILAS: "Five, four, three, two, one! Start marching!"

(MARCH TAKES PLACE) POST-MARCH

MASON: "Welcome back. I hope you enjoyed the march. Wasn't Thaddeus' story powerful? And what a creative wish! It is amazing how organized Thaddeus stayed during his illness, and how he kept such thorough records of everyone he infected. It was also powerful to see the impact that Thaddeus' revelation had on everyone involved. Thank you again to everyone who made his wish a reality.

"Now, before you enjoy the activities and food, this morning you are in for a treat. At this time, we would like to ask Kid Wisher Gada Sneve and her parents Mat and La-Norr to come to the stage. Gada is six years old and lives near Stonewall. Gada's name means "lucky" and even though she has been diagnosed with terminal cancer, she's still lucky because today we are going to grant her wish!"

(LEAD APPLAUSE)

"We would also invite Wish Granter volunteers Marth and Sarai Odden, Johan Krispin from Scorch Steelworks, Bret Sammoth from Shackleford Blacksmiths, and Thomas Tribb from the Black Mountain Fire Department to join us on stage. I am going to turn the microphone over to Hector Damien from Wish Granters for the introduction…"

HECTOR: "Thank you again for being here today. It is inspiring to see so many people from the area coming out to support our wish kids and their families. Our guest of honor is Gada Sneve. She's here today with her parents, Mat and La-Norr, and her big brother, Colby. Mat and La-Norr, could you tell us a bit about Gada and her medical history?"

(MAT AND LA-NORR ANSWER)

HECTOR: "What was your reaction when you found out she was going to receive a granted wish from Wish Granters?"

(MAT AND LA-NORR ANSWER)

HECTOR: "What wish did Gada come up with and why?"

(AS MAT AND LA-NORR ANSWER, POINT OUT ANYONE WHO TRIES TO LEAVE)

MASON: "Again, we extend our thanks to each of our sponsors for your time and generosity in helping to make Gada's wish to come true! Now, ladies and gentlemen, cheer as loud as you can as we bring out the subjects of Gada's wish: Missy Steuben, who is Gada's least-favorite classmate, and Missy's parents, Sam and Allie, and her older brother, Robert!"

(APPLAUSE AS STEUBEN FAMILY IS LED TO AND SHACKLED INSIDE THE CAGE)

Mason: "All right, it's time to make your wish come true, Gada. Light 'em up!"

(NOTE: KEEP BACK TO AVOID BURNS)
(LEAD APPLAUSE AFTER)

(BACK TO MASON—FINAL REMARKS)
"Wow, what a morning! Again, enjoy the activities in the Square at all of the sponsor booths, food and beverages, with all proceeds supporting Wish Granters. Also, stop by the merchandise tent to buy a T-shirt or souvenir photo of today's granted wish, or to make a donation if you have not already. Thank you to our sponsors and to all of you for being here today and for supporting the kids and families of the Black Mountains Chapter of Wish Granters!

"Let's have some more fun!"

(MASON: DIRECT GADA AND HER FAMILY TO THE CAGE FOR PHOTOS WITH THE CHARRED REMAINS, THEN ESCORT YOURSELF TO THE PANEL TRUCK WAITING BEHIND THE STAGE)

# BURIED ALIVE IN A SALLOW GRAVE

by
Alice van Harlingen

*For Harlan*

*One of the strange things about violent and authoritarian regimes is they don't like the glare of negative publicity.*
—Salman Rushdie

The day the fifth war on Tenemount began, we began our own. It had been long in preparation and would have a splendidly violent end, but it started small—with the most powerful thing any rebellion has ever had. It started with words.

The night wind felt like sandpaper thirty-two stories up. It darted and circled like an agitated snake, but the sky was clear. There were no drones as far as I could see, and that comforted me. At least something had gone right.

"We have to hurry," Millie said, and she gave me a quick kiss before covering her face with her Spiderman mask and rushing off to tell Jack what to do. I took a deep breath and tasted her lips for a long, still second, and then I lowered my own mask. Visible drones or not, there might be cameras.

The virus we'd sneaked into New Calastra's system should have taken out every piece of surveillance in the area, but I didn't trust it. The police and the drones and Central Intelligence had ways of getting around technical issues, and I was sure they had more than a few human spies, too. I hurried toward Big Tom and helped him with the rope. "It's gonna be all right," I told him, but I believed that as much as he did. His hands were shaking.

When we'd secured our end, I signaled Millie. It was time. My heart thundered in my temples, and I grew cool with a sudden, slick sweat. *It's gonna be all right*, I told myself.

And then we pushed it over the edge.

The package dropped two or three stories until the ropes went taut, jerking it back toward us. For a split second I worried that it wouldn't unravel, but then the top edge turned over and toppled toward the ground, unfurling as it went.

This was only the first step in the plan, but like all first steps, it was important, maybe the most important. Millie and I had spent the previous few days finishing the banner. It would hang from the Watch Tower, the most visible building in New Calastra, and send one simple message: *Make New Calastra Great Again*. We'd used the same words he had during his campaign almost two decades earlier, but the image below the words, the Don with his face crossed out and eyes removed, would make it clear that this time we were taking it back from him. This time the words weren't hollow.

The banner stopped with a jerk and then lay against the concrete and glass, rippling like waves in a shallow pool, caught in the sick-green ambient light that shone on the Watch Tower's facade. Millie came over to me and I put my arm around her. She slid her hand up the side of my shirt so that the tip of her finger settled against the underside of my breast, and I rested my head on her shoulder.

We'd done it. Beneath us, people were stopping, pointing, and, I hoped, thinking. I took it all in: the distant growl of a hundred worn-out car engines, the starless gray-black of the night sky, the swell of wind and stink of the city, the feel of my love's body against mine, the sense that we'd done something that couldn't be taken back. This last set my heart racing; we couldn't linger for too long. Mayhap we'd already overstayed our window. "Time to go," I said.

Because we'd expected a tight escape, we'd planned ahead. (We'd planned way ahead. It was one of the reasons it had taken us four years to make this first step.) The fire escape would be cut off quickly, so we had set up zip lines on the twenty-ninth floor that ran to the top of a nearby apartment building. From there we'd take the stairs to the ground, exit out the back service door, and slip into the sewer. Everything was ready. If it worked.

As if cued, sirens sounded in the distance.

*No authoritarian leader cedes power easily or turns it over to bodies he cannot control.* —Stephen Kinzer

I cut the zip lines, sending them dancing into the green glow radiating from the street below. Then I hurried toward Millie, Jack, and Big Tom, who were already at the entrance to the stairwell. Millie was waving me over, and when I reached them, she touched the small of my back and closed the door.

The stairwell smelled like vomit and mildew, and the same sick light from the street shone in it. My stomach turned, and I took quick, shallow breaths to combat the smell. We hurried down, each story marked by a number stained on the ruined concrete.

We were about halfway to the street when we heard them. Their boots were heavy, intentionally so, I thought, sounding like the hoof strikes of agitated horses. I took Millie's hand and signaled to the boys.

Floor three's door had something sticky on it that I hoped was spilled soda. I held it open and ushered the other three into the dimly lit hall.

"Come on," Millie said. Her mask puffed out in sharp, quick breaths.

I took her hand again, and the four of us ran toward the other end of the hall. Buildings like this had two stairwells to fit the code, and while I hoped the police wouldn't be in both, I knew they probably were. The whole way, as we passed door after door—some decorated with Christmas trees or dancing children, or the Don, red-faced and screaming—I looked for another way out, but there were no windows, only doors, and all of them locked. Trash littered the hall, and that sick smell from the stairwell was worse in here, like week-old death.

When we reached the other stairwell, I first listened. When I heard nothing, I edged the door open. Time was short. They'd only been entering the building, not yet climbing the other stairwell, when we took this detour, but it wouldn't be long before the police found their way to this level. Millie squeezed my hand.

The first thing I noticed when I opened the door wasn't the sound; it was the lights. The police had laser sights on their weapons, and these swarmed the walls and stairs like locusts. My heart slid to my groin, and I let the door swing shut. We were trapped. They were coming up both sides. There was no way out.

As if reading my mind, Big Tom started checking locks. He moved quickly from one apartment to the next. But it wouldn't matter. Everyone locked their door in New Calastra. Crime was high. The Don liked it that way. It made his policies necessary.

After checking four, Big Tom knocked on one decorated with about a dozen Santa Clauses, each different in some way: some in red, some in green, some fatter than others, some beards longer than others. He rapped his knuckles on the wood three times, quickly, like housekeeping in a hotel. My breath caught in my throat. We'd worked so hard, we'd prepared, we'd planned. Was this the end? Sure, I had faith that the rest would be released—so much of it was automated, and we weren't the extent of the rebellion—but I'd hoped to see it play out. I'd hoped to be able one day to move away to the mountains, away from the cities and politics and people, and give Millie the life she deserved. To give all of us the lives we deserved.

When no one came to the door, Big Tom took a slow step back and then slammed his big foot into it, just beneath the knob. The door flew open, a strip of wood splintering off into the hall. He gave me a wide-eyed look through his Superman mask, as if he were asking for approval, as if he knew what he'd done was wrong but necessary. I'd known Tom most of my life, and he was a kind man. He never would have hurt anyone. That's one of the reasons I loved him.

I almost shoved Millie and Jack through the door, and as I passed Big Tom, I squeezed his shoulder. When we were all inside, Big Tom closed the door, as if this were his apartment and everything was normal, as if the police wouldn't notice the damage from the outside. It didn't stay closed, however. An inch-thick strip of sick green shouldered its way in a second later. In my nervousness, I laughed.

The apartment was a mess. Pots clustered near the kitchen sink and clothes curled in heaps on the floor like scared animals. Roaches scurried from the light. I thought about saying something, alerting the tenant, but then I thought better of it. If he or she hadn't shown already, they either couldn't or didn't want to get involved, and I didn't want to endanger them any more than we already had. Through the balcony window, you could just see the red and blue alternating hues from the police cars in the distance.

I went out first. The wind here was less abrasive, but the temperature seemed to have dropped twenty degrees. Although their red and blue lights first darkened and then bloodied the green glow in the alley, there were no police to be seen and no drones. *Thank the Gods*, I thought. But then my heart sank. When Tom had kicked in the door, I'd known what he was thinking. To keep up to code, apartment buildings needed two stairwells and a fire escape that climbed its way to each balcony like a rusted series of vines. But there was no fire escape. The alley was still three stories beneath us, but there was no way to get to it. We were trapped.

I almost cried. I felt the pressure behind my eyes and in my throat, but Millie, always the clever one, took one look over the side and started down. She lowered herself from one balcony to the next beneath it, then the one below that. She was already in the alley, near the manhole we'd left partly open, when I followed her.

The balconies were spaced so that I could grab the ledge of one, let my arms straighten, and only have a two-foot drop to the ledge of the next. With each drop, I worried that I'd slip and end up on my back, head cracked open on the pavement below, but I didn't slip. I made it to the bottom, where Millie kissed me. Jack came after me, but Big Tom didn't. He stood there, three stories up, looking at us. I waved for him to come, but instead, he turned back inside.

When Jack hit the ground, Millie pulled me toward the manhole. I was waiting for Big Tom to reappear. I wanted to make sure Jack, Millie, and Tom made it to safety before I did, but Millie had other plans. She shoved me onto the dewy ladder. "We have to go," she said. I climbed down a few rungs and Millie followed closely, each rung she took forcing me to the next. Once her head had dipped below street-level, Jack dragged the cover closed. What was he doing? What were they doing? This wasn't the plan.

"Jack!" I shouted.

Millie pushed me farther into the dark and stink and wet of the sewer. There were tears in my eyes now, and it hit me that while this may not have been my plan, it was their plan. I'd imagined all of us getting away together and waking the next morning to see the banner on TV and hear reports about the fliers the others would have slid beneath each apartment door and into each mailbox before morning. I'd dreamt what that would feel like, but the farther down I went, the more I realized that it would never happen that way. No matter what we'd done, it never would have happened that way. They'd known this and prepared. I hadn't.

Before my foot hit the concrete at the bottom, the first shot rang out.

*The stability and security of authoritarian regimes cannot create but terrorism and violence and destruction. Let us accept the choice of the people. Let us not pick and choose who we would like to rule their future.* —Wadah Khanfar

Lisa McAndrew had to say something. She always did. She was sitting at her desk, which wasn't too far from mine but closer to the big windows that opened onto the street. The morning light gilded one corner of her desk, and a small TV sat not too far from that gold. I'd been listening to the TV, trying not to think about Jack and Big Tom, but it was no use. I hadn't slept. Neither had Millie. I'd spent hours wondering if the police had killed them or captured them, how scared they were, how hurt they were—and, selfishly, if they'd talk.

When not listening to the reports or pretending to work, I worried over the next step in the plan. Our next release would be audio files sent to every computer, TV, and radio in the city. It would hit about noon. The files had been recorded the previous week in the run-up to the newest war on Tenemount. In them, the Don opined about the people of New Calastra. He didn't use glowing terms.

"This is shit," Lisa said. She almost spat the curse. "I got one of those fliers. Did you?" I nodded. "How dumb do these rebels think we are? The Don's the only one who can keep us safe. He's fixed the economy, crime, terrorism. He's the only reason we're still here, but these ignorants can't accept that. Liberals. Liars. Trying to take him down my whole life. But we know, don't we? The silent majority knows what's good for New Calastra. He's made it great again. Unpatriotic shits."

I hunched my shoulders and pretended to go over the same file I'd been pretending to go over all morning.

"Let me guess. You agree with them, don't you?" She took a sip of coffee and stood. She clicked her heels against the floor a few times. "I just don't get it. Can't they see all the good he's done? Don't they know how good we have it?"

"Maybe they don't think it's as good as you do," I said. The words squeaked out of me on their own, and as soon as they did, I knew I should have kept my mouth shut.

"I bet they'd rather live in Tenemount. Terrorists." She sat again, took a slug from her coffee mug, and banged a pen against her desk. Her face was red, and a vein showed on her forehead. "Do you think they'll catch them?" she asked.

"Probably," I said, and I did. We'd worked it into the plans. Everything would continue now. There was no stopping it because it wasn't about us, or as Lisa called us, "the rebellion," anymore. It was about the people, and I hoped they'd do something.

When I said it, I thought about Big Tom and Jack. I grabbed a tissue and pretended to sneeze. I wiped the tears from the corners of my eyes with it.

"I hope so," she said. She slammed the end of her pen down again. The TV had switched to talking about the successes of the new war: how much progress we'd made in only a day. Tenemount would fall again, soon. That's how it always happened with the war. We won, and we won quickly and decisively. A few months later, we'd be hit by a terrorist attack, always somewhere outside the core of New Calastra, always densely populated, always poor people. Then we'd launch another war, and everyone would feel safe again. The drums of war, I thought, ran the risk of fading to background noise if played constantly, but the silences, however short, made them seem louder, more insistent, more necessary.

I sipped my coffee and dug into the file for real this time. I did this for two reasons: 1) to get my mind off Jack and Big Tom and 2) because I feared that if I kept going over it without doing anything, someone would notice. For a few short hours, I lost myself in numbers and names and percentages.

It was 1:15 when they came.

I was in the breakroom pretending to eat lunch because I couldn't bring myself to eat anything—I was too nervous and worried for food—and taking as much time as I could away from Lisa, when Central Intelligence came for me.

For some reason, I imagined they'd come armed to the teeth and in large numbers. I thought they'd clear everyone out of the office and shoot first, but that's not what they did. It was one officer in the beginning, and he came dressed in plain clothes and asked for me, like a friend or a customer. Lisa got me from the breakroom. She said someone was out front to see me, and I thought that was weird. No one visited me at work, or at least they hadn't before. As I first put my untouched lunch back into the refrigerator and then made my way to the front, a hundred things played in my mind, but chief among them was the worry that it was Millie with a problem or someone coming to tell me Millie'd been captured.

When I saw him, I smiled. That's how clueless I was. I smiled at him. A big, shit-eating grin I'd only give a customer or a stranger. "Hello," I said.

As soon as the word came out, I knew for sure that something was wrong. Maybe it was the way he stood, a little too straight for a customer, or the blank, wan look on his face, too passive to be normal. Maybe it was a premonition—not that I believe in that stuff; Millie does, or did; I'm not sure which now. The officer was wearing jeans and a plain black shirt under his tan coat. He had sunglasses and a mustache like my father had once worn. He took a step toward me, and his boot clacked the linoleum. He reached under his jacket for his gun.

Without thinking, I turned back toward the breakroom. There was a back exit there, just past the sink and dishwasher. It was alarmed, but I didn't care. I ran, my coworkers' dead eyes following me. The officer yelled, "Stop her!" Behind me, I heard the door scream open and more boots on the linoleum floor.

My boss, Mark, stood beside his desk. As I passed, he said, "Stop right there, young lady," and reached for me. I tried to avoid him, but he had long arms, and one spidery hand snared my elbow. He pulled and twisted me toward him. Police and Central Intelligence flooded through the door. There had to have been two dozen of them with more coming. Cold fear seeped into my stomach. I struggled, but Mark held.

Mark was a nice guy. He'd never made a pass at me, which it seemed all men did, especially in the workplace, and he always approved my time off. He was good for the occasional, vapid work conversation; so, I felt bad about what I did next.

Mark was shouting something to the officers, but the adrenaline rushing through me made it impossible to hear anything other than my heartbeat clearly. I tried to pull my arm away again, but he still held. I screamed in his face, and he snaked his other arm around my waist. When he did, I drove my heel into the ball of his foot. This shook him enough that I could twist toward him. Before he could regain himself, I thrust my knee into his groin. A deflated *oof* leaked from him, and he let go. He toppled to the ground. As he fell, I kicked him in the face.

I made for the breakroom door.

Lisa stood in front of it. She'd put both arms up and spread her legs like a goalie. A fitting sneer sat on her face, and in the split second before I barreled into her, I thought that sneer matched her personality so perfectly that it must have been her face's natural position. I lowered my shoulder so that it hit her square in the chest.

Lisa was bigger than me, and the collision threw me sideways into the doorframe. She fell into the breakroom, her legs going straight up like a turtle flipped on its shell. My breath left me, and I staggered toward the back door, pinprick stars filling my narrowing vision. In the main room, the police and Central Intelligence shoved people out of their way and shouted at me. Everything sounded as if it were coming through a long tunnel filled with fans. My chest felt as if it were caving in.

I was too scared to turn around to see how close they were. I focused as best I could on the door, which seemed to move farther away with each step I took toward it. When I finally reached and opened it, the alarm blared. The sound, which I knew to be deafening, came through the tunnel muted and muffled, a weak squawk. I hurried into the alley. Behind me, Lisa shouted something. (She always did.)

I'd seen war drones on TV, but never one up close. It was the size of a car, but porcupined with guns and artillery. The front exhaust grill looked like a crooked set of monstrous teeth, and it gave off a noxious smell and searing heat. Trash fled from its fans like gazelle from a lion. I had nowhere to go, so I stopped in front of it. It hovered there, swaying side to side, as if contemplating.

*In every country today there is politics. It may be authoritarian politics, but there is politics.* —Hillary Clinton

The room was lined in gold. The Don had gilded the ceiling, the picture frames, the drapes covering the windows; the carpets even had gold thread. Had I been able to turn my head, I was sure I'd see that the ties they'd used on me were gold as well. I tried to move but couldn't. They'd stretched me so tight that the insides of my joints ached.

I wasn't sure how long I'd been here. I was still nauseated from whatever gas the drone had used. The room, one I'd seen on TV a hundred times, was filled with gold light, but the windows were covered. It could have been night; mayhap even days later.

I pulled at the binds, but nothing moved. A sharp pain tore into my side, and I let out a cry. At that moment, I thought of Millie. Was she okay? Was she safe?

A small drone, about the size of a football, floated in front of me. I spat at it.

"Now, now, is that any way for a lady to behave?" the Don's voice came from behind me.

*Authoritarian political ideologies have a vested interest in promoting fear, a sense of imminence of takeover by aliens and real diseases are useful material.* —Susan Sontag

"Fuck you!" I shouted.

"You are the picture of femininity, my dear." I could hear him moving behind me.

"Get stuffed!"

"Oh, aren't you clever? A perky little harlequin." He laughed. "I'm going to enjoy this more than I thought. I don't get to do this that often, you know. It's one of life's little pleasures."

"Fuck you!"

As he passed, he ran a finger along my side. "Perky, indeed," he said. As always, he wore a suit that was a tad too big for him and a long, mono-color tie. He had gold hair to go with the gold room and slit eyes that his fat face had swallowed long ago. Too-white teeth shone in his too-wide smile. "I thought we'd have a chat before I kill you."

"You may as well kill me then. I'm not interested." I pulled at the binds again.

"Oh, my dear, the fun we could have." He tapped a loafered foot on the marble floor. "I want you to tell me about the video."

"What video?"

"I find it impressive. Honestly, I do. To get as far as you have. To have done everything you've done." He stopped and looked around the room, as if buffering, waiting for the next thought. "You're much too intelligent to play stupid. Now, tell me how you got it."

Because I didn't know how long I'd been out, I wasn't sure if he meant the video of him giving his unvarnished thoughts on New Calastrans, which we'd planned to release a few hours after the audio, or if he meant the longer video showing him inspecting Tenemount's war drones and planning the attack on King's Court, which he'd used as an excuse for the latest war. I looked at him dumbly.

'You better be careful, my dear, I prefer my women dumb. You keep it up and we may have a little fun before we're done here."

"Fuck you!" I said again.

"A woman of immense vocabulary. I love it. Let me ask you a question then. Are you proud of yourself?"

"Get stuffed."

"I see. Well, you should be. You've played this game perfectly. Better than I anticipated. It's been, what, four years? That's it, isn't it? You've been planning for four years, right?"

I thrashed at my bonds again, and every joint screamed. A small cry escaped me.

"Four years, three months, two days, eleven hours, forty-six minutes, and twelve seconds, or at least, that's when we first caught wind of it. I like to be precise if I can, don't you?"

"Fuck—"

"—Me. Yes, I've heard it." He clapped his hands together. "Get stuffed, right?"

In that moment, I knew we'd lost. He'd known. The whole time he'd known, and he'd prepared. He'd toyed with us. I closed my eyes and in that red-tinted darkness I saw one thing, Millie's face. Tears swelled against my eyelids, and I did my best to keep them from spilling. I couldn't think about her and what he'd done to her or would do to her. As if she could hear me, I said, "I'm sorry."

"Well, that's a start, isn't it? A good apology never hurt anything, did it?"

"Get stuffed!"

"So, you're not going to tell me about the video." I wasn't sure if it was a question or a statement. "And now you know that I let you do it, but do you know why?"

"I don't give a shit."

"She has new words. My God, she has new words." He clapped again. "But I want to tell you. Can I, please?" He paused, as if buffering again. "It's my favorite part."

A tear slid down my cheek and my chest hitched.

"You've helped me tremendously, you know? It's hard to control a population of this size. I mean, I know New Calastra's not the biggest city, and I know that most of them are bone-stick-stone stupid, but you have to do something to bring them together, to stop their thinking and get them acting on instinct instead. Survival instinct, you know? Get them all going the same way." He paused again. "Nothing does it quite like rebellion. Wars work short term, but rebellions, especially those that get close to succeeding, really drum up support for those in power." He laughed, a sick sound that seemed to leak from his throat.

I couldn't hold it in anymore. "Don't you see what you've done to this city? Don't you care? Look at us. The people are suffering. You're like some disease that's eating away at everything, crippling us. You're destroying our humanity."

"Humanity's overrated, my dear, don't you think?"

"Aren't you afraid of them?"

"Who? The people? No, my dear, I'm not. Why would I be? I'm giving them what they want."

"What's that?" I asked.

"Strength. And between us, the freedom to not think. Most people hate making decisions. They want someone to do it for them. I give them that." Another pause. "You, my dear, are the exception, don't you think?"

"Fuck you!"

"We're back to the clever banter, are we?"

Tears ran down my face and splattered the marble beneath me. I wanted to be strong. I wanted to say something clever. I wanted to fight back, but there was nothing I could do. He'd won. From the beginning, he'd won.

"Oh, my dear, did I make you cry?" His sick smile seemed to stretch the width of his skull.

"No," I said. "You don't have that power. You never did. You never will."

The Don's face flushed red, and he lunged toward me. I thought he was going pull a knife and finally do what he'd promised, but he didn't. He stopped just short. When he spoke, the words came not from him but from the room around him, from everything: the marble floor, the gilded ceiling, the candelabra hung just so between portraits that also spoke, the tiny drones buzzing above us like giant summer mosquitos, the drapes, the podium off to my left where he dictated edicts and injunctions and mandates and fiats, the cameras filming us, the fillings in my teeth.

Before the bombs, our last planned event, shook the room and sent it and the capitol building tumbling and crumbling into the sick-green glow of the New Calastran afternoon, into cloud-heavy skies toward a distant glaucomaed star it would never reach, I knew it was true. It had always been true. The Don was New Calastra and New Calastra was the Don. They were one, the same. They were—

*Let me classify this very definitely. This is not an authoritarian organization.* —L. Ron Hubbard

CODA 1:
A thick fog of soot, pulverized concrete, and microscopic bits of metal and flesh slowly settled into the rubble, which flamed in places and lay lifeless in others. Here, a statue that had stood since the founding grinned half-faced into the pitch-black sky; there, an arm, either marble or flesh (you couldn't tell which), reached bodilessly toward a future it would never know. And everywhere, drones, some as small as baseballs and some as large as houses, shoved aside Sisyphean boulders and the ruin of what had been to rise into that day-made-night, each with one thought, one instinct; each possessed by hope.

CODA 2:
"But that's not an ending," the little girl said. "It didn't end. It just stopped. Mayhap there's more?"

He shook his head.

"That's not fair. How does it end?"

"Who said it was the end?"

"But how could the lady tell her story if she was dead? It couldn't be the end."

"Sometimes endings aren't fair, are they, my dear?"

"But what happened after?"

"We can't know that, my dear, now can we?"

"But it's not fair."

"Who said it had to be fair?"

"But what's the point of it if it doesn't end? What's the moral?"

"I think the moral is hope, Pandora. I think the moral of the story is hope. That's okay, isn't it?"

# CLIMACTIC CHANGE

# HIGHWAY 99

by
I. A. Green

In the heart and belly of California, there are vast, lonely tracks of agricultural land where humans rarely go, despite growing most of their food there.

In one such remote swatch of land, where people only stop to change a tire or take a piss off the shoulder, a small bridge stands unmarked over a small stream. The stream is one of those odd, self-contained tributaries that seem to have a definite beginning, but an indefinite end. It begins in the Sierra Nevadas, pure and distilled from winter snowfall, meandering its way down through the foothills, until it enters the Central Valley.

There, it flows by the dark silo and hunkering warehouse of a roadkill crematorium. Waste from the silo falls into the stream, and under the weight of its refuse, the stream's passage becomes sluggish. Movement slows to a near stop, except for a slow sinking into the wide marshes farther down, dissipating out among the wild reeds. No one goes near the stream except over the bridge for brief flashes, self-contained in their separate vehicles, rushing to get anywhere else.

Lacing around and over the stream are the hard veins of highways and small, rough roads that are a staple of the Central Valley, where billions of tons of agricultural products are transported at all hours. The highways providing this mass movement unnaturally carve the landscape up into sections. The animals living there must cross the roads or remain trapped, unable to mate outside their family groups or find food outside the perimeter. Sometimes, even if they do make it across, the monoculture crops on the other side are equally limited, equally fenced in by highways.

For a moment in the California legislature there was some small talk of building access roads for wildlife. These "green highways" arch over or tunnel under (depending on the species), so wildlife can cross without risking the roads. But in the conservative Central Valley, there is little interest in preserving wildlife, not when human life is barely surviving. Once these farms belonged to individual families, but the land has been eaten up by Big Agro, the agricultural mega-corporations. Farmers are still required to run the machines that till and seed the soil, but no longer earn a living wage for their labors.

The few projects proposed in Sacramento to appease more liberal constituents in the cities tended to end at the point where funding would have begun. The dwindling animal populations remained divided, starving from lack of food, falling ill as a result of forced inbreeding, or risking the asphalt, often leaving their crushed and abandoned bodies dotting the road.

Lying forgotten by farmers and shunned by animals, the stagnant water of the stream is dank with the runoff from the roadkill crematorium that broods over it like a hanged man from a branch. The impoverished farmer who works the eighty acres that surround it had complained about the smell that hangs thick in the air around the crematorium like rancid perfume trapped in an elevator. But this land is owned by the richest, most powerful agricultural corporations, and when the farmer calls, he is met with redirections and then letters informing him his complaints have been noted but, unfortunately, no action can be taken at this time.

And so the crematorium grinds through its work uninterrupted, while the stream and its stench languish.

Remnants of the steady diet of the crematorium float on the surface of the stream. The stream is black at its deepest points, with eerie, iridescent swirls congealing at the shallower depths of the shoreline. It is beautiful except for its wrongness, its unnaturalness. Nothing but algae can survive in it. The fish died years ago; the frogs and insects have long since emigrated to less toxic waters.

The stream has nothing to do with life, now. But, like all of nature—it adapts.

Rachel had two left fingers on the steering wheel of her 2005 Ford Focus sedan, her right hand cradled in her lap. Her eyes rested vacantly on the road. She had been driving north for hours.

The road unrolled in front of her with endlessly repeating farmland and orchards blurring by on either side. The sun was moving west sluggishly. She'd stopped once for gas and a tired burrito at one of the run-down travel centers. The heavy-set Latina who gave her change never smiled or spoke. The woman was trapped in a town no one wanted to live in. There probably wasn't much to smile about.

Sometimes on these long trips through the blankness of the Central Valley, Rachel tried to imagine the lives of the people in these dusty, depressing towns, in their drab motorhomes and tract houses. She'd see these homes lined up in little groups like bands of survivors as she passed on the highway. Some were well-kept, with a certain kitschy charm if you liked that kind of thing. Most, however, seemed to shrink into the tall, waving grasses no one cut, possessing several abandoned cars skirting them like rusting monuments to a lost civilization.

When she imagined the interiors, they always looked like her great grandmother's mobile home. Pictures of family members who didn't visit hung like "before" photos to the "after" of her life. Rachel felt uncomfortable in the yellowing kitchen. The linoleum had a bubble in one corner from water leaking underneath the sink, and sun-bleached gnomes with frozen smiles stood on the small patch of decorative gravel outside. Inevitably, guilt over not having visited her grandmother in forever would surface during these trips through towns like the one her grandmother lived in.

Because without articulating it, she hated visiting—hated the poverty, hated the smallness of her grandmother's slowly collapsing life. Her grandmother had loved the outdoors and working in a small antique store within walking distance, but as her strange illness progressed, she became increasingly homebound. After she broke a hip tending to the garden, she was wheelchair-bound as well. Her life dwindled into watching television and caring for the few plants she'd been able to bring inside. After the hip accident, while she was in the hospital, the rest of the garden died, the plants untended in their planters. That's when the gravel had been installed, the gnomes no longer surrounded by tomatoes, celery, basil, and rosemary.

Rachel swiftly slammed a mental lid on the image and redirected her attention back to the road.

She was good at that—*compartmentalizing*, her therapist called it. She had to be, working in the home foreclosure business. She was a trim, mousy-haired woman in her early thirties, with a long face, and looked older than her age. She worked as a legal assistant at Griffin, McAllister and Steinman, LLC. She had been hired there during the housing crash, and as a freshly graduated communications major from an average college, she wasn't in a position to be choosy. She learned to compartmentalize when coworkers joked about fielding calls from desperate people being evicted—one from an elderly man on an oxygen tank as he stood outside what used to be his home. It was a job, she needed it, end of discussion. And, as her mother had always warned, you have to work somewhere at least three years before moving on or you won't find another place to hire you.

Her therapist had gently challenged her when she had quoted this after a long session of describing how much she disliked (she didn't use *hate,* hate was just such an extreme word) the people she worked with. But Rachel remained convinced. Five years later, it was still a job—and it kept her from living in mobile homes in towns like these.

Soon she'd be at her modest, practical apartment, and could warm up that frozen pizza she'd had the good sense to buy before the trip, knowing she'd be numb and exhausted when she got back. It never occurred to Rachel to order delivery—her mother had been against spending money on frivolities, too.

There were the distinctive Sutter Butte mountains to the left—looming and solitary figures on the landscape, out of place in the surrounding flatlands. She was coming up on the last stretch. *Two more hours till I'm home,* she thought in weary relief.

The twilight deepened. The sun was lingering behind a mountain range so distant that it seemed a mere suggestion, one side of a plowed furrow. The farms surrounding the area had long suffered from the nearly decade-long drought. Amid the usual "Jesus Saves" and scrawled, hand-painted placards proclaiming "Family Farm Jams—Fresh!" One showcased a conservative politician with boxing gloves and a macho expression promising to fight for Central Valley families. Rachel passed other signs denouncing the "Congress Created Dust Bowl" and asking, "Is Growing Food Wasting Water?"

Rachel was far removed from these lives, but she did feel for them, although a part of her (the part that might have used the word *hate*) wondered why they didn't just leave and go somewhere else. In this economy, you did what you had to do. An image of her gray cubicle in the tall building flashed through her mind. She had tried to decorate her cubicle a little—pens with plastic flowers taped to the top; a small picture of wildflowers in a vast prairie, half-buried behind her stack of paperwork; and a poster with a kitten that reminded her to "Count Your Blessings." And always her supervisor, Charlie, leaning over the partition and "delegating" most of the "team's" workload to Rachel (we all have to do our parts, as you know).

*Sure, my part and your part and some of Desi's part as well.* She brushed that thought away. She was still on the weekend until tomorrow.

Her muscles ached, especially her forearms and right leg. The arm brace, which she wore sometimes to relieve the tendonitis she'd earned from slaving away over a keyboard, helped a little.

She stopped briefly at a rest station and got out of the car. Her legs had forgotten how to work and with shooting pains in her joints and muscles, she stumbled toward the soapless bathrooms. Rachel hoped this one at least didn't have flies and streaks of mystery liquid around the seats. She always prayed it was from the toilet bowl spray, but you never really knew.

The sun was gone by the time she was back on the road. Between large expanses of cloud cover the stars were slowly creeping into existence. Sparsely positioned streetlights flickered on and illuminated small pools of the darkening road. Telephone poles disappeared into the night except as brief apparitions when her car headlights illuminated them and then were gone again. There were fewer cars than normal. She saw all this subconsciously. Mostly she was thinking about her bed and wondering if Rob, her boyfriend, had cheated on her while she was gone—again.

The smell hit her first. A rank smell of death and rot and meat gone bad.

"Oh my goodness," she said, startled into speaking out loud as she scanned for the source.

Sour-smelling cow farms were part of the Central Valley experience, with thousands of miserable beasts standing in their own manure, packed shoulder-to-shoulder, waiting for the slaughter. But this was a different smell, one she had noticed before on previous trips, but never so strongly, never with such a presence.

The smell grew until it filled the car. She hit the air recirculation button, but the stench crept in relentlessly. Once, back in college when she'd had her old Honda Civic, a mouse had crawled into the A/C filter and died there. The smell had been so overwhelming that every time she got in the car she'd seriously considered getting it towed to the shop. But having no money, she did her best to just breathe out the window until she finally saved enough to get the mouse removed. This smell was like that, like breathing right next to death.

There—on the right. Small lights blinked on a towering smokestack, with a small warehouse hunched beside it. In the pulse of the lights she could see great billows of smoke belching from the head of the silo, like the streaming hair of a waterlogged corpse. She had heard rumors that all the roadkill in the surrounding area was cremated nearby—this must be the place. All the dogs, cats, raccoons, deer, snakes, rabbits, skunks—they all ended up here, their lives cut short and consigned to the flames.

Her own dog, Miles, had run away and disappeared when she was twelve. Her mom had driven for hours around the sprawling country roads surrounding their house with Rachel and her sister, Lauren, hanging out the windows of the car, calling for him over and over.

Rachel's mom was a thin, anxious woman with eyes like a deer. She was terrified of disappointing anyone, so she had driven them around until well after dark, stopping here and there to let them look on foot.

With her small hands cupped around her mouth to amplify the sound, her eyes searching the hills, Rachel hadn't noticed the small lump until she stepped in it, with a squelching sound and a sensation of stepping into mud and sticks. Leaping back, she trained her beam downward.

The rabbit she'd stepped on had been dead a long time. Its eyes were gone, picked out by vultures, its intestines shredded on the asphalt and partially eaten. Rachel loved rabbits. She had always wanted her own after holding one's soft, shaking body at a 4-H event. Mom had off-handedly said she could have one in eighth grade, assuming

Rachel, at that time in fourth grade, would forget—but she was still waiting to have her own pet rabbit.

Looking closely, she saw small white maggots in its side, raising their heads up occasionally, as though they were turning to stare at her but only had the strength for a few seconds like a baby unable to hold its head upright. They were wriggling in the depression where the rabbit's ribcage had shattered on impact, flattened by the car's tires.

Like a zoom on a camera coming into hyper focus, she looked at her foot, and saw a maggot had fallen on top of her pink sparkly sneaker when she'd stepped on the corpse.

Screaming, Rachel frantically scraped the side of her shoe on the grassy embankment, her flashlight bobbing crazily, carving up the night. Mom and Lauren came running. That ended the search for Miles.

At home, Rachel scrubbed her foot viciously in the shower, searing tears washing down the drain for both Miles and the rabbit (and herself, in that way children have of viewing their pain from the outside in awe, as though they are the misunderstood heroine of a tragedy).

With her foot rubbed raw, she felt weary with grief. Her mother threw out the shoes rather than try and deal with them—she'd read on the internet that rabies can survive in dead bodies for months.

With a smirk, Lauren asked, "Rabies? Nobody gets rabies from a rabbit." Lauren enjoyed proving she was not as big a fool as her mother.

Mom snapped at Lauren to go to her room and stop traumatizing her sister. Lauren's smirk faded and she stomped off. Mom started following and immediately apologizing for having been unhealthy in her communication.

Rachel ran to her room and cried herself to sleep.

They never did find Miles. It would be years before Rachel stopped dreaming of him crushed on the road's shoulder, turning to look at her with picked-out cavities instead of eyes.

She didn't notice the bridge.

Small and insignificant, it blended in with the rest of the landscape and didn't merit her tired attention, now under assault from that awful smell. Her weak beams barely illuminated the road—she needed to replace those bulbs again, they were always burning out. She'd never had a car burn out headlights so quickly. *Next time I'm getting a Japanese car*, she thought irritably. She squinted at the road.

The ghastly smell swelled until it filled the car. The dead mouse had been nothing to this creeping fume. The smell was so thick it was like a fog bank, taking up space in the car previously unoccupied. *The dang car doors must be loose again. Or could be the whole re-circulation system is messed up.*

"For heaven's sake!" Rachel muttered. She popped a sample bottle of pumpkin spice hand disinfectant and rubbed her hands with it, dabbing a bit on her upper lip. It immediately started burning like hell. She gasped and swiped her hand under her nose, which smeared the disinfectant over more of her face. Her eyes welling up from the alcoholic fumes, she frantically reached down for a tissue and the last dregs of her water bottle, keeping the wheel straight with one knee.

She'd crossed over the bridge by the time she'd managed to jerk a Kleenex free and sit upright again. She happened to glance in the rearview mirror, preoccupied with getting the disinfectant off her face, quickly looking forward again to make sure she wasn't veering too far to the sides—when it sunk in. She'd seen something.

Something in the rearview mirror—something in the backseat.

Rachel froze, eyes straight ahead on the road, Kleenex against her face, her left hand white-knuckled on the wheel. Fear hit her stomach like a brick. Every childhood story whispered at slumber parties came back to her—of women alone and unaware in cars, with dark men looming up unseen behind them.

*Good grief,* she thought. *Stop being dramatic. Stop being your mother.*

Darting a glance over the shoulder of the chair, she swiftly scanned the backseat. In the yellow sweep of the streetlights every ten seconds, she could make out a crushed sun hat, some wrappers, a thermos, the cast-aside Kleenex box.

Ordinary. Safe.

"Nothing," she said loudly, turning back. "Just the regular crap you always bring too much of. Idiot."

Wide awake now, she reached out a trembling hand and, turning on the radio, she pushed *scan.*

Like the geography throughout the valley, radio stations shifted on the dial, but essentially remained the same. The station options were: several country; at least two religious, with empathic and outraged preachers; one Top 40 pop; one classic rock and one classical; and a few mariachi bands trilling joyfully, bolstered in their enthusiasm by ridiculous brass.

But while there were the distant sounds of preachers, mariachi bands, and country music, each was drowned out by an insistent, scratchy static, as though sandpaper were being rubbed against their throats. This was unusual—even in remote areas of the valley, a few stations were always able to get through.

After about a minute of cycling through station after station dead with static, she gave up and turned the radio off again.

Out of nowhere, a massive truck zoomed up behind her, the kind of hyped-up compensation for insecure manhood that dominates the backroads and highways of rural California. He (it's always a he) roared up till he was practically bumper to bumper, the massive tires lifting the truck's searing bluish headlights so they glared directly into her mirrors.

"Ow—what the heck!"

Rachel righteously kept to the speed limit, her eyes bleached by the ferocious light. She glared into the rearview mirror, further scarring her retinas, too mad to care. You're just going to have to wait, sir. No dotted yellows for a while yet. Rachel's family all wore glasses. She'd escaped the need for years, but now, in her early thirties, she had noticed how difficult it was to drive at night. Lights from oncoming cars would be haloed strangely, and her eyes would strain to determine how far away they were. It made passing nearly impossible.

Lately it had gotten so bad, she would accept that she couldn't understand where the lights were coming from, and could barely see the road through the glare. She'd begun leaving earlier in the day to avoid driving too long at night, but she'd gotten a late start on this trip. So when jerks like this truck rode her rear end, she was afraid and angry, knowing it would harm her ability to see even further.

Finally, the driver had his chance and, roaring into high gear, he zoomed around Rachel's little car. Rachel glared up at the driver, a twenty-something bro with in a baseball cap with white decals of naked women on his tailgate. He ignored her.

"Typical," she muttered. Glancing in the rearview mirror she saw the distortion again. She stared in the mirror, transfixed.

She saw what appeared to be a large, luminous being, resting in one of the dark corners of the backseat. It looked like light haloed through misty rain, almost an aura. And like fog in the sun, it dissipated as she focused on it.

Fear curled at the nape of her neck like a coiling rope. It must be the retinal blowout I got from that car, she told herself. It had to be.

Turning to look back over her shoulder again, she saw—darkness. Dark seats, indeterminate piles, and a few stars in the night out of her back window. There *was* that burn on her retinas. It must have been that. She rubbed her eyes wearily.

Rachel had been putting off going to the ophthalmologist. She told herself it was because she didn't want to fork over the money but, really, she had a deep-seated fear she would end up blind like her grandmother. After her fall, her grandmother had developed an eye disease where she saw showers of light in her vision, bright blinding lights that could not be avoided by closing her eyes. She could remember visits being cut short, she and her sister shushed out the door as her grandmother, confined to her room at the far end of the dark hallway, wailed in agony under the attack of her own eyes.

Her embarrassment over being afraid of nothing was increasingly wiped out by fear, and she gave in to it. With a trembling hand and her eyes completely off the road, she reached up and adjusted the mirror to the left, seeing only darkness, and a few blips of headlights in the far distance coming over the road. Then to the right—again, nothing she could see. Slowly, instinctively, she looked up.

It was on the ceiling.

Time slowed down as adrenaline shot into her bloodstream and her brain reeled in an attempt to understand what it was seeing. She felt like she was at the end of a long tunnel, where she couldn't hear the rumbling of the car or the low whistle of the wind ripping at the car door's cracks.

With white wisps haloing it, the figure was the shape of a human torso, cut off at the waist. Above the torso, she saw what was undeniably a face, with a snout like a wolf's. Numbly she registered enormous catlike eyes with the greenish reflecting sheen of animal eyes in flash photographs, unfocused but staring in her direction. There was a foaming cut where the mouth should have been. The face shifted, contorting into various animals, none completely recognizable as any one creature. Rachel's comprehension ricocheted back into her, and she screamed.

It drifted down into the passenger seat beside her.

"What are you? What do you want?" Rachel was swerving on the road, the dut-tu-tu-duh-tu-tu of her car tires skidding over the ribbing on the road's barriers a warning that she was too far out of the lane, but Rachel hardly noticed in her panic.

The being's mouth opened, ghostly fangs rimming a dark hole, and she saw through to the window on the passenger side. It exhaled, the foulest stench of decaying, charred bodies with the horror of rotten meat. Its breath reached into her nostrils and filled her throat like cotton.

She gagged and slammed her hands against the window as her brain screamed GET OUT! GET OUT NOW! Tears pricked her eyes as she struggled to breathe.

The wraithlike being lifted its deformed, twisting face and roared.

It roared with the force of every wounded predator's fury against the vultures picking before it is dead, like every bellow of pain, every panicked scream of an animal trying to pull itself off the road when half of it won't come. It roared out pure terror and agony.

Rachel shrieked again and flung herself back, hands flailing against the air as she recoiled as far away as she could. It wasn't far enough.

The car tires squealed as the wheels swerved. The car twisted violently, careening at 80 mph off the road. It rolled, and rolled.

The highway technicians were nearly done with Monday's route. They were close to the animal crematorium, ready to begin unloading an average pile of possums, raccoons, cats, and other animals they'd collected. They'd stopped to scrape up one last gopher before dumping for the day, as the sun had almost set. Accustomed to scanning the roads, they had both noticed the fresh skid marks half a mile back with a trail of glass shards and shattered bits of fender and rubber. But they hadn't seen the wreck itself and decided it must have been hauled off already.

Opening the truck door and stepping down to grab the gopher, the younger and twitchier highway technician paused next to it and then shouted, "Rich—there's the wreck! Over there!"

He pointed off the side of the road to the stream that divided Monday and Tuesday's route of death collection. Stocky and no-nonsense, Rich shook his head.

"There's no way it could have been the same wreck," he said. "This is almost a half mile from those skid marks." Rich was not one for foolish talk or speculation.

Donny stared at the mangled car, wide-eyed. "I dunno, Rich, remember that wreck last year? The bad one, with the kids?" His voice dropped to a whisper. "It was right around here too."

"Shut up, Donny, you dumbass. I ain't listening to your spook stories no more."

"I'm telling ya. I said it before and I'll say it again. There's something not right about this stream."

"Say it again to somebody else, jeez. C'mon, we gotta call the people technicians." It was their morbid joke. The highway techs cleaned up the dead animals, the people techs cleaned up the dead humans.

In the half-submerged car, Rachel's face was pressed hard against the wheel, mouth slack, her open eyes unable to see anything anymore.

Unnoticed by the two men sitting above, reeking bubbles rose up in the oily stream where the car and the woman's trapped body lay in the ghastly remains of all the other roadkill.

They smoked as they waited by the bridge, while the sun slowly set and sirens began wailing in the distance.

And beyond the bridge, the crematorium waited for its next feeding.

# TRINIDAD

by
Jessica Palmer

The beauties of the Raton Pass into Colorado assail the eye and awe the spirit as one crosses from one state to another, for all but the driver who must circumnavigate a series of sharp curves.

The passengers marvel at the view.

Billboards greet the innocent traveler with aphorisms about the town of Trinidad: "The Best of the Wild West" and "The friendliest place on earth." False advertising.

The vista broadens where the interstate meets the city. The Rockies retreat to the west while pine-clad, flat-topped Fischer's Peak towers overhead. Church spires stretch to the heavens. An idyllic sight that even the driver can view in wonder.

*Don't be deceived.*

The visitor's eyes reach for the blue bowl of the sky flanked by mountains and sandstone cliffs. A glance to the side reveals cobbled streets and buildings frozen in time, dating back to the late eighteenth and early nineteenth centuries. The town boasts the amenities—McDonalds, Pizza Hut, Wendy's, Sonic, all the fine eateries—even a Walmart. These were discreetly tucked away under the highway overpass. Nothing to ruin the pristine image of the old west. Nothing to deter the unwary traveler.

Trinidad allows easy access, but this too is misleading. Downtown is a rabbit warren of one-way streets that turn in upon themselves. Signs leading to the interstate vanish with no entrance in sight.

The happy-go-lucky tourist might be tempted to stay.
*This is what they want you to do.*

Lydia drove along the back roads from Alamogordo on I-25 on her way to Colorado. This trip would be the last. She hated the drive. To arrive for the one o'clock close, she'd had to leave at five in the morning. Two hundred miles through the desert without access to either a restroom or a gas station. So, no coffee. Each trip required planning. This time it was far worse. She'd rented a van to carry the livestock and their cat boxes, along with those breakables that never seemed to survive a move.

Blessedly, the rental was air conditioned.

She reviewed in her mind all that she had done, wishing she could eliminate this niggling sense of doubt. She assured herself that she had others on her side representing her interests: The Realtor, the mortgage company, the inspectors. Her inspector had passed everything—plumbing, fireplace, roof, building structure, foundation, and wiring. The mortgage company had also hired an inspector who provided a history of the building. A few alarm bells clanged inside Lydia's head when she read the report. The property had been bought and sold five times in as many years.

The turnover in owners could easily be explained by flippers, and by the time Lydia obtained the information it was too late to act.

Before she made an offer, she'd been thorough in her investigation of the town: census statistics; economy; overall crime rates; history, or what there was of it. She even called the police department to make sure her street was safe.

The officer affirmed her street was secure, although the cross street, a busy road that led directly to I-25, was not. Since the houses on either side of hers faced the street, she thought she was safely nestled between the two and away from danger.

Her welcome to the neighborhood was less than friendly. She and her agent were evicted from one parking place to another until they had to park half a block away from her house. Meanwhile, the seller loaded furniture one piece at a time into one pickup at a time.

Consequently, Lydia could not inspect the home or unload the cats so they wouldn't roast in the van under the hot sun. The Realtor said she fought with the seller about the curtains, which the woman was removing. When Lydia was allowed inside, it was after the close of the business day, and the real estate agent had left while the seller was still moving.

Earlier, the Realtor had asked Lydia if she accepted the house. She replied, "No, not until I can inspect it."

When the seller left at 7 p.m., Lydia was alone to discover the woman had taken everything, light bulbs, toilet paper—even the screws and brackets for hanging the curtains. Even the rods from the closets were missing. The seller had a go at removing the towel racks, but she left the religious homilies behind.

Meanwhile, the people hired to unload the van damaged the lamps she had hoped to salvage. She felt ill, unable to breathe because of the heat. She tried to splash water on her parched skin and the faucet fell off in her hand. She released the cats, set up their scratching posts and waited in the darkness for the movers to arrive.

First thing in the morning, she called the title company and said no dice, she didn't accept this house as is. It was too late. The real estate agent had accepted the condition of the home on Lydia's behalf, and without her consent. The only legal recourse was to sue the seller. Then Lydia contacted the seller's agent. The previous owner had done a runner, taking the check and leaving with no forwarding address.

Lydia captured the cats and placed them in their carriers so they would not escape when the movers turned up. They yowled in protest. The movers appeared and the circus began accompanied by a chorus of disgruntled cats.

Within the first twenty-four hours, Lydia learned none of the plumbing worked. The toilets ran. In the light of day, she lifted the lid to the tanks and found that the mechanism had been mangled. The drains were at best dodgy. There was no hot water. Faucets wobbled and fell off.

Once the movers were gone, she wandered around her house wondering what she had done to herself. The recently freed cats paced and she listened to the sound of snapping wood popping *inside* the walls.

The structure was not sound.

Light bulbs placed in fixtures sparked and blew out. The wiring was not okay.

The inspector was batting a thousand. So far, he hadn't gotten a damn thing right.

The arrival her bulbs with the movers also allowed her to see her face for the first time. She noted all the signs of sunstroke when she was on the curb awaiting entry to her home. Lydia's face was red and swollen, and she found a red mark on her eyelid indicative of a spider bite—either brown recluse or black widow. Both were native to Colorado.

*Crack!*

She stared at the ceiling over her head. It was then that Lydia realized she was doomed.

The old man drove along the interstate from Pueblo back to Trinidad—the pickup bed littered with detritus of pool supplies. The radio played "A Boy Named Sue." He bellowed to the tune.

He was always picking up supplies for his pool. Today's purchase was second-hand. The pieces and parts rattled every time he took a corner a little bit fast.

*This better work.*

Dave Williams enjoyed his little outings. His house was usually littered with human flesh. The Quintana brothers, Juan and Jose, worked around his house, fixing this, that and the other thing. In the end, they'd trashed the garage and littered the yard, with the excess dumped on the adjacent property. The place resounded with sawing, hammering, and the voices of people crawling on his roof.

All he wanted was a *goddamn pool*. The ladies loved it.

Overall, though, Dave liked the parade of family, other Quintanas, brothers, father, their wives and progeny, brothers of brothers, miscellaneous cousins and friends. It was hard to keep track. He didn't really care. He watched and enjoyed the unfolding drama.

Dave slowed infinitesimally as he approached an exit, cast his gaze sideways. Some might look for speed traps. Dave was looking for hitchhikers.

He sighed and farted.

Another exit.

He took his foot off the accelerator. The vehicle coasted. Two people were crouched next to the ramp.

*What the fuck were they doing here in the middle of nowhere?*

He swore in English and Spanish. He swerved with a hard right onto the ramp and hurriedly rolled the window down to air out the cab. Pool parts crashed around in the truck bed. He braked in preparation for a stop. A middle-aged man and a plump woman sat opposite on the curb. A sign proclaimed: "Viet Nam Vet."

The old man cruised through the stop sign without checking for vehicles. Not here. Not where the prairie stretched for miles.

As he sped up the ramp, he thought: *Not his type. Not his type at all.*

Dave Williamson liked the ladies. Young, fresh, tender as they had been his youth. The dollies, that's what *he* wanted.

The mountains around Trinidad have been carved hollow with mines. The county government lists fourteen mining disasters with a cumulative death toll of well over four-hundred. John D. Rockefeller, Jr., owned controlling interest in the mines. When the miners called upon the unions, the militia surrounded their camps and killed many, including women and children, in the Ludlow Massacre.

Lydia huffed. The citizens voted for Trump in the last election, the only county in Colorado to do so. One would think the miners and their descendants would have learned to distrust the wealthy.

The breathtaking scenery disguised a toxic environment. It was populated by cruel people shaped by a ruthless history. Trinidad was a tight-knit community, where families take care of their own and the rest be damned.

And the souls of the dead walked the streets by night.

The peeper pressed his eye against the hole conveniently supplied by Williams. Located in the closet, it gave a panoramic view into the bathroom and the adjacent bedroom. He peered at the couple making love. He was forbidden from using the peepholes, but what others didn't know wouldn't hurt them.

The first week after Lydia moved there, the city of Trinidad had a record hail storm. Electrical service was, at best, dodgy. As more of the house was revealed by emptying boxes, Lydia found holes in the walls where wires were cut and left exposed. Another thing not noticed by the inspector. Elsewhere, she saw burns in the carpet, as if the previous homeowner, with her no-smoking signs on the front door, had used the floor as an ashtray.

The hail melted and the temperatures soared to an unprecedented high of over one hundred degrees.

Her neighbors, those who spoke with her, warned Lydia about Williams and the Quintana brothers who lived next door. Drug dealers, they said. She paid little heed to small-town gossip.

Lydia had other things on her mind besides her neighbors. She didn't care what they did on their property as long as they left her alone. However, she had noticed that the neighbor often brought young hitchhikers home.

*The ladies went into the house and never came out.*

The pace in Trinidad was slow. It took three weeks to get cable, phone, and internet connection, access to the outside world. She called the cooling specialists, the plumbers, the builders, her Realtor, and the inspector. She got a chilly reception from the latter two.

Some, the more greedy, she cajoled into putting her on the list for repairs. Each did little or nothing. Each had call-out charges. Each tried to sell her a four-digit replacement rather than do a simple repair. Each had to be called out multiple times to fix their so-called fixes. Each overcharged for their services. Most called her crazy when she suggested a repair meant an item should work.

The city inspectors refused to help, making jokes at her expense. One city employee told her that she had no right to speak with the building inspector. The government would be no help, but governments never are. They were designed to be deaf to the pleas of the citizens.

One morning, Lydia went out to check the mail, usually a depressing mix of her ever-mounting bills and the collection notices intended for the previous resident. Her jaw clenched. The box had been bashed flat. The broken flag lay on the ground, surrounded by shredded pieces of mail. She called the police.

The officer exited the vehicle and advanced upon Lydia. "Yes, ma'am, what can we do for you?"

She pointed mutely to the smashed box.

"Happens all over town. Not even worth writing up," he said.

Stunned, she gestured at the shredded mail scattered along the sidewalk.

"That's a postal matter. I suggest you report it to the post office."

The screen door in the adjacent house opened. Williams stepped out on his porch, a smirk on his face. The door slammed shut behind him. The cop looked up.

Color drained from his face. "Ah, er," he stammered. "We're very b-busy. If there's nothing else."

The officer nodded to Williams and returned to his vehicle without giving Lydia a second glance.

She added a new mailbox to her growing list.

Lydia visited the Chamber of Commerce. The receptionist scowled when Lydia posed her question. "The Chamber won't make recommendations for any local contractors."

"Aren't they members?" asked Lydia.

"Well, yes, but…" The reception glanced nervously around the empty room. "The official response is we can't afford accusations of favoritism. The truth is you can't trust them. Not a single one. They demand payment up front and won't finish a project, assuming," she chuckled, "they ever show up."

She considered Lydia. "They target the elderly, widows, and the disabled, you know. They get a 'special'—" she raised her hands in the air, index and middle fingers extended to bracket the word—"rate."

Lydia stiffened. "I hardly consider myself old."

"You live alone, don't you? You have no family here or you wouldn't be looking for a contractor. And you're a woman. Sorry, dear, the only way to get something repaired in this town is if you happen to have a skilled relative. You could try another town, like Pueblo."

"With their five-hundred-dollar call-out charges," said Lydia.

"Out of state, maybe, like Raton."

Lydia's eyes narrowed. Trinidad was a hostile environment where the vulnerable were prey.

The city borrowed its history from the fables of the Wild West, claiming connection to the likes of Bat Masterson, Kit Carson, and Billy the Kid. Butch Cassidy and the Sundance Kid hid from the law in the mountains surrounding the Raton Pass. Black Jack Ketchum was executed in Trinidad.

*Wild West* was an apt description, a time and a place where officials operated on both sides of the law. Lawman one day, paid killer the next. While the powerful acted for the city, they lined their pockets and flouted the ordinances against gambling, and frequenting or possibly owning bawdy houses.

Bat Masterson was sheriff of Trinidad for a year, but he was ousted for his extracurricular activities. Kit Carson and Billy the Kid, to whom the city fathers laid claim, traveled through Trinidad along the Santa Fe Trail, but most often, they had traversed the plains branch favored by cattlemen.

The town's official history ignored the Native Americans, who had populated the region since Paleolithic times.

The Purgatoire River ran through Trinidad. The name, Rio de Las Animus Perdida en Purgitorio, meant River of Lost Souls and dated to the first expedition of the Spanish who were seeking the fabled city of Cibola. The story says gold was discovered at Spanish Peaks. The local tribes were enslaved, forced to work the mines, and then killed to keep the location safe. The caves are said to be haunted by their lost souls.

In the 1920s, Trinidad welcomed the Mafia. Al Capone evaded officials hiding in the tunnels and passages that had been dug beneath the city when the city fathers embraced morality. In a mining town when something needed to be hidden, dig deep. The doorways opened to local business where men could pass unobserved to the brothels and the speakeasies beneath the streets.

To this day, the catacombs often resounded with the soft chink of glasses, the louder clink of mugs, and the muted twitter of women. Intermittently a scream, soon silenced, pierced the night. The heavy footfall of boot-clad feet echoed inside the bowels of the town, followed by gruff voices repeating the password that gave entry to the dens of iniquity.

Once beneath the streets, city fathers sat beside miners. Both claimed a need for relief in the moonshine that flowed through the city and release in the arms of a woman not one's wife. Most would wake up the next day to attend church and mouth the words of a hymn or a prayer that they did not believe and listen to sermons they did not heed.

Hatred stirred in the mines above Trinidad. It walked on all fours, although once it might have been human. Love had motivated it then, but revenge powered it now. It recalled the betrayal of the city fathers and those in authority against the land and the people.

Water splashed under its not-quite-feet. The stream led to the cave mouth and wound its way downhill. The creature carried malice and spite in its black heart. It peered through the opening to the twinkling city lights below.

Then the dark mist split, a portion sinking into the water with a bubble, a hiss, and the stench of rotting eggs. The rest returned to the tunnels.

Saws buzzed throughout the night. Sweat dripped into his eyes and blood splashed his face. A leg here, an arm there, until he had a nice, tidy little bundle to fit into the thirty-gallon trash bag.

The elder brother, Juan, wiped his face with a rag, stepped outside the shed, and sprayed himself down with the garden hose. He was tempted to hang the head next to the severed dolls' heads that adorned the perimeter of the yard, staring into its center with their blank eyes, but he squelched the impulse.

Instead, he stuffed the head into the bag, which he tossed into the dumpster to be hauled away the next day.

The peeper stood in the kitchen and watched his neighbor sleep. She kicked off the sheets to reveal an oversized T-shirt that bunched up around her waist.

It wasn't as much fun as leering at a young couple screwing, but it would have to do. They weren't getting many visitors of late.

The window provided the perfect vantage point from above where the peeper could gaze down on the unsuspecting sleeper. The old woman was defenseless.

She sat up, and Juan knew he had been caught. He walked over to the refrigerator and made himself look busy. He found a beer, left the kitchen, and waited.

All he had to do was walk a few feet from the back door, climb the fence, and . . .

The woman sat in her bed, choking and gasping for breath. She had allowed herself a late dessert. It was repeating on her. She leaned forward to let the fluid drain from her mouth and throat. She continued coughing to expel as much liquid as possible, and she prayed that she wouldn't end up with aspiration pneumonia.

She regretted the late-night snack on an already full stomach, but it had been something of a celebration of life for her, or as much as life allowed.

She sensed movement, glanced up and saw a face in the window peering down at her. The figure started, as if caught, and then it turned away.

*Spooky.*

She gasped and began to cough again.

Dave followed his friend into the kitchen. He glared at the neighbor. "Get rid of her," he said.

"You mean?"

"You've done it before. You know we can't work with her around. Get rid of her."

Juan nodded.

The peeper was bent over double, on all fours. His feet remained flat on the ground. His fingertips maintained his balance. He crab-walked, moving sideways, to ensure his head did not appear above the window frame. It was his nightly excursion, through the fence, along the side of a neighbor's building and into street.

He could stand upright once on the sidewalk; however, the former position was the more comfortable, less likely for him to trip over something he could not see. He skulked through yards and down alleyway, hugging walls, keeping close to the ground in open areas.

To pass unseen was a handy skill to have.

Lydia was seated in her bed when a head, or the top of one, floated by the window. She could see the baseball cap. It was cut off at the brim, revealing no face. The sill was four feet from the ground on the narrow strip of land between her home and the fence on the property line.

Her mouth dropped open. Either the person was extremely short or he was scraping along on all fours.

She waited for the hovering cap to vanish from view and slid out of bed to close the curtains...

The creature floated as a mist, searching for the way to the city below that did not require losing pieces of itself to the water or the wind. It represented not only the hatred, but the pain and fear of the many victims, for the specter embraced all who died in the mines.

From the first tribes whose heads were severed by the Spanish to still their tongue—to the miners were blown to pieces. Others perished more slowly. Those with burning lungs and limbs ablaze. Those who choked on noxious fumes and others who expired when the oxygen supply ran out. The creature contained the crushed bodies of the fallen and the spirits of the many who had had time to contemplate their inevitable fate.

The thing thought of itself as retribution. It was of the earth, and it was apart from it. It felt not only the sorrow of mortal souls, but the torment of the land. Much had been disturbed with the coming of the European and naught set right.

Thus, it became like the river of perdition that wound its way through the town's heart.

Lydia awoke night after night. Always in a cold sweat. Always at the same time. Lydia blamed her bladder. *Who knew that it would develop an every-two-hour schedule.*

She blamed her dreams. They scared the pee out of her. The dreams were always the same, or similar, presenting an identical theme. She would sit bleary-eyed while her mind unrolled the visuals for this night's folly.

One night she would be walking through the narrow hall when the floor opened before her feet. In each, though, Lydia ended up clinging to the walls to prevent falling into the crawl space below. The blackness drew her, the temptation to lean over the abyss to see what lay therein.

In other dreams, she listened to the crack of wood and watched the ceiling collapse in slow motion. Then the next moment, she was sitting up in bed, soaked to the skin and heart pounding in her chest. Her cats paced and dug at the walls as if trying to escape.

Sometimes when she woke, she heard the sound of hammering and construction next door, but always she saw the light in the kitchen window beating down on her and a person silhouetted from behind. Disembodied heads floated past her window. These traversed too close, too close to her window by far.

In the morning, the gates would be open, items missing from her yard or moved. The flowers she had planted, dug up, with the tag left behind to ensure she noticed the lack.

Leaping into abyss of her dreams was starting to sound like a good idea.

Most downtown businesses closed on a Saturday night, except the bars and the potteries. The natives got used to the sounds of brawls and occasional gunfire emanating from beneath the streets. The local junkies didn't notice.

Tourists who frequented the saloons after dark listened to the sound of muffled voices and giggling laughter. The woman eschewed the tavern, going instead to the greasy spoon next door. The waitress was in the process of closing up. She rearranged crumbs on the counter with a wet rag.

"Can I get a burger?"

"Grill's already clean," the waitress said.

"How about a piece of pie?" the tourist said.

"Okay, but don't take long. This place should've been closed a half an hour ago." The waitress slammed a plate in front of her and thrust a fork in her hand.

The woman cocked her to listen to the laughter and the tinny strains of Ta-ra-ra Boom-de-ay on a player piano.

She commented on the noise as her fork hovered over her pie. "This place is empty. Where are the voices coming from?"

The waitress glanced nervously at the basement door. "One of those tapes, you know. Some slick salesman from out of town sold it to the owner, told her the recording implanted a memory of a crowded establishment full of happy people and laughter."

"They have the same tape next door." The woman frowned. "And I can tell you it's not working. That place is as dead as a tomb."

The waitress shrugged. "Probably ran into the same slick salesman, and then there's acoustics in this place. It's a high ceiling. Sound carries."

A shot rang out from somewhere beneath her feet. The woman dropped her fork with a clatter. She called for her bill, thrust cash in the waitress's hands and fled into the growing dusk . . .

The sun set behind the mountain. Lydia checked her larder. The cupboards were bare and it was harder and harder to find money for food. Unless she scraped mold from the refrigerator walls and fashioned it into the shape of a festive, green turkey, she would have nothing to eat tonight.

She was out of cat food. *That would never do.*

Lydia settled behind the wheel, inserted the key into the ignition and turned it. The engine whined and groaned. The battery, purchased two months ago, was dead.

"Damn." She slammed the door.

*Bang, bang, bang!* She followed the sound of construction of the never-quite-completed shed being erected around the neighbors' crop of marijuana.

One of the brothers—the eldest by the look of him—jumped when she called across the fence. "Hello, can you help me? My battery is dead. Do you have jumper cables?"

His face blanched white under the dirt. He regained his composure. "Oh, yes, we noticed that. Wondered if you knew you left your car lights on."

Lydia kept her expression neutral. They knew and didn't tell her. "I didn't. I don't drive at night if I can possibly avoid it."

"Oh," he said.

"It must have been the Trinidad Welcome Wagon," she commented dryly as she contemplated the baseball cap pulled low over his forehead.

He turned and shuffled away.

The thing halted deep within the mines. The yellow mist had attained an almost human form, if not mass. It drifted here and there, with an arm or a leg vanishing into the wall. It carried the stench of Hades's fire, brimstone and damnation.

A faint bulge or swelling over what appeared to be bowed shoulders tilted to one side as the crash of gunfire cleaved the night. The creature spun, passed into a tunnel wall and headed in the direction of the blast.

Another soaked night, roused by some disturbance she knew not what, but sensed that left the coppery taste of blood and fear on her tongue. Lydia lifted her gaze to her neighbor's kitchen window and gaped. The neighbors' lights were on, but the blinds were closed. Every other night, she saw one of them standing there and staring down on her as if she were a bug under glass.

Sleeping with the lights on had become a habit for her. Once a matter of survival; she had to see her husband coming. The last two nights, though, she had opted for lights out.

Tonight, the cats slept peacefully at her side. Her eyes scanned the bedroom. With the lights out there was nothing to see.

The fact that the neighbors closed their blinds in response only seemed to confirm what Lydia long suspected. They were watching her, and the floating heads and the late-night excursions were not her imagination.

Voyeurism was a crime of power and intimidation, where arousal was derived from spying on others unseen. The object was to observe people in their most defenseless, most vulnerable moments.

*When was an individual more helpless than during slumber?*

The Trinidad police were useless, adhering to the same work ethic as the citizen. Do as little as possible. Better do nothing at all. Laws were enforced when the victim was a person in power, a family member, or a friend.

A sign of the times when businesses hid behind governments, and computers, answering to no one. The reality was not only sanctioned by the political climate but supported by it. The company got tax breaks and the individual got screwed. Such was life.

Clearly, official channels would not help Lydia except to warn the perpetrator of her report. She wondered if law enforcement believed that the culprit would suddenly become nice. A perilous philosophy, to risk the life of the victim.

Retaliation was swift and immediate, and appropriate. Repairs dismantled. Security measures torn up.

Lydia gave up. She pretended it wasn't happening, as the police had.

With the lights off, the only way to watch her now was if they came into her yard and pressed their noses against the glass.

"Oh, gawd." She slapped her forehead and shuddered with dread.

Malice burbled down the mountainside, finding entry through the cracks and the crevices. The underground river fed the Purgatory as it had for centuries. Previous generations had used the spring as a safe source of water. The mines had contaminated it, and it was safe no more. So, the stream was forgotten, unacknowledged by the city that did not want to admit responsibility for the safety of the citizens nor confess to the poor quality of the town's water.

Malice might have experienced a mild annoyance if it could feel anything else than what it was. The sulfurous gas bubbled, breaking through the surface intermittently while angry townspeople reported gas leaks.

Malice followed the path of least resistance, down, down, down, letting gravity do the work. It missed its twin, who still clambered in the mines to commune with the spirit of the mountain. They would meet again soon enough.

Lydia strode through the house. She sniffed the air. She smelled something, garbage or sewer gas. She wondered if the septic line that she'd been asking her plumber to fix had finally ruptured.

She didn't want to deal with the utilities people again. They came out after her last report, with their meters and their tools, poking holes in the ground and treating her like a royal pain in the ass.

Malice continued with its downhill glide until it was blocked by a concrete wall. It sank into the earth, oozing under the foundations and into the crawlspace.

If it had had legs, it would have paced along the wall, seeking outlet. Instead, Spite released itself as gas and drifted up to the floorboards, but met resistance from the thick layer of insulation.

The creature was trapped, completely contained within the four walls of the home . . .

Still within the mine, its twin sensed the presence of another, one who understood. A spirit that knew betrayal and grief. The tang of fury, the bitter bile of hatred turned inward.

The creature reached out and engulfed the other, assimilated it, taking the soul unto itself.

Spring had begun with Lydia charged and ready to create the garden that was one of her goals. Last summer, her yard work consisted of killing the crop of weeds that seemed to be the only thing that grew in this soil. This year she had a blank slate.

She policed the yard for the neighbor's wastes daily. Glass glittered in the sun on the bare earth. She found bits of broken glass, pieces of rust barbed wire and old bed springs. Every time it rained, more rose to the surface.

She had wondered how long this phenomenon might last.

The couple that lived behind her house was doing as she did, as most people did when the weather turned mild, working in their yard. She stopped them and asked why so much broken glass and rusted metal.

"Don't you know? Didn't anyone tell you?" said the husband.

"Tell me what?"

"For decades before this house was built, the lot was used as an unofficial dumpsite. People would bring their garbage from miles around, and when the pile got too high, they'd douse it in gasoline and have a bonfire."

"This house was built in the seventies," she noted. "That means leaded gas."

"Yes, but nobody knew about lead pollution then."

"Yes, but people knew about lead poisoning," Lydia said.

"Well, it was all perfectly legal," added the wife

Lydia went back to the house and recoiled. A decapitated squirrel lay on her doorstep. On shaky legs, she walked into the house to get a pillow case in which she could wrap the corpse. The cats, now locked up in her bedroom, yowled in protest at their confinement.

"Quiet!" she shouted. She stooped to pick up the small body. The hair on the back of her neck rose. She turned slowly. Williams stood at the fence line, grinning at her.

Lydia sat in front of her computer, trying to put the poor creature out of mind. She concentrated on her original mission. Decades of cumulative gasoline poured upon her property. Her research indicated that the hydrocarbons had long since evaporated, but left lead, which would be leeched from the ground by judicious planting.

Okay, she thought, no vegetable garden this year, but maybe the next.

In the following days, Lydia soldiered on, buying and planting flowers to detoxify the soil. And trees. Lots of trees. Each new hole revealed the extent of the problem. She unearthed glass, with some bottles dating back to the early 1900s, two feet deep. Her heart sank.

She wanted a dog. The cats stayed inside, but she could not release a dog in this yard where the pads of its feet would be shredded.

Lydia had also unearthed coal, coal ash, and cinders covering the entire property. She had dismissed it. It was a coal mining community, after all, and Lydia remembered her parents spread ashes from the fireplace on the garden as a fertilizer. Charcoal was used as a neutralizer and a beneficial additive medically.

In the front, she dug her holes deep enough to accommodate the roots of the spruce. Within three inches of the surface she found huge chunks of coal. The more she dug, the more she found. She went to another location and began to dig. Same thing. Again, and again. And again. The entire front yard consisted of coal some three feet deep.

This was too much. She abandoned her tools and returned to her computer to look up coal, coal ash, and coal cinders online. She found that the legacy of coal is cobalt, arsenic, lead, mercury, bromide, cadmium, and thallium, to name only a few. The articles said that these chemicals lowered the IQ, caused birth defects, and poisoned the populace slowly.

It explained a lot, such as an entire community with the cumulative IQ of a carrot. It explained other things, too, like her steadily declining heath and her loss of strength. Ever since she had rid the yard of weeds and exposed the soil, Lydia had been breathing arsenic and lead.

Lydia contacted both federal and state environment protection agencies to see what she could do. Both confirmed what her neighbors had said. It wasn't illegal then and the city had never claimed it as a legal dump site. They could not be held accountable.

"I've been smelling gas lately," she informed the agent.

"If it was a dump site, one must presume that organic matter was also discarded there," he replied. "The decomposition would create a sulfurous odor very much like the additive used to give natural gas its scent. Happening so long ago, though, you wouldn't be held accountable either."

Another problem solved, if not satisfactorily. She didn't have to fix it, but she had to live with it.

Dave lumbered over to the shed.

Juan straightened. "What's up?" he asked.

"Clean up. We need to make a garbage run."

"Ya want me to get the trailer ready?"

"No, just bring the bag," Dave said.

A few minutes later, Juan joined his benefactor in front of the house. The door to the truck was open. His gaze went to the blanket spread across the passengers' seat. An icy finger ran up and down his spine. "What's this?"

"You're wet," said Dave.

Juan hefted the bag onto his shoulder and climbed into the cab. He settled on the seat, hauling the bag onto his lap.

The two drove in silence along Highway 12. Dave spoke for the first time when they were far enough away from town. "Time to start dumping. Hands first."

Juan grinned as he threw the hands, still attached to the arms, out the window. Next the legs.

Dave turned down a gravel road that ran along the base of the mountains. "We need to talk. You've been falling down on the job a lot lately. I thought I told you to get rid of her."

"I've tried, boss, but this bitch keeps calling the cops. You know I've used every trick."

"It doesn't seem to be working," said Dave.

"It's worked in the past," Juan grumbled.

"This woman is made of sterner stuff," Dave said. "I want her gone by the end of the month."

"It's not my fault," Juan protested.

Dave pulled over to the side of the narrow track. "Remember what happened to her," he indicated the bag on Juan's lap, "can happen to you."

Juan broke into a cold sweat as he slid from the pickup. "S'not my fault," he mumbled.

He extracted the head from the bag, dragged the top blanket from the vehicle and wrapped it up. Then with strength powered by adrenaline, Juan tossed the bag into the dense undergrowth far from the track.

They took the head to the state park . . . .

Her garden tools disappeared one by one. She took no note, for other facts had arisen during her internet research. Only handful of mines around Trinidad had been reclaimed. Each mine contributed a deadly gift.

Lydia slumped in her chair. She had chosen this house because it was no fixer-upper; it was safe, secure, and the right size. It had a fenced-in yard for a dog and room to grow vegetables, with space for an office if she ever started work again. Now she ran at breakneck speeds to stay ahead of the repairs, and she lived atop a toxic stew.

What had become of her intuition? Shouldn't she have received a warning from somewhere?

A divine bolt of lightning, or something?

She'd hope to mingle among the community. Now all she knew was anger and she hated them.

She stared at the blinking screen. She had given up so much to get here—a large chunk of her savings to buy the place and the rest in an attempt to make it safe. She hadn't expected to win popularity contests but it was not unreasonable that she might find peace. Instead she had been harassed and targeted.

Rage burned in her bowels. It had taken a while to get used to the idea that she could never get a dog. Even then, she'd comforted herself thinking that the condition of the soil was a temporary situation, but not when glass penetrated feet deep and chemicals measured in half-life permeated the ground. Her yard was toxic, unable to support the growth or life.

No safety, anywhere. Her home collapsing around her ears. No security with hostile neighbors living right next door. Not even the potential for income while her funds dwindled. Nothing to call her own.

Lydia stretched her arms toward the heavens to call down a curse upon the land that had taken so much from her.

Somewhere inside the mountain something stirred.

Lydia dropped her arms. No god would listen to her. The Almighty, she decided, was at best apathetic, at worst laughing up His silvery sleeve.

She deflated. She'd be better off dead.

Days came and went. Lydia remained inside the darkened house, with curtains closed and no desire to view the mountains. She had barely moved from her recliner except to fix another drink. The cats avoided her.

She dumped their food on the floor. She steered clear of the windows. There was nothing to see except the creepy little man who stalked outside her bedroom and the faces leering down at her from her neighbor's home.

Lydia didn't eat. What was the point? It would only prolong the agony.

If she slept at all it was to descend into inebriated slumber.

Lydia did nothing, for there was nothing she could do. Nothing would remove the toxins and the continual disintegration of her health. She inhaled the lethal cocktail daily.

Nothing would prevent the neighbors from calling her yard their own.

She gave up. She didn't care anymore.

Her hopes—even the semblance of them or the delusion that she might attain them if she worked hard enough—were gone. No dog. No garden. No income. No safety inside her home or outside of it. No justice. That required a certain measure of honesty on the part of the city fathers, which was lacking.

Trinidad was evil, pure and simple. Based on a malevolence that seeped into the soil and was ingested by the people until it rotted minds, and their hearts.

Lydia inhaled deeply. Her throat tightened at the ever-present stench of methane. She could only hope that her neighbors smelled it as well.

Her eyelids fluttered. Her psyche curled around the hard kernel of hate which was all Lydia had left. She stood, slid along the wall to the kitchen, and fixed herself another drink. She spun, overbalanced, and spilled it. She made another one.

Lydia stepped over the puddle, staggered through the dining room, and lowered herself into the chair. Her stomach rumbled, but she had no food. It was a waste of money, anyway. The only thing the refrigerator contained was a fretwork of grey fungus, along with her precious supply of rum and Coke.

Better to die by her own actions than let the house kill her.

She lit a cigarette and slipped into a waking dream, picking up the action exactly when and where she had left it. Lydia raged inside the mines above the city. She was not alone. Here she had found refuge. She found acceptance and comfort. Wrapped in the arms of darkness, she knew love, of a sort, a kindred spirit with a hatred for the city as strong as her own.

The walls around her began to vibrate and heave. Lydia rose and stumbled to the back room, her eyes still closed. Then she did something she had never been able to do before. She hefted the trap door to the crawl space and tossed it aside.

She lay down prone, listened to the trickle of water beneath her house, and shouted into the dark space. "I am sorry. You are trapped down there. I did not know. I set you free."

Lydia sat upright. Escaping gas hit her in the face. Wood snapped overhead. She threw back her head and laughed for the first time in weeks. A chunk of ceiling fell to the floor.

She crawled back to the recliner, grabbed another cigarette and lit it.

The world exploded around her.

The night manager checked the kitchen and wiped down tables and countertops. She helped herself to a drink as she tallied the night's take. Some nights, it was nice to be alone, without the clatter and clang of dishes and pans.

*This was not one of them.*

She lifted her head from the books and peered into the umbra around the basement door. The sound of human merriment penetrated to the first floor, with the clink of dishes and the soft imprecations of women.

The specters of Trinidad past were getting lively of late. The ghosts were popular with the tourists, but she wouldn't mind if the spirits would give it a rest.

The creature squeezed through the last crevice leading into the tunnel system under the city. It was not alone. Roaring laughter echoed through the halls.

Ladies leaned in open doorways. Some young and fresh, with slow brown eyes and ebony hair. Others old, with timeworn faces and hopeless, haunted expressions.

The apparitions reached out toward the specter, their arms passing through it. "Do you want a ride?"

They thrust out their breasts.

The creature adapted the form of the many it had known as they died in the caverns. They provided the specter, if not solidity, a measure of control.

Somewhere ahead, a brawl broke out. The sound that had drawn the creature thus.

And the walls under the city began to shake.

A fissure opened in the side of the mountain. It ran like fire, both down and across, linking mine to mine, mines through boiling aquifers into the city. Pockets of poison never meant to link crossed. The surrounding peaks collapsed into the valley.

Gases that accumulated over a century in the long-dead mines blew, expelled with such force both above and below that they filled the cracks and the crevasses inside the mountain.

The superheated air mixed with the clouds of dust overhead and fused the particles into sprinkling shards of glass. Nature was not finished with her defilers. The mountains left standing rocked back and forth. The city was engulfed under a shroud of gray.

The building shuddered above the manager's head. She grunted.
*The ghosts were getting too damned lively.*
She stepped outside and turned to lock the door behind her.
The buildings swayed. A piece of the old Trinidad Hotel toppled onto the pavement. Church spires did a slow dissolve.
She had been through this before.
*An earthquake, a damned earthquake.*
She ran into the empty street, hoping the falling debris would miss her. Her head swiveled on her neck, swinging this way and that. A pillar of flames shot into the sky from the area around Spanish Peaks, and Apache tears pattered down on the city.
The cooling drops of obsidian pelted her. She gasped, inhaling a mouthful of burning dust. The next thing she knew her lungs were on fire and the street buckled under her feet.
Then she knew no more.

Lydia drifted above her home. Fire buffeted her; it cradled her. She rode the conflagration, and she had never felt more serene.
She was gratified when the neighbor's garage, damaged in the last earthquake, split along the two-inch seam created then and collapsed into the eyesore of a shed where they grew their marijuana. The partially dismantled chimney disintegrated, plunging through the roof of the home.
Something in the junked trailer where it was rumored the neighbors cooked their crank detonated and pieces of metal shrapnel rocketed across the yard. One of the brothers, she could not see which, was skewered by a pipe. Piles of lumber burst into flame.
In the distance church spires toppled, a condemnation of the mountains' gods. Trinidad's precious historical buildings left stand-

ing for eventual repair crumbled and fell into the cavities made by man's greed.

Dark arms surrounded her and carried her away to the city center. A fracture cleaved Trinidad in two. The River of Lost Souls plunged into the resulting chasm with a mighty roar. More fractures formed, radiating outward like a spider's web. People erupted from their homes across the city and burst into flames, caught in the inferno of the pyroclastic blast. Their shrieks were cut short and they were consumed by the buildings' descent.

Lava cascaded from some of the breaks, and the entire valley shivered, like a dog trying to shake off a tick. With a final agitated flick it was done. The overpass folded in slow motion upon itself, and the mortal gods of Shell, Pizza Hut, McDonalds, and Walmart ceased to exist, while the interstate became a tangle of concrete and steel.

Lydia—or what was left of her—smiled as the earth swallowed the city whole.

# DESTITUTION TERMINATED

by
Catrin Sian Rutland

It started with the MicroOrbs, the so-called Bad Medicine, Brilliant Medicine. Everything had changed the moment they were released, and now we are left with this world. The MicroOrbs had been designed to kill the rich, the power-hungry, and the armies.

We are taught now that this was a noble idea, but it had failed in the initial stages. The intended had indeed died as desired. The rich, the evil, the violent, the greedy, and the richest of criminals were gone.

The drug had been created in two batches, the first designed to genetically modify victims and kill, the second batch to fix genetic abnormalities and improve health. The second batch had been tested on volunteers to prove its benefits; the rich had then clambered over each other in order to receive the drug. They received the killer drug but it took a while for them to die. The second batch was then given to the rest of the population, who saw cancers cured, heart disease become a thing of the past, and harmful mutations fixed.

Technically it was brilliant. Improve health and make wealth obsolete, and the population are happy. The concept was to use the money from the now-dead rich and power-hungry people to create equal and fair communities for the rest of the population. The creators had made some compounds in advance but the plan had been to create more communities, safe and peaceful places of equality and sanctuary.

The problem was that the world panicked. People hoarded food and water, gathered weapons, and started killing those around them.

Fear became rampant. With no authorities, no armies, police, or peacekeepers, the people desperately tried to stay alive, gathering what riches they could from the dead, and did not trust the company, Adpacemgenomics, which had created the MicroOrbs.

Dr Eliza Simpson who had designed the medicine had used the mantra 'One world, one cure, one peace', but only the cure part became reality. The world was divided, and war ravaged every village, town, and city. Dr Eliza had lived in the first Adpacemgenomics designed gated community, building the pharmaceutical company and entire community around her over the years prior to the Orb release.

At first glance the Adpacemgenomics looked fantastic. A company that cared so much about its employees that it housed them, had a small medical centre, shops, childcare, even a school on site. History showed that it was a great deal more than anyone would ever have realised. It had security, great glasshouses designed to grow food, and water collection and purification stations. It had laboratories which were designed to keep the population healthy, to let them live long lives free from disease and death.

Eliza had designed these communities in several countries. Of course back then pharmaceutical companies made huge profits and she had inherited a growing and vibrant corporation. Her parents had schooled her in biochemistry, genetics, economics, and business management from the minute she could read and write. Eliza had a brilliant mind.

Initially named MicroOrbs, in the first few years they became known as a 'Bad Medicine' by the world, but now we know better. MicroOrbs were a 'Brilliant Medicine' not a 'Bad Medicine'. 200 years is a long time, though; most of us are members of new generations, the Post-Medication War offspring.

As I grew up, in the years following MicroOrb release, I was lucky enough to be taught by Dr Eliza herself. When I was a child she instructed a few of our classes. Of course, we all sat in awe as she discussed postmodern ethics and socialisation. Her enthusiasm and brilliance shone through with every word she spoke.

My classmates and I were enthralled; we desired to be just like her. We memorised every word, asked so many questions and were treated as the equals we aspired to become. A world of equals was an impossible dream, but this woman had managed it. Yes, there had been some death, the Post-Medication War was regrettable and humans had killed other humans, but it just showed how horrific life had been before. Humans will do anything to live.

Our present-day communities were clean. Technology after the wars had declined a little but over time the founder generations rebuilt the machines. The blueprints were resurrected and materials sourced from the remnants of the old societies. The 3D printers were reinstated and the modular apartments were rebuilt. They were once again clean, spacious, and easy to build. Materials from the old world were recycled and everyone knew that each and every module was the same.

All of us were equals, fairness ruled, we had true egalitarianism. Each community was built in places far from natural disaster zones. Earthquakes, floods, hurricanes—nothing could stop Mother Nature from her course, but history and geometrics had ensured that each housing zone was in a low-risk area. Despite this, the building modules were designed with these possibilities in mind. The materials used could withstand most of what nature could throw at them.

The apartments themselves were well lit, clean, and practical. Each south-facing wall contained a holograph zone. We could still watch the old movies, but few people wanted to see the dirty old world. Hologram viewing taught us more. The older generations still watched the devastation, murder, death, and disease in the old films, but we younger ones preferred science, game shows, interviews, and visualising the latest technology.

I liked the interactive sports games. I could fully immerse myself into the crowd and even competed from time to time in the 3D athletics. It was much easier than actually training for the real games but it still took time to perfect the online skills. That being said, competition was not really an issue these days, or when I was growing up. Each person had their rightful place and everyone worked together to increase momentum on new developments.

Regular hologram shows portrayed problems with the latest machine, material, food discovery, or medicine. Everyone could try to help solve these issues. These shows made you think. If you had an idea, you could send in a hologram message or even wander along to the dedicated discussion groups. I preferred the latter; it was more sociable. I would send along my hologram, use my 3D set, or sometimes pop along in person if the show was being created within my community.

Teamwork, strategic thinking, discussion—these helped to modernise our society. We would wait with expectations and hope for the update shows, to find out which ideas had been successful and which concepts had failed but had been worth attempting at the very least. Such hype was created when our leader appeared live in any single programme.

Sometimes I wondered why, as Eliza was fairly omnipresent, but you always knew which problem was the most important to solve. She would utter a few words about the project and the altmetrics, the method by which everything was measured in our new world, would show the instant and rapid increase in participants. She just always knew what was important. If you were really lucky she would name a few people who had been instrumental in solving the problem. My name was mentioned ten times before I was even twenty-four years old.

I left schooling at fourteen years old. They say that people prewar attended until they were in their twenties. It seems that those who stayed longer were frequently undertaking further education whilst others were enjoying life or unsure as to which avenue they wished to pursue.

I think kids grow up much faster now. We are healthy; perhaps that makes a difference. We are also taught all year round and undertake specialist subjects from an early age. I personally had hoped to follow in my parents' footsteps, working in the cryogenics unit. One day I saw that dream come true—but I should tell you the rest of the story first, otherwise you will not understand the point of everything. You might not believe me.

As I have said, I loved science and still do. I would quietly work on problems, attempting to find solutions. The only real way to advance our society was through technology and medicine. As health was no longer an issue, due to the MicroOrbs, living was the major problem. Ensuring food and water availability was the key to success. As Elisa said, those with enough food and water would never need violence in their lives. It was so true.

Death was not really an issue either. With countless years now available to us the death rate was tiny, so we continually faced a growing population. Each new mouth needed feeding, each little body needed clothing, and so expansion of the communities was required. We all worked hard to create this environment. From a very early age we each took specialist pathways which would help us to excel in our eventual areas of work. Why bother learning electronics if you were to head up the soil laboratories? There was nothing to stop you changing jobs, but really it was better for our new society to advance knowledge in each field and sustain our precious lifestyles.

Our government were fair and wise and always did what was best. The past corruption was long gone. Those self-serving politicians were gone. Nobody much liked the thought of Eliza killing off corrupt politicians again, and we normal folks liked the security that this ever-present threat gave. The politicians were not dishonest, fraudulent thieves.

Eliza maintained her position as president of the new world, but most issues were voted on by the world or individual community populations, and the politicians were mainly there to share the facts and carry out the wishes of the people. Just as in previous millennia they could be voted out, but no one ever bothered. They had been fully trained for their position and were good at it.

As their children grew up, the older politicians would retire and generally continue teaching the younger generations. The same was true in most vocations. With people staying fit and healthy there was no reason to stop working, and besides we all wanted to earn our place and expand our possibilities. We knew that without infrastructure growth we could not have more young enter the world.

People were fairly content with the two-baby rule. It was there to protect us. Eliza had convinced older generations it was not the same rule as dictated by previous countries in the old days. We had to expand civilisation at a healthy rate or risk the famines and lack of adequate housing and resources again. As most babies stayed alive it was not a real problem, and if you lost a child you could have another, it was only fair.

Likewise, some people still died from accidents and even the old new virus or disease, but we did not have to fear these situations. The cryopreservation techniques were outstanding. If anyone died or got sick, you could simply preserve them until that day when a cure was found. Plenty of people these days make the conscious decision to go for cryo. If you lost a loved one, if the crops did not do very well, or if you just wanted a break from the real world, you could check in to the centre, sign the agreement, and freeze down for a while. It was also done by people who wanted to maintain skills and memories for future societies and many still think it is a good method for so many of these reasons.

Of course, every small detail was always stored on computers and cortex memory sharing devices, but many thought that just wasn't the same as having real people who could share their experiences. Every cryo was voluntary and on average around five to ten percent of the population entered it each year. Every decade or so some were woken up and sent out to new communities throughout the world.

We grew up hearing of these new havens. Their technologies were not as advanced as ours and they grew slowly, but we heard great things about them. We would know we were not isolated in the world. Travel was still a problem, so few people risked it, but our dedicated explorers would risk their lives outside the walls of the communities in order to bring back news from others who were willing to venture out. Sadly, we never enjoyed visitors as we were the central hub; our explorers took news and technology to all other hubs.

My own role would lead to helping these amazing people to awake from their frozen slumbers. It was a very important job. Only my family had ever been trusted with this demanding and privileged profession. My parents explained it was like the role of an undertaker or priest in years gone by. Care was needed to help those who were ill, precision was needed to ensure that each person was cared for and frozen appropriately. The entire community trusted you.

If we did our work well nobody would fear death because death did not exist. People were either alive or frozen. When death does not exist, you do not need religion. The government existed to ensure morals and behaviour as guidance and bereavement help were no longer required for relations of those who had passed away, because death did not exist. Even animals did not die since Eliza had opened the pet cryopreservation unit.

It was a brilliant solution and I knew my family had a huge responsibility. If the cryo systems ever went down, generations of humans would be lost and the grieving would be immense. My future role in society was clear: I would keep both hopes and humans alive.

Although we left school at fourteen, I was not allowed to start my role until much later on. Like the future politicians I had to wait another ten years. Maturity of the soul and mind they called it. I stayed with the ministers and leaders, learning about laws, psychology, how to communicate with the community, media relations. It was all pretty interesting but I was not entirely sure how it would help me.

I was assured that media communication was very important; I had seen my parents and grandparents in hologram rooms and giving out messages and doing tours about the cryo works so I suppose it is important. I really wanted to understand the science behind storing and keeping people frozen and how it was applied but I was told it was top secret and that I could not commence it until I was more mature.

Patience was a virtue; that old saying was still true. So, like everyone else I worked five hours a day, did various community activities for two hours, and then socialised and rested. My favourite activities were helping to bring up the newly born pets. Each person was allowed a pet animal. It helped to preserve the mammals, reptiles, and birds. I am not sure how well insects faired in this system but small mammals and reptiles certainly did well.

Most of our meat was grown in the labs in order to reduce energy requirements, so the odd person kept cattle and sheep. These were usually housed in the little farms spread out across the community so they were not usually popular pets. We all wanted something that could live happily in our apartments or nearby.

My friend Ben used to say 'cows are just not very cuddly' and I agreed, I still do. He went on to look after the animals following his training. Even animals had been given MicroOrbs over time, so they were not ill.

Ben was to work with me, ultimately, but doing the cryopreservation of animals and storing their DNA in the databank. He had to start with both civics lessons and training in basic animal sciences and husbandry. Neither of us were very sure why husbandry was necessary. I mean the animals did not need straw or care when frozen but it filled time until we could begin working properly, and he enjoyed caring for them.

Ben and I spent more time together as the years passed. In between extra classes, various work assignments, and watching the general law sessions, we got to spend our leisure tokens together. Each person had five credits a week to spend as they wished but as we were under twenty years old we were given a couple extra.

The public hologram rooms were always free but we enjoyed golf, the gym, and synthetic substances rooms, and took occasional visits to the old-fashioned Irish pub. The swing doors and wooden bar always amused us. There was plenty to do but sometimes we wished we could travel.

Some of the old movies we had seen showed people visiting exotic mountains and beaches. Our own beach and mountain were pretty, but honestly a little change now and then might have been nice. Ben and I started taking our vacation times together. The benefit of having our allocated unlimited leisure credits to spend on those twenty-three days a year was so valuable, a benefit of our training schemes.

It didn't take a genius to work out that we would get married. It was always so easy to talk to him and we loved the same activities and science. We would even be doing similar jobs in a few years, it was so natural. Our parents were delighted. Everyone told us how happy they were for us. We would be cryo geeks together, be able to discuss our work with each other, and some even said that together we would create new innovations in frozen health and preservation. At the time we thought so too. We had no idea of the science yet but it seemed to make sense. Oh, and we were in love; we still are.

Eliza herself came to see our first daughter. Her naming ceremony was a glorious event with so many people turning up from all over our community. One of the explorers even gave a great announcement. She had told one of the French communities the news from our side and one of Ben's aunts had sent a message of congratulations. She had been frozen years before but to hear news that she was now in a new community brought us such joy.

As usual we pressed the explorer for updates, but they have to give so much news out when they return that it is always difficult to get specifics. The new community was doing well, though, and to hear such news always made us happy.

The next evening the explorer was on the news discussing some of the new laws created in other communities. A couple had banned travel completely in order to save much valued food and save the lives of the explorers. This seemed sensible but our people were not fond of the idea of giving up on travel completely. We did all agree that for a few years fewer explorers should be sent abroad.

Another community had voted in new laws pertaining to people who were less able to work. They were routinely being frozen until medicine advanced enough to help them work again. We had seen a few men and women slowing down, less able to cope mentally, and a few who were just not inclined to work. It was a valuable discussion as they still needed food, water, clothes, entertainment.

In this blossoming new world everyone had to do their part. We put off making this change to our laws but there was a renewed enthusiasm for work in all departments. I was young but I could understand how work could become boring or tedious for those still in post after a century.

Ben and I settled into life with our gorgeous daughter. She was a constant joy and never before had we been so grateful for living a safe and happy life. We watched her gradually growing and taking her first steps. We wanted to take a few years of enjoying her before trying for our second child so we both had our contraceptive implants put back in.

Her MicroOrbs worked well and she stayed healthy. No nasty little childhood illnesses, no vaccines; the Orbs took control of everything. Ben and I were doing our 'jobs' but these days they mostly consisted of society and ethics classes and coursework. So much reading and writing about our community, keeping society safe, understanding ethical and legal decisions. We took exams most weeks and endless personality and ethics tests. Soon our baby was big enough to attend her compulsory childcare sessions, and Ben and I started to begin our roles in the cryopreservation section.

After years of being together, first as school friends, then as husband and wife, it seemed natural to take our first steps into the cryo unit together. We were not alone though. We entered with both of our families. It would appear that the first few months would be spent understanding the cryo liquids, body preparation and counselling sessions. We had entered the 'public gallery' numerous times before, of course, but now we would be understanding how to speak to the public. What the tours consisted of, how to inform folks about the process.

We watched as our parents talked about the technical aspects of the procedures. We were allowed to sit in on the sessions designed to guide people through the process if they showed an interest in being preserved. We sat next to families who had lost loved ones and learnt how to support them through the distressing times.

Although no one ever truly died, families would miss their loved ones until they saw them again; this was to be expected. Ben and I sat through all these sessions together. Although he would mainly deal with animals it was understood we would be supporting each other through life and it was sensible to have the same training.

Life was busy. We would work, take some leisure time with our daughter, do a little community work, listen to any news about other communities or the increasingly unusual and dangerous animals and plants living on the other side of the walls. We now understood why we had been forced to wait until we were older to start our jobs. We were dealing with emotions. Emotions were not very common in the normal world. People were healthy, happy, had enough in life and no longer grieved, so we probably saw the greatest amount of fear that now existed.

Everyone wanted reassurance. Would they definitely be looked after whilst frozen, was the success rate honestly one hundred percent, and would they be stored with other family members if possible? We showed people around the public gallery. They could see for themselves the latest frozen bodies stored in the pale blue liquid; they could see with their own eyes that the bodies were not decaying.

We showed them the great maps of the underground vaults which housed every single person ever born and frozen. Every individual in the entire community was assigned a potential place at birth. Space was made for each new person. Each space was ready for the day when it would be filled with its owner. Families kept together, husbands and wives next to one another.

We would explain how the space was kept forever. We explained how movement around the unit was entirely possible if you changed partners. Many people had been frozen and moved to start new communities but their space was kept here and a new one made in their new cryo unit too; it would be their choice as to which they would return to.

Eliza told us of people who had emotionally broken down just prior to the freezing technique, but also reassured us of the numerous drugs available to calm those folks down. A technique sometimes used was extremely serious. On very rare occasions we would be presented with criminals. In these cases we were to give the calming drugs and proceed as normal. We all knew of criminals and knew that the geneticists were working on ways of changing their genes to make them safe; so far there had been no criminals unfrozen, but one day, hopefully.

Ben and I dreamed that the first criminals might be cured on our watch. There were not too many lawbreakers though. Without power or resources needing to be fought for as they were freely available and shared, and with the prospect of being frozen if they did break the rules, most people conformed to society rules.

The last month before we entered the massive freezing facility beneath the ground was fascinating. It was spent entirely with Eliza, the ministers, and in ethics and morals classes. We were nearly ready to start our final jobs and nearly trusted to play one of the most important roles ever assigned. So, few people had ever been honoured with such positions. We knew this as most of the people who had worked in the unit were still alive, but then most high government officials tended to stay awake rather than be frozen. We knew why. They were wise and needed to stay around to give advice and train the youngsters. One day Ben and I would become the wise teachers, but for now we were the young learners.

A couple of days before we went into the facility we were told we would have to remain inside for a month. We could take our daughter or leave her with our parents; it was our choice. We questioned the need for the confinement but the ministers insisted it was for our benefit and for the benefit of our society. We would get to know secrets, play with life and death, the weeks would be complex and confusing, and it often took new generations a while to understand the situation. Reluctantly we agreed.

Our little girl was to stay outside and our parents would get extra vacation in order to fully care for her. She would have a wonderful time whilst we were learning. A month seemed such a small price to pay. We packed up a few bits and bobs and some clothes and finally entered the unit. We had waited our entire lives for this moment. We were apprehensive, excited, and frightened.

As we walked through the public gallery we passed the newly frozen. The gallery was so clean and quiet. Every step taken on the white tiled floor echoed around the room. It felt peaceful and clinical.

The blue liquids within the cryo units were gently stirred inside the vessels. Each frozen person hanging within their container, eyes gently closed but their bodies moving ever so gradually in time with the circulating liquids.

We saw a criminal, a couple from a much older generation who had decided to sleep for a while, a lady who had decided that she wanted to help start another community elsewhere, and a young mother with her stillborn child. She wanted to wait with her baby for the inevitable cure and wake up alongside him in order to start his little life afresh. Those people would gradually be moved into the underground zone we were about to enter. Once moved, visitors would not be allowed to see the frozen again until they were awoken.

We moved in through various sets of doors, each requiring DNA, iris, or fingerprint scans. The final door was controlled by two passwords and voice recognition. All the necessary arrangements had been made in advance to ensure our first trip went smoothly.

Upon entering the bunker zone, we changed clothes into the suits provided and went into the little apartment which had been prepared. It had food and water, a hologram screen, a comfortable little bedroom and a separate lounge area, even a few old-fashioned board games on the tables next to the chairs. Due to limited electronic transmissions, apparently the hologram screen would only allow incoming data, but Ben and I could forgo our little trips to chatrooms and discussion banks for a month.

We were enormously disappointed to be left alone in the apartment for the night. The new surroundings underground had unnerved us slightly but our family members had been called away to a new patient and we were left to grab some food and have a shower. The next morning we were up bright and early. We were not used to getting a full night's sleep; our little girl woke so frequently that it was a luxury. I think we both agree it was our last-ever luxury.

As we entered the unit we were guided in by our parents with a hand on our shoulder. Our parents led us through the corridor and into the great cryo vault. What we saw was not what we had expected. A dim concrete room containing just a single vat of blue cryo liquid. As we stared at the liquid, the body of the criminal was wheeled towards us.

Carefully our parents hooked up the clear container to a hook on the end of a vast chain and it was drawn up using a winch towards the ceiling. The blue cryo liquid was released into the great vat and the body of the latest criminal to be sent for cryo preservation just hung between the vat and the clear container. My parents lowered the body down and carefully placed it on the trolley to the left of us. I looked around but could not see a single needle, transfusion kit, or piece of medical equipment. I needed to understand how they drained the blood and replaced it fully with cryo liquid. Surely it needed to be carried out quickly.

Instead, Ben and I followed our parents and the trolley through another badly lit corridor via three more security doors. The temperature was increasing steadily; I recall thinking it must take a lot of energy to keep an entire vault frozen, so perhaps the heat dissipated into the corridors. Once we arrived at the final chamber we saw the truth. A fire was burning in a large hearth. The body was wheeled over, the trolley tipped up, and the criminal started to smoulder. Our parents turned sharply and left the room, taking us with them.

We did not sleep that night. Each day a new body was burned and each night Ben and I would fade in and out of nightmare-infested fits of sleep. Everything was a lie. Nothing was real anymore. The new communities did not exist, the explorers did not explore, death was real and final. The young mother and her tiny child would not return in decades to come or start up a new community.

Eliza had prepared the world for a religion-free existence but could not overcome the fear and worry of death; she could not remove the grief Religion was required until she had overcome death by fabricating an eternal existence for all. An eternal existence which science could not yet provide.

Despite the years of work on the cryo techniques, the cells within the bodies simply exploded, shrunk, or deteriorated. So the lies began. First the cryo bank, then explorers, then the sightings of once-frozen people who had started new communities.

Eliza knew, her highest government members knew, and so did our two families, the human and animal cryo bank families. We now understood why our families chose to remain awake. Death was real, death was final, and they all kept it a secret. The political method of silencing the people worked and was protected.

Destitution had been terminated, but at what cost? We were presented with two choices, to die or to continue with the deceit. We were afforded six weeks to make our decision, after which we would have been killed if we had not made a choice. We had been betrayed by everyone we knew and loved and by our politicians. If we lived we would have to continue the betrayal to both society and our own daughter. After a month we chose life, for us and our daughter. We also chose to lie to our community. Humans will do almost anything to live.

# UNFAIR AND UNBALANCED

# EACH NEW TWIST OF FATE: FOUR DETACHED VIGNETTES FROM THE DEATH OF AMERICAN POLITICS

by
Bob Freville

## I. Polite Society

Lindsey cracks a PBR and goes to take a slug off it, but something occurs to her. She removes the can from her lips. "Did you put Tahini Goddess dressing in the hummus again?"

The sound of chickpeas being shelled sharply ceases. "No," Jeff replies curtly.

A bowl slides across the countertop and the sound is quickly followed by the clank of a wooden cutting board coming down on the marble finish. The rapid-fire succession of chops lets Lindsey know that Jeff has moved on to preparing the scallions for the main course. Moderately satisfied, she returns to typing up her latest blog entry on marijuana legislation.

After a beat, her fingers stop hitting the keys. It's still nagging at her. "Because you know the reaction he had last time."

"Christ, Linds. Whose friend is he? I've worked with the dude for five years. I think I know about his anchovy allergy."

"Didn't at last year's cookout," she reminds him.

There's a knock at the door.

"Can you get that?" he says. "Maybe it's the salad dressing police come to take me away."

Lindsey smirks and sets her iPad down, crosses the room and turns the doorknob. Before she opens it, she shouts, "Forgot to lock the door again."

Jeff sighs. "On this block? What's gonna happen? Some soccer mom high on yerba mate's gonna break in and steal your yoga pants?"

Lindsey doesn't answer him, instead turning her attention to the tall black gentleman standing in the doorway. He greets her with a smile and she him.

"Law," she purrs.

"Lindzer tart," he cracks, holding out a Glad-wrapped bowl of greens.

"Never heard that one before," she replies sarcastically. Lawson laughs and enters the foyer. Lindsey closes the door and eyeballs the bowl. "Baby spinach?"

"Kale and summer crisp," Lawson says.

"Summer crisp," she says. "Sounds appropriate."

"Had to steal the thunder from Reg. He's bringin' honey-roasted summer squash."

"Want a beer?"

"Yeah, whatever you got."

They go into the kitchen, Lindsey playfully smacking Jeff on the ass on her way to the fridge.

"Hey!" Jeff gives Lawson some skin. "What's up, man? How was your vacay?"

"Eh," Law shrugs. "What's there to say? A week at my mother-in-law's is like a month in Guantanamo."

Jeff laughs. Lindsey takes two cold ones from the fridge and hands one to Law.

"Thanks, honey. Nah, can't complain. The country air was nice. Makes you tired, though, when you're not used to it."

"Tell me about it. I was in a coma the last time we went to my pops' cabin."

Lindsey dinks cans with Law. "So where's Reg? I thought he was coming with you."

"No," Law says. "Stupid bastard broke up with his boyfriend yesterday."

"Jesus. Another one?"

"That ain't the least of it. Dude's cryin' in his beer at the club last night? Picks up some bridge-and-tunnel fuck boy, brings him back to *my* house. Sonya's trying to sleep after workin' a double and this motherfucker's grindin' in the guest room."

Jeff doubles over, wheezing with laughter. "Reg."

"I swear, man. Dude gets more mangina than me or you gotten blowjobs."

"Nice," Lindsey says, swigging from her PBR and shaking her head. "What about you two? Manny told me you took sick leave."

"Yeah," says Law. "My back's been acting up something fierce the last couple weeks."

"I told you stop liftin' that heavy shit in the warehouse. Ask a brother for help." Jeff rolls his eyes and drinks from his beer.

"Yeah, yeah. Sometimes I think the two of you conspire to emasculate me."

Lindsey shoots Jeff a look. "Babe, if you're that easily emasculated, maybe it's time for the hormone treatment."

"Oh!" Law chokes on his beer. Jeff shakes his head and grumbles, returning to the cutting board.

After dinner, Jeff, Law and Reg are playing some pool in the rec room.

Reg says, "You still thinkin' about buying one of those stupid drones?"

"Nah," Jeff says. "Lindsey wants to start a college fund in case we ever have kids."

"Little premature," Reg says.

"Yeah, that's what I said. But who really needs a drone anyway? I'm not twelve."

"I'm sure Lindsey would debate that," Law says.

Reg chimes in. "Everyone needs a drone, dude."

"For what?"

"For what? You jokin' my ass? For fucking spying on the drones that are spying on us. The government's got them all over the goddamn place. Some George Orwell shit's going on day and night all across America."

"Hear that," Law says.

"Guess you got me there," Jeff says. "So much for the Land of the Free."

"Hey, don't give me that Land of the Free crap," Law snaps. "This shit's been free for you a lot longer than it has for me and mine."

"Law, you grew up in the 'burbs. Don't start that Kunta Kinte shit."

Lawson scratches on the eight ball. "'Scuse me?"

"You scratched, man."

"You just call me a slave?"

"You're the one that brought up slavery, dude."

"No, I fuckin' didn't! *You did* with that *Roots* shit. That ain't funny, Jeff. I know we're friends, but that don't mean you get a hall pass to drop an N bomb or no bullshit."

"I'm just saying, man. Don't start the whole righteous black man thing. You went to college on a full scholarship."

Law tosses his pool cue down on the green felt. "And what the fuck does that mean? That I forfeited my right to speak on behalf of the black community?"

"Law, we're in Riverdale. You *are* the black community."

"You're crossin' the fuckin' line, man." Law advances towards Jeff, but Reg throws an arm up in his chest, effectively blocking his path.

"Alright, alright, calm down. Law, chill. Guys, you're boys, okay? Let's stop this shit before it gets out of hand. C'mon, man. We've been pals forever. This is stupid."

"I know," Jeff says. "I'm not a racist or anything. You know that. I'm your kid's fucking godfather."

Law takes a deep breath and exhales. "Yeah, I know. Just be a little more sensitive, man."

Jeff nods deferentially. "Yeah, I know. Don't worry, I'll vote for Ben Carson."

The two laugh and shakes hands, a shake that turns into a half hug. Jeff slaps Lawson on the back. "Rack 'em, scratcher."

Later on, after a civil conversation about health care and several well-intentioned jabs about each other's skills on the basketball court, the boys join Lindsey in the living room for a nightcap. As she sets out a pitcher of sangria, she hits the power button on the TV remote.

"That pawn shop show on tonight, Lins?"

"No," she says, handing Law a glass with ice in it. "Tonight's the night." The boys look at her quizzically. She tunes the television to CNN. "They're about to announce the presidential candidates."

II. The Voter Base

Rusty and Tank are at the post-rally tailgating party, sitting on lawn chairs in the back of Rusty's pickup, gazing out at the crowd of supporters and protesters as if on their very own thrones. Clutched in their hairy knuckles are rally flyers and cans of Natty Ice.

Tank takes a swig off his can and spits the foamy head at a Prius parked on the passenger side of Rusty's rusted Dodge. He swallows, then looses a belch, adjusting his American flag belt buckle so that it ceases to dig into his pendulous gut.

"Really sunthin', iddn't it," he says.

"Wuss that?" Rusty asks.

"All these people here for one man. Kinda burns your eyes, no?"

Rusty looks around pensively, then shakes his head in the affirmative. "Sure is, Tank. Imagine the amountuh pussy juice that's flowin' right now. Lotta undies goin' in duh wash tonight.'"

Rusty and Tank both laugh and guzzle another pair of Natty cans. As cars begin to snake their way around the bend, bound for the highway, Rusty spits in a brown yellow arc off the side of the truck bed. "You believe my cunt sister refuses to support the man because she says he doesn't respect women's rights?"

Tank shakes his head. "Fuckin' bitch."

"Thass what all *I* said. Crazy chick can't get it through her head that he loves women just as much as the rest of us. Sonovabitch's been married three times, for chrissakes. He knows a thing or two about the fairer sex."

"She's got it all wrong," Tank says. "Ain't that he hates women or nut'n. He just understands we need a strong man in charge-uh shit. Who the hell wants a pantsuit in charge-uh the nuclear codes? They can't make the tough calls like we can."

Rusty discards a crumpled can in a black garbage bag and takes a fresh one from the cooler. As he rips the top open and it suds up, he raises it in the air and looks to Tank, who raises his can in kind. "Preach it, brother."

The pair dink their cans together in a toast.

"To freedom," Tank says.

"To freedom," Rusty agrees.

Three co-eds walk by in bikini tops and Daisy Dukes. They grimace at Rusty and Tank.

Rusty and Tank flash them tobacco-stained smiles and shout, "To freedom!"

The girls giggle and shake their heads in disbelief. One says to the other, "Oh my *gawd*!"

Rusty watches them go and sends another brown yellow streamer over the side of the pickup.

"Bitches."

Tank cuts a dangerous-sounding fart. "Women's rights," he says mockingly. "Who says they know what to do with their privates anyways? Ain't it a man who has to pull babies outta their nasty gashes at them godless clinics?"

"Yep," Rusty says with some apprehension. "I mean, I guess. Shit, I don't know." He pauses, deep in thought. "But whatever, all's I know is it's a man's gotta put up with their shit and it's a man's gotta work his balls off to support their fuckin' decisions whether they kill that poor fool baby or they decide to keep the goddamn wailin' thing."

"And where does it get us?" Tank asks. "Beggin' for a BJ 'cause it's our birthday? Soon as our sperm's up in them, they close up shop faster'n a part-time mechanic. Spend the rest uh your life negotiatin' with them for a little poon."

Rusty agrees. "They already own our asses at home, they damn sure don't deserve to own the whole goddamn country."

Both shake their heads and go quiet for a while, stewing about the wrongs that women visit upon them. Then Tank asks Rusty when he got laid last.

"Shit, man, my balls got barnacles on 'em at this point. I ain't had a slice of hair pie in longer'n I can remember."

Tank laughs his head off at this. Rusty slugs him in his bulbous bicep.

"Don't be laughin' at me, asshole. Your lard ass hasn't seen yer dick in years, much less had it serviced by no muff."

Tank paws at his arm and scowls at Rusty who cracks another can of Natty. "Whatever," Tank says under his breath. Then, "You know what really pisses me off?"

Rusty doesn't answer him.

"I'm tired of these snowflakes sayin' how he ain't fit to be president because he hates the towel heads. What's so wrong with that? Far as I'm concerned, we should bomb 'em all back to the Stone Age."

"You got that right," Rusty concurs. "No moose limb ever done nothin' for me. And shit, these people think this dude's bad because he grabbed some snatch? How about what them brown motherfuckers do to their women? Putting them in those veils so they can't see nothin'? I don't trust a bitch I can't see."

"Yeah," Tank laughs. "You don't put the brown paper bag over their head till *after* yuh seen they got a butter face. I ain't takin' some towel head's word for it."

Rusty guffaws. The pair continue to drink. A few minutes later, a pair of thin, well-kempt boys in their mid-twenties walk by, holding hands and sipping wine coolers.

Tank stands up with a start, rocking the truck like a canoe. He takes an empty Rolling Rock bottle from the cooler and chucks it in their direction. It shatters on the blacktop, spooking the both of them.

"Fuckin' cocksuckin' homos," he shouts. "Get the fuck outta my country, you filthy bitch faggots!"

The two well-kempt boys pick up the pace, weaving in between vehicles and setting off a car alarm in their haste.

Tank settles back into his lawn chair and shakes his head, sighing deeply. "Lost my train uh thought," he says.

"Yeah?" Rusty says.

"What was I sayin'?"

Rusty shrugs.

Tank scratches at his goatee then says, "Right, so like I was sayin', I was blastin' her in the ass and guess what happened next?"

"What?" Rusty asks uninterestedly.

"I'm pumpin' away and just as I started to pull out, this meatball bitch cuts a fart like you wouldn't believe." Tank clutches his stomach, laughing to the point of tears.

Rusty looks at him and winces. "Did she shit?"

Tank sighs. "A little . . . but it was worth it. Made the orgasm that much more intense."

Rusty shakes his head and laughs weakly. "Like our man said at the rally, brother. You gotta . . . *drain the swamp.*"

Tank and Rusty both double over in a fit of laughter, dinking their Natty cans together anew. When their cans are empty, they toss them into the cooler beside the decomposing head of a seventeen-year old black girl who was just askin' for it by wearing Daisy Dukes to a Dairy Queen.

## III. The Journalist

They blamed it all on the Correspondent's Dinner. One second-rate late-night host had cracked too many jokes about the "titan of industry" and the next thing you know, the son of a bitch is in the running.

In truth, it may have been all my fault. At least the higher-ups thought it was. At the time, I never thought the bastard stood a chance of winning. I was simply blowing off some steam and taking the piss out of him for the sake of balancing the weights, as it were.

If I'm being honest, the campaign trail had been a hard day's night. There is no demoralizing atrocity on earth quite like a gig following these buffoons on the road for seventy-eight goddamn days and having to describe it in legible detail.

If you've stayed in any of the same hotels as political lobbyists and pundits, you have borne witness to the basest bacchanalia to ever be played out on the bloody grounds of human history. It is a humorless, emotionless orgy of airplane-bottle drunks and dull screams by barely legal whores that penetrate your bedroom wall at three forty-five in the morning.

When I filed my final copy about Herr President-elect, the results weren't quite in. They were playing it close to the bone and I was fed up and stoned for sleep. The decision to give the son of a bitch one last good ribbing before we sent him back to his golden skyscraper was one that washed over me out of sheer frustration.

The headline read, "Gold-Obsessed Presidential Candidate Receives Golden Showers." The story quotes an anonymous source who claims that Herr President Elect spent time behind enemy lines, paying Russian tarts to empty their bladders on his face.

As associate editor, I was able to slip this one into the paper by burning the midnight oil. By the time it ran, it had been picked up by the AP wire and spread like syphilis. The editor-in-chief demanded to know why I would write such a thing. I told him there had been a rumor on the campaign trail.

Which was true . . . because I had started the rumor myself after seeing a funny meme in which someone taped a photograph of Herr President-elect to their toilet tank.

I was promptly sacked, which was fine with me. A vacation was all I really needed after lo these many days of having to hand in quotes from the maw of such a monster and do it all with decorum. But that's where I thought it would end. I was wrong. And I now blame my stupid story for sending the monster into a rage.

After my rumor spread, the monster's minions used it to dismantle the free press and rallied his supporters to get out to the polling places and fake news be damned.

And now, here we are, at what I can only describe as the omega of existence as we knew it. As I load the chamber of this Desert Eagle .50 caliber, I hope and pray that the memories of what led us here will be flushed out of my skull and left on the wall for the minions to clean up.

God help you all.

IV. The Man in Power

Do you smell the ashes, brothers and sisters? Can you feel their warmth on your cheeks? I keep my promises.

I've said it before, but I'm gonna say it again and there's nothing you can do about it, you understand? What separates the winners from the losers is how a person reacts to each new twist of fate. That's it.

And boy, understand me when I say I'm a winner. No matter what they tell you.

Fuck you! You don't understand! You're a deplorable nothing of a person. You know *nothing* of what I am capable of.

Here I am, folks! They told me I couldn't do it, but I have. It's been hard, but the triumph of my will put me right where I said I would be. They said I wasn't qualified. They said I was a joke. They're the jokes! They're not qualified to be *me*, you understand?!

When I was just a boy, I faced adversity from these worthless losers. They fucked with me, but they fuck with me no more! Huge, *huge* adversity! I faced it face-first, you understand. I picked myself up by my boot straps and I took a ridiculously small million-dollar loan and I turned a mountain into a mole hill and then I turned a mole hill into a monolith! I built an empire cast in gold while the *losers* drooled and *wished* they were me.

I evicted the colored element from my properties to turn a buck, sure, but that's just good business acumen, okay? Where did they go? How did they survive? That's every man's responsibility. I refuse to feel sorry for losers who don't work to get where they are.

I'm the most empathetic person you'll ever meet. Nobody cares more than me.

No, you understand. You're not *listening* to me! I have all the answers, but they don't want you to hear me, so they spew lies and brainwash you with falsities.

I am your leader, you *understand*? It's all about each new twist of fate. Are you getting me, Jack?

This is the big leagues and I'm no baby. They say very hurtful things. *Very hurtful* things about me. But a winner reacts. He reacts to each new twist of the blade.

I'm the one twisting the screws now, you get me? They say I'm not a man of my word. They don't know *jack*. They're a gaggle of nobodies and loser liars.

I paid two hundred and seventy-five bucks for a plate at their stupid dinner back when that immigrant was your president and I sat there and watched as I was mocked by people whose names I'd never heard of before. They're nobodies. But they say very hurtful things.

But I react to the twisting of their blades. I'm a natural-born winner. I've been winning my whole life. I take their mockery and I curl it into a little fist and I bring that fist down on the power structure.

I *am* your leader.

I wonder what you're all thinking when you're asleep and I'm in here, pacing the carpeted floors with my gold phone clutched in my fist. My thumbs run wild. I can't help myself. I see the opportunity and I have to have it. It's mine. Everything's mine.

Why doesn't anyone get it? Why can't you see how amazing I am? My kids know it. I make them know it. Maybe not my youngest boy, but I'll beat it into him sooner or later. He'll pay for his lack of enthusiasm. They'll all pay.

It's lonely up here, but don't feel sorry for me. What we have here is ginormous. I'm a giant. My home has turrets at the top sharper than a twist of the blade. I've built myself up. And I'll keep building and building and building until all you good people are safe and secure.

Those who wish to do me harm will be unable to see our world. The sun will not pierce our gates. And no Trojan horse will gain purchase to my palace. They'll be shot down trying. Good luck, Jack! Nice try! Gotcha!

They're always laughing at me. Cackling from somewhere behind the camera.

That's okay. I refuse to shake their hands. I spit in their eyes, the cunts!

This is my world now, Jack! You will not break me. I do not bend.

You know, I say I worked to get where I am, but the truth is, you put me here. Sometimes your best investments are the ones you don't make. I laid the groundwork, but you're the ones who rolled out the carpet and invited me in.

I watched a movie on the late-night channel last night that said a vampire can't enter your home unless you let him in. I thought that was funny.

They keep laughing at me. It's not funny, but I'll have the last laugh.

I'll take their women by force and throw their children to the wolves. Ol' Benny Franklin once said, "Democracy is two wolves and a lamb deciding what to have for lunch."

I like that. I think about it when I'm flossing in the mirror. There is blood on my teeth tonight and I like it. Blood is the life force of our great country and I can taste the possibilities.

I will make my world the greatest world ever. Period.

My enemies say that I am wrong to keep the hordes from storming into my world and sullying it with their brown skin and bad intentions, but I don't care if you tell me that their religion is one that promotes peace. The dirty, stinking truth is that a couple sour apples spoil the whole bunch.

Spoils. I take all the spoils for myself and that's the way it's supposed to be. Winner take all!

I take my cues from the tundras where leaders rule with an iron fist and the people know their place. Know your place. But fuck! Each twist of fate makes me tear my hair out. You're all so hurtful. You just don't understand. Winning. Fate. Power. You have to know your place. Love it or leave it. Get out of here! I say. Take the losers with you. You challenge me and you challenge me and you expect me to do so much with so little. This is the hardest job in the world and you just don't appreciate how much I can do.

It gets to where I have to take a vacation. I've gotta get away.

My team spirits me away to my favorite golf course and I take my anger out on the nines. But I still can't quell this ire that rises like bile in the back of my throat. I tell my team to go home.

My team. My staff. My house. This is my house! I am the man in charge and I am legion! But I can't trust my minions. I can't trust that they're not colluding to try and hurt me.

They know what I've said, they know what I've done and they're all bullies. I know they're up to no good so, one by one, I take them out like pieces on a chess board.

Checkmate!

I will not let them speak for me anymore. I will shred every word that they have written about me. I'll tear them all to twisted ribbons and seal their twisted fate. Hail to the king!

It's quiet in here tonight, but I can hear the chatter outside these windows and I know what you're all up to. That is why I will burn it all to the ground. I've built it and I can tear it down. In the end, you will all know that you were sore losers and I was always meant to win. I will rise like that stupid bird from your ashes.

Can you taste the blood now? It's gushing forth from your wherevers as I twist the blade of faith and fate. Do you believe in me yet?

If it's all over it's your own fault. You shouldn't have worn that rubber. You losers are the death of humanity, not me! I am legion. You lose. Checkmate!

You don't want some slit to be in charge, you want a man and that's what I am. I win. Take your rights and stuff 'em up your skirts!

In the end, you will know I was righteous in my choices. I am a human Bible and I will cast all the sodomites and lame jerk-offs into the fiery pit they belong in. You will all be left with no idols to pray to but me and I will not be merciful. Sometimes the best investments are the ones you didn't make.

As I punch the keys on my cell and prepare to send this message, I can't help but laugh. You get what you pay for, losers. I am your king of ashes.

# HOW I'LL LOSE MY CAREER

by
Edmund Colell

My career began after I graduated from the University of Arizona's College of Law at age twenty-three. The same age my daughter was when my son shot her in the face, misusing the twelve-gauge I kept under the mattress. He went to prison, and my wife fled as far as she could without a passport.

The first morning I woke up without my family, I couldn't move from my bed until eleven. Five missed calls from my chief of staff. Ten from my campaign manager. A collection of text messages I feared to read.

The State of Arizona could probably function without a governor for a couple of hours. It may not look good in a run for Senate when you don't show up to work at the job you were already elected for, but neither does losing your family in an act of household gun violence when you're Tom "Cowboy" Watts. The embrace of the deerskin blanket once donated to me by a proud huntress seemed the last bit of warmth and comfort available in the world.

That woman was likely watching the news that day, as were hundreds of eager liberal bloggers and Facebook brats, as well as folks on the right questioning my friendship with them. I imagined my email full of requests for interviews. Enemies wanting to kick me for defending hundreds of self-defense court cases and for upholding Second Amendment legislation throughout my time in smaller offices. Even the Gabrielle Giffords shooting, I claimed, was the fault of a bad man abusing a safety tool. Loughner was one of millions of boogeymen who could only be answered by bullets. I used to call characters like that "Stabber Jack." Something like Meyers or Voorhees or Krueger. I used to say, "No one in those movies had an AR-15, did they?"

My fellow GOP rival, Lieutenant General Greg Peters, wooed my former NRA donators away from me. He went on record saying, "Tom's done playing cowboy. Join a soldier!"

I crawled to the edge of the bed and held my phone. "It's over," I wanted to text my campaign manager. I didn't.

There were thousands of things I wanted to do, hundreds of more things that needed to be done regardless, but I couldn't move. Not until my phone buzzed with a call from my office again, when I answered, "I'll be there," and hung up.

No shower or breakfast, only a dab of cologne and a thermos of cold coffee sitting in the percolator from the day before. The house had remained untouched since the former matriarch flipped it here and there in search of her things. Hiring help seemed like an unnecessary expense before, but a great idea then, if I could pick up the rest of my life.

Ringing phones raise my blood pressure. Of course, several calls were eager to greet me as soon as I walked in the door. The gently flowing miniature fountain on the corner of my desk, surrounded by pictures of my children, did little to minimize the effect. Though I felt down, the core of my chest was rocketing. These were the filtered phone calls, at that. I shudder to think what else my public liaison endured. I placed ten calls on hold until I could answer the first one. "Office of the Governor, Tom Watts speaking."

"Hello, Governor, this is Amy Sanchez with the *Arizona Daily Star*. I'm calling today because our paper wants to cover your current stances on policy."

"Thank you for your call, Amy. At this time, I'm upholding my policies until further notice."

"Would you still have time to answer a few questions?"

More calls started blowing up. "Please send all questions through the contact form on my website. Thank you and God bless."

At least press calls tend to maintain decorum. One of the other calls came from an older mother of three, named Martina. She started with, "I'm sorry for the loss of your girl," and ended with, "You know, you killed my Chuy. He never did a fucking thing. I hope he finds that little *puta* in hell, because if he *ever*—"

"God bless." I wrote a note for later: no more calls from anyone identifying themselves as a parent.

I remember one other call from the public: "Hello, my name is Jennifer Nguyen. I work in the coroner's office. I examined Mara Watts. There are details about your daughter I need to discuss with you."

Ten more calls demanded my attention. I asked Jennifer to confirm Mara's birthday and the number on her toe tag. When she proved her legitimacy, I said, "Please give me your phone number. I will have to contact you outside of my office hours."

"Personal or work? I'm only here until five."

Offering her personal number seemed strange after the fact, but I said, "Maybe both. I'll call you back as soon as possible." The notes in the autopsy seemed final. I already knew more than a few things they didn't, like the nose piercing Mara had gotten the night before, the winged eyeliner style she experimented with in the days leading up to her death, and the subtle unease in her eyes whenever she had to hug Brett for pictures. That last detail, I can only see now.

The phones calmed down toward the end of the day, but the damage had already been done. I had been worn to the bone over giving the same answers and politely side-stepping the press's dissatisfied responses.

The bottle of water I'd brought to soothe my voice ran out too soon. Much remained to be done, including the reading, signing, and/or vetoing bills that had been drafted long ago. The requests for pardons. The petitions every other citizen of Arizona felt necessary to pile high with signatures. The inbox overflowing with questions I directed away from the phone. Only an eighth of what my workload often entails, not including the pressure of my comatose campaign.

And as soon as I thought of that failing run for Senate, my campaign manager called me: "Tom. Pal. With every last ounce of respect due, I beg you. Give them a fucking statement."

I remained silent. Head in one hand.

"I hear you breathing. Good. At least they'll know you're not fucking dead."

I finally said, "It's over, Joe."

"Tom. You've taken too many contributions and given too many speeches. So you can't stay the course. Fine. But you will get on the phone, the microphone, Twitter, whatever, and you will announce *some* kind of course."

"They'll eat a flip-flopper alive."

Silence, then: "God made you flip-flop, Tom. You're a prophet now. Sell it."

Said a better way, those would have been the funniest words I ever heard. No way anyone else would take it seriously, either. Pious evangelicals and smarmy atheists alike would write me off, at best.

Maybe God had a plan. If He did, I wasn't privy to it, but science has trouble explaining the senseless. If he had to punish my children for their father's advocacy, then I needed to do the right thing. The hard thing. The coffee felt dead as it flowed all the way to the bottom of an empty pit, but nothing else would help me out of the chair.

Deep breaths. Light stretches. I paced the room long enough to keep my blood pumping and my thoughts straight. I scheduled a speech in the southern end of Phoenix for the following Tuesday, then took a secret swig of bourbon from a flask hidden in a book of law.

More microphones and cameras that day than any before. The audience hungered. In each of their eyes, I gauged who would be delighted and who would be disappointed. A woman wearing a cross on her necklace and a Make America Great Again hat pointed the baby in her arms to look at me, waving the little one's hand. A college boy in a polo shirt sat next to a grizzled trucker, both of them smiling practically the same despite their backgrounds. A twenty-something girl with messy black hair streaked pink and teal and wearing hipster glasses sat with a tape recorder and a notebook, eager to write retorts for every line I had prepared. Yet I gave them each my warm, home-grown wave and smile.

Deep breaths. Light stretches.

"My fellow Americans, it has been an honor to serve the State of Arizona as governor, and I would be even more humbled if the people of Arizona choose me to serve in Congress as senator. This country needs a strong man who will help us keep a powerful military, dedicated police forces, and a rock-solid border to protect our friends and families from our enemies. Today, as every other day, I am ready to prove my might. We are a country in need of strength."

Much of my speech fed on those feelings and policies, and I meant every word. The crowd ate it up, applauding after nearly every sentence. On her own cues, Hipster sighed and wrote. Damn near every rally I've hosted and attended has been a family reunion between strangers. These people would beat my own security to the punch if an assassin came my way, and I would open my house to them if an earthquake swallowed the city whole. To them, I was good ol' Cowboy Watts.

"It's no secret to anyone that my wife and I suffered great losses. No parent should ever see their child for the last time at breakfast. Neither should any parent work hard to instill honesty, integrity, and a love for mankind in their child, to later see them in court for an in-human crime. Of course, I'm not alone. Worse, I have helped those awful things to happen to others.

"We're aware of the bad guys around us. The street mugger. The drug dealer. The terrorist. And, yes, the monsters lurking in our state and federal governments."

My throat had dried to jerky by then. Some observers who already guessed my incoming point started whispering to each other, puzzled. I hid my shaking hands behind the slope of the podium.

Hipster stopped writing and waited.

"But it doesn't take much homework to realize that most victims of gun violence aren't the bad guys. I only wish that fewer families have to endure the pain I carry every day. Through my tragedy, the Lord our God has shown me the truth. This is why I am coming out in favor of greater funding for family counseling services and stronger firearm regulation."

Collective mumbling. More camera flashes. Maybe a vein had popped on my face, or I had gone pale, or a drop of sweat had beaded. MAGA lady's excitement had fallen, and she hurried her child toward the back. Student shook his head while typing on his phone. Trucker stared, mouth hanging. Hipster watched, enrapt, pen held tight.

"If elected, I promise the average American safety abroad, safety on the streets, and safety at home. This can be, should be, a bipartisan effort. God bless you, and God bless America."

I stepped off the podium. A great noise swelled in my people.

Not applause.

Reporters brandished microphones and barked questions. Fiery voices hurled curses and insults. The rancid toe of a sneaker struck the corner of my eyebrow. A well-dressed middle-aged professional elbowed his way through the crowd to spit on me. Police and security forces closed the gap and raised their riot shields. An officer with a megaphone demanded peace and order while I was led by each shoulder to a black Ford Lincoln. Pepper spray streams brought tears, convulsions, and screaming to the tribe that had welcomed and trusted me. A rock slammed the rear-view mirror, opening a spider web of cracks behind my head.

Once the safety of the car silenced the rally far behind us, one of the guards chuckled and said, "Jesus. Did you spoil the new *Star Wars*?"

Living in a house on the end of a road in the middle of the desert gave me the advantage of seeing Phoenix far enough away for me to feel both close and separate at the same time. On a good day, I could stand outside and admire my old home as if it were my proud father taken under my care. On the day following that speech, I hid inside, where my father can't belt me for saying the dirty words I said in public and making him look bad. No desire to confirm the social media wildfire or to turn on my phone. The air conditioning kept a gentle seventy-two degrees while I cleared the trash in my home, washed dishes, gathered laundry.

With a sink full of silverware and a loaded washer, I tried to call my wife, Emily. Straight to voicemail. I said, "Hi, honey. I'm going to make things right by you and by our children. I love you. I miss you."

I immediately got a call. I answered, "Baby?"

"It's Joe."

"Oh. Hey."

"That was an interesting interpretation of my advice."

"More grieving father than prophet, Joe."

"God, guns, country. If you have to sacrifice one, pump up the other two. We have one more month to win back our support and we can't afford to do anything else that will put memes on Facebook."

Much as I wanted to give him my own command to go fuck himself, I said, "Noted. Thank you. God bless."

Remembering Mara recalled the need to reach Jennifer. I beat myself up for forgetting her. To my surprise, she was still interested when I called and asked about my daughter. She said, "I'd rather meet in person. I'm not sure I can describe it well enough right now." The company of anyone neutral seemed better than loneliness, so I offered to rendezvous at Jones' Espresso Bar the following evening And told her which car to look for in the parking lot. Before we hung up, she said, "What you did yesterday took a lot more courage than anything I've seen from anybody." I was glad that she didn't know how I'd cowered since.

That night, as I ate a frozen pizza alone in front of Netflix, I thought of the voicemail I left Emily. Probably deleted before anyone could listen. To her, I was as dead as our girl and as wicked as our boy.

After a calm Thursday of hiding, I put on a gray hoodie and thick glasses, and shaved my beard before I left home to meet the girl who works for the coroner. I'd kept the old sedan I drove before I changed careers, in case a threatening public became reality. None of its luster returned in the moonlight, and its black-tinted windows guaranteed that every part of me but my lights would disappear into the dark. Security presence would have spoiled the disguise. Sure enough, on the ride there, nobody looked at me twice and nobody shouted my name.

I waited in the parking lot by Jones'. The heat trapped in my hoodie forced me to try cracking the windows, then rolling my side down and cranking the AC when that didn't work. Darkness and the noise of traffic kept me safe. Some of my campaign signs on the street corner had been torn out of the ground. Even though I told her how I would look, I didn't get those details on her. Most of the women on the street had company, and none of the cars coming in after me opened to someone who didn't immediately leave. I held eyes with a pretty young thing getting out of a Volkswagen, but turned away before one of fifty bad possibilities could happen.

Ten minutes into waiting, I wondered if she forgot, if she was being followed, if she wasn't who she said she was, or if she had been bait.

"Stick 'em up!"

Deep bark out of nowhere. Narrow shadow jabbing for my face.

The shadow was a finger. The attacker was Lieutenant General Peters, and he was laughing.

So, I punched him. Right through the window and into his bullshit hole. And he laughed again. Wiping his mouth, he said, "You're lucky. Real men don't press assault charges."

When my breath and heart rate settled, I said, "You earned it."

"Would've been funnier if you shot me." He took a bite of a wrapped sandwich in his other hand. "Mmm. You get the chance, you should try my little shop down the street. Open Season Subs. If you haven't tasted venison in the middle of a whole grain bun, lovingly blanketed with fresh ingredients, well, you just haven't lived." He winked, then returned to the dark, eating all the while. At least he left with a fat, purple lip.

Peters had gone long before Jennifer pulled into the lot. She apologized that something came up, "something stupid," and left it at that. Cute Vietnamese lady, her modest makeup, girlish short hair falling around her neck, and simple black shirt and shorts over her soft features making me wish, for a moment, that I had been a fresh-bodied law grad again. I would have also wished for better meeting circumstances.

I gave her cash for our order and waited alone at a corner table, facing the wall. I hoped this would be quick.

While the coffee cooled, she said, "What happened at that Walmart yesterday was crazy."

"Oh. I haven't seen the news."

"Five dead and fourteen injured. Some kid with an Uzi."

"You can imagine how I feel about it now."

"Some people think you planted him."

The rumor mill didn't take long. I glanced to make sure the other customers were isolated in their own conversations. An older man-made eye contact with me but didn't linger. "Short answer's no. So, you had something to say about Mara?"

She took a long draw of her coffee and searched for a place to start. "Did she used to have a tic? Muscle problems? Anything off like that?"

I listened.

"She was fine when we brought her in. No vitals. Hole in the face. You know, the parts that are already on paper. And when other people were around, taking measurements and filling out stuff on clipboards, that's all that happened. The only thing unusual to anyone was her dad.

"Sometimes corpses twitch from the expanding gases. Sometimes they even groan, like a gentle 'ohhh.'"

A couple sitting in the table ahead had the backs of their phones facing me, cameras and all, but it seemed they were taking selfies.

"She twitched, too. Her hands. Her palate was shattered, but the rest of her mouth made a noise, too. Not a groan, but a quiet 'jik-jik-jik-jik.' Sort of a chatter. No one else seemed to notice the 'jik-jik-jik-jik' whenever it happened, and I caught weird looks whenever I pointed it out."

Some guys talking in line looked my way more than twice. Expressionless. Then inquisitive. Grins. One of them pretended to project onto no one in particular while half-shouting, "Holy shit, what if Tom fucking Watts came here tonight?" His buddy said, "I'd call him a giant pussy." "Puuussyyy."

Jennifer kept going. " . . . How no one catches anything like that . . . " and " . . . That kept popping into my dreams . . . " were most of what I remembered while half of my senses read the room for anyone paying attention to the hecklers.

"Crusty old pussy." "Can you believe my dad voted for that guy?" "Fuck your dad. He still says Chevy is better than Dodge."

" . . . I mean, what do you get from something like that?" she finished.

I came back with nothing, my innards twisting. Someone would pay attention to those boys. Someone else would recognize me. The barista turned. The couple took out their phones again. The guy passing me from the front looked at me a little too long.

"Are you okay?" she said.

"I'm fine."

She finally understood the noise behind her and said, "We can take this somewhere else."

Smiling as politely as I could, I wrote my email address on a napkin and said, "Let's continue this electronically."

She sighed, ripped up the napkin, and walked out.

One of the boys went, "Oooh."

I pretended to adjust my glasses on the way out, blocking as much of my face as possible. It wasn't until after I hurried out of town, keeping watch on my rear-view, that her words sank in. And as I sat in bed and processed it all, the only conclusion I had was, "So your little girl makes a weird corpse. It happens."

Just like it happens that a young man named Harry Owens killed the barista, then himself, shortly after I left.

My written public statement the next day was, "I am in shock over the violence that has risen in my city over the last few days. Public safety must be secured. I will work with the mayor and chief of police to employ any means necessary."

I edited those three sentences for hours. It used to be much longer. Any accidental word or punctuation could have signaled the worst. I don't even remember the original words.

Sometime after I finished the final draft, before anyone could read it, I received this message through my contact portal. I remember it most above any I had read that week:

> just because your kids fucked up doesnt mean you can threaten a fundamental american right. do everyone a favor and switch sides. hug an abortionist . . . marry the hombre of your dreams and open a reefer farm together . . . because you wont just go down. youll go down alone . . .

The last time I went outside for something other than work, it was for supplies. Pulling cash from the bank, filling a few cans of gas, and buying groceries. I sent help for the first two errands but chose groceries as an effort to publicly strengthen the end of my campaign with some hello-there-citizen moments. This outing, however, I didn't shy from bringing security. They pretended not to be with me, wandering and waiting to intercept anyone who showed anything much hairier than a friendly greeting. Good deal of success at first. Selfies and handshakes here and there, some signed items, reconciliation with a mail carrier who hated my guts while I was the Cowboy.

Then I stood in line at check-out. A young man got close and said, "What did you tell her? What did she tell Owens?"

Heart in the back of the throat. One of my guards took notice.

"I won't tell anyone. I'm just curious. Why did they both have to die?"

I said, "I'm sorry to say I'm not sure what you mean."

He pulled up his phone to show a video, hosted from YouTube. It shows a side from opposite the selfie couple where I am speaking to Jennifer. She tears up the paper, and leaves. I leave shortly after her, and the footage skips to Owens inaudibly raising hell with the barista before peppering his chest with 9mm rounds and then eating a bullet himself, ending with no one standing at either side of the counter.

One of my guards, Jose, said, "Sir, I am going to ask you to maintain a three-foot distance from the governor."

Once far enough away, the kid said, "Why did you give the order?"

Another amateur documentarian in the store was likely recording their own evidence of something I never thought of. Three of those filmmakers might have been there. Seven. Every single person there, even those who embraced me, might have been one.

I said, "Sir, you are begging the question. Good day."

"What?"

I sensed attention from people beyond my field of vision. To seek them would be to validate having their eyes on me. Any eye twitch—a possible admission of guilt. Louder, I said, "Good day," and Jose escorted the kid away. I wish he hadn't.

I pretended the only people there were myself, the cashier, and the bagger, no matter that I heard faint mumbling in multiple directions behind the beeping transactions.

My phone went off on the ride home. Jennifer. She had woken up that morning to threatening text messages. Her address and contacts had been spread across the internet. Anywhere she'd go, she'd be subject to the same. No one else but me seemed to have armed security. So, I picked her up from a Circle K, where she had been disguised as well as a pair of sunglasses and a headscarf can allow. She stomped on her phone and threw it in the dumpster before we took off.

I had another ring en route. Joe. He was resigning as my campaign manager and wished never to work for me again. Thank God.

Jennifer asked if she could see Mara's room, as well as Scott's. I told her neither place was ready yet, but the living room, kitchen, and yard were free to roam and forage. While she got set up with soda and TV, I chose to clean Scott's room first. Surprisingly well-kept room for a boy of sixteen. Much better it had often been. His bed was already made, his backpack ready by the door, his Safeway uniform clean and hanging. No dirty clothes. Everything in its place.

It stank of planning.

I inspected every crevice and seam, opened his computer files, and researched his online posts from the last few months. Nothing surfaced. Like when I visited him and begged for his reason. All he did was shrug. This kid once said he'd give up his initial dream of joining the Air Force for fear of accidentally killing the wrong people. I yearned to seize his prison shirt lapels and demand an explanation of why his sister was the right person. But it looked unlikely that any evidence of motivation would be found, even if his room was ripped apart.

Next, Mara's room. A little messier. Still smelled of cheap perfume. Could never keep on top of dusting her furniture or her electronics. Makeup supplies were scattered across her desk, having collected there in her last few weeks. There was a lighter hiding in plain sight among some lipstick tubes, but to my knowledge, she had stopped smoking.

Her green carpet was bleached where she bled out. A few auburn hairs remained between the fibers. The wall by her bed had taken worse damage. While the crime-scene cleaners were careful to remove my daughter's remains, they could do nothing about the scattered holes. The forensic team determined that she had answered the door just before he pulled the trigger.

While cleaning, I found a snack bag of pills under her bed. A quick Googling revealed them as Xanax. I would never know the name and address of the greaseball who supplied her, but I found the awful sense in it. Mara used to say she was tired and "out of it" all the time at home. And of my two kids, she was easily the most anxious. We had to pull her out of school once for panicking on an exam, beating her hands on her desk, and shouting curses at her teacher.

When I told her about Stabber Jack as a child, to playfully explain weird noises in the night, she wouldn't shut up about him for weeks afterward. I made the guy up to put a face on anything suspicious I sensed while alone at night, but she didn't understand that until she was seven. It gave her little comfort to know that my father used to warn me of a monster crawling in the dark, waiting hungrily for me to leave my bed.

If her fate could ever be reversed, maybe she would have brought up her own kids without making up monsters. Of course, nothing stopped me from using ol' Jack as my favorite political shorthand for "he who attacks your family at night." Gun lobbies and manufacturers love a little help from boogeymen.

After finally cleaning Mara's room, I flushed the drugs and asked Jennifer to pick up where she left off at Jones'.

With her shades off, I finally noticed that her face was less made up than before, paler and more sunken. She said, "You didn't answer me. What do you make of what Mara did in the morgue?"

I said, "It's just as much a mystery to me."

Her voice began to fail here and there. Deep breaths and choking pauses. While I can't replicate her rhythm, she said, "Fucking nightmares every fucking hour. I eat when I remember to. No-call-no-show almost got me fired. Please. No one else has even listened to me."

I sat there, lost for a way to comfort her. "It's all senseless. I still need answers, too."

She hid her sobs in her hands. I offered a hug, but she hurried to Mara's room and locked herself inside for the rest of the night. Her cries ended quickly, and there was silence from there until long after I went to bed.

When I saw her the following morning, she cheerfully offered me coffee.

Peters had a fantastic turnout for his rally in Tucson the night after our encounter, as I found when I dared to check the internet again. Interesting for a town so liberal that it ought to replace each Elk Lodge with a Planned Parenthood. He still had a scab on his lip, and he opened his speech by saying, "Some of you may be surprised to know that Tom Watts can throw a solid jab. God knows if he learned that in law school or if he actually had to get his hands dirty once or twice. 'Cowboy.' If he ever rode a horse in his life, it was probably polo." Some scattered laughter, then he continued: "Even so, I'll give him the victory for that fight. It's the last he'll have for a while."

He reaffirmed his oaths to the policies he planned, then said, "Arizona still has a Republican candidate committed to our right to bear arms. Now, my heart goes out to the Watts family, but I don't think my rival ever served. Sure, he talks a good deal about strong military, but had he survived a deployment or two, maybe he would understand how ready access to a rifle can, in fact, *prevent* tragedy."

Roaring applause, and he bathed in it for a good minute. Someone in the audience chanted, "Fuck Watts, fuck Watts," which didn't take long to spread, and Peters gleefully let the crowd take over. When he was ready to speak again, he said, "My goodness. I had at least a little more left of my sermon here, but I don't think I can win any more votes out of you. Have a good lunch, Tucson."

It didn't take long to find some of the memes Joe had mentioned earlier. One of my face Photoshopped into a painting of Benedict Arnold. Another of a bull rider getting gored, with the caption, "We need stronger horn regulations." Perhaps my favorite was two pictures of me side-by-side, the same one on my website, of me standing in front of the American flag. On the left, "Troubled kid guns down mall in Tucson . . . 'Man bad! Guns good!'" On the right, "Own kid kills one person . . . 'Guns bad! Bad bad!'"

But I had also seen a shared article written by Lily Morrow, whose picture before the text revealed that she was the hipster writing at my last rally. It had been published the day after. Title, "Mister NRA Is Human After All: What I Did and Didn't Expect from Tom Watts."

Apparently, what she did expect was "a repeat of his plans to divert more tax dollars to war and to raise the already-racist immigration laws," and she "had also expected that the murder would change him, but, "I figured he would still spin it like he did with so many other shootings. No 'if only she had a gun,' no, 'my son needed help.' Just an announcement to completely flip on his pet cause. And he didn't walk it back after the audience wanted to rip his skin off. Maybe I'm celebrating too early. Maybe he will excuse this speech and jump back into the gun lobby's lap. But until we see more, I hope this will give him cause to be born again as a completely different politician."

Most of the shares on that article came from people who also didn't want the cowboy anymore. In that moment, neither did I. Browsing a little more proved that some people supported my change. Enough, at least, to prevent me from quitting altogether. Those who were Arizona voters probably already had a Democratic candidate in mind, or third-party, but with elections so close, I had to seize the opportunity.

I groomed, dressed, and asked Jennifer to help aim Mara's webcam at me as I sat on her bed, in front of her ruined wall. There was no speech prepared. I began:

"Hello, fellow Arizonans. Americans. Anyone around the world who happens on this video.

"I understand the confusion. After all, I showed off a shiny new shotgun maybe two months ago. I come from a hunting family. My grandfather sold skins and meat to help pay for my father's education, and my father continued the tradition as a sport. He taught me how to take down a deer when I was eight. He always emphasized that you can do any dumb thing you want as long as you're safe about it.

"Of course, I passed that all down as well. Yes, I taught Scott how to shoot. If anyone has responsibility for his sister's death, it's me."

Saying that last sentence was like punching myself in the stomach, up to and including how my breath shortened and I wanted to cry.

"You see the damage behind me. This is Mara Watts' room, where it happened. I can think of no better way to explain what it has all meant for me. To explain, to those who have viciously attached me to other recent events, that I could never wish this kind of pain on anyone.

"Even our armed forces try to avoid harm. At least, to minimize it.

"I honestly wish I'd experienced a change like this sooner. It showed me just how difficult that change is. And each of my contemporaries is vulnerable. I can only hope they will come around without suffering as I did. Now I only hope to do right by my family.

"God bless you all."

Jennifer stopped recording and sat down to hug me. Then to hold me. She kissed my temple and said, "You did right by her."

The video spread from my accounts to other's pages, then to news outlets, and beyond. The conspiracy theorists hadn't let go of their convictions, but it seemed like my message traveled further and faster than theirs. I declined interviews, but it seemed not to matter too much to public opinion.

I edged out Peters in the polls, one week before the voting booths opened.

I wasn't yet comfortable enough to go on the town for pleasure, but I was able to give my security staff more time to live their own lives, and Jennifer and I celebrated with delivered pizza and a marathon of a show neither of us had seen before, *American Samurai,* and we joked about how I'd carry it as my new nickname.

In our quiet moments, Jennifer questioned me more about Stabber Jack. What he is; why he is; what I would see, hear, smell, or feel if he were close. Details I'd never thought of. Once she said, "Do you hear chattering sometimes as you're falling asleep? That jik-jik-jik sound?" Her tone reminded me of Mara asking two days before her death if she would ever feel normal again. Softly desperate, like she would never have an answer if I didn't know.

"No," I said.

No more from her. She began to avoid me, keeping an undefined distance. Beyond the occasional "Hey," she hardly spoke, no matter how often I offered to listen to what was bothering her. One time I passed too close while she left the bathroom. She gasped and said, "I can't. Please don't."

The night before the results, as I showered, I caught a faint whiff of gasoline. Not long after, there was the sharp cry of a man outside. Then the smoke alarm blew up. Deafening. The smell mixed with burning carpet. Dirty gray clouds seeped through the top of the door.

I ran out of the bathroom, wet, naked, and calling for Jennifer against the noise. Dust and ash racked my lungs and coated my skin and hair. Flames flickered in and out of the blinding smoke.

I felt around for my shotgun, the metal barrel scorching. The plastic stock was barely cooler. I continued to seek Jennifer, to neither a response nor a vision. If the carbon monoxide hadn't taken me yet, it probably didn't have her either, but someone ought to have been outside. And probably not just the one who screamed.

The gun hurt my hand, but I kept it close as I fled into the cold of November. I suppressed my own coughs, torturing my body with short spurts instead of the drawn-out hacking it needed. In the moonlight, Jose laid bleeding in the driveway. He'd had no backup. There was a deep slit in his stomach. I took his radio, signaled the others, and prayed those who were asleep would wake up.

I searched my grounds, gun at the shoulder. No band of terrorists. No assassin. If there were, they were waiting for me in the desert. But all signs pointed to Jennifer being kidnapped. That was inescapable. And the keys to my car were far from safe to grab.

I simply trusted that whoever had her hadn't gotten far. The police would not have acted quicker than I could. There could have been a million eyes on me in that moment, and just as many crosshairs, for all I knew. For all I cared. I continued calling her name, listening for any kind of response, as I climbed the tallest hill near my house to find her.

Blurred in the shadows, Jennifer had been alone. Fully dressed. Wandering. I called her name, to no answer. Once I descended to her, she turned and hugged me. Soon after, she wept into my shoulder. I asked her what was wrong. I asked if she had seen anyone. She only chattered, as if cold, while wearing a jacket. "My security's on the way," I said. "We'll be okay."

Sharp pain scraping my left rib. Then another. I shoved her.

I shot her.

The detail I remember most, as I left, was soft chattering in her mouth. I still hear it.

Panicked, yet numb, I dragged the weapon off and dropped it in a random place, hoping never to find it again. Soon after, I wandered back to my burning home, where security intercepted me. In their reports, which the police may soon discredit, Jennifer is still missing. The perpetrator behind the fire and Jose's murder is, on the record, still at large.

I won by a hair, but I'm waiting. Someday they will know as much as you, and none will believe certain parts. By telling this story, I know my time will end.

# CROSSROADS

by
Michelle R. Lane

"You're late," I said.

The Devil laughed, his hands encircling my waist. "I've been busy. The end is coming, you know."

I clutched the lapels of his dark coat, pulling him closer. "That's why I'm here. I wanted to witness the end of everything with you by my side."

His mouth found mine in the darkness and that familiar spark of excitement ignited a bonfire inside me. "Beside you, or inside you?"

I shivered in his arms, hungry for the pleasure I had been craving since the first signs of the Apocalypse appeared: storms ravaged the Caribbean and sent the southern tip of Florida floating off into the Gulf Coast; fires raged out of control in the Pacific Northwest and Northern California, leaving nothing but scorched earth and mass graves in their paths; earthquakes in the Midwest killed most the surviving firefighters trying to save folks trapped under the rubble. I wasn't a religious person, and until I met the Devil, I never really believed in the Apocalypse. But now that I had a reason to look forward to it, the end couldn't come soon enough.

We stared at each other, oblivious to the howling icy wind buffeting our bodies, the spiraling pillars of black, toxic smoke, and the stench of decay. Surrounded by death and destruction, all I could see was my lover.

He kissed me again, slower, with purpose, stoking the flames of a raging pyre at the junction of my heart, soul and cunt. "I've missed you, Beatrice."

He pressed his growing excitement against me, a welcome intrusion. My head swam with the knowledge that I wielded enough power to arouse the Devil.

Reluctantly, I broke away from his kiss. "How long do we have? You promised we'd make love until the trumpets sounded."

His laughter was tangible. It caressed my skin like a velvet glove. "Oh, darling, we aren't going to make love. We're going to fuck like there's no tomorrow, because there isn't one. When Gabriel blows his horn, you'll be mine forever."

Hunger and a flicker of fear collided inside me. Eternity in Hell wasn't something most people looked forward to. I wasn't like most people. The Devil had seen something in me years ago when I sought to sell my soul. Neither of us was a stranger to betrayal. Like him, I had learned that when you speak your mind, take a stand, do what you think is best, the people you love will sometimes turn their backs on you and walk away when you need them most. Our broken pieces fit together in a glorious mosaic of pain, loss, and unmet needs. What he saw in me made him feel something he hadn't felt in a long time: Love.

I had been desperate for help, and the Devil was my last hope. My child was dying. He suffered from what should have been a rare disorder since birth. He shouldn't have survived. Hell, I shouldn't have been pregnant in the first place.

After the government colluded with insurance companies and whittled health care down to the point of being nonexistent, insurance companies decided that birth control would no longer be covered. Some evil bastards in Washington decided that being female was a pre-existing condition, so most female reproductive health care services were no longer covered. That meant only the wealthiest women had access to safe, reliable methods of birth control.

My husband and I weren't wealthy, and although we loved each other and had a comfortable life, we agreed that we didn't have enough money to raise a family and provide for a child. William agreed to have a vasectomy, since we couldn't afford birth control. Oddly enough, his vasectomy was covered by our insurance. At least, it would have been if he'd actually gone through with the procedure.

The day I discovered I was pregnant, I waited for him in the darkened living room, curled up on the couch until he got home.

"Hey, Bea. What's going on? Why is it so dark in here?"

"I'm pregnant."

He didn't say a word. He just sat down on the loveseat, still clutching his briefcase.

"Did you hear me? I'm pregnant. How am I pregnant, William?"

He remained silent.

"I spent the afternoon reviewing all of our benefit statements. You know what I didn't find?"

"Bea, I . . . "

"You fucking lied to me. You agreed to get a vasectomy so this wouldn't happen. Why didn't you?"

"I got scared. I thought, what if a new government comes in and puts everything back to the way it was? What if I . . . what if we wanted to have children in the future?"

"Well, William, the future is now. You got your wish."

"I'm sorry, Bea. I fucked up."

When my lab work came back positive for in utero virus, or IUV, everyone I knew, including my husband, encouraged me to terminate the pregnancy. I would have gone to Planned Parenthood that day, but the government had shut down all the Planned Parenthoods the week after they outlawed abortion.

I didn't have a lot of options. I knew the risks. Risks to my health and the baby's. If both of us survived the birth, my child's illness would require constant care, and his lifespan would still probably be short. The only way for me to terminate the pregnancy was to find someone willing to give me an illegal abortion. Even if I could find someone, the cost of the procedure along with the risk of imprisonment were too high. Every day there was another news story about unlicensed clinics being raided. Medical professionals trained and willing to perform abortions were being rounded up. Prison sentences started at five years and went up depending on how many procedures someone performed. If they were willing to give up the names of their clients, they'd receive a lighter sentence. Most doctors kept their mouths shut.

William was adamant that we shouldn't bring this child, our only child, into the world. He accused me of being selfish and irrational.

"I'm being selfish and irrational? You're the reason we're in this fucking situation."

"Bea, I love you. But there is no way in hell I'm going to stand by and watch you sacrifice your life for the life of that child."

"So, what? You're going to leave me because I'm taking responsibility for your fuckup?"

"How many times do I have to say I'm sorry?"

"If you didn't want the vasectomy, the very least you could have done is wear a condom. How hard would that have been?"

"I'd take this all back if I could. I just want us to be the way we were. We were happy, weren't we?"

"I was happy until you lied to me and put my life in danger. It's too risky to get an illegal abortion. Nearly as many women are dying at the hands of greedy butchers with zero medical training as there are women dying from IUV."

"I think those numbers are being inflated by the media, Bea."

"Fine. Let's just do it here at home. I think we have some wire hangers in the closet upstairs."

"That's enough, Bea. If you want to keep this baby, go ahead, but I'm not going to watch you commit suicide."

When he left, I felt a surprising sense of relief. I hadn't realized how exhausted I was from the constant arguing. With William gone, the house was peaceful. I slept better. I had more of an appetite. I felt better than I had in months.

Like William, my obstetrician tried to talk me into seeking help illegally, even though he would lose his license to practice medicine if the government found out about his stance on abortion. "Why tempt fate? You're risking your life for a child that might not live, Beatrice. I know you aren't religious, so why are you doing this?"

"No, I'm not religious. But when you create a life and share your body with another soul, it changes how you view the world. At least, on some level, it should."

I always believed that I had the right to choose when it came to my own body. I was choosing motherhood. Not because some Bible-thumping asshole said I had to, but because I wanted to. The idea of becoming a mother terrified me. That didn't change the fact that it was my responsibility to care for the life growing inside me.

When Jacob came into the world, we thought he was stillborn. He didn't move. He didn't cry. The doctor was about to pronounce him dead and hand his tiny body to the nurse when he took his first weak, shuddering breath. His breathing reminded me to breathe, and the doctor handed his pale little body to me. My tears mixed with the blood and afterbirth still coating his nearly translucent skin. They let me hold him for a few moments before the nurse cleaned, weighed, and measured him. I didn't need to wait for the results of his bloodwork to know how advanced the virus was in my newborn son.

Because there was no known cure, and because millions of pregnant women had contracted IUV, insurance companies refused to pay for the expensive care of the infants if they lived. Since IUV was contracted during pregnancy, it, like being female, qualified as a pre-existing condition. Besides, the babies usually didn't live beyond their first few weeks. What was the point in trying to fight a losing battle? The hospital staff told me there was nothing they could do to help my sick child and sent me home with him.

I refused to give up on him that easily. I consulted everyone I could think of to get the help I needed: doctors, nutritionists, herbalists, spiritualists, and even God. I begged God to save my little boy. He never answered.

One night, after listening to Jacob cry for six hours, my prayers still unanswered, I decided to seek help elsewhere.

Long before I met William, I dated a man who enticed me down a darker path and provided distractions from my boring, small-town life.

I'd been invited to a post-Apocalyptic costume party in the woods. I don't think I was more than 16 or 17 at the time, but I was no stranger to partying. With less than an hour's notice, I pieced together a costume from things I found in my closet: a leopard-print bra and matching skirt trimmed in black fur, a black cloak left over from an old Halloween costume, a raven mask with black feathers, combat boots, and a walking stick with a human skull for a handle. Voilà! I was a dark sorceress à la *Mad Max*.

The moon was full that night. Its pale light made maneuvering through the dark woods a little easier, but I still managed to trip over my skirt. My eyes adjusted to the bright glow of firelight when I entered the clearing in the trees where three large bonfires blazed. I joined a small group of people passing a joint around the closest bonfire.

A girl I met dancing at a local club hugged me, handed me the joint, and then checked me out head to toe. "That's a great costume." We talked, smoked more weed, and then the whiskey started to flow.

An hour later, a guy named Bingo tried monopolizing all of my time. He was a handsome rockabilly god with blond hair styled in a DA and a leather jacket with a motorcycle gang emblem painted in white on the back.

I liked Bingo until he followed me to the mobile home where the bathroom was located and tried to assert his dominance. One minute we were talking about the Stray Cats, and the next he had his hand up my skirt. Somehow, I managed to sweet-talk my way out of the claustrophobic trailer with promises of a future peek at my panties. He was either stupid or crazy enough to accept my lie. Just before I bolted back to the bonfire to surround myself with more people, a man clothed all in black slithered out of the woods, almost in slow motion.

"Everything all right?" His voice was deep and smooth.

Bingo wrapped his arm around my waist and pulled me tight up against his side. Startled by the near violence of his touch, I almost screamed. I knew fear was plainly displayed on my face. I looked to the stranger for help.

Bingo buried his nose in my hair and took a deep breath before answering the stranger's question. "Everything's fine. Mind your own business, Frank."

An easy smile spread across Frank's face as he took two steps toward us. "I was talking to her, Bingo. I'm concerned about this young lady's safety. I know you well enough to know that by the end of the evening, she'll regret meeting you."

Bingo grasped my face and forced me to kiss him. I tried to pull away, but his grip was too tight. When he was done kissing me, he turned back to Frank and said, "If you want her, take her from me."

Frank was now close enough to touch Bingo. His hands balled into fists at his sides. He shrugged and said, "If you insist."

Bingo released his grip from around my waist and took a swing at Frank, and nearly punched the side of my head. I ducked and moved a few feet away. Adrenaline told me to run, but a calmer part of me needed to see the outcome of the fight. Frank was right. If Bingo won, I wouldn't be safe. Bingo's punch missed Frank. Frank took a swing at Bingo and his fist connected hard enough to snap Bingo's head back. Bingo laughed, wiped blood from the corner of his mouth, and then held up his hands.

"I guess you want her more than I do. She's yours, Frank." Bingo turned to me with a smirk. "Maybe another time, sweet cheeks. I won't bother you again tonight."

His emphasis on the word "tonight" sent a chill through me. I never wanted to find myself alone with Bingo again.

Bingo headed back to the party, leaving me alone with Frank. I didn't know Frank from Adam, but I stayed by his side the rest of the evening. I didn't know why he'd chosen to intervene. I didn't care. I felt safer with him than I did with Bingo.

By the time Frank offered to drive me home, I was really high. I couldn't stop laughing, and he seemed to like the fact that I found his macabre sense of humor so amusing. He pulled his pickup in front of my house and turned off the engine. We sat in silence for a few minutes listening to the engine pinging as it cooled down. It was late. Most of the houses on my street were dark. I'd told my parents I was staying at a friend's, so they didn't expect me home.

I liked Frank. His hair was naturally black, not dyed like many of my friends. He wore a Vandyke beard like a cartoon devil, which made me giggle and turned me on at the same time. The beard made his features seem more angular, but the softness of his dark, almond-shaped eyes spoiled the menacing quality he hoped to achieve with his appearance.

Good looks aside, I knew I could trust him, even though he made me nervous. He was older, more experienced. He hadn't laid a single finger on me during the party, but I knew he was interested. Despite all the partying I did and chances I took by catching rides home with strangers, I was still a virgin. Sure, I'd made out with guys and done other things, but somehow I'd always managed to talk my way out of having sex. Judging by the look in Frank's eye, I wasn't so sure I'd be able to talk my way out of his truck without at least giving him a kiss.

Frank patted the seat between us, suggesting I move closer. "You aren't afraid of me, are you?"

"No." The tremor in my voice betrayed me.

He grasped my chin and leaned in for a kiss. Before his lips met mine, he said, "I'm not going to hurt you, I just want a little taste." Then his mouth was on mine. The kiss was intense, leaving me dizzy and breathless.

I stroked the stubble on his cheek. "You taste like malt liquor and bad decisions."

He laughed. "Well, you taste like cheap whiskey and jailbait."

He pulled me onto his lap. He smelled like leather, cigarettes, and Old English malt liquor. There was no denying that he wanted me. His jeans were fitting a little more snugly, and his hardness pressed against me through my damp cotton panties, sending shivers along my spine.

I lost myself in his kisses, and when he slid his fingers past my panties and inside me, I gasped at the delicious, calloused roughness of his skin. With his fingers inside me, his thumb found the spot that made me cry out.

He kissed me again, his fingers never stopping their relentless motion inside me. "Does that feel good, baby?"

I bit my bottom lip and nodded at him. No one had ever made me feel so alive before.

"Then be a good girl and come for me." His fingers stilled inside me, and his thumb worked in maddening circles around my clitoris until I began moving against his hand. I clung to his shoulders as my climax began to build. He deepened the kiss and my body responded to his touch. His panting and growing excitement pushed me closer and closer to the edge. "I've been thinking about making you come since I first saw you in the woods."

His words and the huskiness of his voice sent me over the precipice, with tears streaking my face. No one had ever been able to make me lose control like that. "That was fucking wonderful. Is there anything I can do for you?"

He smiled and guided my hand to the bulge in his jeans. "You think you can help me with this?"

My fingertips traced the outline of his cock. I was excited, but worried he'd want more than I was willing to give. I couldn't look him in the eye.

He stroked my face and made me look at him. "I know you're a virgin, and that's nothing to be embarrassed about. I don't want to make you do anything you'll regret. I'm not like Bingo. I want you to trust me, because I want to see you after tonight."

Something about his tone told me he wasn't bullshitting me. He meant what he said.

"How do you know I'm a virgin?"

He slid the fingers he'd had inside me into his mouth and moaned. "Because your sweet little pussy is so tight, I barely had room for two fingers."

We had only been dating for a few weeks when I discovered how deep Frank's obsession with the occult ran. He read everything written by Anton LaVey, Aleister Crowley, and anything to do with the Golden Dawn. He taught me to read tarot cards and shared my love of horror flicks, and when we weren't partying or going to local hardcore shows, we were having sex in the basement of his mom's house.

I cherished my memories of Frank. So why, fifteen years later, was I standing on the doorstep of his cozy little cabin in the dead of night, afraid to knock?

He'd been surprised to get my call. I hadn't been sure if he'd be happy to hear from me. We hadn't spoken in more than a decade, but he offered to help me any way he could.

When Frank opened the door, he wrapped me in his arms and squeezed me tight. Then he held me at arm's length to look me over. "You're still as pretty as the night we met."

Frank's flattery was welcome balm to my psyche even though I knew I had bags under my eyes. Nursing Jacob was a full-time job. I never seemed to have enough time to sleep or feed myself. I'd lost weight and my clothes were hanging off me. Taking care of a sick child alone was wearing me out.

I smiled at him. "I see you haven't lost your charm."

He laughed and swung the door open wide to let me in. Strings of orange Halloween lights along the upper border of the dark wood paneling provide the only lighting. Black Sabbath played in the background with the volume turned down. He disappeared into the kitchen. "Can I get you a beer? Something stronger?"

I sat my purse on the floor and tried to make myself comfortable on the end of the couch. "Um, sure. I'll drink whatever you're drinking."

He returned with two bottles of Red Stripe and handed one to me after opening it. Then he made himself comfortable in a well-worn black leather recliner. "So. What brings you to my humble abode?"

I took a deep pull from my beer and savored the cold liquid before swallowing. What is it about the first sip of beer at the end of a difficult day, or the first swallow of coffee after a sleepless night?

Nothing tastes better in the whole wide world. "Look, Frank, you occasionally show up in my sex dreams and I often wonder how you're doing, but we both know I wouldn't be here if things were going well for me."

Things hadn't ended badly between me and Frank. We just had different ideas about where life was taking us. I went away to college and he followed in his dad's footsteps and became a mechanic. We didn't split up because we stopped loving each other. We split up when I decided I wanted more from life.

He nodded with a smirk on his face and took a hefty pull from his beer. He sat the bottle down on the end table near his chair and sat up a little straighter. "True enough, Bea. Things must be pretty bad if you're coming to me for help."

"It's my son, Jacob. He's really sick. Dying, if I'm honest. Everybody told me to have an abortion. Get rid of him. I couldn't bring myself to do it. I ... I need ... no one seems to want to help me." I fought back tears and nearly choked on the lump in my throat.

Frank's face contorted with sorrow. "I'd heard things, but nothing certain. What does your husband think about all this?"

Tears fell down my cheeks and my shoulders shook. "He left before I had the baby. I don't want him to come back."

Frank got up from the recliner and sat next to me on the couch. He put his arm around me and I buried my face against his chest. His T-shirt had an image of some demonic entity in white against the faded black cotton fabric. He didn't say a word, just let me cry.

When I finally stopped crying, I became more aware of his arm around me. No one had touched me since William left. After his betrayal, I didn't want him to touch me.

I shifted away from Frank, suddenly conscious of how easy it was to be close to him. "I'm sorry to bother you like this, but I've run out of options. I need to try something else, and I think you're the only person who can help me."

He stared at me for a moment, thinking. "I'm not a healer, Bea. I can't save your boy. All I can offer you is the comfort of my bed if you want it, and I'm still a good listener. If you let me, I can help you forget your troubles for a few hours." He rested his hand on my thigh. Familiar, comforting, not demanding.

I covered his hand with mine and didn't push him away. "Frank, is the Devil . . . real?"

He laughed. "Is that why you're here? You wanna talk about the Devil?"

The look on my face made him stop laughing. "No, I want to meet him."

The following week, I returned to Frank's cabin to learn how to summon the Devil. He was happy to see me even though he wasn't exactly thrilled about why I was there.

"Bea, summoning Lucifer isn't a panacea for all that ails you."

I listened and let his words sink in. "This is my last hope for my son, Frank. If the Devil won't help me, I don't know who else to ask."

He stared at me in silence for a few beats. "Fine. The Devil is in the business of collecting souls, not helping people. He makes bargains. You trade your soul for whatever it is you want, and then that is the end of the conversation. There's no haggling or compromises, but he'll trick you if he can. Choose your words carefully. Once you make a deal, there's no turning back."

When I left Frank's, I had a Tupperware container of dried herbs, a silver knife, a black candle, and step-by-step instructions with an incantation in Latin. I thanked him, kissed him on the cheek, and went home to prepare.

Typically, when you make a deal with the Devil, you seal your fate with a kiss. You summon the Devil to a crossroads, ask for what you want most, and kiss him, and the deed will be done. That's not exactly what happened when I met the Devil at the crossroads nearly 10 years ago. Yes, he agreed to give me what I wanted in exchange for my soul. However, when we kissed, the kiss lingered much longer than I anticipated. In fact, the kiss frightened me. I tried to pull away, but he wouldn't let go.

The kiss turned into caresses and groping and groans laced with unbridled need. He stopped kissing me long enough to look me in the eye. My fear slowly ebbed away when I saw the raw look of need in his eyes. The pain in me recognized the pain in him. No one had ever looked at me like that before. No one had ever wanted me like that.

He let me go and fished a pocket watch from inside his coat, checking the time. His hand trembled. "Why have you summoned me, Beatrice?"

I took a step toward him, reaching to caress his face, and he backed away. Was I making the Devil nervous? "It's my son. He was born with IUV. He's very sick. Dying. I want you to save him."

His gaze traveled up my body slowly until he met my stare. There was lust in his beautiful amber eyes. He shook his head slightly, as if he were struggling to focus. "That's a fairly standard contract. Your soul in exchange for your child's life. A classic act of selflessness with a very heavy price. It seems almost a shame that you'll be going to Hell. Have you thought of contacting my father instead?"

I laughed. "I tried that. He never answered."

He shuffled from foot to foot. "Am I to assume that I am your last hope?"

"I think you already know that."

He smiled and nodded. "Desperate times and all."

I reached for him again. He grabbed my wrist, squeezing it tightly before I could make contact. "Please," I said.

He pushed me back away from him. He didn't hurt me, but I almost lost my footing. "Don't, Beatrice." The tone in his voice was a warning.

"Don't you like me?"

He made a sound like a strangled chuckle. Before he turned away from me I saw anger and frustration etched on his face. When he turned back to look at me, his face had softened. He seemed lost, uncertain. "I am finding it nearly impossible to keep my hands off you. I'm sorry about your son. I wish I could help you, but you don't deserve the punishment that awaits you in Hell. You don't deserve . . . me."

It was my turn to get angry. "I summoned you to sell my soul. I don't care what awaits me after I die. My son is dying right now. I can't bear to watch him suffer. Please, help me."

He looked away, wringing his hands. "You're supposed to be afraid of me. Why aren't you afraid?"

I touched his face and made him look at me. "I know I should be afraid. I don't understand my feelings either. I know that making a deal with you means that I'll go to Hell. I still want you to touch me."

I knew there would be consequences for giving myself to him, but I didn't care. When his mouth met mine again, it felt like we were canceling out each other's loneliness.

You might think the Devil would be a violent and selfish lover. You'd be wrong. Despite his expertise in sin, he worshipped my body like a religious relic. He watched with awe as I undressed for him, and gently kissed every inch of my bared skin. My blood pulsed through my veins like a river of fire when his flesh melded with mine. We touched and tasted and sucked and bit and kissed and fucked until I thought I would go out of my mind. No, the Devil is nothing, if not a generous lover. I gave him everything he asked for and more. Saying no to him seemed like blasphemy. I don't know how long we reveled in each other's flesh, but when we finished making love, he knew me inside and out. There were no secrets between us.

We dressed in silence. What was there to say that hadn't been communicated between our bodies? My heart ached at the thought of leaving him. And, as if he sensed what I was feeling, he held me close to him and said, "I will see you again. At the end of days. When the world ends, you will be my bride."

Tears streaked my face when he kissed me for the last time that night. He promised to fulfill our agreement, but he wanted more than my soul. He wanted my heart as well.

A few days after my encounter with the Devil, Frank called to see how the meeting went. "Did the spell work? Did he show up?"

"Oh yes." I was conscious of the carnal tone in my voice, and did nothing to hide it.

Frank was quiet on the other end of the phone. The ticking of the clock in my kitchen counted the seconds before he spoke. "Did he . . . make a bargain with you?"

"He did." I was a little shocked by how happy I sounded about it.

"Bea, are you all right?"

"I've never felt better. He was nothing like I expected. I'm actually looking forward to seeing him again."

Once more, Frank was silent. "Seeing him again? I don't understand. He doesn't actually come to collect your soul when your time's up. He makes the deal, grants your request, and that's that. When the time comes, you'll just go straight to Hell."

I laughed. "Well, in my case, I think he might make an exception. We got along like a house on fire. He wants to see me again."

"He told you that?"

Frank's questions were beginning to get on my nerves. "Yeah. Why?"

His tone changed from concerned friend to possessive lover. "What exactly happened at the crossroads, Bea?"

"I followed your directions to the letter and summoned him. He showed up, we talked, and then sealed the deal with a kiss."

"Uh huh. And then what happened?"

It was my turn to be silent. I wasn't embarrassed about what happened between me and the Devil, I just wasn't sure if it was any of Frank's business.

"Bea, what did you do after that?"

I should have been ashamed for what I did, but I wasn't. In fact, I was ecstatic. Still, I didn't answer his question.

"Did you . . . did he . . . did you fuck the Devil?" I couldn't tell if he was angry, in awe, or just jealous.

My tone was even and matter-of-fact. "I didn't fuck him."

He let out a huge sigh, and then he laughed nervously. "You had me worried there for a minute."

"We didn't fuck. We made love."

There was a sputtering noise from Frank's end, followed by coughing. "You what?"

Jacob moved in his crib, waking up from his nap. I lowered my voice. "I have to go, Frank. Jacob's awake. I'll talk to you later." I hung up.

A few days after making my pact with the Devil, Jacob appeared to have completely recovered from his illness. There were no signs of IUV. He finally had an appetite and was gaining weight. He was alert, made cooing sounds, and smiled like a normal healthy baby. His complexion was now closer to the color of my own caramel-colored skin. My son was healed. Not because of science or medicine or God's intervention. Jacob was healthy because I sold my soul, and the Devil keeps his promises.

While the infant mortality rate climbed worldwide, my son and I thrived. No pregnant woman was safe from IUV. Mothers died in childbirth, babies were stillborn or died within hours of birth. Stupidly, the government continued their campaign of ABSTINENCE SAVES LIVES, and refused to make birth control free and easy to access. Most of Europe, parts of Asia, and even parts of South America managed to stop the spread of IUV by providing birth control at open clinics or providing sterilization to those who requested it.

Regardless of what the right-wing government thought, the threat of death wasn't going to stop people from having sex, but it did stop them from having babies. In fact, no one was getting pregnant if they could help it. Over a five-year period, there were no successful births. Across the globe, women took necessary precautions, but in America, women who didn't have access to birth control gave birth to dead babies, or died.

Jacob grew and grew, amazing his doctors, my friends, and our family. When William found out about Jacob's miraculous recovery, he begged to be forgiven and to be let back into my life. He wanted a second chance at being a husband and father.

After a week of relentless phone calls that I ignored, William showed up at the house and banged on the front door. I had the locks changed after he moved out. "Come on, Bea, let me in. I just want to see you and my son."

"Go away, William. You left us, remember?"

His banging got more aggressive but his tone and words were that of a man desperate for forgiveness. I just wanted him to go away. I called Frank. I suppose most people would have called the police. Unlike most people, I was raised not to trust cops and didn't want them in my home.

Frank was at work when I called. "Don't worry. I'm on my way. I'll make sure he doesn't bother you again."

I felt so stupid calling Frank, but I didn't know what else to do. I wasn't afraid of William. I was angry at him for having the audacity to come to my house and demand to be let in. Until Jacob's health improved, he didn't want anything to do with us. Now that our son was healthy, he wanted to try being a family again. The thought of him touching me or holding Jacob made my flesh crawl.

When Frank showed up, William went ape shit. All of a sudden, I was a bitch and Frank was the lowest lifeform who ever walked the Earth. Frank attempted to solve things peacefully, but each time William said something negative about me it made him angrier. His breaking point was when William called me a whore. Frank didn't say a word. He just beat the living shit out of my ex-husband, put him in his car, and told him if he ever showed up at my house again, he'd kill him. I don't know if Frank would ever really kill anyone, but after seeing the ass-whooping he gave William, I wouldn't test that theory. William got the message loud and clear and never came back.

The rains started on a Monday afternoon and didn't stop until fourteen days later. The water kept rising and rising. There were freak storms, earthquakes, tidal waves, wild fires and other natural disasters happening all over the planet. Apocalypse enthusiasts were basking in their glory.

As much as I looked forward to seeing my demon lover, I also knew my time with Jacob was coming to an end. When the time came, he'd be going to Heaven and I'd be going to Hell. A heavy sadness fell upon me. I thought I had reached my lowest point when I was in danger of losing Jacob to IUV. Apparently, no matter how low you get, there's always the possibility of a deeper level of sorrow.

The Susquehanna rose higher than ever in its history, and the flood waters reached above the first story of our house. Jacob and I took shelter in the attic, hoping we were high enough to avoid drowning or being swept away in the surprisingly fast current.

On our third day in the attic, just before dawn, the house shifted with an ear-splitting groan. Wood, brick, and concrete collapsed under the pressure of the rushing waters that had weakened the foundation. I woke up just in time to see Jacob slip through a gaping hole in the side of the house. The flood waters had finally reached the attic. He was gone before I could even sit up. I watched, helpless as my 10-year-old boy disappeared into the swirling black water. He didn't cry. He didn't scream. He simply said, "I love you, Mommy." Then he was gone.

I cried until I threw up, heaving until my stomach was empty and there was nothing left inside me, and then I cried some more. I cried until I exhausted myself, but sleep wouldn't come.

A few days later, after the floodwaters subsided, the dead began to rise. Jacob stood in the yard, staring at the house. I called to him from the attic window. I'm not sure what drew him away from the house, but all the dead seemed to be headed toward something, no longer interested in the living. Saying goodbye to Jacob the second time was a little easier.

When the last of the dead had shambled past the house, I decided it was time to return to the crossroads.

With only the clothes on my back, I walked the nine miles from my crumbling, water-soaked house to the place where I believed I would find my salvation. Nine miles of burning buildings, abandoned cars, and screaming people running in every direction with nowhere to go. After the flood, the sun didn't rise. It's as if the sun went on strike and left the moon to watch over us.

The lunar eclipse began at noon and bathed the Earth in darkness. Only a red halo could be seen around the blackened orb. Traveling alone in the darkness should have frightened me, but all I could think about was meeting my lover at the end of time.

I don't know how long I sat there waiting for him. It was enough time to count my blessings and accept the fact that there would be no tomorrow. I realized I had no regrets, no remorse, and no fear. Sitting there, waiting for the Devil, I was at peace.

Ten years may not seem like a long time, but I was given ten more years with my son than anyone had predicted. Everyone else gave up on him. Gave up on us. The same government that refused to provide access to birth control to protect women against contracting IUV did nothing to come up with a cure to save the millions of women and children affected by the virus. Even God turned his back.

None of that mattered when the Devil came to claim me. He was more handsome than I remembered, and I nearly wept at the sight of him. There were so many things I wanted to say to him, so many words of thanks that were forgotten the moment he touched me. His fingertips burned my clothes to cinders. "You won't need these," he said.

I rode the Devil until Gabriel's trumpet sounded, in a blur of flesh and fire. Passion burned me from the inside out. Consumed me body and soul. Our lust never flagging, the Devil fucked me like he would never be satisfied until we became one. A literal beast with two backs. My laughter at the perverse thought gave him pause, but it was the scent of brimstone that brought me back to myself.

Still thrusting inside me, slowing down only long enough to pull me closer, my back to his front, he whispered against my ear, "Welcome home, Beatrice."

# INSIDER TRADING

by
Ken McGrath

"Didn't you ask me about this already?" Lauren Golden, her brow furrowed, looked up from the clipboard her assistant had just handed over. "I'm sure we haven't gone through all the details yet. I'm still very anti this proposal."

Annie angled her head to read the title on the top page.

"Authority to rezone the 22-acre conservation site in the east of the city for commercial purposes. Yeah, that's the one. And you've agreed to it already, remember?" she said with a shrug, absently twisting her long hair into a loose plait at her left shoulder as she spoke. "Misters Heady and Cairns from the wildlife commission were in yesterday afternoon to confirm everything's been approved. They sent you those flowers as a thank-you and everything."

Lauren looked to her right and noticed a large vase of fresh sunflowers which dominated the corner of her desk.

"Were they there a second ago?" She pointed at the flowers.

"Been there all morning, Madam Mayor. I really think you need to take a break." Annie said. "Beautiful, aren't they?. They say that sunflowers symbolise spiritual guidance and that you're on the right path. I think you should sign the forms, then see about taking the rest of the day off, maybe. Clear your head."

Lauren sat back and folded her arms.

"So, they've rolled back on this proposal, have they, Heady and Cairns? I can't believe that. Who bought them out, I wonder?" Lauren shoved the clipboard back towards Annie, as if she couldn't stand to have it on her desk. "I can't sign this. I won't sign it."

Annie's face darkened. "You have to."

"Excuse me, I think you'll find I don't have to do anything that I don't want to. I was voted in to this office on a pro-environmental stance and I intend to stay true to that. Regardless of what those two so-called colleagues of mine decide to do." Lauren stood up and walked around the desk. "Now if you'll excuse me I have a birthday party to plan."

At the door Lauren glanced back to see Annie glaring at her and shuddered.

"I have a birthday party to plan," Lauren repeated as she pulled the door shut and hurried away.

Outside, on one of the quieter back streets between her office and The Colander, Lauren thought about what she's just seen. For Annie Capullo, her assistant for the last five years, her friend, to have stared at her with such venom—Lauren couldn't make sense of it. She pulled her jacket tighter and looked up to see if the clouds seemed like rain.

On one of the first-floor balconies above her a woman was lighting a cigarette. The smoke that wafted from her nostrils made Lauren think of dragons.

The woman looked down at Lauren and her face curled into a sneer of wrinkles and bared teeth. The smoke swirled around her head and seemed to grow thicker. Lauren took a step backwards as the woman rolled up a sleeve, removed the cigarette from her mouth, and ground the lit tip into the flesh of her forearm.

"Get out," she rasped. Lauren took another step backwards and stumbled over her own feet.

"Get out," the woman repeated, voice rising in pitch and volume until it was a scream. "Get out. Get out! *Get out!*"

Lauren turned and ran.

The Colander was one of the city's top restaurant's and a favourite of Lauren Golden and her family from way, way back, from before she was ever elected for public office, let alone mayor. Situated in the city centre but on a small side-street that was mostly home to other niche restaurants and art galleries, it offered the opportunity for a nice break away from the public eye.

Lauren stood at the reception desk and waited for the maître d' to come out and greet her. As she waited she looked around. The restaurant was a little under half-full, the general chatter and clatter of cutlery on plates a nice background noise.

"Madam Mayor, welcome. How may I help you?"

Lauren smiled at the maître d'. He was tall and slender, with a mouth like a slash, dark eyes, and a smooth, bald head.

"I'm sorry, do I know you?" Lauren asked.

"No, madam. I'm new. Would you like me to escort you to your table? Your party is waiting."

"My party? What are you talking about? I'm here to book a birthday party. For my husband."

"You are over here with Misters Heady and Cairns from the wildlife commission," he said and gestured to a table where they indeed sat. "I believe you were going to discuss the rezoning of some waste land."

"It's conservation land," Lauren said automatically, yet distracted. Her attention was drawn to a giant blackboard that took up one whole wall of the restaurant. "Is that new too? I've never seen it before."

"It's just the menu, honey, where they write the specials. Now come on, sit down." She felt a hand on her arm and turned to see her husband standing there, beaming at her.

"Adrian, when did get here? It's supposed to be a surprise."

"What is?"

"The birthday party."

"We're not here for a birthday party, love," Adrian said, and put a guiding hand firmly on her lower back. "We're over here with Misters Heady and Cairns, from the wildlife commission."

Lauren looked down to see she had on her favourite little black dress, her Audrey Hepburn in *Breakfast at Tiffany's* number. The one she kept for only the most special of occasions.

"Really?"

"Yes," Adrian nodded. "Are you okay?"

"Sure, sure," Lauren said, sounding not one bit of it. "Wait a minute. I just want to take a look at that."

She pushed away from her husband and went over to the blackboard. The left-hand side had the day's menu written in solid script while the right was dominated by a huge, chalk drawing of a tree whose branches swept out across the board, reaching like fingertips. Lauren craned her neck to make out what was drawn amongst the tangle of twigs and leaves.

"I think it says something. Yes, it does, there's definitely something written here," she said. "Can you see this, Adrian?"

"It's just the menu is all, love." He placed a hand on her shoulder. "Now come on, sit down, we need to talk about those rezoning documents."

"No, not yet." She pushed away from him. "Look, seriously, there's something written here, in the branches. It looks like the word *up*."

"It probably just says *soup*," Adrian laughed. "I'd say they have all sorts of subliminal messages hidden around here to try and get you to order different things."

Lauren squinted at the picture, forcing herself to see between the lines, then she pointed.

"Look, there, it says … it says, 'Get out, Lauren. You have to wake up.'" She froze. "What?"

The letters lit up bright red, like neon, then everything else faded into smoke and disappeared.

Lauren spun around to find Adrian—and stared at herself. She gasped, turned, looked frantically about. Everyone in the restaurant lifted their heads to look at her. Every single one of them was wearing her face. Then, as one, their jaws dropped open and they screamed.

"Get out!"

It was as if the restaurant was suddenly filled with the noise of a thousand seagulls. Lauren fell backwards and looked on as the walls parted. Helmeted riot police swarmed into the restaurant. They were countless as they advanced on her, their identities hidden beneath reflective silver face-plates that ended at the nose, lips set in harsh lines above stern jaws. Each held a stubby black baton, the tops of which danced with blue sparks.

On her knees, ears ringing, Lauren focused on the message, on the glowing red words.

Lying on her back in bed she could feel her arms flat and heavy by her sides. She could feel her eyelids closed tight. She was aware of every part of her and she was suddenly aware that she couldn't move any of those parts. Her throat was phlegmy, constricted. She tried to scream but wasn't able to control the muscles.

In the restaurant the guards jabbed the shock-sticks into her. On the floor of the restaurant she jerked about as her body was wracked with electricity.

In bed she felt her body tense and she pushed her eyelids upwards with all her might. She felt the strain in her jaws, but despite it all she couldn't pry them apart.

The guards stood over her, their brutal faces unmoving as they shocked her again and again.

With a final push and a shout, Lauren got her eyelids open and lifted her head off the pillow. She gasped, still convinced she could feel the tingle on her body where the shock-sticks had been used.

Lauren rolled onto her side and fumbled the bedside lamp on. The room was unfamiliar. A hotel bedroom, with no one beside her. She sat up, thinking, tried to remember where Adrian was. The door to the bathroom was open, the light off. No sound came from inside. Then she remembered Adrian hadn't come on this trip. She had come alone to meet the wildlife commission.

She caught her breath and lifted her hand, felt the sweat on her brow.

No, wait, that was wrong. She wasn't here for a meeting. She never left home these days without Adrian, not since his accident.

There was the click of a key card outside and the door opened slowly, a widening strip of light slicing through the darkness.

"Who is it?" she called, hearing the fear in her voice.

"Madam Mayor, Madam Mayor," a man's voice said from the bathroom. "You really do seem quite intent on making this difficult for yourself."

Lauren pulled the covers up tight around herself as her gaze swiveled from the dark doorway of the bathroom to the slowly opening one into the hallway.

"Who are you? What do you want?"

Then she saw, illuminated in the hallway door, the man from her dream, the maître d' from The Colander. He tilted his head and smiled. The light in the bathroom flicked on and what could have been his twin stood there. The only difference between them was the one in the bathroom had hair, black and slicked back, like an elderly solicitor.

Lauren Golden screamed.

The two men looked at each other, smiled broadly, and waited silently.

When she had finished screaming, the one at the bathroom spoke.

"Madam Mayor, allow me to introduce myself. I am Mister Sound and that is my colleague, Mister Tight. We are your Influencers for this evening. Sometimes we are playfully referred to as the Agents of Sleep. There is a rather good joke in there if you care to try and figure it out," he paused for a moment. "I doubt you have heard of us. We are hired to work with people like yourself when they need to have their minds made up about certain things. We take our…"

Lauren jumped out of the bed.

She flung a pillow in Mister Sound's direction as she made a burst for the still open hallway door. Mister Tight tensed, his arms raised to tackle her, but she swiftly took his legs out from underneath him and drove the palm of her hand into his jaw as he fell. Then she was out the door and into the corridor.

She turned blindly, ran down hallways that all looked the same. Banged on locked bedroom doors as she went, shouting all the time. She didn't look back until she was at the lifts. She hammered the call button with her thumb.

"Come on, come on, come on," she muttered.

She looked up and saw the two men come around the corner at the end of the hall.

"Oh God, come on, come on," she whispered. She bashed the button, glanced up at the LED display as the numbers crawled slowly, painfully upwards. The two men advanced at a leisurely pace.

"There is no point in running Madam Mayor," Mister Tight said in a sing-song voice.

"We are going to get you," Mister Sound harmonised, his mouth parted into a wide grin that showed off far too many teeth.

*Why weren't any of the doors opening? How had none of the other guests been woken by the noise? Where was the lift?*

Lauren felt a scream rise up her throat, but before she released it the doors parted with a ping and she fell into the elevator.

She jabbed the ground-floor icon and began hitting the close-door button. It was an agonisingly long time before the doors finally came together. Heart pounding, she leaned back against the far wall, her breath ragged. Somehow, she noticed the soothing tones of a pan-pipe version of "Tears in Heaven" being played in the background.

When the doors parted on the ground floor, Lauren pushed herself upright and looked out into the lobby. With a deep breath, she stepped forwards from the lift and found herself standing in the doorway of her hotel bedroom once more.

She looked behind her. The corridor stretched away to her left and right

"There really is no point running Madam Mayor," Mister Tight said, stepping out of the bathroom.

"You're only going to find yourself back here again," Mister Sound whispered in her ear. She jumped, skin prickling with gooseflesh.

"Please sit down. It's easier that way." Mister Tight gestured towards the bed.

Lauren moved into the room but away from where Mister Tight was pointing. She kept her back against the wall, trying to keep both men in sight at all times. They looked at each other and smiled their wide, rictus grins.

"Madam Mayor, I warn you, there really is no point in running," Mister Sound repeated. "So please, save your energy. We will only have to rerun the scenario again."

Mister Sound smiled. It made Lauren think of a cat trying to make friendly faces at a mouse.

Behind his thin lips, Mister Tight ran his tongue over the front of his teeth. Lauren watched in disgust as he spat at the wall, and then recoiled as the wet spot sprouted legs and scurried away at speed. Mister Tight smiled a wide, yellow-toothed smile that didn't reach his eyes. The more he smiled at her the bigger his mouth was getting. It looked like it would break through his cheeks if it continued that way.

"We are in control here, Madam Mayor," Mister Sound said. "Don't ever doubt that."

"What do you want from me?" she said, unable to keep the fear from her voice.

"We have been employed to ensure that your mind is made up about a certain decision," Mister Sound continued, in the voice of a stern teacher. He nodded to his companion. Mister Tight's face remained frozen in that overwhelmingly, overwide grin. "My colleague and I have some very special skills that allow us to visit people in their dreams. There we can use our influence to imprint ideas on a person's subconscious. Just like we are going to do with you."

"Do you ever wonder why public figures do things that are out of character or politicians break their campaign promises?" Mister Tight said. He nodded and pointed at both himself and Mister Sound. "Not always, but quite often. We're very good at what we do. When we're finished you might even believe you came to the decision yourself."

"You expect me to believe there's some cabal that runs everything from the shadows?" Lauren snapped.

"Quite frankly, I don't care what you believe, Madam Mayor. You're not going to remember any of it tomorrow anyway," Mister Sound said. "We're the ones who are in control here. We've always been in control. We have been through this before with you and you have always proven to be difficult, but you have never failed to take our treatment and follow the path we were instructed to guide you down."

Mister Sound clicked his fingers. Lauren was lying in the bed, arms flat by her sides. She tried to scream but her throat was locked. She could hear them moving around the room out of her line of sight. Nothing she tried to do worked, no part of her responded.

Then Mister Tight stepped into view on her left. He lifted one of his hands, the fingers long and thin, the fingernails pitch-black and pointed. He seemed to be growing taller, skinnier, more imposing. She felt as if the bed was growing up around her, sucking her in deeper.

"We can make this very uncomfortable for you for as long as it takes, Madam Mayor," Mister Tight said, his voice very matter-of-fact. "You won't remember it tomorrow when you wake up, but while you're here we can put you in a nightmare that will last a lifetime."

Mister Tight's eyes glazed over, fully black, and Lauren's heart felt like it was about to burst in her chest.

"Now," Mister Sound stepped into view. A forked tongue flicked out between his lips. "We are about to run some scenarios and we would very much like for you to take on board the lesson we want you to learn."

Lauren's eyelids closed.

"Hello, knock-knock?"

"Huh?" Lauren Golden blinked rapidly. She looked over at the entrance to her office where Annie was standing.

"Are you okay?" her assistant asked.

Lauren paused for a moment before responding. "Yeah. Yeah, I am. I must have just zoned out. I don't think I've been sleeping well this last week. Is everything okay?"

"Just wanted to let you know that Misters Heady and Cairns from the wildlife commission are waiting for you in the Oak Room."

"About the rezoning of the twenty-two-acre lot, right?"

"The conservation site," Annie corrected her. She stepped into the room and gave Lauren a concerned look. "I can get rid of them if you want."

Lauren stood up and brushed at her shoulders, fixed her shirt. "No, no. I'm ready for them. By the way, I like your hair. When'd you get that done?"

Annie touched a hand to where her hair ended just under her jawline and made a little uncertain face.

"Do you like it? Really? I just went for it over the weekend. Fancied a change. You don't think they took too much off, do you? I keep going to plait it, forgetting it's all gone now."

"No, it suits you. It really does," Lauren said with a smile. "And you're right, sometimes we just have to follow our instincts and go with what feels good, don't we? Now let's go talk to these gentlemen and see if we can finally resolve this rezoning issue. It seems to have been the only thing on my mind this last while."

# FREEDUM

by
James Musgrave


I got the Freedum delivery job through my broinlaw, Sid Edelstein. He works at It's a Mall World over by the river. The fortyyearsofgreen didn't work too well. Water had to be filtered by a reputable company. Instead of going podtopod, the way I deliver Freedum, his delivery method gives his customers their choices on different levels of the mall. His customers are mobile. They work for the gubment and are kept busy going around the country getting votes, so their legs are still functional. And, there were always the protectors of Corporate Gubment, and they were lurking everywhere.

On the other hand (or leg), my customers are the majority of our country's working stiffs: the Freedum Flyers. These are the folks who run most of everything in our society. They control all the computerized Freedum such as Instabanks, Instashops, Instagames, Instasports, InstaTV, Instamovies, Instablogs, Instasex, Instamarriage, Instadivorce, Instamortuary, and the hundreds of thousands other "Insta" websites. This makes up our World Freedum Network. I serve the 90 percent of the working stiffs who run this online virtual world.

In our post-green world, the only room we have for mobile humanity is on the tiny Paths of Nature that weave through the millions of pods where the Freedum Flyers work, keeping our social fabric running and our Freedum Malls supplied. We lost most of our space for moving around long ago. The majority of the elders cannot even remember what it was like before we became a nation of Freedum.

They did remember that there were no android spies of the Corporate Gubment the way there are now.

Some of the oldest of the mobile ones tell crazy stories on late-night talk shows about places called National Parks where they say they could leave the cities to visit Nature that was being held captive inside huge enclosures called parks. They had trees growing, wild animals frolicking, waterfalls falling over mountains, and places where one could actually sit out in the middle of all that green and cook over an open fire!

A fire in the middle of trees, can you believe it? We know all about the fires that stormed the path of destruction that led to our fortyyearsofgreen, just as we know about the flooding of the oceans caused by Global Warming that led to our fiftyyearsofwars. Our wars were fought over the rest of the natural resources left after the floods, and I guess back then our population was down to a reasonable size, but after the wars, we started going at it again, and our numbers soon increased until we were back up to our usual overflowing and suffocating size. That's why we needed Freedum.

I guess I like my job. If I didn't do it, then these Freedum Flyers of mine would have no life at all. As I drive down the paths between pods, I try to focus on the music streaming inside my Freedum Flyer Greenmobile, but sometimes I can't, and I look outside to see all the deliveries being made across this great land of ours. All of our fish are now farmed, all of our other complex protein was long ago converted to cloned Instamammals, and all of the vegetation is also bio-engineered and delivered by podmobiles to the pods housing our Freedum Flyer workforce. The mobile gubment workers are the only ones who are allowed to go "shopping" in the Mall Worlds. They can also, of course, get deliveries made to their gubment pods, but that is considered a low-class thing to do for a mobile person. The pods are all around me as I drive down the path to make deliveries. My Freedom Flyer is over two blocks long, and when I arrive at a pod, it swivels into a vertical tower, wherein my assortment of "choice modules" are raised to the level of the Freedum Flyer worker bubbles, and the busy little bees can then partake of the only enjoyment they ever have in their hectic lives.

What do they get to choose from? Why, they choose from the same variety of Instant Freedum that they are in charge of on their computerized network! Isn't it beautiful? The logic of it all? It's a giant feedback loop. There is no need for advertising because we deliver the choices directly to the consumer. And, of course, the consumers work at providing those same choices to the rest of the world. It is a perfectly programmed circle of capitalism at its finest. The Corporate Gubment reaps the benefit, of course, and this often makes me a bit sad. I wonder what those mobile gubment workers do with *their* profits? Sometimes, I even speculate if they deserve their profits, but even thinking such subversive thoughts can get one arrested and sent to one of the thousands of Terrorist Detainee Pods.

However, today is my Freedum Flyer friend's birthday, and I am going to propose something to him in the way of a celebratory act. My friend's name is Caleb. Freedum Flyers are not allowed a surname, as they are considered part of the working infrastructure of the Corporate Gubment and not really in its corps of leadership. I, however, dissident that I am, believe the Freedum Flyers and other working stiffs deserve better treatment. That's why I am doing this. My friend Caleb and I are going to perform a celebratory trick on the gubment mobile employees that will teach them a lesson.

Here it is, pod number 6855273-C-36657. As I open it, I can see my friend still at work, typing frantically on his keyboard, his face a picture of stern concentration, his tiny, useless legs dangling over his seat like the *tzitzit on my tallit prayer shawl*. Yes, I am a Jew. My name is Jacob Weisberg, and I am going to cause a ruckus in the world of the gubment. I will not be alone in this effort, as we Jews insinuate ourselves throughout society, keeping a record of our activities, and we are obligated by our religion to constantly work for "Justice." The treatment of the Freedum Flyers like my friend Caleb is not just.

"Caleb, my friend! Happy birthday! Stop working for a moment, will you? I have a proposition to make."

My friend's huge, bald head rises up from the keyboard, like a moon over Jupiter, and I can see his reflecting, human eyes of green-blue staring back at me. He is intelligent, inquisitive, with a great sense of humor. That's why I am doing this. I know his kind must get some respect in this world order, or they will surely eventually die, and I will not be part of their destruction!

"Jacup Wiseburp! How the hell are ya?" Caleb waves at me, weakly, as his hands are conditioned, through many thousands of repetitive hours, to type only at a keyboard and not to wave in the air at a friend.

"Listen, Caleb, I have a plan that I've been working on for many months now, and it's going to make the gubment pay attention to your plight as a Freedum Flyer."

"Here we go again. Jacob, buddy, it's all good. I know you Jews invented guilt, but we InstaCatholics perfected it. We Flyboys look at our job as just another cross for Jesus, that's all. Don't be so sad. It ain't all bad, you know. We get a week in the Instasex game rooms with our choice of thousands of celebrity women—hooray!"

"That's not *real* human contact, Caleb. It's a programmed hologram that tricks your body into secreting its holy juices in a masturbatory sin! It's worse than Onanism. It just feeds into your narcissistic tendencies. Don't you want to run free out in the world? Don't you need to touch another imperfect human and love her as a truly married person and not in one of these fabricated Instamarriages that are just virtual lies?"

"Jake, you don't really *get* it, do you? Our virtual world gives us more Freedum than the real world! That's its beauty. Before the Insta-world we had fewer choices, and we were killing each other over the limited natural resources. Now we all live in harmony in the world, we all get fed our fill every day, and we all get billions of different choices to make to bring joy into our personal lives. I'm glad to be growing older in this world. Why can't you just relax and enjoy it too?"

"Look down at your legs, friend," I tell him, making a last effort to break through his wall of denial. "You can't walk. You can't visit any other place but inside your own head. They *made* you this way! And they don't care, either, when your pods get destroyed by earthquakes or fires. It's not broadcast over the Freedum Network, but I've seen the results. Thousands of your friends and their bald heads and spindly legs are crushed like maggots inside a loaf of bread. Get wise, Caleb! Don't be a martyr for Corporate Gubment."

"All right, Jacob. Let's just assume for a moment that you can show me the world you propose is better. What is this plan of yours? How do we show the gubment up?"

"Now you're talking!" I pulled out the walker that my broinlaw, Sid, created for Freedom Flyers to become mobile. It is a solar- and biofuel-powered hovercraft that could propel a small Flyer anywhere he or she wanted to go. It could maneuver the stubby body at up to ten miles an hour, and it could fit snuggly on the thighs of the Flyer so they wouldn't tip over. "We're going to organize a mass demonstration of Freedom Flyers, and we're all going to march on Corporate Gubment offices. But first, my friend, I am going to take you with me so you can see how our leaders are living at your expense!"

On his thirty-fourth birthday, I took Caleb to see what was going on inside a gubment pod on the outskirts of our city. I had, one year earlier, visited the gubment workers' domicile through a servants' entrance that snaked through the rows of buildings that served as their living quarters. I, of course, was not an authorized servant, but another of my broinlaws, Mel Appel, was, and he was able to get the correct chip implanted in my arm to get me into the buildings as a delivery person. So, on this day, I took my little friend Caleb for his first look at how the other half lived.

Actually, like most of what humanity created (and as our King David once pointed out much earlier), it was nothing new. In fact, as my grandfather Sol, who keeps the ancient collection of history books, told me, "That's just like the ancient Romans, Jacob. They live like the Romans once did."

The first building I showed Caleb was one where the gubment employees ate and enjoyed themselves as a group. The walls were covered with mirrors so they could see themselves as they stuffed their mouths with every imaginable food and drink. They sat in a wide circle, slobbering, spitting, splattering and swatting each other with the liquids from chickens, turkeys, pigs, cattle, fish, fruits, wines, liquors, and many other consumables we had never even seen before.

Also, against the wall, were a row of tubs, where the gubment imbibers threw up when they were full so they could then engorge themselves some more. And, as they partook of this ungodly feast—in total nudity, I might add—dozens of dancing women pirouetted across the front of the assembly, also sans clothing, in a disgustingly sexual equivalent of the gluttonous display. The pale white women were kissing, fingering, and flopping against each other, moaning and groaning like ghosts from Hell. As we gazed upon them from the delivery chute, I turned to my friend Caleb and muttered, "Would you like some Sodom on your Gomorrah?"

"Revolting!" he said.

"Don't worry, pal, I've got it all on video," I said.

Although I showed Caleb many more buildings that day—buildings where the gubment mobile employees strolled in natural splendor inside hermetically sealed-off arboretums and aviaries, relaxed in furnished comfort in giant four-poster beds, frolicked in heated pools, sweated in luxurious saunas, commingled in romantic showers, and kissed each other inside fragrant gardens—we just watched them in complete silence, and I could hear Caleb's stomach begin to growl in a sort of primeval protest.

"Let's go back," I told him, and we left the gubment employees inside their world of real, physical delight.

That's when the android protectors began to follow us, and their data processors kept up an internal and infernal din of noises.

All my Jewish friends wore their blue *talit* shawls when they delivered the thousands of Freedom Flyer hovercraft to their new owners. We were making a religious as well as a political statement. I must admit, when I saw the rows upon rows of Freedom Flyers queuing up on the Nature Path that led to the Corporate Gubment headquarters across the river, it was quite a moving sight.

The androids standing outside were ready for the final entrapment. But I had my evidence inside my sealed container—digital videos of the insides of the gubment buildings where the truth of their exorbitant lifestyle could be shown for the entire world to see. I also had many more copies made, and my friends in Freedom pods around the country were ready to stream them over the network if our demands were not met.

My grandfather Sol told me the story of Jacob in our scriptures, and he said that my namesake had to wrestle with an angel in order to gain a spiritual blessing for his people. He became the spirit of Israel and he defeated the material Rome. That's what I was now doing, or so I believed, and as we rolled down the Nature Path, I could see the thousands of bobbing, bald heads of my Catholic brothers, and the ruffling blue tallitot of my Jewish brethren, and my heart was at peace.

When I showed the videos to the President of the Corporate Gubment, he was honestly surprised at what he saw. He immediately ordered that the android protectors following us be shut off. He told us he did not realize that profits were being used in this way, and the corporate leaders behind him immediately agreed to our demands.

What were they? They were actually pretty simple. I wanted the Freedum Flyers to be able to exercise and to marry each other in real marriages, and to be able to grow real legs and take real walks in actual gardens and other places built for their public enjoyment. I wanted us to have access to Nature again. Perhaps a public nature reserve, such as the National Park, could be again preserved for us? I told him our bodies were crying out for spiritual release, and our only enjoyment on earth could come from friends, from family and from the warm hugs of their bodies. Never again should we be shut inside secluded pods to work until our bodies became frail and disfigured. "Our bodies," I told him, "are temples of the Creator. We, in fact, are created in His own image."

I guess it was this last statement that really got to the president. I saw tears come to his eyes, and he gave the orders that would result in our freedom. Yes, we have reverted back to the ancient spelling of the word. Some gubment advertising man had created "Freedum" because he thought it was an ingenious way to show superiority over the "dumb" workers.

As my friend Caleb's legs grow stronger with each passing day, his head also seems to be getting smaller; perhaps it is the special hormones and medical care from the gubment that is causing his hair to grow out and his smile to become authentic. I don't know. I just know that I enjoy taking him out for walks inside the new Freedom Garden in his neighborhood, where we exchange jokes about the gubment employees who were terminated from their jobs—or, in some cases, as with those who were the planners behind the theft of the money, were thrown inside a Terrorist Detainee Center to live out their lives in the shadows of miserable anguish.

The lesson we learned from this experience was that freedom is not choice. Freedom is the leisure to walk, to assemble, to sing, and to dance, and to do all the other physical things that our souls need to join with our bodies. For, after all, our spirit is wed to our body, and whenever cruelty or injustice tries to separate them, my people, and any people who understand, will always rise up to fight the injustice.

# AFFECTION BY PROXY

by
Jay Seate

All is reality. All is truth. Truth, the whole truth and nothing but the truth. Truth can hurt, but in Timothy Van Knott's world, reality *is* truth. As radio-babble fills his bedroom he is up and showering.

"I hate that fucking, maudlin song," the DJ shouts, "but you pricks have made it number one and so I spin it."

Timothy eats his cereal.

"Traffic's the same as always," the radio voice spews. "Tied up, screwed sideways, and if you're driving, plan on playing with yourself for an hour because we've got major delays all over the system. So, what else is new?"

Timothy slaps off the radio and dresses in his cord trousers, shirt, and tie. He goes out the door and walks to the trolley stop. He rides five miles, and then walks a final two blocks.

The world changed during the first half of the twenty-first century. Timothy had not yet been born when society fell victim to age-old idiosyncrasies rampant on our socially malformed planet. Politics in particular became based on nothing but misdirection and lies. Truth had been lost. This cancerous proclivity eventually brought a second wave of upheaval and change before false deities could drive the world into false realities. There was a nonviolent cleansing of sorts, a revolution to clear away those who thrived on deceit.

A new order was established while Timothy was still a child. Its edict was a simple one—upon penalty of incarceration or worse, the truth must be told. Eventually the populace succumbed and the world became a relatively peaceful place. Governments still made decisions based on self-interest wrapped in the always familiar sanctuary of patriotism. Corporate goals still drove the system, the difference being that they made no bones about it, no false promises.

Protests over one thing or another occasionally arose, but the appetite for social issues had mostly departed with the wind of truthfulness. No one really gave a shit. Haggling over questions of promiscuity, religion, or moral decay were things of the past. Prejudices were out in the open. The truth had set people free, it was said. Thoughts that once dare not speak its name were no longer stifled. Expressing opposing opinions were all but extinct, all of this for the common good of defeating the untruths that had brought society so close to chaos.

As Timothy strolls to his building, men and women are preening on the way to wherever they will spend their day, some striking the pose, awaiting their critique, as it were, on the GQ or Vogue meter. The men are worse than the women about stopping others and requesting the sign. One man with a gold tie and suede jacket gets the signal that he has missed the acceptable fashion boat today, the dreaded thumbs down. He glumly walks away in the direction he has come.

Timothy stops no one. He already knows he's an oddball. He knows his wardrobe relates only to those who do not care about style or appearance. His considered nerdiness and Tweakish tendencies place him on the outside of the "insider" caravan. The insiders—the celebrated ones that have been accepted as cool and tasteful. Being on the outside doesn't feel that bad, and in all honesty, if he had a choice, it is the side he would choose to be on, free of any wish to be GQ or Vogue.

Those humans who feel like sideshow freaks no longer suffer the indignity of whispers or side glances. People are truthful about their proclivities and prejudices. Those who cannot find ways to deal with such truths usually find ways to leave this mortal coil. Beyond the task of earning a living, life in wealthy civilizations is about pleasure, which is allowed to flourish without restriction. In Timothy's modern world, most everything is legal. In spite of the inordinate time the GQs and Vogues spend grooming themselves and admiring their clothes, he has no doubt society is better off today, when humans can pursue their pleasures and vices without judicial fear, and without having to play like they have the same dreams and virtues as everyone else, because human beings clearly do not. The age has been reached when no one has to lie about his or her proclivities. Every aspect of existence is so honest you could just shit.

Once inside his Silicon Valley compound, Timothy steps out of the way as three GQ men in tailored suits walk briskly down the corridor on a mission. They are cool, confident, their right to the hallway unquestioned, their correctness infallible. They are followed by a second wave of three high-level technicians who walk just as majestically, their lab coats flapping, their positions secure because they passed their reality check long ago—loyal and devoted to their projects. They don't fuck around.

Timothy hangs his windbreaker in his locker and slips into his own lab coat, thinking prison must look suspiciously like his cubicle. Someone taps him on the shoulder. He turns and there stands a girl named Brenda. He was introduced to her when she first joined the team several months ago, but he'd forgotten about her.

"I'm ready to talk to you," Brenda says to Timothy.

"Oh, okay. Make it quick. We're on in seven minutes." This is something different in Timothy's day. He has little to say to the people he works with and they have little to say to him. Truth gets in the way of conversation.

Brenda speaks again. "I'd like to get together if you're interested in a coupling. I'm clean and have had limited sex partners. I've had no major surgery or implants. My breasts are small but sensitive and responsive. I'm a confirmed outsider, a weird duck like yourself, and have no ambition to be otherwise."

She does not have to tell Timothy this, of course. Tweaks such as themselves are obvious to everyone. There are no niceties of common ground between the insiders and outsiders. They get along fine because their roles are clear; truth in advertising is the hallmark of society, perhaps even a badge of courage, because he or she does not have to pretend, and people do not have to say pretend things.

"Uh...sure. I'm not with anyone. How old are you, Brenda?"

"Twenty-eight, and you are thirty. I checked your file. You look like a good match on paper. Just one thing, I'm a nut about cleanliness. I'd like to do a quick exam before we make a date. Is that okay?"

Timothy looked at his watch. "You'll have to make it quick." He opens his lab coat and Brenda pulls down his trousers and underwear. She examines his penis and raises his testicles.

"Turn around, would you?"

Timothy obliges. Brenda bends him forward at the waist and examines his anus. It is the first time he has met anyone this strict.

"All right," Brenda says. "Your hygiene is excellent. No fecal matter." She smiles. "You can get dressed now, as the doctor would say. I'd like to invite you over for dinner and sex whenever you're available."

Timothy appraises Brenda's appearance for the first time. He thinks her unusually attractive for a Tweak and she has nifty little tits. "I'm usually available."

"Well then, let's not drag it out. If you have no cats or anything to feed, why don't you come home with me after work?"

"That will be fine," Timothy answers. "We better get to work though. I'll meet you out front at five o'clock." He shakes the small, warm hand she offers him. "Very nice seeing you again."

"Nice seeing more of you," Brenda answers with what sounds like a harbinger of things to come in her voice.

The corridors are now clear of traffic with the exception of Tony Atiffe, the top GQ lady's man of the company, quick with a smooth quip. He is standing alongside two Vogues. One of the women's breasts have been liberated from her blouse. Her nipples protrude stiffly like two-oversized eraser tips as Tony teases them with his fingertips and tells her a sweet nothing. The other woman stands near Tony as if anxiously awaiting her turn for his affection.

They glance at Timothy, unconcerned, as he scurries past them to his workspace just as the eight o'clock chime hums through the building. He is momentarily distracted by the invitation for sex, reminding him that although he's not a GQ, he is certainly a *Homo erectus*. Brenda seems the sensible kind of woman to mate with and her precautions show awareness of the issues of modern times. Soon, he settles into his routine. Fitting Brenda's profile makes for a pleasant workday expressed in the trace of a smile. He tries not to think about five o'clock.

Timothy's job of testing the chemical makeup of products is mundane, as are most occupations as he sees it. He spends most of his free time just walking and watching the insiders pose, or he listens to the old music. The songs speak to him of a time before conversation was mostly four-letter words and when a person's thoughts were a mystery. The songs he listens to describe expectation and heartache, feelings that no longer carry much relevance. Now that people are blatantly honest, they are far enough ahead of the curve to avoid disappointment.

There is crime, but rates are lower than they used to be because desires are more attainable, and people usually tell what they know about wrongdoers. It's not a case of brotherly love. People have been programmed with something similar to a truth serum. Consequently, prejudices are clear and accepted. At least people know where they stand. Timothy can barely imagine the old world where people only pretended to like you. Society dumped those notions long ago and Timothy gives it little thought except for times like today when something unusual happens—when another person reaches out to him and asks for something. And this request has a return. Real sex *is* pleasurable, after all.

At precisely three minutes after five, Timothy hangs up his lab coat and walks out of the compound onto the busy street, feeling a vibration of excitement. Perhaps Brenda will be the one, a soul mate of infinite layers and endless revelations. Her proposal has lit something within him. He thinks beyond the act of coupling to the fantasy of pulling her toward him and burying his face in her hair.

He waits for her, but she doesn't appear. He goes back to his locker to make sure he hasn't gotten his signals crossed. No note or sign.

Truth is the maxim of their society, so he can only wonder if she has become ill and left early. Sometimes the chemicals they work with can do that. He is unsettled, however, because people like him and Brenda, the outsiders, the ones who don't meet the GQ or Vogue qualifications, don't usually plan one thing and then do something else. Information is an obligation.

Timothy finally shrugs it off and schleps to the trolley, halfway expecting Brenda to call out. He watches GQs drive past him in their asshole-mobiles until his mode of transportation stops and opens its door and he gets on. Though surrounded be unknown people looking grimly forward, he feels distanced from the world around him and has felt that way for a long time.

Back in his silent cavern of emptiness he calls home, he mopes around trying not to dwell on thoughts of Brenda. The room fills with shadows as the sunlight fades. He eats his plasma dinner of synthetic beef, creamed corn, and peas in front of the plasma screen. He has a drink to relax, but it doesn't improve his frame of mind. Finally, he puts on the sad and soft old music, and goes to bed. "Brenda is actually attractive in a pixie sort of way," he tells the walls. With a change in hairstyle and a laser trace rather than her outdated eyeglasses, she could be quite acceptable to the GQs—and even the Vogues, if she swings both ways.

Willpower has never been one of Timothy's strong points. He thinks about Brenda to the point of strapping on his cyber-female sex buddy. The wonders of modern technology have given this piece of equipment every lifelike quality a person could hope for. It consists of a rubberized, female torso beginning at a belly button and ending at mid-thigh. In some formidable laboratory, science has reproduced the texture of human skin to the point where, at first glance, only the lack of blood and rough severed edges separates toys such as this from a grisly crime scene. Fortunately, that type of depravity seldom occurs and even less seldom goes unsolved thanks to cadaver brain-tracings and advanced crime detection technology.

Secured by a stretchable band, Timothy lies down on his bed and holds the custom-designed artificial torso away from himself long enough to insert his penis into its perfect vagina. He lowers the toy onto himself until it fits snugly. He begins to move it up and down as the torso secretes fluid. His cyber-buddy also comes with a wet clitoris and real pubic hair sown around the vagina, one hair at a time. "You should be Brenda tonight," he tells the synthetic marvel. "At her place. Dinner and then sex."

Even though he is speaking to his artificial partner, he doesn't think of it as a replacement for the real thing. That would be silly. There are a few things that the present world cannot replace completely. Metal bats almost sound like wood striking a baseball. The speakers under the hood of some vehicles make the electric engine sound almost like an illegal gasoline engine revving up. But they have not developed cyber drones with a warm heartbeat to go along with a wet pubis. Not yet, anyway.

He pumps the rubber-compound vagina. Its walls secrete additional fluid. His hands move faster on its hips. He looks at its labia, wondering how similar Brenda's imperfect genitalia might compare. He begins to arrive at the point of no return. His desire overtakes him in the form of watery squirts into a receptacle within his synthetic concubine. Later, he'll remove the container and put its refuse in a recycle jar for spent semen which will be deposited and used in stimulant and beauty products. Remarkable that society has learned to recycle almost everything for some positive use—better living through chemistry.

Timothy's passion ebbs. The episode was quick, clean, and without sentimentality. He then gets up and slips out of the device, trying to decide if he feels better. It's clean sex for sure, but the occasional bit of mess created by two live bodies would have its appeal.

He sterilizes his cyber-sex buddy and slips her back under his bed. He goes to sleep remembering Brenda's impromptu exam, the slight shiver that passed through him when she lifted his scrotum and penis for a look-see, and realizes he actually looks forward to the next day.

The posers are in fine form as Timothy walks to work. Most get thumbs up, some, thumbs down. He marvels at the importance of this ritual to the insiders. Sometimes truth seems to have been manufactured by Madison Avenue, but his thoughts return to Brenda. *Just a few changes in appearance and attitude and she would definitely be close to Vogueness.* He is glad that desire is not in her character. He looks forward to talking with her again, and hopes the invitation is still open.

He doesn't see her until lunchtime. He takes his tray to the space next to her. "Hi, can I sit here?"

"Suit yourself," Brenda answers.

"I hope I didn't screw up after work. I waited out front."

"You didn't. Something came up."

"Oh. Well, how about our plan? I'm still available."

Brenda looks at Timothy and smiles. "We can still do it, but not for a while."

"I hope nothing's wrong. No one's sick or anything?"

"No," she says pensively. "The truth is, Tony Atiffe copulated with me last night. He just sort of came up and started talking to me and I took him home. It won't last long, but I mean…it was Tony *Atiffe.*"

Living in a world of truth did not prevent hurt or even bad hair days. Timothy does not know what to say. Suddenly his values are scrambling around inside his skull. "But you…you're not a Vogue. You approached me and…"

"I know, but Tony said I was just as good a lay as any of the insiders and he wants to treat me like one of them for a while. Maybe in a few weeks—"

"Did Tony meet your hygienic standards?" Timothy spits, suddenly outraged without knowing why, experiencing an emotion he can't recall.

Brenda takes a bite of her sandwich and rolls her eyes at Timothy. "Who cares? I got laid by the hottest outsider I've ever known." Then she adds, "Even I couldn't say 'no' to that opportunity."

"But you said—"

Brenda looks Timothy straight in the eye with a look that might have been called the fish-eye in earlier times. "I have a suggestion, Timothy. Get your ass off the pity-pot and accept the situation."

Timothy picks up his tray and walks away. He dumps his lunch—uneaten—into the trash bin, not knowing what to do next, not understanding these new sensations. They could be disappointment, frustration, disgust, outrage—words he has heard, but susceptibilities he hasn't been forced to feel and knows little about. They make his stomach ache. He walks from the cafeteria to the restroom and tries to throw up.

Forty-eight hours ago, he didn't know Brenda personally, so why this feeling of...betrayal, is that it? Something has been taken from him. He isn't sure what exactly, but it is something that validates his worth. To whom can he express his loss? Who will care? Tweaks do not cross over. Insiders do not take what is left for the outsiders. Tony came on to Brenda and quite honestly, Timothy guesses, told her he found her attractive, in her own way, and wanted to fuck her.

"She broke the rules and let him take her...let him take my spot. She'll change. If we ever *do* get together, she'll think about that GQ prick."

It's true people no longer lie to each other, but one can lie like hell to oneself. He'd let her get away, causing more new feelings like cowardliness and hopelessness and shame to slip in. For the first time he feels terribly alone in this world with truth but without sentimentality. Timothy splashes water on his face and decides what to do.

For Tweaks, the people who scurry through life like mice in a maze, sometimes resentment of the assholes is the only revenge one ever gets. Not this time. After lunch, Timothy mixes chemicals that are not supposed to be mixed. He might appear a trifle distracted, but no more than that. It's a good thing no one asks him what he's doing, for he would be obliged to tell. Then, for the first time in years, he steps away from his workbench before the afternoon break. He takes a canister of the potent blend and walks down the corridor to the management offices.

Tony sits at his desk. He is on the phone, wearing his tailored suit, his hair perfect, comfortable with his freewheeling life and the favors that come with being a cocksure GQ who can sleep with as many females as often as he likes, whenever he likes. It's clear no one is off limits for Tony.

Timothy approaches Tony with a smile. Tony swivels around in his chair. His eyes meet Timothy's. Timothy's Adam's apple jerks in his throat, but that is the only indication of unsteadiness. At first, Tony looks surprised then his lips give way to a smirk, revealing perfect teeth. Without saying a word, because if he spoke he would have to be truthful, Timothy opens the canister and throws the liquid in Tony's face. Tony drops the phone and screams.

Timothy then says, "Take this any way you want to. Any old way at all."

The acid is already eating away at the flesh on Tony's handsome face. He falls out of his chair and onto the floor, screaming, and clawing at his eyes. Timothy ducks out of the room before anyone comes to Tony's aid. He breathes slowly and deeply, maintaining complete control of himself. Then he heads for the stairway.

He is not finished. Oh no. As someone wanders into the corridor, they ask Timothy where the screams are coming from. "Down the hall," he answers truthfully. He climbs the stairs to Brenda's department. He hides the second canister behind his back and steps aside as some lab coats walk hurriedly down the stairs. Some look at him blankly as they pass. He climbs to the next floor and runs into a group of people peeping out of a doorway at the echoes of Tony's painful lament float up to them. Among them is Brenda.

"Come with me right now, Brenda." He takes her arm and walks her to the end of the hall.

"I can't just leave work. Why would you ask such a thing?"

"Because I'm quitting, and I would like to have one time with you. We could leave right now down the back steps. I thought about you all night, and when you didn't meet me, I was totally bummed out. I won't ever see you again after today, but if we could have our moment of honesty and sex, one outsider to another."

A smile carves its way across Brenda's lips, like she's a nurse about to break bad news. "Things changed for me last night, like I told you. If it had been any other day… Just bad timing for you, I'm afraid, but the world is full of sex mates for your type. What is going on downstairs, do you know?"

"My type?" Timothy says in horror. "Your head can be turned that easily? One night of having a GQs prick shoved inside of you?"

"Take it easy, Tom. It is Tom, isn't it?"

Timothy knows this is the final kiss-off. A new emotion turns him into something like a wolf when it first smells blood. "Cyber-surgery can fix the two of you, but it will take time and money."

"What are you talking about?"

He takes the second canister from behind his back and tosses it into Brenda's face. Her composure departs as she becomes something with twitching lips and rolling eyes, a character out of a horror movie. The desire to bury his face in her hair is gone. Her screams are of a strangled higher pitch than Tony's.

Timothy spits words at her. "You've spent your last day as a Vogue apprentice."

The people in the hallway gasp at what they are witnessing. In that moment, Timothy is all-powerful. The techs stand and stare as if they were observing a genie rise out of a magic lamp, its wonders to perform.

The moment doesn't last long. Some of them start toward Timothy and Brenda. Timothy throws himself back into the stairwell, but not quickly enough to avoid a piece of burning flesh Brenda has torn from her face. It slaps against him and slithers its way down his lab coat. He brushes it to the floor and walks downstairs, leaving Brenda's screams behind while contemplating his reaction to this new wave of emotion caused by Brenda's infidelity.

He hopes people will hide in pockets of his building, but instead he hears the smack-smack of shoes against the linoleum floor. "He's the one!" someone shouts amid the chaos. "Van Knott. He must have made the acid!"

Co-workers multiply in a hallway, but no one rushes Timothy, their eyes wells of terror. No one takes control. Maybe they think he has more hot liquid hidden somewhere. Timothy notices that the Tweaks and the GQs/Vogues are all mixing quite nicely in their shared crisis. His feelings are releasing themselves with an energy that surprises him, like a spring thaw after a winter of frozen, dead emotions. He might still be a Tweak, but he's someone to be feared now. *Happy, happy. Joy, joy.* A wry smile twists the shape of Timothy's mouth as a man finally grabs him from behind and pins his arms. Someone else calls the police.

The question as to why Timothy has committed such a horrible act is one that he almost salivates like Pavlov's dogs to answer. "Because with truth comes pain. The truth will set you free, my ass."

Timothy wonders if those in authority will let him play his music in prison or let him bring along his cyber-buddy. He wants his music because now he understands all those lyrics about heartbreak and disappointment and hurt. He wants his toy because it can't disappoint him. He also understands that honesty is not always the best policy and that the truth doesn't always prove to be liberating. The truth is that it's only relative to the circumstance.

Anyway, he won't have to be witness to any more posing, unless his prison guards are GQs.

# SECRET BALLOT

by
Frank Oreto

"Get your coat on, honey," called Randall. "Time to go vote." He flipped off the radio, silencing a local congressman in mid-rant. He was glad Election Day was here. "If I have to listen to one more campaign commercial I think my head will explode."

Randall's daughter, Caroline, fumbled with the zipper of her purple jacket. "Why don't I get to vote?" she asked, as the zipper finally slid up with a buzz.

"You're too young. You have to be eighteen."

The six-year-old's face scrunched up at the injustice of age.

"It's kind of boring," said Randall. "You're not missing out."

Chill November air blanketed them as they left the house. The sky threatening to drizzle any minute. They were alone on the street. Randall remembered the last election. That year the yards had been full of "Vote My Way" signs and there had been so many people walking to the polls, he had felt like part of a parade.

This year it was mostly unopposed locals. *Why even bother?* he thought. *Because I've got nothing better to do?* Caroline's school acted as the local polling station. They had canceled classes, so Randall had taken the day off. He always stayed home on school cancellations and sick days. Holly couldn't. She made real money. He felt resentment flare up. "It's my civic duty," he said aloud.

"Is there going to be a bake sale?" Caroline asked.

"Oh yeah, there's always a bake sale." An image filled Randall's mind—a table covered with brownies and cupcakes, Wanda standing behind it. She would be there selling sweets for the PTA. Randall imagined her looking at him with that smile she always wore. She was a good-looking woman. *So is your wife*, he thought. But Wanda had a kind of fragile beauty. There was nothing fragile about Holly.

A wave of self-loathing chilled Randall's warm thoughts. *Am I that guy? My wife is successful, so I need somebody on the side to feel like a man again.* It wasn't as if anything was going on. He didn't even know Wanda's last name, and he would never put his family at risk. *But a man can dream*, he thought. So, Randall dreamt of brownies and fragile, beautiful smiles.

The school stood only a couple of blocks away. Its proximity was one of the reasons they had bought the house. Caroline grabbed Randall's hand and made an exaggerated show of looking up and down the one street they had to cross.

"Go ahead, sweetie. I think we're good."

Randall scanned the parking lot. Only a few cars, and they probably belonged to the people running the polls. He didn't think there would be a long line.

Caroline skipped over to a scattered pile of long yellow placards. She picked one up and brought it to her father. "Hal Philips for Mayor, Hal Phillips for Mayor!" she sang, waving the placard over her head. She held it out to Randall and waited for the inevitable praise he gave her whenever she read something aloud.

"Put it down!" His voice came out harsh, and Caroline's face clouded. Randall plucked the card away and stared at it. Right after the candidate's name was what looked like a big red exclamation point, but it wasn't. It was blood. Randall threw the card on the ground. He knelt beside Caroline and gave her a reassuring hug while his eyes played connect the dots with the numerous brown-red spots scattered over the cement entryway. *What the hell is going on?*

"It's okay," he said aloud. "That paper was dirty. I didn't want you touching it."

There would be people through the doors—retirees working the polls, Wanda with her table full of treats. Out here, they were alone and there was blood on the ground. He wanted to pick Caroline up but settled for holding her hand as they walked in the school.

"Bake sale," Caroline squealed and ran to the long table full of confections. She reached for a Rice Krispies treat, all unhappiness forgotten.

"Not yet baby," Randall said. "We've got to vote first." He tried to shake off his own unease, wishing his emotions were as mercurial as Caroline's.

He heard the tap of shoes on tile and turned to see Wanda approaching them. The sight of her lifted him like a wave of warm water. *Maybe I'm not that different from my daughter after all*, he thought. His face stretched into a pleased smile, then froze.

Wanda's eyes were wide and rimmed with red. Her mouth a hard, thin line. She nodded at Randall as she passed him and took her seat behind the table. She attempted a smile for Caroline, but it only lasted an instant and never made it past the corners of her mouth. Caroline only had eyes for the treats and didn't notice.

Randall took his daughter's hand and gave her a gentle tug toward the gym, where the voting machines stood. His eyes bored into Wanda's, trying to convey his concern. The look was wasted. Wanda stared down at the snacks with all of Caroline's intensity but none of her joy.

Inside the gym stood two more tables. Instead of cookies, these held files containing the names of all the registered voters in the area. Randall was the only voter there. He walked up to the gray-haired woman at the closest table and smiled at her.

Isabel Gracie was his neighbor and had worked the polls every year since Randall and Holly had moved to Collier's Run. She did not smile back, but Randall didn't expect it. Isabel took her responsibilities very seriously.

"Isabel, was there a fight outside or something? I thought I saw blood on the cement."

"No, nothing like that. Probably one of the voters had a nosebleed. Now, what's your last name?"

"Deerhorn!" yelled Caroline.

"What she said." Randall still felt uneasy, but if something bad had happened surely Isabel would have told him.

Isabel patted Caroline's hand then scanned the pages of names in front of her. She turned the book around and pointed to Randall's name and the empty line beside it. "If you could just sign there, Mr. Deerhorn."

Isabel looked at the signature and nodded. The only other poll worker in the gym, a heavyset man with a gray goatee, sat at the second table. The large sticker on his shirt read "Hello, My Name Is Al." He watched Randall and gave a curt nod when their eyes met.

Randall followed Isabel to the line of black voting machines near the gym wall.

"You're familiar with how this works?" Isabel asked after she had prepped the machine.

"Yes, ma'am."

Isabel nodded and then walked back toward the table.

"Bake sale," Caroline said, her voice a plaintive whine.

"Just hang loose for a minute, babe. We'll get there."

Randall watched the screen fill with voting instructions. He pressed NEXT until the actual ballot came up. He knew almost none of the names, not that it mattered. His usual strategy was when in doubt vote for the women. They seemed less likely to mess things up. He worked his way from mayor to sheriff to various judgeships.

Randall pressed the NEXT button again. In the center of the touch screen, the shape of a hand appeared. It blinked on and off, the words PLACE RIGHT HAND HERE written below it.

"That's new," Randall muttered to himself. Usually, after you filled out the ballot, the computer asked if you were sure about your decisions and let you see all your choices on one page.

Randall pressed his palm to the screen. A surge of dull pain throbbed from his fingertips to his elbow. The kind of pain you get when you give your funny bone a good whack. He snatched his hand away, expecting it to be red. *The goddamn machine shocked me!* Randall rubbed his fingertips against the palm of his hand. Had it been a shock? A tingle might be more accurate, but it had been a strong one. Caroline stood near him staring at the gym door, no doubt dreaming of sweets. She obviously hadn't felt anything.

Randall looked down at the thick wires snaking away from the machine—no sparks. "There's something wrong," he called out.

Isabel walked over.

"There's nothing wrong, Randall," she said. Her voice was low even though there was no one else near enough to hear her.

"I beg to differ." Randall held up his hand. "It shocked me. Are you telling me getting electrocuted is part of the process?"

"Don't be a baby. It's not that bad."

Randall's mouth dropped open. "Really? You know, Isabel—I think I'm done here. Let's go, Caroline." He stepped from behind the booth. Isabel stood in his way.

"I'm sorry, Randall," she said, her voice softening. "I know it's unusual, but please could you finish voting? I did it. It feels . . . odd, but there's no damage."

Randall looked at his neighbor of five years. He'd been ready to walk out, more over the way Isabel had spoken to him than the tingling in his hand. Now, he felt undecided. Isabel must be in her seventies. If she could handle this, what did that say about him?

Isabel took Randall's hand and stepped in even closer. "Randall, please, you have to vote. I thought it was some sort of joke at first, but it's not. It's deathly serious. I'm worried that—" Isabel's voice tightened into a hiss of pain. She let go of Randall and pressed her hand to the side of her head.

A thin stream of blood trickled from her nose.

"I can't talk about how you should vote," Isabel hissed. She pressed a palm against her eye and groaned. Blood pattered onto the gym floor.

"Jesus, Isabel, hey!" Randall looked for the other poll worker. "She's bleeding!" he called out.

Al was on his way, moving fast despite his girth. As he reached them, he plucked a monogrammed handkerchief the size of a hand towel from his pocket and pressed it to Isabel's bleeding face. Isabel crumpled into the big man's arms.

"You know we aren't allowed to influence the ballot, Izzy," Al said, patting her on the back.

"Is she okay?" Randall asked.

Al locked eyes with Randall. "Not so much," he said, his voice hard.

"Is there anything I can do?"

Al had already turned and was leading the sobbing Isabel back to the polling tables. He didn't bother to look back at Randall. "Vote," he said.

Caroline stood with her hands pressed to her mouth. Randall went to her, wrapping her in his arms. "It's okay, sweetie. Mrs. Gracie just had a nose bleed."

Caroline shook her head in an emphatic no. Bleeding was never all right. Randall kissed her cheek. He looked toward the tables. Isabel sat next to Al dabbing at her nose. The bleeding had stopped.

"Come with Daddy," Randall said. He led Caroline to the table where Isabel and Al sat. Al's hard eyes softened when he saw the little girl.

"Mrs. Gracie," Randall said. "Caroline wanted to make sure you were okay."

Isabel took Caroline's hand in her own and gave it a squeeze. "I'll be fine, dear."

"Hey," Randall said looking at Al. "You think Caroline could hang out over here while I finish up?"

Al nodded.

"Honey, I'll be right back."

Caroline gave him a perfunctory "Okay, Daddy" and began describing her new winter shoes to Isabel.

Randall walked back to the voting machine. The blinking hand still filled the screen. He looked at it and felt his stomach turn over. "Civic duty," he said and pressed his hand to the glass.

The tingling returned. He expected it this time and did not pull away. The tingle spread like a brush fire over his nerve endings. It wasn't pain. Close, but different—something between a bad itch and a tickle. It swept over him and then disappeared. In its wake, Randall felt languid, almost high. *It's tranquilizing me*, he thought, but couldn't work up any objections to the idea.

The gym grew dark and then went away altogether. A word floated around in Randall's head. He reached for it and the word came into focus—CHOOSE.

Suddenly Randall found himself in a crowd. It was real, he felt them brush against him. Heard their snatches of conversation. They were marching and he felt himself pulled along with them. It was a parade, a celebration. In the center of the marching throng, like stones in a brook, stood angels.

Maybe *angel* was the wrong word—there were no wings—but it was what Randall thought when he saw them. They were tall. Eight, maybe ten feet, but perfectly proportioned. They wore no clothes and their skin had a pale, golden glow that radiated out from them. Randall wanted to bask in it. They were beautiful, but it was a terrifying beauty, like the ocean during a storm. The crowd moved around the angels, each person straining to reach them, to feel their power and then pass on before being overwhelmed. Randall drew near one. He felt its presence for the barest moment, then found himself rising above the crowds.

"If we vote to invite them, the angels will come." The words rang in Randall's head as clear as thought, but not his own. More like an announcer—that guy who voices all the movie previews—broadcasting directly into his mind.

"The angels will come, and with them, we will change the world."

Randall saw that new world—like his own, but perfected. He flew above it and everywhere there was abundance, beauty, and smiling people.

The scene changed. Randall now stood on the outskirts of a burning city.

"But it won't be easy," the announcer said. Now, music—an orchestra playing a theme in minor chords—accompanied the voice. "There will be dissenters. Those too mired in their own pride and beliefs to accept the changes to come."

Randall did not march this time. He ran. He had voted against the coming of the angels, and his side had lost.

The stench of blood and decay filled the air. Randall felt the lash of a whip on his back. He joined a stream of beaten, half-starved figures being herded toward a mass grave. A bullet tore through him and he fell, rolling onto the still forms of those who had gone before.

"This is the cost of making the wrong choice," the announcer proclaimed. "Do you wield the lash or feel its bite? The angels understand. They know the pain of choosing."

Randall found himself on a wide plain, an angel standing before him. Behind it stretched a perfect world and its smiling inhabitants.

"You live in a hard, uncertain world. It doesn't have to be that way." The announcer and his music were gone. This was the voice of the angel and it held its own music. "Together, we can remake your world into a paradise free of pain and worry. All you have to do is make the right choice." The angel smiled and the feeling of love and compassion in that smile flowed over Randall like warm summer rain.

Randall blinked and took his hand off the voting machine. He swayed for a moment, finding his balance. He could see the gym again. Caroline stood by Isabel, still talking away.

"Jesus," he whispered, then shook his head and looked back at the touch screen. There were now two small glowing squares. One said "yes," the other "no."

Randall took a long shaky breath. The odd thing, if he had to name just one, was that he believed it all. There was no doubt in Randall's mind he was about to vote on whether to invite some sort of supernatural beings to take over the earth and make everything perfect. And anyone not with the program would be wiped out. Moreover, he believed the vote was binding. The angels could not just show up. There had to be a vote.

"It was a god-damned campaign commercial," Randall said aloud. He looked again at his daughter and the people near her. Al stared back. He looked worried. That worry pissed Randall off. It had been a good campaign commercial. Hell, he could still smell the wildflowers from the paradise-on-earth scene. But you don't sell out humanity to some angelic super-race just because they're pretty and know how to garden. The so-called angels were going to lose by a landslide. Humanity would muddle through on its own.

Randall jabbed his finger down on the no button. The choices disappeared, and the screen flashed red. The words "Thank you for voting" appeared.

Randall walked to his daughter. Isabel had joined Al in looking at Randall. Their eyes bored into his for a long moment, and then Isabel let out a sigh. Al stood and slapped Randall on the back.

"What, you didn't think I'd . . . ?"

Al held up a hand. "No, son, it's a secret ballot. You aren't allowed to discuss the details." He gestured toward the bloodstained handkerchief now folded neatly on the table.

"Oh yeah, right," Randall said, now understanding the drying blood on the cement outside.

Al took his seat. His momentary smile faded into grim worry.

"Come on," Randall said. "It's going to be fine. No one's going to—" A tiny jab of pain behind his right eye cut off the words. "You know."

"Yeah, sure," Al said, but he didn't look any happier. "Thanks for voting, Mr. Deerhorn."

Randall took Caroline by the hand. "Let's get a brownie, kiddo."

Wanda sat at the bake sale table, dabbing at her eyes.

"It's going to be okay," Randall said. "They have to abide by our vote. You can feel that too, right?"

Wanda nodded, but couldn't muster a smile in return. She handed Caroline a folded-over grocery bag. "Here you go, I put a little of everything in there."

Caroline grabbed the bag before Randall could argue. She reached in and pulled out a Rice Krispies treat. "Thanks so much!" she squealed before taking a huge bite.

"How much do I owe you?" Randall asked.

"Don't worry about it."

Randall was at the door when it hit him. *They knew how I voted—Al and Isabel, probably even Wanda. They're here every election. Watching people make decisions. The ballot may be secret, but they looked me in the eye and knew, just like they've looked at every other person who voted today.*

Randall turned around. "Wanda?"

She looked up.

"You've been here all day, right?"

Wanda nodded.

"Has it been busy?"

"Off and on."

Randal swallowed. "How we doing?"

Wanda opened her mouth but no words came. Her face filled with pain. She shook her head once then began rubbing her temples.

"Okay, sorry." He turned to the door, pulling Caroline along with him. *They stuck it on the ballot on an off-year election. Nothing but retirees and stay-at-home dads with the time to vote. People without a lot of power. People who maybe were a little resentful. People like me.* On the way home, he fished his cell phone out of his pocket. He pulled up his contacts and dialed Holly.

She answered after the fourth ring, sounding annoyed. "I can't talk now, Rand. I'm in the middle of a half-dozen things."

"Did you vote?"

"What?"

Randall could hear voices murmuring in the background. "This morning, did you vote?"

"No, I had that early meeting. I probably won't bother. I've got way too much on my plate."

"Listen to me. You have to stop on your way home and vote."

"Aren't you Mr. Civics all of a sudden."

"God-damn it, Holly, promise me you'll vote. This is important." Pain pulsed behind his eye again. He had to choose his words carefully.

"Okay, Randall, I'll cast my freaking vote. Can I go back to work now?"

"Yeah, I'll see you tonight. I love you." Holly had already hung up. Something wet ran over Randall's upper lip.

"Daddy you're bleeding," Caroline said.

"It's okay baby. Daddy's okay." Randall wiped the blood from his face and dialed the next number.

# AUTHOR BIOS

## ABUTTU

Querus Abuttu or "Dr. Q." is a retired U.S. Navy veteran, Forensic Nurse and Certified Nurse Midwife with a Ph.D. in Public Health and MFA in Writing Popular Fiction from Seton Hill University. She is a member of the Horror Writer's Association (HWA) and often writes dark tales under what she calls "speculative bio-horror." When she's not writing, Dr. Q. explores the wilds of Virginia and hopes to capture local phantoms and make their stories her own. You can find her at conferences such as Stokercon and Bizarrocon, and on Facebook at: https://www.facebook.com/DrQAbuttu/. Follow her on Twitter at: @Querus_Abuttu

## CAMPBELL

Broos Campbell has written or edited more than a dozen books, and has a particular interest in ships and the ocean. His Matty Graves novels concern the triumphs and disasters of a mixed-race American officer during the early years of the U.S. Navy. He's currently working on a novel about a teenage girl hunting for her mother's corpse.

## CHAMBERLAIN

Gregg Chamberlain lives in the True North Trump-Free Canada with his missus, Anne, and their clowder of cats, who care nothing about politics so long as it does not interfere with their nap times. He has one other political-sf satire piece regarding POTUS45 in the Alternative Truths Vol. 1 anthology and has other less political sf and fantasy stories and zombie filk in various magazines and anthologies.

## COGHLAN

Stephen Coghlan is an ever expanding Spec-lit author who writes from the Maple Syrup region of Canada's National Capital. Feel free to check out his website at http://scoghlan.com, or find him on Facebook and Twitter as @WordsBySC, where you can find out where his written wonders will take you next.

## COLANGELO

Michael R. Colangelo is a writer from Toronto. Visit him at http://michaelrcolangelo.blogspot.com/

## COLELL

Edmund Colell's work has appeared in Bizarro Bizarro: An Anthology, New Flesh Magazine, LegumeMan, and elsewhere. He survives in Arizona, hoping never to be targeted by legislation.

## DAY

David Day believes the future is a paradox, simultaneously representing beautiful hope and terrible possibility, and that we are on an ever-constant journey to resolve that paradox into the now. David received his MA in Writing Popular Fiction from Seton Hill University in June 2011. He is the author of one novel, Tearstone, as well as several short stories. Find out more about him at his snazzy but woefully neglected website: http://www.davidlday.com.

## DUCHESNEY

Morgan Duchesney is a writer and karate instructor with deep roots on Cape Breton; a large island on Canada's Atlantic coast. Morgan continues to be inspired by the oral tradition of Gaelic story-telling that yet endures on this "rock in the sea". His fiction has been published in *Static Movement, Morpheus Tales, Death's Head Grin, Blood Moon Rising,* the *Danforth Review, Canadian Stories* and the *Naashwak Review* and the short story "Wrong side of the River" recently received an honorable mention from the Ottawa Crime Writers Association. As well, he writes political essays and contributes a monthly column to *Baddeck's Victoria Standard.*

## FERGUS

Sin Fergus is evil sister to the owner, editor and anthologist at Scary Dairy Press. You can find her at various horror/sci-fi/spec-fic conferences and local pubs representing the company and seeking out fantastical stories to listen to and tell! www.ScaryDairyPress.com

## FLOWERS

Leadie Jo Flowers authors novels, short stories and poetry in the genres of science fiction and horror. She makes extra money for traveling by teaching English in Moscow, Russia. Traveling helps diversify her knowledge of the world and many differing cultures. (Yes, this does reflect in her stories and poetry.) Her background includes playing piano (Not in a long time!), selling high end wines, working in doctor offices, sales, making chocolates, mothering three sons, watching her many grandchildren grow up, and more. Oh, and she's a great cook!

Leadie Jo is a member of the Horror Writer's Association and you can usually find her at Stokercon, World Science Fiction and Eurocon conferences as well as a few others. Her poetry has appeared in HWA Poetry Showcase Volume IV, and a short story in Hazard Yet Forward. You can follow what is happening with her writing at these links.

https://www.leadiejoflowers.net/
https://www.facebook.com/Leadie-Jo-Flowers-198085643573595/

## FREVILLE

Bob Freville is the author of "Battering the Stem," an urban crime novel from Bizarro Pulp Press, and the writer/director of the minimalist vampire opus "Hemo" from Troma Team Releasing. His work has been published by Akashic Books, Bizarro Central, Creem Magazine, Clash Media and others. Freville's dark satire, "Celebrity Terrorist Sex Bomb," is now available from Journalstone. Bob lives in a crummy apartment overlooking a crumbling Babylon. To send him dirty pictures or death threats email: intrepidaspirationsllc@gmail.com

## GENEROUS

Eddie Generous is a coauthor of the slasher collection *Splish, Slash, Takin' a Bloodbath* (written with Mark Allan Gunnells and Renee Miller) as well as of *Dead is Dead, but Not Always* (available this spring from Hellbound Books), he runs Unnerving and Unnerving Magazine, and he lives on the Pacific Coast of BC with his wife and their cat overlords.

## GREEN

I. A. Green is a writer, poet, and social justice warrior. She is new to horror writing but found herself inspired to dive in after living through the horror of the recent election. She lives in Los Angeles with three cats and one partner, and she has prepped a Trump Exit bag for all of them. Ish also works for The Trevor Project and as a State Correspondent for 50 States of Blue writing about progressive politics and social justice issues. Find out more at www.iagreenwriting.com.

## HARDY

Stuart Hardy is British internet comedian and TV critic from the YouTube channel "Stubagful" where he's known for his popular Doctor Who reviews series "He Who Moans". He also makes bizarre horror cartoons and adaptations of his speculative short stories about technology and social media and the way in which they affect society and the online political discourse. He's also worked as a satirical sketch writer and commentator for various community radio projects over the course of the last ten years. His primary influences include Charlie Brooker's Black Mirror, Douglas Adams, Philip K. Dick, and the short stories of Robert Shearman.

## HARRISON

Kev Harrison is an English teacher and writer of dark fiction, living in Lisbon, Portugal. He has had stories published in Lost Films from Perpetual Motion Machine Publishing, Beyond the Infinite: Tales from the Outer Reaches from Things in the Well and has also had tales featured on The Other Stories podcast. His story 'Muscle Memory' will be included in the forthcoming Frankenstein-themed We Shall Be Monsters anthology from Renaissance Press. His first novella is currently with a publisher.
www.kevharrisonfiction.com
www.twitter.com/Lisboetaingles

## HEMMELL

Russell Hemmell is a French-Italian transplant in Scotland, passionate about astrophysics, history, and speculative fiction. Recent work in Aurelis, The Grievous Angel, Third Flatiron, and others. Find them online at their blog earthianhivemind.net and on Twitter @SPBianchini.

## HODGES

Larry Hodges is an active member of SFWA with over 90 short story sales and four novels, including "When Parallel Lines Meet," which he co-wrote with Mike Resnick and Lezli Robyn, and "Campaign 2100: Game of Scorpions," which covers the election for President of Earth in the year 2100. He's a graduate of the six-week 2006 Odyssey Writers Workshop, the 2007 Orson Scott Card Literary Boot Camp, the two-week 2008 Taos Toolbox Writers Workshop, and also has a bachelor's in math and a master's in journalism. In the world of non-fiction, he has 13 books and over 1800 published articles in over 150 different publications. He's also a professional table tennis coach, and claims to be the best science fiction writer in USA Table Tennis, and the best table tennis player in Science Fiction Writers of America! He's also an amateur presidential historian, which inspired him to write "I've Been Waiting For You" and many of his other works. Visit him at larryhodges.com.

## LANE

Michelle R. Lane writes dark speculative fiction about women of color who must battle their inner demons while falling in love with monsters. Her work typically includes elements of fantasy, horror, romance, and occasionally erotica. In January 2015, Michelle graduated with an MFA in Writing Popular Fiction from Seton Hill University. Her short story, "The Hag Stone," was published November 2014 in the anthology *Dark Holidays*, available from Dark Skull Publications. She lives in South Central Pennsylvania with her son.

Feel free to stalk Michelle online at Girl Meets Monster: https://michellerlane.wordpress.com/.

## LOGAN

Thomas has a variety of literary and genre stories appearing online and in print and has worked in various capacities for Fictional International and smaller journals, including as Fiction Editor for the Portland, Ore. journal The Grove Review. Otherwise semi-reclusive and secretive, he'd prefer you not to know that he has lived and taught across the country, earns a living in the renewable energy industry, that the last four of his social are 1233, was never a vegetarian but rather was never fond of your family's cooking, or that he often ends his thoughts and sentences awkwardly.

## LUCAS

Andrew J Lucas has contributed to books published by Fasa, Dream Pod Nine, White Wolf Games, Rebel Minis and Atlas Games among others. He has twelve solo books for various publishers and while his creative output is often blunted by his day job and the enthusiasm of his young daughter for distracting him, he does manage to get produce a few prime works each year. The last few years he has written and line produced books for Rebel Minis, as well as contributed five short stories to various short story anthologies. Andrew has also been writing poetry and fiction for many years and had a number of poems and stories successfully published in that time. He enjoys biting off more than he can chew and often writes for emerging markets and RPG publishers he finds cool… When not working, writing or playing with his 12 year old daughter he works on his wargame armies and occasionally finds time to field them in battle. He lives in Langley BC Canada likes cats but has none. Andrew can contacted @ this facebook page https://www.facebook.com/bladestalker or @ charonp@telus.net

## LUDENS

Adrian Ludens is the author of Ant Farm Necropolis (published by A Murder of Storytellers). Recent publication appearances include: Blood in the Rain 3 (Cwtch Press), Corporate Cthulhu (Pickman's Press), and Whispers of the Apoc (Tannhauser Press). Adrian a rock radio announcer and a fan of reading dark fiction, watching hockey, listening to all types of music, and exploring abandoned buildings.

## MANZOLILLO

Nick Manzolillo's writing has appeared in over forty publications including *Mother's Revenge, Haunted: An Anthology of the New England Horror Writers, Grievous Angel, Red Room Magazine*, and the *Tales To Terrify* podcast. He has an MFA in Creative and Professional Writing from Western Connecticut State University. By day he works as a content specialist for TopBuzz, a news app. A native Rhode Islander, he currently lives in Manhattan where he spends the little free time he has growing a beard. You can follow his publications at: nickmanzolillo.com

## MCGRATH

Ken McGrath is from Ireland, originally Thurles, Co Tipperary but now Dublin, where he lives with his wife. His fiction has appeared in or is forthcoming through The Arcanist, Daily Science Fiction, Cirsova Magazine, K Zine, Bards & Sages Quarterly and Spaceports & Spidersilk among others. You can find him online @fromthebigface if you want.

## MUSGRAVE

Jim Musgrave has been a Finalist in the Bram Stoker Awards, and he won the First Place ribbon for his historical mystery, *Forevermore*, in the Chanticleer International CLUE Book Awards. His works have also been a Finalist in the Next Generation Indie Book Awards and the Eric Hoffer Awards. All of the mysteries in his Det. Pat O'Malley series were selected as "Featured" titles by the American Library Association. He has a new mystery series out featuring *Chinawoman's Chance*, the first volume, set in 1884 San Francisco. He lives in San Diego, California, and he owns EMRE Publishing. Website: https://emrepublishing.com

## MUNRO

Donna J. W. Munro has spent the last seventeen years teaching high school social studies. Her students inspire her every day. An alumni of the Seton Hill Writing Popular Fiction program, she published pieces in Every Day Fiction, Syntax and Salt, Dark Matter Journal, the Seton Hill Kindle anthology *Hazard Yet Forward* (2012), the new anthology *Enter the Apocalypse* (2017), *Killing It Softly 2* (2017), *Beautiful Lies, Painful Truths II* (2018), and several upcoming 13 Press anthologies. Contact her at https://www.donnajwmunro.com

## NIKITINS

Tahni J. Nikitins completed her degree in Comparative Literature with a minor in Creative Writing in Uppsala, Sweden. Her essay wrote her honors thesis on the role of trauma in Mark Z. Danielewski's *House of Leaves* and her essay 'The Deconstruction of Narrative Framing in David Markson's Wittgenstein's Mistress' was published in the Comparative Literature department's annual journal Nomad. Her recent publications include 'Is It Any Wonder' in the magazine *Gods & Radicals* and 'School District 375' in the independently published anthology *FLASH!* She is currently working on revisions for a couple of novels as well as piecing together a collection of long-form poetry.

## ORETO

Frank Oreto is an author and editor of weird fiction living in Pittsburgh, Pennsylvania with his wife and numerous children. His writing has appeared in numerous publications including Metaphorosis, Owl Hollow Press, and Pseudopod. You can follow him on Twitter @FrankOreto or on Facebook at fb.me/FrankisWriting

## PALISANO

Author John Palisano has a pair of books with Samhain Publishing, DUST OF THE DEAD, and GHOST HEART. NERVES is available through Bad Moon. STARLIGHT DRIVE: FOUR HALLOWEEN TALES was released in time for Halloween, and his first short fiction collection ALL THAT WITHERS is available from Cycatrix press, celebrating over a decade of short story highlights. NIGHT OF 1,000 BEASTS is coming soon.

He won the Bram Stoker Award© in short fiction in 2016 for "Happy Joe's Rest Stop". More short stories have appeared in anthologies from Cemetery Dance, PS Publishing, Independent Legions, DarkFuse, Crystal Lake, Terror Tales, Lovecraft eZine, Horror Library, Bizarro Pulp, Written Backwards, Dark Continents, Big Time Books, McFarland Press, Darkscribe, Dark House, Omnium Gatherum, and more. Non-fiction pieces have appeared in BLUMHOUSE, FANGORIA and DARK DISCOVERIES magazines. He is currently serving as the Vice President of the Horror Writers Association. Say 'hi' at: www.johnpalisano.com and http://www.amazon.com/author/johnpalisano and www.facebook.com/johnpalisano and www.twitter.com/johnpalisano

## PALMER

Jessica Palmer has had twenty-eight books published in both fiction and nonfiction. Her fiction spans genres of horror, fantasy and science fiction for all age groups. Her works have been released globally by such publishers as Simon and Schuster's Pocket Books, Harper Collins's Element Books and Scholastic UK. Each have been reprinted and translated into several foreign languages. Her nonfiction includes university-level textbooks on Native American culture, an encyclopedia of natural history and engineering textbooks. Palmer was employed as a journalist where she won awards for crime reporting. She has been licensed as a wildlife rehabilitator for sixteen years, in four separate states and by the federal government, in order to take care of sick and wounded animals in preparation for their release to the wild.

## RUTLAND

Catrin is a scientist. As an Associate Professor, she teaches, lives and researches science. Her fiction pieces explore the world beyond what is (presently) possible, known, proven or in existence. Writing allows her to explore these ideas and understand society and the world around us. When Catrin is not researching, teaching or writing, you'll find her reading horror, science fiction or dystopian books with a cat sat on her lap.
Author webpage: http://catrinrutland.weebly.com/
Twitter @catrinrutland
Amazon author pages: http://www.amazon.co.uk/-/e/B017XTOMOA and http://www.amazon.com/author/catrinrutland

## SCHRAEDER

E. F. Schraeder is the author of two poetry chapbooks, most recently Chapter Eleven (Partisan Press). Schraeder has an interdisciplinary Ph.D. emphasizing applied ethics and lives in the rustbelt. Schraeder's work has appeared in Mummy Knows Best, Haunted Are These Houses, The Literary Hatchet, and other journals and anthologies. Schraeder serves as contributing editor to ananimal advocacy webcomic and is online at www.efschraeder.com. Current projects include a monster's coming of age novella and a collection of weird stories.

## SEATE

Jay is a writer who stands on the side of the literary highway and thumbs down whatever genre that comes roaring by. His storytelling spans the gulf from Horror Novel Review's Best Short Fiction Award to Chicken Soup for the Soul books. His tales and essays may incorporate hardcore realism, fantasy, horror, or humor featuring the most quirky of characters. His longer works can be found online at Amazon and B&N.

## SULLIVAN

This is Rider Sullivan's first sell. He lives in Alaska.

## TAMASFI

Laszlo Tamasfi is a comic book writer, a husband, an LGBTQ+ ally, and the lover of the strange and unusual. He›s the author of Invisible Hands, The Observatory, and The Last Panel for The DarkSide Magazine.

Originally from Hungary, he now lives in the United States.

## VAN HARLINGEN

Alice van Harlingen is a recovered musician and baseball addict who lives in Central Pennsylvania. This is her first published story.

VOTE

Made in the USA
Lexington, KY
03 February 2019